COUNTDOWN TO DOOMSDAY

Brandon Rolfe

ISBN 978 1 905553 93 8

Printed by Dolman Scott

www.dolmanscott.com

Dedication

For

Annita Crestina and Enrico

About the Author

Brandon Rolfe studied optometry at university in Glasgow, before working in hospitals and medical centres in Coventry and London. Initially he practised as locum, around the Greater London Area, before becoming clinical director in the city's south eastern sector. Between professional duties, he created and marketed his own patented product. (patents USA, UK, S/Africa). Qualified also in engineering and psychoanalysis, he later opened a private psychotherapy clinic. As a further diversion from work, he ran a confidential intelligence service. Having completed a second novel, The Analyst, he is currently working on a third novel.

1

02.40hrs, 23rd June, North Sea. The Royal Navy Harrier Mk3 thundered onwards at 600 m.p.h., into the crimson dawn, anxious to reach its mission-point in the bosom of the rising sun. Like a great seabird, its 'plumage' bristling with 25-mm GU-12 cannon and AGM-65E Maverick missiles, the plane tore on through the sky, its Rolls Royce Pegasus turbofan engine screaming out its fiery fury with 21,500lb thrust, to ripple the cold air with its 0.7 Mach anger. Sunbeams pounded the great bird's beak and tickled its belly, while others exploded into diamonds of coloured light on the glass-fibre wing tips and around the Perspex canopy, where a helmet bobbed and turned. The pilot's helmet bore a black arrow and he aimed it 90 degrees to starboard to look out. Trained eyes darted about behind the rubber mask in an overall check along the wing; from the glistening rods to the hooded mouth of the engine nacelle, where the sun lingered, but dared not enter, to be churned by the roaring turbine blades. The head turned to port, swinging the convoluted oxygen tube like a wrinkled proboscis.

The same expert eyes judged the velocity below with their own up here, at 300ft above sea level, and returned to the front with a bob of the head. Land and sea rushed past, where minutes before, HMS *Dover*'s dull grey deck had been. At 02.31hrs precisely, the signal had come in from the Nimrod on RAF Coastal Command Reconnaissance, Flight 301, reporting the sighting. Flight 301 had reported the plane going down south of the Muckle Flugga rocks, just off the northern headland of Unst. Within two minutes of receiving the coded signal, HMS *Dover* had jettisoned the Harrier, codename PETREL, from its deck and had it racing north on Blue Alert urgency.

HMS *Dover* was part of Naval Strike Force Command and as such, was part of Britain's contribution to Nato's Greenland/Baltic maritime air-arm. On constant patrol in these waters, the 20,000 tons *Dover* was equipped with conventional and nuclear missiles and four Sea King helicopters and three Harriers, to investigate, intercept and 'nullify' if necessary, any incidences of 'hostile influence' --- what had been the former Soviet Bloc's Baltic fleet --- and could well be again, the way things were cooling into another Cold War between East and West. The pilot consulted the time: 02.42 hrs. He would soon reach the target.

Zetland's southern tip slid rapidly over the gilded silken sea below, nearer and nearer. The pilot's head bent over the Ferranti Blue Fox radar display screen to check the electronic land map. He spoke into his rubber mask. 'Zetland, CONTROL. About another seven minutes and we'll be bang on target. Changing twenty one degrees west.'

The pilot tipped the ailerons with the Boulton Paul actuators, to swing the plane round smoothly and follow the spinal line of the islands. These scattered out ahead, beyond the 60th parallel and Greenland's toe, in a sprinkling of emerald gems encrusted with golden sun and the rust of Pre-Cambrian cliffs. They were the uppermost jewels in the crown of Her Majesty's British Dominions and all under the protection of Her Majesty's Royal Navy. Hundreds of birds flew out in squawking flecks from the furrowed brows of the cliffs, to watch the great royal bird zoom over.

The radio began to crackle with static, just as the mainland began to splinter up into bronzed fragments: 'CONTROL calling PETREL. Do you read me, PETREL? Do you read me?'

'Loud and clear, CONTROL.'

'What is your position, PETREL?'

The pilot looked down at the sea, sparkling gleefully while it rent the land asunder. 'Just leaving the mainland now. Flying over the Yell Sound. Should be there pretty soon.'

'Can you see anything yet, PETREL?'

'Not yet, CONTROL. It's too early and the angle's too wide at this height. Don't want to fly any higher and spot somebody's radar.'

'Very well, PETREL. Report as soon as RED WHALE is sighted. Back-up on the way.'

'Okay, CONTROL. Will do.'

As the islands flitted past beneath them, the pilot watched their ghostly flight on the radar screen, checking them aloud to himself: 'Yell -- Fetlar -- Uyea -- Unst. Nearly there now.'

02.49hrs. Sure enough, as CONTROL had promised, support appeared as two dots in the sky far behind the Harrier. They were growing larger by the second. Eurofighter Tornadoes, sent up from RAF Leeming, Yorks, they were catching up fast. Closing in, they flanked the naval plane, right and left. The Harrier pilot held up a thumb to the other pilots.

On the last island now, the great 'seabird' dived down for a scavenger's look at 100ft. The two Tornadoes climbed up steeply into the sky, to bank over and circle down and round while the other plane went below. Straight ahead, the island began to split on cue into the four-mile-long Burra Firth fjord. The Harrier swooped down the glacial valley with a thunderous scream and there it was, in front.

The gigantic US Rockwell B-1B Lancer strategic bomber, bereft of its right wing, lay up on the right bank of the loch, like a monster ray fish. Entrails trailed out from the fuselage tail-cone to the GQ ribbon-type parachute brake that floated at the water's edge. Twisted wing pieces, gleaming and smooth, fitted the scene like discarded claws. The dark General Electric turbofan engine poked out from the belly, like fish roe, dangerously close to the bomb itself. The B83 thermonuclear stand-off bomb lay dislodged to one side of the belly, with the island's annihilation nestling in its unexploded mercy.

With the bomb safe for the moment beneath them, their mission was to fend off RED WHALE. Off-shore, the massive 8000 ton 'whale', black not red, basked in the sun with sinister glinting silence, while watching its 'spawn' scramble from the dinghies and scurry among the wreckage. The Harrier banked up steeply into the sky, blocking out the Russian sailors for a second, as it went into a tight turn. The whole North Sea spun round slowly, driven by the giant 426ft submarine in its 'screw slot', the binoculars winking on the 47ft long 'sail' of a conning tower.

'PETREL calling CONTROL. Do you read me, CONTROL'

'CONTROL receiving you. Go ahead, PETREL.'

'Circling RED WHALE now. Delta class, by the look of her. She's quite a giant. Easily four hundred feet.'

'She *is* Delta class. Left Gdynia in Poland six days ago. Last seen patrolling the Icelandic waters until she was reported 'shadowing' the plane when it came down.'

'They've landed a party on shore. About twenty, I'd say.'

The radio pipped patiently during CONTROL's hesitant silence before coming alive again: 'The bomb must not fall into their hands. Repeat. The bomb must not fall into their hands. You have full permission to intercept, PETREL.'

'Understood, CONTROL. Going in now.'

'Good luck, PETREL.'

'Tally-ho, CONTROL.'

The jet fighter screamed down in a warning swoop, leaving only sixty feet clearance for the sailors to duck their heads in reflexive fear. Everyone cringed down for a second and then straightened up to watch the great fire-bird climbing high into the sky. The officer snapped them out of their trance, waving his arm and barking them back to work with a voice as broad as the wooden Mauser holster that dangled beside the transmitter slung over his shoulder.

'Spishitye! Mi spishim!' (Hurry up! We have no time to lose!)

The guttural Slavic gabblings recommenced and they clambered over the plane. From high above in the sky they looked hardly more serious than romping children on a picnic treasure hunt. But they didn't carry wooden pirate swords. Instead, they attacked the bomber with oxy-acetylene torches and heavy duty cutters, while those with the cameras climbed into the cockpit. Like Lilliputians, they worked frantically on their great 'Gulliver', more afraid of their commander than the Harrier, as it shattered their eardrums with another 600m.p.h screech.

Ignoring the Harrier, the men worked on feverishly, their tensions hidden inside. The great bomb was beginning to move as the two men in goggles cut away at the fuselage fastenings, behind a deluge of sparks. It looked a frightful load to move, being ominously long and fat with devilishly pointed tail fins. That was why the other team was assembling the eight-wheeled hydraulic bogie, attaching buoyancy tanks to its sides and finally a tackle to its end and that to the cable that ran down the beach, into the water and out to the submarine.

Swooping round for another dive, the Harrier pilot prepared to fire the air-to-ground missile. He judged with lightning speed. Distance was too short for visual guidance by the missile's aft end flares. He operated the Ferranti Airpass -11 computerised radio command-link lock-on, watching the display screen and fired. The missile rocketed away from the wing with fire-ball fury, to home in on its target, while the plane curved away. The 300lb warhead exploded in the rock-face 100yrds from the men, showering the place with rocks.

Everyone stopped work and looked around for orders. The officer had none to give, and looked round at the submarine, waiting for his transmitter to speak. No-one went back to work and anxiety mounted as the plane came in again. Everyone dived for cover just before the second warning missile was let loose. The Maverick screamed over their heads and exploded 50yds away, spewing up a shower of rocks that narrowly missed most of them.

The veteran seaman with the cutter's goggles looked up at the bomb's suspension and shook his head pessimistically. It was touch and go whether they could cut it free in the little time that they had. He didn't think that they could manage it and looked round at the officer and then at the plane circling in the sky. The officer took the message, but didn't flinch. He kept his stalwart stance, surveying his men in their predicament. He was a seasoned officer. Although too young for the Second Imperialist War in '39, or to have looked nuclear war in the eye, when America had later blockaded Russia's aid to Cuba, he had first seen military service, mostly through binoculars, as a junior 'naval advisor' offshore from Cambodia, in the Mekon delta, in the Vietnam conflict. Like any good officer, he was not afraid. But he did respect the safety of his men.

A startling cry from one of the men, above the Harrier's roar, solved the problem.

'Smatritye! Smatritye!' (Look! Look!)

Shading his eyes from the sun, the officer followed the arm pointing down the valley. After a second's focusing, the two optical smudges became real solid objects. Popping up and down like wind-hopping dragonflies and coming on at them at 130m.p.h. Sure enough, they were the two Westland Lynx helicopters promised by CONTROL, and sent out from RNAS Unst. Both were armed with machine-guns, torpedoes, and Nord SB3.11 air-to- surface missiles. They each also carried twelve marines.

That was it. The officer swung his arm and ordered immediate withdrawal from the beach. Grabbing their tools, the men crawled out of the bomber like maggots from a sore host. The artificer with the camera carried a leather shoulder satchel hurriedly stuffed with top secret flight command codes confiscated from the Lancer's cockpit.

Somehow sensing the general rush to escape, the massive bomb shuddered and suddenly broke free under its own weight and slithered down the slope, knocking the bogie aside. The old sailor's eyes widened in alarm at the danger and he yelled to his mate. 'Vnimaniye!' (Look out!) But it was too late. Like a killer shark, the huge finned bomb pinned its victim down by the hips, squeezing out his agonised scream. Those that heard, stopped to look. The officer turned round, at the same time stopping two of his retreating men.

Everyone rushed in to help the injured comrade, but found that they could do nothing. The ground was too steep and the bomb's angle was wrong for wedging the bogie's hydraulic jack. The old man knelt over the younger one --- a mere lad. 'Ni bispakoityes, ni bispakoityes.' (Don't worry, don't worry.) Perhaps it was a stupid thing to say, the old man thought, but he didn't know what else to say in the circumstances. He gave the lad a fist to grip and rambled on with coarse jokes to distract him from the pain.

Squirming with excruciating pain, the young sailor gasped out his words slowly: 'U minya galava kruzhitsa.' (I feel dizzy.) Speech was difficult, not just because of the pain, but because his native tongue was Arabic. Pressure became too great and his head slumped down into the soft sand.

'On upal vobmarak,' said the old man to nobody in particular. (He's fainted.) The officer stood up and looked around for the jet fighter. It was circling around waiting to see if the retreat would recommence. He then looked round at the helicopters. He guessed that they would most likely have winches on board that were capable of shifting the bomb. That was his decision, then. His injured party would have to be left behind, to be tended by the British. Their doctors couldn't be any worse than those 'butchers' in Yerevan, back in Armenia, he reasoned bitterly.

The radio transmitter crackled out the mounting urgency and so he signalled his men to move out again. All but the old man obeyed. He stayed put, by his 'apprentice'. The officer saluted with understanding in his dark Armenian eyes. 'Da novi fstryechi,' (Till we meet again,) he said, and then was gone, running down the beach to join his men in the dinghies. The cable, disconnected from the bogie, snaked down after them, and disappeared into the water.

The Royal Navy helicopters landed with a whirlwind commotion, spilling out their twenty four marines onto the red garnet sand. M16 assault rifles, with M203 grenade launchers attached, swung about in all directions. The Russians were well out in the water by this time and so the men stood and watched them bobbing up and down in their dinghies. When they turned and went among the wreckage, they were surprised to find an old sailor in a black sweater and *Yalta* on his cap, standing in their midst. Only an odd rifle pointed at him, as he spoke in a heavy Uzbeck accent. 'Prashu vas pamoch mnye? Praizashol nishchasni sluchi. On siryozna ranyen.' (Will you help me? There has been an accident. He is badly hurt.)

Nobody understood. They simply stared on tensely as he babbled and gestured in his strange ways. The chisel-faced Welsh sergeant pushed his way through to the front. 'What's goin' on, then? Who the hell are you, then? He understood as soon as the Russian pointed to the black 'thing' trapped beneath the bomb. They both knelt down quickly beside the still body.

'On patiryal saznaniye,' said the Russian. (He's lost consciousness.)

'He's lost consciousness,' said the Welshman.

The sergeant stood up and bellowed out to the helicopter. Its winch paid out the cable and they fastened it, with nerve tingling care, around the bomb, behind the anterior fins. 'What yer bleedin' all peein' for, then?' shouted the Welshman in jest. ' 'Fraid of meetin' the angels, are we? An' all of us all regular little choir boys, too.' The Wessex lifted into the air, straining on the cable, until the bomb rose up at its front. Gingerly aware of the nuclear menace hovering beside them, they put the stretcher down beside the sailor and placed him carefully onto it. Some would have said none too carefully, but everyone was in a hurry, with 'something else' on their minds. 'Watch it, now. We don't want to break any ruddy bones, now, do we?' chided the sergeant, monitoring every single move.

The Russian felt relieved, as he watched his young charge being stowed in the helicopter's stretcher bay. The sergeant touched the Russian's arm lightly, and with a hard smile ordered him with a nod onto the aircraft. Appreciating the casual discipline, the Russian adjusted his cap into a more formal position, with *Yalta* facing defiantly to the front. He climbed on board beside his mate. The helicopter cluttered away into the sky with its urgent load, leaving the others to guard the Lancer and its nuclear charge.

03.10hrs. Her Britannic Majesty's Forces were once more the sole occupants of Her northern-most shore. Off-shore, the great Russian 'whale' blared its warning horn and dived, disappearing in a mighty swelling of waves and foam.

2

05.01hrs, 23rd June, Unst. The knife and fork clinked and grated, cutting the small room's silence, as well as the two golden kippers on the chipped NAAFI plate. Grilled with a generous knob of butter, the fish looked delicious, infusing the blade and prongs with hungry gusto, to thrust and parry, flashing their scars like proud sabres. Now and then the fork stabbed at the plate of steaming mussels garnished with chopped onions and white prawn sauce. John Sherman watched all this this from his chair by the window, when he wasn't looking out at the transport plane being serviced by the RAF ground-staff maintenance crew. The eyes looked on, while the mind worked elsewhere, running the facts over and over again through its treadmill. Not fully satisfied that there was nothing to worry about, he tried to ignore the burning unease in his mind, relaxing until his grey concentration began to drain away. He began to take more note of the other man's 'involvement' at the table.

Amusement poked through his dark mood for a few seconds, as did the awakened pang of hunger in his stomach, as he watched the other devour the kippers in a miniature martial arts display. He now wished that he hadn't turned down the NCO cook's offer of a similar golden breakfast from the island's culinary waters. But it was always the same when you were called out early on an assignment like this. And stomach habits changed no more than work did. You took it all in your stride, with no more fuss than that shiversome early morning pinch of Andrews liver salts, until it became second nature.

Called out of his shallow sleep, in London, at 02.46hrs this morning, he had been airborne and racing north to investigate, on coded instructions, at 03.04hrs. The message had been short and precise. A US Bomber in Operational Flight had gone down; flying out from RAF Fairfield, destined for Iraq. His job was to look into it; to 'get it and vet it'. Nothing more was needed to set up the alert signals in his mind. All aspects of terrorist sabotage spiked up in his mind, like those tiny pin-pricks of light you try to comprehend on a radar screen. These had given way to pressure points of frustration, where impatience with the monotonous flight left you no more to do than occasionally tap your restless feet.

Sherman's companion over at the table, Wing Commander Fodlow, from RAF Intelligence, had shared the flight. Neither of them had exchanged much conversation. What few words they had uttered had hardly managed to leave the strained jokes stage. Fodlow seemed to have no inclination to see the serious side of things. A jolly pear-shaped product of the 'Biggin Hill-Bader' school, with about as many flying hours as a frightened hen, he saw all problems remedied with a tap on the knee from the M.O.'s rubber hammer. Sherman, himself, was a staff officer on the Directorate of Service and Intelligence. A mind-jangling job where you had to correlate all the information gathered by all the secret intelligence services. That could often be a wearisome chore, when petty bickerings among the rival intelligence officers caused snippets of information to be snipped even further. This caused needless delays and certainly saved nobody's tax-money. That was why he had to investigate points for themselves, on the spot, and gather all the data into a form that kept everybody happy, especially department heads --- and let the nation sleep peacefully at night. An optimist's folly, perhaps.

They had flown into camp, here at Unst, at 04.11hrs, to join the technical team already working on the wrecked Lancer for signs of sabotage. That was just under an hour ago. Since then, two reports had come through from the team, at progressive stages, completely dismissing sabotage at that stage. They were waiting now for final clearance. Sherman fingered the crisp notepaper with the coded message which the radio operator had given him on the plane. The two latest reports should have set his mind at rest. But they didn't. He was still uneasy about something, somewhere, at the back of his mind. Nothing specific; nothing more tangible than that faint thread of tension that you can't dismiss until you've finally put the lid on the job. Totally irrational, of course. He knew this, but accepted it as the habitual uneasiness that others called 'alertness', that always waylaid you at this unfinished stage of the investigation. Besides, it was his job to be suspicious. That was what he was paid for; to be suspicious and safe, rather than satisfied and sorry. He went over the points again in his mind, while watching Wing Commander Fodlow contentedly champing away to his palate's delight.

The wall phone rang in the stone passage between their room and the staff kitchen.

Fodlow jumped up and chewed his way over to the phone. He picked up the receiver and grunted into it, while sucking around noisily for particles between the teeth. 'Uh-huh.' He waited, searching the gums with his tongue while the phone spoke. 'Uh-huh,' he said again and found time to blow out a particle, which stuck on the phone's wall unit. 'Uh-huh -- All right -- Thanks -- Fine -- Right.' He went back to his seat, completely oblivious to all but the noisy searchings in his mouth. He took in another mouthful of fish before sharing the information with his companion. 'It's all clear. That was them on just now. Seems it was just a freak malfunction in the engine thrust units, or whatever it was he was saying in his technical jargon. I, for one, just can't keep up with this new fangled blah blah of a technical language that's developing these days. But anyway, one thing's for sure --- it's definitely not a bolt of Allah's fury cast down on us, courtesy of Al Qaeda's champion zealot, Osama Bin Laden and his lot. No trace of devious technical tamperings anywhere. A routine Board of Inquiry lot will have to be gone through, of course. Otherwise, okay. Does that sound all right to you?'

Fodlow's nonchalant manner, with its matter-of-fact sum up virtually meant that he was taking full credit for everything being 'okay'. Sherman could have bet that he harboured a secret yearning for the simplicity of a bygone era of Biggles gung-ho chivalry in the clean clear air. Perhaps a lot of us did. But he didn't like the way the Wing Commander's final remark had come. With its hint of a chiding, as if he was being blamed for everything. But he resisted the urge to show his annoyance. 'Yes, I suppose so. Commander. It *sounds* all right. What about the bomb, itself?'

'Will it go off, you mean?'

'Yes, something like that.'

'No, not a chance of it, from what I gather. At least I shouldn't think so. Not with this latest integrated link-on set-up they have on it now. I gather that it works something like the principle of Nobel's dynamite. Kick it, beat it, but it still won't go off without its programmed detonation.'

'That's just as well, then, I suppose. It wouldn't do to overgrill the fish, would it, Commander?'

Sherman's faint personal stab had got through. Fodlow, for all his apparent gastronomic preoccupation, took the message sharply and cast a wary glance at Sherman, over the mussel impaled on his fork. He wiped some more prawn sauce onto it. 'But I guess you really haven't seen any real action, have you? Not like we did in the Gulf and the Falklands. With flak and anti-aircraft tracer bullets strafing your arse, you had to count your balls regularly, I tell you. No titanium in those days.'

'Titanium?'

'Armour plating --- American A-10 Thunderbolt. Not that you would have been through anything like that, eh?' The aggressive hold sparking up in the tired eyes struck Sherman as a boyish challenge to swipe and bash his conker.

'No, not quite, Commander. Strictly speaking, Biggles Books were my line of fire in those days.'

The casual small talk lost its edge as suddenly as it had begun and immediately dried up. Both minds came back to the more important matter in hand. With his fork nakedly empty, Fodlow hunched over it with a philosophical look, ready to speak after he'd swallowed his mouthful. 'You'll no doubt be wanting to see them yourselves, after our Intelligence Section has interrogated them?'

'Faster than fast. As soon as your people are finished, we want in, without a second to spare. As it happens, we know quite a lot about them already.'

'Such as?' queried Fodlow, with a note of disbelief in his raised eyebrows.

Sherman already knew his notes and read them off from memory before his fingers found them, dashing any doubts Fodlow may have had. 'They're from the submarine, *Yalta*; 'Delta' class, nuclear powered; first launched in seventy-nine; captained by one Mikhail Yeltsov; born in Yerevan, Armenia; two children; the son graduated from the Timiryazev Agricultural College; the daughter died from polio, aged three. The submarine left Gdynia in Poland, on Thursday the seventeenth, to take up watch on our NATO Summer-time

Operation off the Jan Mayen Island, off Iceland.' Sherman paused for an apparent mental breather, looking at the floor with his inner puzzle, before looking back at the Wing Commander. 'At least that's what it's *supposed* to have been doing after leaving Gdynia. That's our official statement for keeping face, so to speak. Where the thing went to after the seventeenth is pretty much unclear. Damned well anyone's guess, really.' Although Sherman's words came out in a constantly calm pace, Fodlow could virtually hear the situation gnawing away like a true rodent across the room in the younger man's mind.

'Delta class? They're quite big, aren't they? remarked Fodlow with what sounded like faint touch of envy.

'Very big, Commander. Almost twice the length of ours. Forty thousand tons dry weight, or else nine thousand tons displacement submerged; sixteen SSN-8 missile launchers, single warheads, though. Nautical range, four thousand, two hundred miles.'

'Hmm, pretty impressive. Still, they never quite got the bomb. That's the main thing,' said Fodlow, with a sudden halting fall of voice in the last words, pulled down by the gravity of the situation.

Sherman saw the change of mood and took the opportunity to stress his question urgently, without having to pull rank with priority orders. 'Can we go over again what exactly it is they *did* get, so I can check for anything I've missed. No room for errors, right, Commander?'

'Yes, quite right.' Fodlow's cough seemed more for embarrassment than for any particles bothering the windpipe. 'Well, in actual fact they damn well nabbed all the Strategic Nuclear Strike Command codes. Targets, codenames, the lot. Damn bloody horror of a nuisance.'

Sherman scribbled down what codes he could remember in his notebook and put a stroke through each of them. 'A tiny bit of a problem there, Commander. Only double shift work for the poor 'technics' having to reallocate routes and targets and reshuffle codes. There again, maybe Putin won't be too happy, himself, when he discovers that we know the strategic codes for his 'mini' Cold War with recommened cold front patrolling of Western air space and waters.' Sherman's calm words did nothing to reassure either of them in their minds, as they both visualised the mountains of paperwork and headaches that would have to be suffered to put things right again. Not to mention having to face and satisfy angry enquiry committees.

Made no difference that it wasn't *their* plane; it had crashed in *their* back yard. And with a nuclear bomb. That would have the politicians 'exploding' their anger on the Defence Minister.

'Just as well the crew survived, all but the pilot, that is. It could have been a lot worse if he hadn't stayed on board to bring it down as best he could -- and perish, poor bastard. They could have been picked up by the sub', if the trawler hadn't reached them first. Were they *really* going to drop that nuke, to fry Bin Laden's lot, as well as everyone else, I wonder?'

Sherman pondered the implication, with its uneasiness, in the Commander's words.

'Presumably having it on operational flights, without actually using it, is the President's new muscle-flexing tactic to match Putin's recent stepped-up show of strength. At least to God, I hope so.' Clearly not fully convinced with his own answer, he drummed his pen down sharply on his notepad. Fodlow caught the unsettled motion. He wasn't feeling too happy himself. Sherman looked up from his writing and stared out of the window. The mobile compressor chugged and shuddered away, all by itself. Standing over it was the brilliant white B.Ae 146 transporter that was to take them and the B83 bomb back to the Nuclear Strike Command base in Buckinghamshire. There, it would be examined for damage by the team of nuclear fission specialists. Let's hope to God, it gets there in one piece, Sherman thought. Otherwise, a team of 'mushroom' specialists would be more appropriate.

05.11hrs. Sherman watched the flight-sergeant strutting briskly towards their building, to tell them that the plane was ready. Zipping up his leather writing case, he stood up to go. Fodlow looked up at Sherman. 'Ready at last, are we? About time, too,' he said. He looked at his watch, then down at his plate. Sherman followed the other's longing look at the unfinished breakfast. Any faint pang of hunger he may have felt earlier, when offered breakfast by the corporal, was now gone. He had to 'stomach' other things first. 'You finish that, Commander. After all this, I think we can spare a few more minutes. I'll go on ahead. I've still a couple of questions I want to put about before they fly us back.'

3

12.17hrs, 23rd June, S.E.London. The eerie whine of the electric motor grew louder as the yellow Coventry Climax fork-lift truck ghosted up out of the abyss of darkness. Darkness was all around, where only a few tungsten lamps winked feebly from the warehouse roof that spanned 31,000 square feet. The Climax hummed up closer, along the passage between the mountains of of wooden crates, so that nervous pigeons fluttered away to safer positions among the spiderwork of steel roof beams. Cool as it was, the sound of the wings flapping in the invisible dust inspired an even more chilly air to the place.

The truck came right up and Sherman stepped aside to let it pass, with its two tonnes load of ten inch diameter oil-valve camshafts bound for Abu Dhabi. His eyes were not fully adjusted from the blazing sun outside, and he had a little difficulty in seeing what other kind of components were stored in the boxes around him. There were obviously many different kind, judging by the varying sizes and shapes of the boxes. The components made under official Government contract looked no different from the rest, except that they were sectioned off behind thick wire partitions with the gates heavily padlocked. Even Sherman didn't know what he was passing, when he passed the wire mesh area with the KEEP OUT: CALL OFFICE FOR KEYS notice in large red lettering.

He did know, however, that Ancol Engineering Ltd., like many firms in the United Kingdom, was commissioned by the Ministry of Defence to make various specific parts of an integrated armaments programme. Each part, isolated this way, looked innocent enough to its production team, giving no indication of how many cities it could help to raze to the ground. The idea was also to cut down the risk of security leakage. That was becoming more of a headache, with the increasing number of foreign, particularly Russian and Middle Eastern, factory inspectors coming into the country to supervise their countries' contracts with British firms. Money was always a blindfold to problems like this. Some Government sources were stirring to the issue and one MP had even approached Sherman to ask him to compile a report for the Home Secretary. But that wasn't why he was here this morning.

Sherman ducked under the low wooden door, out into the bright daylight. The narrow corridor connecting the warehouse to the office block had glass walls and a glass roof.

He took in the panorama with a hand shading his eyes for a few seconds, to spy out his contact. There he was, standing on the second stage of the steel staircase that zig-zagged up the gable end of the building like a giant ivy climber. The man had sounded anxious on the phone and he'd openly stated that he was anxious for someone from Security to come along to help him out. You couldn't help but conclude that the man *must* have been anxious, considering that he had come all this way to Deptford from the top secret base in Buckinghamshire. Sherman felt that horrible tingle you have when bad premonitions start up in your mind.

At a closer look, up the last few clanging stairs, the man in his duffle coat and broad frame plastic spectacles looked the exact stereotype of the school swat. Nicknamed 'Thinker' or 'Stinker' probably. With his long pale sexless face, he looked ten years younger than he was written up as in the classified Official Secrets dossier. Sherman smiled inwardly at the thought of the man suddenly whipping out a stink bomb and catapult from his pocket. The man's feet shifted with nervous impatience and he consulted his watch to hide his uneasiness. 'You're early,' he said. 'Seven minutes, to be precise.'

Sherman had nothing against the man, but he tried not to be initially too friendly. 'Miracles do happen. I'm usually late. You *are* Mr Blenning, I take it?'

'That's right. Graham Charles, to be precise. Here.' He handed over the wallet with its three plastic windows flashing their credentials. The photograph in the middle panel was a right nightmare snap, but it was enough to confirm that the man was indeed Graham Charles Blenning. The third panel had a statement from the Science Research Council proclaiming that G C Blenning Ph.D, M.Sc., was a senior physicist in the Daresbury Nuclear Physics Laboratory, who also worked in part-time liaison with the Ministry of Defence as a nuclear fission consultant. That meant that he bred nice little atom bombs.

Sherman snapped the wallet shut and handed it back smiling. 'That seems to be in order. So exactly what is it you think that we can do for you, to have me running along here, when I could be a hundred other places instead?'

'To be precise, you can get them to let me in here, for a start.' Blenning thumbed at the building behind him. 'I told them that I was a Government employee and I showed them my passes. But they just wouldn't budge. They said that I had to have someone from the Ministry "to endorse an official entrance onto the premises," to use their precise words.'

Sherman nodded with a neutral cold face. 'I'm sure that you'll understand that we can't be too careful in these matters. But then you can tell me all about it. Let's go inside first. These open stairways can make you feel naked, even with shoes on.'

They went in through the glass storm door, through the semi-glass Staff door and through the first fire door, before the receptionist looked up from along the passage. Sherman halted for a second between the two fire doors. 'It's to do with that American beauty of a B83 bomb, isn't it?' he said warily, feeling the answer already burning in his stomach, as he searched Blenning's face.

'Yes. Well, it started with that. Yes.'

Sherman's mind buzzed. *Started?* Only *started?* Christ. Don't you just love these guys who can't keep things simple. There was that uneasy feeling coming over him, when you know -- just *know* -- that it's not going to be your day. Not by a long chalk. He wondered if he had been wrong, rushing lunch in the canteen to come out here, now that it was trying hard to climb back up his throat. A packet of Rennie tablets materialised in his hands, and he popped one under the tongue to suck slowly with a rueful twisting of the mouth. Just like when you concede argument to the warhorse mother-in-law. 'I wonder why I don't think I'm going to like what comes after "yes".'

Sherman's frown deepened as he turned and pushed through the second fire door.

'Yes, you see, to be precise ------'

'Later.' Sherman snuffed the man's remark with a sharp wave of the hand, at the same time holding up his MoD security pass to the girl. 'Sherman. I phoned earlier. I need to speak to your Mr Darrel? It's important.'

Her eyes didn't jump at the sight of the security pass, but her voice was extra hushed. 'I'll tell him you're here. If you'll just wait a moment.'

Mr Darrel, the Senior Administrative Executive for Ancol, took them along to a door marked with Senior Technical Executive, and disappeared inside. They waited until he reappeared, gave them a nervous nod, and retreated along the corridor. The Senior Technical Executive had a few private words with Sherman, before taking them along to yet another door, marked Drawing Office. At Sherman's request, he left them on their own. The office's inner walls were glass and wood and looked on to a warren of similar glass and wood offices in the bygone style of the '40s Ealing Studio Films era. Breezy George Formby was surely around in the background somewhere, strumming his ukulele? A small panel on the third wall looked on to the factory floor, where lathes turned smoothly, snivelling out long curly snots of gleaming steel.

Sherman sat down on the cold radiator with his back to the glass panel and toyed with the cactus plant named a whole mouthful of *Opuntia monacantha*. He let Blenning rummage around with the drawings he'd been given from the Classified filing cabinet. His patience thinned out as he waited, the seconds ticking by into minutes on the wall clock. The secretive rustling of the papers didn't help much, no more than did Blenning's maddening low mutterings. Sherman could stand it no longer. He sat bolt upright, staring into Blenning's bent back. 'So what is it that you so urgently needed to tell me about the bomb, Mr Blenning?' The statement came out with just enough measured control to make the command sound like a polite question.

'To be precise, it simply won't explode.' Blenning's remark was clinically precise and unemotional, unaware as he was, that he could be annoying anyone.

Sherman felt his goodwill plunging rapidly down the tube like mercury, and folded his arms resolutely. 'So let's get this straight, now. Am I to understand that you've dragged me all this way out here just to tell me *that*?' His annoyance was out in the open now. 'Forgive my ignorance on the technical side, Blenning, but isn't that what it's *supposed* to do? Namely, to explode only when programmed to do so?'

The horror that his analysis could be so misunderstood clocked up like sacrilege in the scientist's systematic mind. His pale placid face fired with feeling and his manner became anxious, with awkward gesticulating hands. 'No, no, you don't understand me. This bomb has been designed so as never to explode. *Never*. Not even when programmed to do so!'

4

12.29hrs, 23rd June, S.E. London. Sherman stood up from the radiator and stared at Blenning, letting the words sink into his brain. The alarm bells began to ring out behind the eyes that took on a new hardened look. 'If I understand you correctly, Blenning, the bomb is, in fact, a dud?'

'Well yes, to be precise, there is no way in which the mechanical components can be activated to bring together the two critical masses needed to initiate the atom bomb which acts as the absolute bomb's detonator.'

'Like I said, it's a dud.'

'Well yes, I suppose it is,' said Blenning, as if seeing Sherman's definition in a new light; as a discovery somehow different from his own. 'I must confess that it took me some time to tumble to the conclusion. You see, since we were inspecting the bomb for damage, then it was only natural that we should not be surprised by any of the parts failing to function. They did, in fact, fail to function as you know, but without cause from damage. Instead of being damaged, these parts were perfectly cut and shaped as they had been designed and drawn in these very plans. In fact, they were performing as instructed, to function perfectly as the imperfect bomb, if I may use the paradox.'

Sherman leaned forward on the large desk and flicked a blueprint pensively. He clearly understood what Blenning was saying and he didn't like the idea one bit. A new thought suddenly struck him. He pushed the heavy, now 'useless', papers away and looked up at Blenning. You said that the bomb was failing to function because of these designs; then that means that ----'

'Precisely. It means that with all the component parts manufactured from these blueprints, different parts by different manufacturers, this is not the only bomb which will not go off. In fact ---'

'They're all duds!' Tearaway fire engine sirens now wailed in Sherman's head, pushing the original impatience aside. Christ! What more was to come? At first you can't get the ruddy guy to speak; now you almost wished you could choke the bastard, to stop him giving you more of his disturbing scientific titbits. The irony hit him like cold rain on a drunk's face. How Maureen had often fired the same temptation in him when she had let loose with her volley of words in one of her histrionic 'period' moods. And he *hadn't* been drunk on those 'hell' nights. Only once. The last time; when he had almost lost control and returned her scream; but he hadn't. That was when she wanted the divorce. He had suggested trial separation. Her mother could only look pleased at the news when it got out. That was three -- no -- two years and ten and a half months, now.

'Well, not quite,' said Blenning, breaking into Sherman's distraction. 'Say perhaps ninety-five per cent of the Blue Steel deterrent programme. You see, these 'annexe-plans' are the recent improvement for the bomb that was agreed upon by majority decision of the Nuclear Armaments Council two years ago, and brought into actual production only this January. Since this decision was taken and acted upon, only about ninety-five per cent of the Blue Steel programme has been refitted with the new design so the five per cent of Blue Steel is still operational.'

'Whatever way you put it, it all boils down to the fact that for the last five months we've been operating the country's nuclear strike force like a box of dud Christmas crackers. No -- correction -- a box of ninety-five per cent dud Christmas crackers. I suppose we should thank Heaven, or perhaps more appropriately in this case, *Hell*, for small mercies.'

Blenning had said his piece as a diagnostic scientist and now considered that the prognosis was a matter for Security and Mr Sherman. His eyes shone with great interest as he scanned over the blueprints. To Sherman it all looked like a daft cut-out print for a cardboard boat or puppet that you found on the back of the breakfast cereal box.

'It's all really quite clever,' said Blenning at last. If he gave no appearance of being upset by the findings, it was only because he was preoccupied with the scientific implications. He was in his element now, where a lecture was fitting to explain the very mastery of the technique used. 'Quite fascinating really. The principle of the design has been left untouched. Only the dimensions have been altered by the microscopic minimum necessary to inflict the maximum degree of disorder.'

'The dimensions?'

'Yes, a few millimetres here and there, added or removed and the intended co-ordination of the system breaks down. For instance, take my watch here. The overall resultant function of 'time' being told on a silly dial is brought about by the co-ordinated teamwork of the individual pieces. Not only is shape important, but size also is very specifically limited. Thus, change a few teeth or escarpment levers in size and the watch ceases to function. The important thing is that we notice that the watch ceases to function because the watch is an actively employed piece; its performance is regularly checked when we consult it for time. On the other hand the blueprint, when divided and subdivided into separate drawings, offers no reliable means of detecting any errors.'

'You put it all very nicely, Blenning. What we don't suspect, we don't see.'

'Precisely. It's only fortunate that your Ministry asked me to examine the bomb.'

'It's only fortunate that my Ministry has its freaks as well, Mr Blenning.'

'Sorry?'

'Something else. Doesn't matter.' Sherman was thinking how 'errors' had to be substituted by deliberate tamperings. He smiled inwardly as he folded the blueprints and thought of the freak malfunction that the RAF engineers had said had caused the Lancer to crash. Well it was an absolute blessing in disguise that the plane had crashed. And to think old Fodlow had been worried by a few scraps of paper being taken by the Russians. If he'd known what those sailors had really left behind when they left the bomb! If the *Russians* had known! So much for Strike Force Command's strong arm role of defence of the realm. You could just as well imagine that legendary 'Thin Red Line' holding back the Russian assault at Sebastopol with rubber muskets and rubber musket balls. Not quite a rib-tickler, alas.

With the blueprints folded under his arm, Sherman opened the door for Blenning, ushering him out.

'Are you taking those drawings with you? Won't we get into trouble?'

'You let me worry about things like that, Mr Blenning. I'll take care of that side of things, don't you worry. My Ministry, as you put it, is going to be asking you to recompense by solving some of their little problems in the next few days. Come on, let's go. We've seen all we need to see here. I've a feeling we're going to be watching out for "bullets strafing our arses".'

'Sorry?'

13.18hrs. Their car bowled along Evelyn Road and on along Jamaica Road, before Sherman decided to turn off, towards the Old Kent Road junction. It was a necessary change, he thought. He had originally intended going on back the way he had come, via Tooley Street and Tower Bridge. That way, he could have turned off before the bridge, to drop in at the pre-arranged dockside local to meet the contact. But that was off now. Things had changed. Keyed up into this new situation, he frowned as he tried to think how much they had changed. The contact was high risk material, too sensitive to allow for phoning on the mobile. The man was familiar with the procedure, with the danger it entailed, and would know how to look after himself. Standard action was for contacts to disperse after an agreed time lapse, if the other side failed to turn up. That hadn't changed. If only you could change the damned traffic lights! Sherman thrummed the steering wheel, but the traffic in front paid no attention. It remained stock still. When the twisting snake of vehicles did move off again, it was at a snail's pace, bumper to bumper.

13.28hrs. The junction spread out ahead of them, with its giant concrete tentacles waving its new generation's hard farewell to an older gentler London. It was awkward, as well as sad. With its great labyrinth of concrete stairways and pedestrian underpasses, spotted with coded signs, you definitely needed an honours degree in geography to navigate your way to the public lavatory.

They drove on, along New Kent Road, along St George's Road and then onwards along Westminster Bridge Road. All the while Sherman was tossing this new information about in his head, deciding the best signals to put out from the Directorate's Central Intelligence Exchange bank to the other departments, without dropping the egg. Somewhat tricky, considering it was an inside job. He needed to make a phone call. But not on the mobile. An outside phone was safer.

The traffic was slowing up again for the lunch-time period. They slowed down before the bridge itself. Sherman leaned over the wheel to crane up at Big Ben. 'Nearly quarter to.' He looked round at Blenning. 'In view of the circumstances, Mr Blenning, I think it would be a good idea if we went and consulted Sherlock Holmes.'

'Sorry?'

'They do a nice bar lunch. Nice atmosphere too.' It was only two minutes away from the office and he needed to make that outside call. He could do that and then be in the office without having to account too much for himself and his whereabouts. More to the point, it was also off the beaten track from those droves of news hacks sniffing around for sensational scoops in the lunch-time watering holes along Whitehall.

5

14.15hrs, 23rd June, Northumberland St. Sherman checked his watch with the pub lounge's wall clock. Broaley was late. He'd said five past. The fact that he was fussing over the time made Sherman admit to his edginess. Maybe it was nearer the time for his scheduled medical check-up. He made a mental note to have his secretary make an appointment for him with the Department's counsellor. Soft name for 'shrink'. Probably he needed some iron tonic pills to combat the effect of mountains of paperwork and endless interim committee meetings. He was certainly due for some leave, but that would have to wait. In normal circumstances involving a security leak he would have gone straight to the office and set the machinery in motion. But this was different. The damage was done, five months solid, as Blenning had said in his unwavering thermonuclear certainty. Twenty minutes more was not going to make any difference in stopping the boat from floundering on the rocks. More accurately, Sir Richard Hossley, Director General of the Department, would still be in session with the Minister himself, helping him tidy up and sweep 'awkward things' under the carpet, in preparation for the monthly Parliamentary Committee for Internal Security. One hell of a big hoovering job was going to be needed for this.

But this wasn't the only reason for holding back. If you jump forward with a report like this now, the general enquiries that ensue are going to lead to more selective investigations, and that is tantamount to putting the cat among the pigeons. No, to catch the pigeon, rather than frighten it away, you need a certain degree of stealth. You need to make a few 'discreet' enquiries on your own, through round about channels, rather than through the direct central channel. That was why he was waiting for Major Broaley, from MI5.

'It's two minutes fast,' said a voice beside him, cutting through the hubbub of lunch-time chatter like a knife. Sherman looked round at Blenning. The man was beginning to irritate him with his precision sharp remarks; just like a knife, right enough. Blenning took another sip at his water like a school sports day pop, and then became more serious. The scientific problem was undoubtedly troubling him and had suddenly aged his sallow soft face in minutes, where a lifetime had been content to leave him boyish. 'Have you any idea who is responsible?' he asked Sherman.

' "To be precise", no. Probably the lot of us; the whole damn human race, if we care to look at it that way.' Sherman pulled his annoyance back and forced out a neutral smile. 'No, not yet. It's quite difficult to hold a one man vote on who gets the noose at this early stage.'

'I see.' Blenning bobbed his head up and down in deep thought to the statement and went back to his drink.

Sherman tilted his head back and tried, meantime, to think of the best words for dropping the news to Hossley and the other departmental heads. He looked at the Great Detective's etching on the glass pane and wondered how he had put his many awkward cases to Queen Victoria and Europe's many noble personages. A television newscaster standing at the bar looked his way and Sherman wondered exactly how *he* would put his words across to the public if he knew what the situation was.

Major Broaley's face, with its heavy black moustache, stood out in the babbling crowd as he came in the door, looking around with that suspicious air of the school janitor finding glue-sniffers in the boys' toilet. His eyes met Sherman's, and Sherman rose to elbow his way through to him. 'Put that away, Major,' said Sherman, handing Broaley a chunky glass of his favourite malt whisky. The gesture, with its brevity of words, allowed Sherman a few seconds to put up his guard against Broaley's astute senses. There was perpetual rivalry between them, where Sherman had come into the spy game, from out of nowhere, over Broaley's head. Sherman had had no field experience whatsoever, whilst the Major had put in a good many years active service. Having left Cambridge somewhat hastily with only a Second, and possibly because of a don's distraught wife in his wake, Sherman had landed in this lot with the official right to *think* that he was one white-collared level higher than Broaley. But for his lack of Socrates and Sophocles, the Major should have been sitting behind Sherman's desk, and in all fair probability would have made a better job of it. Sherman accepted this, and knowing that the Major thought likewise, was forever on his guard against the Major's acid humour.

Broaley's tight-knotted Artillery tie and broad striped three-piece in worsted charcoal grey, summed up the man for what he was and wasn't. The conservative colours and cutting spoke of the desk-ridden civil servant; whereas the unkempt sleeves with their extra wrinkles in the crooks of the elbows spoke of the active field agent. The tight waistcoat, pulling up towards the armpits, would have looked slightly overweight in another person, but in Broaley, it warned meddlers not to meddle. Broaley eyed Sherman for a moment over the glass then lowered it. 'You sounded anxious on the phone,' he said with the question loaded in one raised eyebrow, searching Sherman's face for what it was holding back.

'You could tell that, could you?' Sherman said cautiously, wondering if, indeed, he had sounded anxious, over exited. He knew Broaley would like that.

'Usually that, and a lot more.' Broaley's iron blue eyes twinkled with cunning anticipation as he sensed that he was on to something, as well as touching a raw nerve in Sherman's otherwise controlled composure. His chin went up slightly to verify this point on Sherman. The light at that moment touched Broaley's face at the right angle and you saw, with a little imagination, a Lord Lucan looking back. Quite fitting, where rumours said that his people had lent a hand in that infamous exit. But that was strictly off the record. Although perhaps not quite with a foot in the door at the Palace, there were still a few faint blue-tinged corpuscles coursing through the Broaley bloodline. A point he never failed to allude to when the opportunity arose. And that was often. Made no difference that he didn't actually mention it, or press it upon you; you just felt it. Perhaps just stopping short of bending over to receive the cane across your lower end. That natural smooth aplomb for doing everything better and superior to you. One of his distant lot had been pally with Lord Cardigan at Balaclava. Apparently sharing the spoils of liquor, cards and last and least, women. A trifle ironic perhaps, since *that* Lord Lucan had been Cardigan's hated brother-in-law, and immediate commander in the field, with very little respect reciprocated between them. Broaley also had a couple of his very own bright-ribboned gongs in his cupboard alongside his skeletons. Well earned, 'beyond the call of duty', they said.

'Let's go over there,' said Sherman, and they shifted to a small space at the bar's end. They both looked round themselves instinctively for eavesdroppers. But this was not really necessary. Firstly, nobody could hear what anyone else outside their own conversation was saying; secondly, the general clamour of voices and clinking glasses made bugging an impossibility. Besides, in public places like these, if you were going to suspect anyone and everyone of talking shop over their Perrier and garlic baguette, you were going to have to put in a colossal amount of bugging time. 'Truth of the matter is, Major, that somebody has taken the corks out of our pop guns.' Sherman went on to deliver the gist of the matter, watching Broaley's face for developments. Broaley conceded no expression beyond the occasional jump of an eyebrow, looking down all the while into his liquor as he swirled it round in its glass. Sherman finished and waited. After the lull, Broaley looked up.

'And you want me to do a little shifting of things down the line; upset the dust, ahead of your report?' Broaley half closed his eyes in mock forethought. 'As far as I can see that's going to call for a lot of unauthorised door opening between the departments. Unofficial and all that. Stepping on people's toes, give people indigestion. Some people are not going to like that. Somebody can get his fingers caught in the door in something like that.' He shook his head slowly and blew a mock silent whistle.

Sherman shifted uneasily as he recognised Broaley's game of playing awkward. 'Not unofficial; just off the Index and without a file, for the time being.'

Broaley saw the chance to be dogmatic to the points in the rule book and jumped in sternly for shear devilry. 'If it's not unofficial, it's official, and how can it be official if it's not entered in the Index?'

'Don't be bloody awkward! You know damn well what I mean!' Sherman was openly vexed now, and Broaley was enjoying it.

'I know what you mean and I know only too well what can be difficult.' Broaley sniffed, with the mischievous twinkle in his eye spreading out into a cheeky smile. Sherman all but felt it burn into his own face. 'You make it sound as if you don't want to be the bearer of bad tidings. Am I right, Sherman?'

Sherman gave him a fiery stab with his eyes, before gulping down his drink and looking away. Of course he was bloody right! He knew that Broaley was bang on target with that point as well as the earlier one. Bearers of bad tidings, as he had put it, were almost inevitably lumbered with the task of salvaging the sunken ship. If they failed, their heads generally rolled. He may have been Broaley's superior on a piece of paper, but off that paper, unofficially, he couldn't make the man wag his tail an inch. Broaley enjoyed that thought as much as he was enjoying his drink. Sherman scratched his face to hide that fact that he was lost for an answer. The small victory was enough for Broaley and he stepped down his attack. 'Do you think it's anybody in your department?'

'It doesn't look that way,' said Sherman, surprised at Broaley withdrawing his wedge so soon. He usually liked to push it in as far as he could, to inflict the maximum discomfort. 'No, with all the technicalities involved, it has the smell of somebody on the extra-departmental Ancillary Register.'

'What have you got out of him so far? *Anything*?' Broaley jerked his head to indicate Blenning, seated at the far wall, whom he'd noticed was staring at them during their talk.

'I'll introduce you; see for yourself,' said Sherman.

Broaley listened to Blenning repeat the details and wondered all the while if the pale faced scientist could do anything else but stir tea with a slide-rule. He ventured a question to Blenning. 'So far you've mentioned only the mechanical components. What about the electronic programme? Has that been tampered with, at all?'

'Oh, but most certainly. To be precise, that was the more difficult to detect. Since, after all, the bomb was involved in a physical acci ----'

'Keep it down,' cautioned Broaley.

'Right, sorry,' whispered Blenning, leaning in closer.

'No, don't whisper. That's just as bad, said Broaley. He shot Sherman a glance to see if he was sharing the same irritation. He was. 'Just talk ordinary, but watch what you say, or don't say.'

'Of course, of course, you're quite right. Yes, well the --- ah -- 'thing's' electronic programming was least suspect because the 'thing' had been roughed up physically.

However, once the mechanical discrepancy dawned on me, then tests were made on the circuits. Most rigorous tests, I can tell you.'

'I believe you; Jesus Christ, I believe you, even if I don't want to. So the circuits have definitely been fucked up? said Broaley.

'Most certainly, without question.'

Sherman thought for a moment. 'And Ancol doesn't handle the electronic side of it. In fact, only a few pieces of the mechanical side. Which means more than one factory is involved unknowingly. Probably a neat handful. Does that make sense to you, Mr Blenning?'

'Yes, I have to say it does hold its logic. But to be completely sure, I would have to compare my findings with the original master blueprints which your Mini--- which your 'people' keep. This would enable us to root out the very factories which are involved in this misdemeanour. However, if I may venture a thought, this is only a small part of the matter. The complete cystic growth must be performed elsewhere, if you follow me?'

'I think so, but clear our doubts.' The slowness in Sherman's words betrayed the fugged-upstate of his thoughts. He looked round at Broaley.

Broaley held the look for a moment before rocking back in his chair, shaking his head in mock amazement and turning back to Blenning. 'Yeah, go on; cheer us up with more good news. Then we can all die laughing.' The words rang too close to ominous for Sherman's liking.

'Well,' said Blenning, 'the party involved must not only have free, inconspicuous mobility between the factories involved, but must also have access to the master-plan before it is subdivided for contract among the individual manufacturers. If it weren't so, then discrepancies in the specific factory workshops would be uncovered if the person to whom they were referred did not already know of them.'

'So it's got to be someone who has access to the masterplan and sub unit component plans, makes copies of the sub unit plans, this time with faults in them, and then submits them for manufacture? Am I correct?' It wasn't the kind of thing you could feel chuffed at being correct, Sherman thought. 'Yes. It was an absolutely astronomical stroke of luck that I came across the flaw.

After all, how do you see what you have no reason to suspect; how does an assembly or inspection team find flaws when everything looks as well as it should on the sub unit plans and assembly plans? It's not as if you can take one out into the backyard and explode it to see if it works, so to speak. Heaven forbid!' Blenning paused to let his words sink in. 'No, it's only on some of the minor component plans submitted to small industrial workshops that flaws will be discovered. That's why I had to go to Ancol to verify my suspicions. Those manufacturers who work in accordance with flawed plans have no knowledge of what it is they are manufacturing. They simply obey instructions.'

'Light the blue touch paper and stand back.' Broaley's mock horror remark had all three sitting quiet for a moment's deep thought. Their silence brought the noise of those around them in closer. Sherman looked round at the surrounding crowd of people, happy in their collective drinks euphoria, totally unaware of the cataclysmic nature of discussion taking place in their midst, under their very noses.

'Doesn't sound very much like the disgruntled shop steward trying to get an extra ten minutes tea-break time for his fellow Trade Union workers, does it?' remarked Broaley sardonically.

'I should think that the guilt lies very much in the higher echelons,' said Blenning.

'Yes, I think you could be right, Mr Blenning. Very much higher,' said Sherman, intoning his suspicions.

'And most certainly a scientists, or someone along the chain of scientific connections,' concluded Blenning.

Broaley stabbed a finger in Blenning's direction to nail a point. 'And you're telling us you got all this when you were comparing *our* notes, *our* plans, with the fucked-up job on the *Yankee* bomb? So it's not just us who are in right shit of a mess; the Americans over there are in just as deep a hole with *their* hardware. Right?' For a moment Sherman thought that the Major, the way he was leaning forward aggressively, was going to grab Blenning by the shirt, and put him through the wall. But he didn't. It wasn't Blenning's fault; except only that he had discovered the fault that was giving them this bother. Broaley apparently had grasped this, sitting back again, clasping his knees tightly in his usual iron grip.

'I wouldn't be so sure that their situation is quite so acute as ours,' said Blenning, once again off at a galloping in his inner assessments. 'Their system of manufacturing and periodic inspection is a little different from ours, to say the least. Access to their nuclear arsenal is also made more difficult by the fact that their stockpile is partly always in active service. Ours, on the otherhand, have only been upgraded from their inactive state to the preparation stage, in the last five months for what I can only see, in my own personally limited capacity, to be the renewal of a Cold War tactics situation.' Blenning paused for yet another moment's inner calculation. 'I would say that a much lesser percentage of their nuclear weapons has been rendered inactive.'

Sherman was surprised at Blenning's knowing about the government plan for the redeployment of nuclear weapons. 'How long have you known of the upgrading programme?'

But Broaley cut in first. 'I only learned of them being taken out of moth balls since ---,' but he didn't want to give a date, '-- since recently.'

Sherman looked at both of them, quietly surprised at both of them knowing what he had taken to be his exclusively horded lot. The conversation was over; like a wisdom fruit having given up its last suck. They all three tried to digest what they could of it in a moment's silence. It was a long heavy silence. 'Well,' said Broaley, clunking his glass down on the table and sidling towards the door. 'I'll keep you informed,' he said cryptically, nodding to Sherman.

'Do,' said Sherman to the Major's back, as he elbowed his way through the crowd and disappeared out the door.

With Broaley gone and Blenning steeped in thought, Sherman went back to the phone. He deftly jabbed in the Grosvenor Square cover number of the American Embassy's CIA extension 'safe house'. With their gross number of agents the system they worked was like picking your contact for the job off a supermarket shelf. That was good old American 'commerce' for you. Sherman gave his pre-arranged cover name and that of his contact and waited. His attention came away from the general noise in the lounge as the tiny metallic voice pricked like an insect in his ear. He listened as the monotone voice of the duty officer gave the rendezvous and time and then clicked off again. He put the phone down with mixed feeling stirring inside him; relieved that things were starting to move, but a little uneasy over *where* they were moving to.

They walked up Northumberland Avenue towards the hub of the 'Empire', where Nelson still stood, undisturbed, on its supposedly unshakeable axle. Sherman turned to Blenning. 'That sure was one hell of a mouthful you gave us back there. Now I'm going to have you repeat it to my boss. He's of the finicky sort and likes things put to him with a straight logician's tongue. You can do that better than me, with your first hand experience.'

'Who exactly is it you're taking me to see?'

'No-one you would know, or waste a second glancing at in public. Actually, he's a Knight of the Order of the Thistle, and he can be just as prickly when he's in a nasty mood.' Sherman halted abruptly to turn and lay a hand on Blenning's arm to stop him. 'So I don't want you just pouring out your horror story findings. We want answers. We need answers. Even if it's just suggestions, at least. That would be something --- at this stage anyway. Right?'

Blenning wasn't quite sure how he was supposed to answer that.

23.33hrs, Whitehall. A clock ticked away sedately somewhere in the shadowy perimeter region of the large room that was lit only by a desk lamp. Sherman was bent over the desk in earnest writing and the nineteenth-century oil lamp gave off his enlarged furry outline like a great Troll. Outside, Big Ben had just lulled out to the nation that all was well, and Sherman was now working desperately to keep that assurance to mothers, fathers, grandchildren and all. Sounded like a ruddy nursery rhyme, except that there was no cheery jingle to it. The room, in spite of its calm surface appearance, had been the centre of one of the biggest security shake-ups they had known for some time. Sherman reflected how Sir Richard had taken it all rather well, considering how he had merely quivered and snorted occasionally like a roused dragon, without actually breathing out any of his usual tongues of fire. He had then lumbered Sherman with the responsibility of 'rectifying the situation' and submitting triplicate reports of the 'good news' to all other appropriate departments. They had spent some time discussing, if not arguing, how to minimise 'appropriate'. Sir Richard had also made it acutely clear that were he to reach for an axe later, to chop off a head, he would not be reaching far; there would only be one name on the executioner's short list: J Sherman. The initial general reaction to the situation had been nervous scoffings of disbelief, followed by minor stupefaction at the overall implication. You can just see that expression on Adam's face when he first lost his leaf and looked down to see that one of his precious pair was missing.

A starker nakedness pulsed in Sherman's mind at the thought of the country's 'defensive' weapons being blunted --- Trident missiles with power no less mythical than old Neptune's watery fork. And how many of Uncle Sam's great 'bald eagles' in the sky were removed of their beaks and talons? This, against the growing awareness of a new menacing Russia --- and China ---and---? Immediate Emergency Priority was now flashing in the country's security network nerve centres. Messages raced to and fro, only failing to melt the telephone lines with their urgency. How the situation was to be remedied had not been fully ascertained in the avalanche of orders that had followed, but Sherman was working on that now, with some help from Meeson, downstairs, from Strategic Strike Force Command. Sherman jerked out of his thoughts and leaned forward again to finish the report file he was doing for Meeson. He finished it, gave it a quick run-over, then threw it in the wire tray on the floor, to be collected later. In the meantime, lights would burn late in many MoD offices tonight. Elsewhere, in the ghostly gloom of government workshops throughout the country, ghoulish figures worked behind masks and shields in a race with time to make new fittings. The Lion could well roar, but it needed teeth, and these, they were hastily trying to give it.

But you couldn't affect a total recall of all weapons in the field for refitting without arousing suspicion in the enemy camp. That would be virtually broadcasting the situation, just short of picking up the red phone and giving the gossip to Putin personally. Most heads had nodded in agreement to this at the meetings. But the news would leak soon enough, if not sooner. It was a statistical fact, backed by psychologists and computers, that no intelligence system, whatever the country, could hold down such hot news involving so many departments and industries alike. Sooner or later, in the shadows of the marginal risk that all intelligences had to allow for, the mole was apt to poke his head above the ground to put his information in the dead letter box designated by the embassy's 'cultural attache'. Sherman thought of his discreet meeting that afternoon with CIA agent, Jeff Monks. As with Major Broaley, he had contacted Monks in order to get an unofficial lead, before sending out his own official interdepartmental report and setting up the investigation machine.

With the reports now in, there was less need for clandestine meeting with contacts, but he still liked to have a personal hold with his acting field officers. Monks, in his typically colossus philosophy of America versus All, had cynically whistled his "sweet jeepers" at the Russkies moving in, now that the Limey-Lion was toothless. You had to see that the man had the old sores over his cousins across the 'Pond'. You always soon, if not rapidly, tired of his jokes. You didn't so much see this guy carrying a chip on his shoulder, as a sack of potatoes, puns allowed. His anger came down more on Britain messing it up and needing a leg-up as usual; never mind any small damage that may have been done in the States. They had massive resources, as usual, to cover for any minor hiccups in their own backyard. He was greatly annoyed at the chance imbalance that could come if Russia took the temptation to move its threat closer to Britain and Europe. Monks' lies were as broad as his Illinois drawl. But that was okay when you knew that behind all that double-talk Monks would get his people up off their fat 'asses' to help turn the wheel and look into things. Time was vital. The thought itself was a gruelling enough workload.

Sherman looked at his watch and saw that Broaley was late with his field call. That would probably mean nothing. Broaley always operated loosely on his schedules. He looked at the other reports on his desk that had come in throughout the evening, without any great cheering. He decided to give Broaley another fifteen minutes, then he would put out a call. No, on second thoughts, he would do it now. Picking up the phone, he buzzed the Exchange Officer.

'Yes?'

'Have Signals put out a call for Major Broaley. Have them put him on to me as soon as his call comes in. Okay?'

'Right.'

Signals was the Department's short name for the Communications Room in the basement, which monitored field agents' progress. Sherman could have called downstairs direct to Signals, but he'd shrunk from doing so at the thought of Pamela waiting down there for him. She worked down there as a Section II Officer, and her official shift had finished at ten thirty. He was supposed to have collected her and taken her out for a meal somewhere, anywhere, at eleven o'clock. He sighed loudly at the thought of her waiting and looked at the work he still had on his desk. Christ, if ever there was a crueller tightrope to walk. You either fell to the enemy, or you fell to Pamela's sulking, with its inevitable bitchy bickerings creeping out by the time they had put the dessert away and were selecting from the cheese trolley. But then maybe she was right; maybe he *was* treating her badly. He probably would have been debagged as an 'absolute rotter' by Broaley's former officer mates at the regimental dinner. Or in an earlier generation, maybe.

Sitting upright, Sherman pressed his eyes with his fingers. He yawned and stretched, looking round at his Sagittarian cup. A present from *her*, back in Cambridge, just before he had left under dire force of events. Hell, that was a long time ago. Maureen had never seen it; she'd have gone bananas, even though it was only a piece of painted clay. Better kept here on his desk. There was still some coffee in the cup, but it was stone cold. Forgotten, when he got engrossed in his work. There wasn't even enough water left in the carafe for him to take a Solpadeine tablet. All those hours of solid concentration. The headache was beginning to make itself felt with the growing stiffness in the neck muscles.

He looked at the long dark Italian walnut dachshund with its bloodshot eye, that was the intercom with its solitary red eye. No amount of jabbing would bring him a fresh cup of coffee at this late hour. Before he could get up to stretch his legs about the room, the scrambler phone trilled out with an icy foreboding. He looked at it while slowly re-rolling the pin-stripe sleeve up his arm to the elbow. He picked up the receiver: 'Yes? Oh, it's you, Major. What new spine-janglers have you got for us now?'

A low guttural that you knew was Broaley's steely laugh when he was in his high-charged mood scraped its way out of the earpiece. 'Listen, Sherman, if you thought that was a rough package we got earlier from Blenning, let me tell you that was just the paper wrappings.'

'Well let's have it.' Sherman's dark forehead deepened its lines and the temple veins throbbed.

'What may have seemed like half a blessing in disguise, with bombs being made inactive, instead of going the other ----'

'Give it to me straight.'

'We've reason to believe ---- hold on a second.' The voice broke off to talk urgently with someone in the background, their words drowned by the roar of a passing aircraft. Sherman looked over the pile of paperwork and felt the horrible pang that all this effort to rectify one problem was about to be swept away by an even greater catastrophe. He was right.

'You still there, Sherman?'

Sherman shut his eyes for a second, as his patience waned. 'You were saying?'

'It's going around that something big is about to happen --- the Jihadi lot are looking to get their fingers into this one; that's if they haven't already. Our translator couldn't get anything out of the Russian sailor before he died. That's because the *Russian* sailor was *Iranian*. No need to mull long over that. Speaks for itself. '

'Big? You mean ---'

'The mushroom pies, themselves. Full-blown nukes.'

'Is this connected to what's already happened?' The silence at the other end was Broaley's answer. 'Is that it, then? Nothing else?' Sherman's understatement was a measured self control to stop the floor from opening up beneath him, at the horrifying news.

'Hell, Sherman, isn't that *enough*?'

'Right, Major. Stay around where we can get to you. I'll call you back shortly. All ri----'

Sherman almost felt his tongue being clipped, with Broaley cutting off bluntly. The Major was not one to waste time standing around for nice cheerios. Sherman put the phone down and leaned forward on his elbow, cupping his chin in his hand. Tapping his teeth, he thought for a second. Little fingers of electricity poked his inside, where panic tried to hack a hole through his self control. He would liked to have gouged the intercom's red eye out with his pencil. Instead, he flicked the pencil up into the air, watching it clatter against the Waterloo battle map print on the wall and fall down onto the table below it. Leaning across, he stabbed the intercom.

'Yes?'

'Get Communications on to me, will you. I want them ready to issue new prime priority signals for a Number One Alert. Have them ready for re-briefing and re-allocation of those already out in the field. Have you got that?'

'Yes. Right away.'

Sherman went to the gleaming triangular stainless steel sink in the corner and splashed some water on his face. Rolling down his sleeves, he put on his jacket and was about to go out, when he changed his mind and made for the intercom again.

'Yes?'

'Change that message to Communications I gave you. Have the call put through to me in Signals. I'll be down there for the next few minutes if anybody needs me. Got that?' As he waited for the girl's reply, he heard the voice coyly ask someone in the background what the extension number was for Signals. He realised that the nightshift change must have just been made, with a 'temps' operator from another department taking over. He didn't waste time. 'Get Mr Cochrane to fill in the details for you.'

'Yes.'

Going down to the Communications Room always guaranteed a drop in your temperature. Not just because it was colder, but also because of the psychological effect of the massive stone walls all around, which gave a chilling dampness to the air. Even after the installation of the new heating system there had been no complete escape from the chilling chastisement you felt when descending the stone stairs. The bill still went to the taxpayer, and various departments upstairs lost some fringe benefits in an insane attempt to balance the payment. Sherman reflected that they had been denied a new electric kettle.

Pamela was perched side-saddle on the corner of the table, huddled over a copy of *Vogue*. She had on a cream cotton skirt and a coffee nylon blouse, with the white bra straps showing through it, pushed into bold outline by her bent back. Sherman put his hands on her shoulders and felt the sudden tensed withdrawal in her body. He prepared himself for the onslaught. It would come, slow at first. She put on a brave face and smiled up at him. 'Ready?' she said, jumping up and piling things into her suede shoulder bag. She didn't wait for his answer, but rattled on about where they were going for their late night meal. It washer usual way of swamping him in words and commitments, so that he had all the more to pull himself out of when he couldn't manage. She sensed that something was up, and that he couldn't manage -- yet again. Not just because of the time she'd waited, but by her shrewd instinct from that momentary contact between his hands and her shoulders. She pulled her comb through her silken black page boy hair. 'So where are we going? I'm starving, now that I'm eating for two.'

His eyebrows quivered. 'You're *not*, are you? Eating for *two*?'

'That had you worried, didn't it?' Her eyes shone with that soft beauty that never failed to draw you in; but the spite behind her teasing showed through in the brief tautening of her lips. You could expect more when she was in that mood. He shielded himself by picking up the duty roster and sifting through the sheets. 'Something's up?' she said, the cheer dimming on her face and the comb strokes slowing down. 'You can't manage?'

The shortening remarks, with their feigned surprise, were meant to slip out her hurt feelings, so he played his part of preparing to put on the tar and feathers shirt. 'Yes, sorry; something *has* come up. A right cropper you couldn't imagine. *Really.*' If only it *was* imagination.

'But that was hours ago. You said you could manage by eleven. And I've waited all this time. I even put in an extra half hour's duty with Norma, to fill in the time. They both looked at the other Radio Officer seated in front of the transmitters, playing mute to their conversation, and stolidly attacking the blue checked wool pattern with her crochet needle.

'No, you don't understand; this is something that's just come up a few minutes ago. A Number One Alert, no less. I've called for an emergency meeting of officers upstairs in ten minutes, and a general recall by Communications on all allocation codes for current missions. This is too big for both of us.' He shook his head. 'No can do; sorry, love.'

She stared for a moment and then pulled herself together. She was the Radio Officer this time. 'I see. Do you want me to stay on here, on extra duty.?'

'No, it's all right; we'll manage. You get off and catch some kip.' He was going to say that she looked tired, and could do with her beauty sleep --- in the kindest possible way; but she would have found some way to be offended by that, so he left it out. 'I think we're all going to be needing sleep and extra vitamins by the morning.' He handed her his car keys. She looked at them without taking them. 'It's all right,' he said. 'I'll get a car from the pool. Go on.' He shook the keys insistently in front of her.

'All right. ' She took the keys and hooked her bag resignedly over her shoulder. 'You look as if you could do with some sleep yourself.' The huff in her voice was almost undetectable.

'I know.' He shifted restlessly before her last plea. She was almost about to dart forward to kiss him, or smooth his shirt or something, but she pulled herself back. He flinched at the gap of indecision between them, hating these theatrical moments when they came. She strode resolutely to the doorway, stopping there to rap the keys sharply against the door-jamb. Ouch! He felt that.

She turned around. 'Will you be long?' The pussycat had softened a little and drawn its claws in.

He pursed his lips playfully and blew a silent whistle. 'I'll be as soon as I can,' he said, then thinking more seriously, 'but I've a feeling it's going to be a long, long night.'

6

06.47hrs, 24th June, S.E. London. The great 15 ton haulage truck thundered on further into the great metropolis. Just like the neutron speeding into the centre of the atom to cause fission from the colossal impact with the nucleus --- the atomic explosion, embryo of the nuclear explosion. These thoughts burned in the mind of Jihad zealot, Maneesh Hassani, seated beside the driver. As he watched the buildings around them racing past, he imagined them doing just that, only with greater velocity of fury as they were ripped from their foundations by the nuclear blast.

Hassani, yet only seventeen, was immensely proud of his advanced schooling, Allah be praised, that gave him this important scientific understanding of the atom and its great power. So infinitesimally small, yet so powerful. Just like their nation, so tiny, yet able to strike out with omnipotent force through the will and power of Allah. Allah be praised. It had always puzzled him why this great instrument of Divine retribution that was theirs, atomic fission, should have been discovered by a Christian, Enrico Fermi, when he first split the atom. But Maneesh did not question this mystery. He obediently accepted this confusion, in his limitations as a mere mortal, as part of the unfathomable mystique that manifested as sacred purpose.

Allah had his reasons for everything far beyond the finite reasoning of man. Allah be praised. By the will and power of Allah, a truly Divine purging would be delivered upon the infidel Christian worshippers of these lands. Allah be praised. They would be smote down and cast into the ultimate dark damnation of their Devil. Allah be praised. Maneesh avoided looking at the medallion dangling from the rear view mirror which bore the image of the traveller, Christopher, carrying the infantile form of his god. He glanced aside at the driver. Cursed infidel! For the alcoholic breath reeking from the man's mouth and the profane pictures of naked females displayed about the cabin, he too would be smote down. Allah be praised. It was unfortunate that a brother Jihadi had died in the course of his duty in the Russian submarine since he had been receiving invaluable training from the Russian nuclear technicians. But that he had died, and he, Maneesh Hassani, had been chosen to serve in his place for this grand mission of divine retribution was the unquestionable will of Allah. Allah be praised.

Wrathful thoughts of righteous slayings were interrupted by the gears growling down as they slowed and finally stopped. 'This is as far as I can take you, pal. That's Putney over that way, away along that road there. Best I can do for you. Okay?' The driver had originally not meant to give the lift. But the Paki or Arab bugger had promptly handed him a very large sum of money with no sign of reluctance. It occurred to him that anyone who could deal out that sort of dosh with such great ease without blinking an eye must be well off. So why the hell come here, to this country, where things were overcrowded enough. He'd had a mind to put this question to the young lad, but something about the lean face, something tense and dark had made him hold back his query. He'd kept his mouth shut and smartly stuffed the money away in his shirt pocket. 'Cheers, mate.'

The truck moved off, receding rapidly down the road into the distance. Hassani turned away from the sight of the disappearing vehicle and looked around. Totally new to the area, indeed the *country*, he felt somewhat disorientated. But he would be guided. Not just by the address on the paper he held, but by the Divine intervention of Allah. Allah be praised. An empty silence hung around him. The buildings, by their very orderly stillness, gave off an aura of calmness that Maneesh found somewhat disquieting. In the desecrated land that he'd just left, his homeland, the air was continually rent by the scream of war, of bombs and heavy weapon-fire. The sound of mass slaughtering of muslims by the demonic American and British military forces. Buildings that were fortunate enough to be still standing simply shuddered as they waited for their turn, or that of a neighbouring structure, to fall. Children born there now barely took a breath between such horrific wrenchings of the air and knew of no sound that was peace. Most surely an almighty vengeance that was the wrath of Allah would be wreaked upon the infidel Americans and British, to their ultimate destruction. Allah be praised.

Maneesh praised Allah one more time, invoking further holy salutations for his guidance, before crossing the road to walk off in the wrong direction, along a road that wasn't the shortest route to the intended address.

11.16hrs, Whitehall. Sir Richard Hossley was just closing his statement to the Committee: 'In all, gentlemen, what we have is a holocaust imminent in our very laps. So there it is. Any comments forthcoming? He took his hands away from the table's edge and rested them over the white blotter. He peered, owl-like, over his gold-rim half-eye reading spectacles for a second, before taking them off to look down the long table. Sherman, seated beside him, supported his quiet survey of the others, lined there before them like two rows of legless chessmen. Once was not enough, and they doubled their splendour in dimmer, inverted, reflections along the table's sides. Even ignoring the colours, the linear primness of backs, moustaches and ribbons, fitted the straight table and the high backed chairs like only the military could. Their chests together boasted enough fruit cocktails of campaign ribbons and 'gongs' to knock the bottom out of the dealers' market. Civvies were in the minority.

Down Sir Richard's side of the table sat Brigadier E J Guthrie-Manning, GCB, DSO; Air-Marshal J L Wainright, DSO, DFC; Field-Marshal J H Harcow, VC, MBE, KCB; Major C E Broaley, VC, GC; and Captain J Mallison RN. Facing them on Sherman's side were Admiral H C Smillsoe, CB, MBE, DSO; Maj-General Sir James Greeley, KCB, CMG, DSO; Sir David Hopeson, KG, MBE; Colonel J L Frewnhurst-Dovett, DSO, MBE; Flight-Lt R Grovensby and Sqd-Ldr J B Goddfrey. Sherman was the only person present who had not done any military service. The nearest he had come to soldiering was his lead dragoon miniatures in his study.

It was an impressive assembly of distinguished services. More acutely, it was all the urgent contacts summoned from Air Intelligence, Naval Intelligence, Army Intelligence and Counter Intelligence for the 10.45a.m. meeting.

Several eyelids blinked and the odd finger twisted a blotter's ear, as they considered Sir Richard's words and all that they had discussed over the last thirty odd minutes. Sherman especially considered the scathing looks Sir Richard had given him, like a Gothic gargoyle, with his foreboding of the looming disaster, singeing him like a serpent's tongue. Between the two of them, there was no doubt into whose lap this great ruddy mess was being thrown. He looked down the table, examining the faces for something, anything, that was more than a wrinkled service despatch. He looked at Broaley, who was studying his watch more than his notes and who seemed more distant from the meeting than the rest of them. Whilst the others seemed content with the written reports and pieces of paper in front of them, Broaley appeared to be preoccupied with activities elsewhere. His mood swung between restlessness and a studied boredom, making him conspicuous among the rest in Sherman's eyes, as he shifted from elbow to elbow. When he looked up and caught Sherman's eye, his face offered no expression or signal of communication beyond the long defiant stare. He fingered his moustache all the while, haughtily holding back what he was thinking, and then looked back down his notes. Sherman returned his attention to the meeting.

Air-Marshal Wainright glanced at Sir James and turned to Sir Richard. 'We have, in fact, as you know, had Operation SHIELD in operation since 14.00hrs yesterday. With this new development, I think we are all agreed to go ahead with a Section One stand-by on Operation BLOWTORCH.' All heads nodded and Sir James continued with the counterpart: 'It is, in fact, the best foreseeable measure to be taken. The crux of the matter is that this latest development only narrows the margin in which we can be allowed to fail. And we mustn't fail. To meet this new crisis, we must supposedly cut a few tight corners, but otherwise, the best plan is already in operation. We can only wait and see now.'

Sir Richard, having heeded the words and already acquainted with SHIELD, now turned to Sherman to be handed the new file on Operation BLOWTORCH. He rolled his eyes up at Sherman, and Sherman sensed the momentary brooding fire burning through the old bloodshot eyes, where fish nets of dilated blood vessels pulsed away over the yellowing white sclera. The old man's mood had worsened to this, following the new developments and the Number One Alert emergency Sherman had set up. The file was like a slab of lead to Sherman as handed it over. Sir Richard took the folder and turned away, resuming once more the eloquent air that could have been compared with the best in the Royal Shakespeare Company. He donned his spectacles once more and ran his eyes over the sheets with their bright red CLASSIFIED stampings. Even as simple words typed on simple paper, the details of strategies to countermand nuclear devastation razing hundreds of square miles with multi-megaton fury, were parching to the throat. Sir Richard's eyes twinkled with quiet wonder and he shook his head in gentle disdain. He looked up at the others with his benign smile. 'I must be getting old, gentlemen, but I suddenly feel the need for water at the table, which I see has once again been neglected.'

Polite strained smiles broke out all down the table and everyone took the message to shift the topic to another stage. Admiral Smillsoe looked up to the top of the table. 'What do we have on this Dr Linsdale?

'Up until now, from what we have here, that is, he could only be classified as ideal,' said Sherman, sliding his file about pensively with his finger. He wasn't happy with the scant details it gave. Like an out of date bus timetable, it may have had its use in the past, but it didn't satisfy their purpose now. There had to be more. Something that would give some rational explanation as to why an otherwise sane man would suddenly do the insane thing and sabotage his country's nuclear defence system, so threatening millions of lives. But *had* it been suddenly? Sherman pondered over this. He continued his delivery on Dr Linsdale's dossier: 'Respectable middle-class background; grammar school education; first class honours at Cambridge in nineteen ninety; went on to take doctorate in research in the Cavendish Laboratory, Cambridge; took up lectureship in Quantum Physics and Nuclear Plasma Fission Mechanics at Cambridge in ninety six; screened and appointed to full scale salary by the Ministry of Defence in nineteen ninety nine; thereafter allowed full access to all of the Ministry of Defence Nuclear Armaments establishments.' Sherman flipped the file's cover shut. It's job was done. It had simply put a name to the man under the spotlight. Now they had to get on with the real gritty stuff of finding out *why* the man had done that for which he was under the spotlight.

'Are we to understand that he's been allowed exclusive personal access to everything?' said the Admiral.

'No,' said Sherman, 'he worked all this time in conjunction with his superior, Dr Hollingsford. And, of course, the other members of the staff.

However, Dr Hollingsford was taken ill some eleven months or so ago and is now in Guy's Hospital with lung cancer. That situation, in all probability, has obviously afforded Dr Linsdale the opportunity to take over as Head Physicist with a total freehand in exclusive access to Top Secret material.'

Someone muttered and tapped a pen.

'As far as motives are concerned,' Sherman went on, 'it would appear to be personal, so far. From what material we could gather, it seems that Dr Linsdale was discreetly promised an MBE in two thousand and one. That, alas, didn't materialise. He was also turned down in his application for a professorship at his Alma Mater two years ago.' Sherman paused, tapping his pen, not fully persuaded by what he'd just read out. 'Still seems a bit weak --- as a reason to go playing about with bombs.' His continued tapping spoke as much for his mind's searching thoughts.

'Political?'

Heads swivelled round on their bright uniforms, looking towards the dark blazer and neat Artillery tie set with a sharp symmetrical Windsor knot. Perhaps the one, if not the only one, decent legacy left behind by the Duke when he relinquished his crown to abdicate. Broaley didn't bother to look up from his folder, toying with its flap. 'You have something further to say on that for us, *Major?*' said Sherman, his tapping suspended in anticipation.

'A possibility; widening the scope.'

'And ----?' But Sherman didn't expect anything else from the Major. You knew he didn't waste time promising what he didn't want to give. If that was all he gave, then that was all you got. Broaley simply looked up with his usual expression of restless impatience as an answer to Sherman's question. He then looked pointedly at his watch. Sherman got the message. He tidied his papers into his folder, picking it up, giving a curt glance to Sir Richard. As chairman of many meetings, Sir Richard was accustomed to closing them with a slower mode of casual conversation. He didn't much like being hurried -- pushed -- especially by a subordinate. But he appreciated Sherman's haste in getting on with things.

Sir Richard stood up. 'Same time again tomorrow, everyone? Unless, that is, something else gets in your way.' The icy intonation in the words were for Sherman's benefit. Ignoring Sir Richard's loaded remark, Sherman affected to look down the long room for any further comments. As they rose slowly and put things away in their cases, it was apparent that most were not satisfied, wanting to go off with something more substantial to chew over.

'Haven't we managed to apprehend Linsdale, then?' said Brigadier Guthrie-Manning.

Sherman looked to the Major. With a little reluctance that only Sherman recognised, Broaley took his cue. 'We haven't managed to pick him up just yet, but a constant vigil has been mounted on all airports and seaports since the alert went out yesterday. In fact, a single flight ticket in his name, by British Airways to Munich was confiscated by our officers at Gatwick Airport last night. Our enquiries into his whereabouts, with casual contacts, has revealed a latent urge to leave the place. To leave the country, in fact. Now we know why. The chances of him doing any further damage to the nuclear defence system would appear to be remote, now that he knows his little ploy has been unearthed.'

'Can we be so sure that he won't resort to other tactics for escape, Major?' asked the Brigadier.

'Yes, well we have kept this in mind and have taken the precautionary measure of -----'

Speech halted and all attention went to the bright red scrambler phone perched on the elegant Sheraton side-table, flashing its light and 'peep-peep-peeping' beneath the quiet Turner water colour. Broaley stopped sidling towards the door. Sherman stepped over promptly and picked up the phone. He listened. 'Yes, one moment.' He turned and held out the phone to Broaley. 'Major, it's for you.'

The Major came away from the door, to take up the phone. 'Yes, speaking --- Yes --- Yes --- All right.' The click of the phone being replaced on its rest cut the room's electric silence. Broaley took a few moments splaying his moustache with forefinger and thumb. 'That was one of our field operatives reporting. It seems that Dr Linsdale has gone to ground. Possibly with a Russian cell. Vanished completely.' To Broaley, the news, with its untimely interruption, was like a power-cut in his report. To Sherman, it was more like a complete disconnection, his cable and plug being yanked out rudely from beneath him.

The Air-Marshal broke the silence. 'Dr Linsdale or no Dr Linsdale, the task's not yet lost. I wouldn't put it down entirely as bad decorum to pressurise the Embassy, to release Linsdale. In the meantime, I suggest that we all get out of here and get on with it.'

Murmurs of approval went out all round and Sir Richard took over. 'Very well, gentlemen, if we have no more to discuss, I once more declare this meeting closed. If we could have your attendances tomorrow, at the agreed time of ten forty-five. Thank you.' He shuffled up his papers and handed them to Sherman.

Everyone started to leave and their informal talk bubbled out along with the general rustle of things being put away. Just as the door was opening, all the noise suddenly ebbed away to an expectant silence. The scrambler phone was once more calling for their attention. Sherman took up the phone calmly and held everyone's attention on his back for an eternal few seconds. He then turned to face into the room, summoning everyone one back with his pen held in the air. 'Yes -- Right -- All right.'

They waited as he put the phone down.

'A letter from Dr Linsdale to his solicitor has just been confiscated and opened. It was to have been read by the solicitor some time in the future. The message is grim. Linsdale was intending to blackmail the country to tone down its political stance of military aggression or else suffer the havoc of nuclear disaster. He doesn't say in the letter how such a disaster was to be brought about, but a separate intelligence report has just come in to say that the material for roughly four fifteen megaton nuclear bombs has been found to have gone missing. Apparently done over a long period of many months.' Sherman paused to take in the dismayed expressions all around. 'Further to this, reports are coming in that a Jihadi terrorist operation is underway to take over from where Dr Linsdale left off, bringing in the necessary material for completion and fully assembling the remaining two bombs, making them ready to explode in a combined programme with the first two bombs.' He took a long breath to let the news set in. 'There are also unconfirmed whispers going around of a sixty hour countdown from noon today. We're not quite sure about that; needs some looking into.'

The Air-Marshal blew into his handkerchief. Nobody was able to give a better answer than that.

11.41hrs. Sir Richard stood in the doorway of Sherman's office shaking his head in disbelief. 'The man's obviously a lunatic; a complete paranoid lunatic.'

'Probably.' Sherman's perfunctory answer was an attempt to shrug his boss off his back, so he could get on with his work. He didn't agree with the old man's hasty diagnosis. The man was often short-sighted in his judgements as well as being a pest. There had to be something more to Linsdale's behaviour than a few loose marbles. Okay, it was just a gut feeling, but he just knew that there was something else. Something he had missed out -- had overlooked. He opened the safe and took out the folder with that day's secret telephone codes, turning a deaf ear Sir Richard's words. There were a lot of calls to put out, lunatic or not. He was surrounded by lunatics, if you put it that way, in the filing cabinets lining the walls. Except that these were classified as personnel and belonged to military powers whose actions may have been alien, but otherwise not lunatic.

Sherman found the codes he wanted and prepared to dial, looking up at Sir Richard to show that he was busy. Sir Richard missed the message and went on: 'And you say there was nothing else in Linsdale's letter? No ransom, no ultimatum?'

'None whatsoever,' said Sherman, wondering over this himself, at the same time managing to put the first two codes through to switchboard. From there they would go to the officer in Communications, who would put out the calls and have them returned at his prescribed intervals. 'Like you said, the man's probably a lunatic. All it needed was that little bit of something to push him over the edge. But what *is* that something, eh?' Sherman's last remark was a subdued muttering, more to himself, as he worked on, head down, through the pages of his codebook. 'It doesn't really change our position. We were after the man before. We're still after him, and we'll get him.'

'You've lost the bloody man, damn it! How do you explain that?'

'We have everybody out on the job. We can't tread too warily if we've already frightened the man and forced him to go to ground. If we mount too fierce a search, he may never show his head above ground,' Sherman paused and tapped Linsdale's file, 'until it's too late.'

'You're slipping,' insisted Sir Richard.

'We're going out full stretch.

'You're slipping, and it's got to stop.'

Sherman didn't answer the remark, but went on putting the other three codes through to the switchboard.

Sir Richard came up to the desk and tapped it pontifically with his podgy forefinger. 'You would do well to consider that when others before you went "out full stretch", they stretched until they broke and had no more to give. That's what you're paid for, Sherman.'

Sherman got up and put the file back in the folder back in the safe. He turned round to face Sir Richard. 'Major Broaley's the best man for the job. I wouldn't have put him in charge, otherwise.'

Sir Richard nodded, playing on his lip with his finger. 'So long as you think so. Nobody is disputing your judgement on that aspect.' He paused a moment to think and then glanced sharply at Sherman. 'Perhaps your trouble is that you have a whip but you don't know how to crack it.'

Sherman went back to his desk considering that there might certainly be some truth in Sir Richard's observation.

A knock on the door broke the thoughtful silence and Broaley came in. He looked at each of them in turn, suspended in their aborted topic, waiting for them to finish their business. Sir Richard looked at the other two, knowing the tussle that went on between them. He went to the door and then turned round for a parting remark to Sherman. 'A good dog can be told to sit down or else be plumped down on its rump. The position is the same in either case, but the dignity is acutely different.'

Sherman acknowledged the inference with some embarrassment, seeing as its subject, Broaley, was standing there listening. Broaley had no inkling what the words meant, but he did catch the odd deliberate way that Sherman avoided eye contact. Sherman noted that of all the others, Broaley had been the one least perturbed by the horrific news they'd received earlier in the Committee Room. In fact, it seemed to have bucked him up with a new surge for action. Perhaps their being on the edge of a precipice situation was the personal catalytic whistle blast that Broaley needed to prompt him up and over his own individual trench top.

Broaley looked at the bulging folders fighting to stay in the wire baskets on the desk and decided to balance the folder he'd brought on top of the intercom. 'That's the report you wanted. It's all in there, the best we could rake up so far, on schedule to the hour.'

Sherman stared deadpan at the green file then turned away to walk aimlessly about the room with his hands in his pockets. 'It's what's *not* in there that worries me, Major. The rules have changed, as we all now know, with that last call. We're now playing the game to his, or should I say, *their* rules, to *their* deadline, and when the final whistle goes, there'll be no extra time to play.' He suddenly stopped walking and leaned an elbow on the filing cabinet to turn and look at Broaley.

Broaley put a filter tip cigarette to his lips and lit it, closing his eyelids slightly, to scrutinise his 'superior. He leaned over to open a window, without taking his eyes off Sherman. He was keen to see what this college boy, stuffed with his congruent triangles and Euclidean theorems, could suggest that could possibly improve his own methods of ferreting out traitors and terrorists.

'You're slipping, Major, and it's got to stop. We've got to get him now!' Sherman wondered if Broaley could detect the tinniness in his voice as he used the second-hand words borrowed from Sir Richard. Broaley cocked an eyebrow and smoked on slowly, watching intently. Sherman leaned his head down, to run his fingers through his hair.

'Have we no idea where he is, at all? Has he really vanished into thin air, like you say?'

'We've got surveillance teams out there scraping shadows off walls and streetlamps, on the chance that one of them turns out to be him. Precise spot checks on all the places he would go to, or could go to. It's all a matter of diligent checking and back checking. A few minutes can make all the difference. If we miss him, we can re-locate him again by more systematic back checking, until we get him by elimination.'

'And if he's vanished, that simply means that you've missed him momentarily, and that you'll get him by simply back checking? Is that what you're telling me, Major?'

'No, that's something different altogether. If he's vanished, it means, in all probability, that he's using a different bolt-hole. No, we allow for a certain period of back checking to come up with positive results, before we apply the term 'vanished'. If we still come up with negative results after that period then he's ---'

'----Vanished. I get the picture. So if he's gone to ground or using a new bolt-hole, as you say, and it's not in any of the regular known places, how do you know where to look? Tell me that, Major.'

Broaley evaded the direct question with its loose ground, where there were uncertainties, and fell back on the secondary sense of past experience with its proven ground. 'It can be an advantage, in a way. If we know for certain that he's no longer in any of the regular places, we can remove our attention from these locations and concentrate our strength entirely on new ones.'

'Like groping in the dark, you mean? Sounds dangerously vague to me, Major.'

'It may seem vague to *you*, but there's a sound, methodical system involved in it, I can tell you. It's not easy,' he paused, looking with innuendo at Sherman's empty chair, 'as you well know, or *not* know.' He blew out the smoke, examining the hopes and doubts switching on and off on Sherman's face. 'You don't seem convinced. Maybe you'd like to make a field inspection? Be on the spot and see things for yourself?' The smile crept out on Broaley's face.

Sherman straightened up. 'You know what, Major, I think I'll take you up on that.' He went over to the intercom and jabbed the button. 'Have the calls from Communications put through to Signals when they come in. Have Signals put them through to me via Major Broaley's field code number.' He looked round at the Major, for his number.

'Seven one nine.'

'Seven one nine,' repeated Sherman. 'Got that? I'm going out; don't know when I'll be back.'

'Right.'

Sherman pressed another button and told the secretary to let Sir Richard know that he would be out indefinitely. He grabbed the files and virtually threw them into their cabinets, locking them away securely. 'All right, Major, let's go.'

As they went down the stairs, Broaley gave Sherman's arm a sharp prod. 'Your file on Linsdale wasn't quite up to scratch back there. It seems he spent a sabbatical at the MIT over in the States. And who knows, maybe a lot more time outside of that known period. That would tie in with them having *their* knuckles bruised as well, and not just us on this side of the water. Langley are looking into it. I'll put a sure bet that that's where the seed for this whole damn mess was planted. Mark my word, Sherman.' Absolute conviction was another hard prod to Sherman's arm. You always knew Broaley hadn't yet lost his rag when it was only *one* new sleeve that you needed refitting onto your Saville Row jacket.

7

11.43hrs, 24th June, Notting Hill W11. The antique/curio shop door jerked open with a shy 'ting', to shatter the inner serenity of dust-laden neglect and possibly that of the outer street as well. But nothing else moved in the languid hot air of the summer morning, except convection currents twisting around the bright red pillar box growing out of the dull pavement like a long septic polyp. This was a safe distance down the street and so anyone going to post a letter was hardly likely to disturb them. Overhead, chirping sparrows hopped among the forest of chimneys, disturbing no-one but the insects peering fearfully from the gutter pipes and slates.

The man took all this in with a sweeping scrutiny and was satisfied. He turned and pushed on in, into the shop's dark interior. There wasn't much to stop the eye in its search of the junk, except a handsome bronze-cased stick barometer and an elegant eighteenth century lantern clock. He gazed up at the lovely brass dial, suspended there in doleful silence, and appreciated his own taste for brass and metals. Woods and earthenware he invariably left to others. And others would invariably come for them. That was extra certain on days like this, when the weather was so fine. He glanced out the window and half expected to see a crowd of American tourists descending on the shop with their loud frenetic chatter. Working with semi-professionals like this always made him feel edgy.

Just as he was about to whistle his presence, the inner door opened in a happy bustle of noise. George Maunders, the owner, appeared in cardigan and leather elbow pads, laughing and talking to someone. He was trying to hold something back with his leg against the wall, but it escaped and he called out after it: 'Here, boy; here, boy. Come on, boy.'

In a brown and white flash of yelps, the young springer spaniel was out through the counter gap and bounding up and down the shop, rocking the curio pieces and scarring the linoleum with its claws. It finally stopped in front of the stranger to look up at him, its eyes loaded with mischief, like its thumping tail. Maunders laughed all the while at the dog's antics, while the stranger looked on in stern silence. He was plainly irritated by such wasteful acts of energy, where a more specific act of precision could be more efficient. He found it irritating even in animals lower than humans. Maunders' mind registered the situation and he lifted the counter flap to step smartly through the gap. Still laughing, he slapped the dog's rump playfully and chased it into the back. He was back and sealed behind the counter in an instant, never once changing his cheery image and glad to have overcome what he'd judged to be a dodgy moment. 'He'll be the death of me one of these days, he will,' said Maunders. 'What, with those teeth of his on the furniture, he'll give me a heart attack, he will. Still, what can I do for you, sir?'

The man looked at Maunders for a second, before taking the flat paper bag out of his jacket pocket. 'I'm in a hurry and I've got to play cricket,' he said. 'I always play cricket in June. Do *you*?'

The code words sent an electric sensation through Maunders' inside. He realised that he was once more being summoned for active work, as 'sleepers' like himself occasionally were. His good cheer evaporated from within him like the methylated spirits he used for cleaning his pieces. Before he could reply, the man slid the small china plate from the bag. It was a quaint Staffordshire piece, three and a half inches in diameter, with a blue and white transfer print of a little kitten. The man's hand came away from the plate's edge to reveal a triangular piece missing where the hind legs and tail should have been. He glanced up to see Maunders' reaction.

Maunders' eyebrows twitched slightly and he thought for a moment. The hollow phrases were seldom used and tumbled out of his back memory like clumsy jigsaw letters from a dusty shelf. 'No, I don't, but I watch it on TV unless I've got repairs to do.' He ambled over to the drawer beside the till and took out an old Swan Vestas matchbox. He took out the small triangular fragment and fitted it in perfectly. The kitten now had two hind legs and a curly tail. Maunders straightened up and looked the man in the eye. The man couldn't resist a smile at the positive outcome of his unannounced arrival. Maunders' cheerful expression faded only a little. There was always that mixture of duty and fear in his stomach on these occasions, when he had to venture forth from the cocoon of respectability that was his sleeper cover, to do his *real* work.

'Section Three sent me. They thought it safer to operate independent of the Embassy,' the man said.

'You'd better come in, then.'

Rather than wait for Maunders to come round in his casual slow manner, the man stepped over to the door himself and snapped the Yale lock shut and turned the 'closed' sign to the outside.

'You're just in time for a cup of tea. I was just brewing it for my elevenses before you came in,' said Maunders over his shoulder, as he went in the back room. The man was in no mood for tea, no more than he had time to waste, but he followed on into the sleeper's den.

No sooner had the door to the inner back room closed, than a 'collector' came into view, pausing warily outside the window. Close on his heels came another 'collector'. One of them seemed more interested in the door lock than the antiques within. Broaley turned to Sherman. 'Closed,' he said.

Sherman looked at the sign for a second and then, still keeping his tight-lipped silence, he cast his eyes round the shop's interior, searching its dark walls and corners. For exactly what, though, he didn't know. 'There doesn't seem to be anyone about,' he said quietly. 'You're sure this is one of the sleeper houses where he could be hiding?'

'Either that, or it could be a link to where he's gone. We're pretty certain that it's a unit of the cell that's taken him in.' Broaley took out a thin strip of plastic and moved nearer to the Yale lock. 'If you could just move in a little closer, behind me, to give me cover, I can get at this lock.'

Sherman put his hand on Broaley's arm to stop him. 'No, don't'

Broaley straightened up and nearly spumed. 'For God's sake, Sherman! Don't bother me with 'breaking and entry' nonsense. This is no time to wail about legalities. You're the one who wanted to go all out and get the bastard!'

'No, it's not that,' Sherman said, still looking about the shop, trying to marshal his thoughts.

'What then?'

'I don't know exactly. I just think we should wait and watch where there's nobody there. You said yourself that we can't be too careful, lest we frighten them away. Well there doesn't seem to be anybody here. So all right, grab -- what's his name? --Manders, did you say? -- when he comes back ---'

'Maunders; his cover name.'

'All right, we grab him. Then what? Isn't there the chance that we could interrupt his signal interval to the others in the cell and blow the whole thing? You're the ruddy expert, Major!'

'Don't get clever with me, Sherman! It's the chance we've got to take.'

'How about mounting a watch and moving on to the other suspected cell units?'

Broaley breathed in deeply, holding his temper at the other's interference in what he considered was inept judgement. Yet he considered the other side as well. 'All right, we'll go back to the car and radio for a surveillance unit to take over here meantime.' He checked his watch for the rough time of entry on the report. 'Okay?' His bark was just a little touch short of insubordination, but for the fact that it was Sherman who was the subordinate in the field.

'Okay.'

They moved away, as casually as they had come, back to the car parked round the corner.

Back in the shop's back room, the man sank back in the leather armchair and studied Maunders standing there, in his typically domesticated image, fiddling with tea bags. George's simple philosophy was an affable one that made him the perfect friend that you so often sought in a whole lifetime but very seldom found. Being born a Londoner, in Stepney in '41, two days after the bombing of Pearl Harbor, how else could it be, except that he should be a friend to unburden his fellow Londoners. And that's how it had been since he'd opened up his business here, in '74.

But the man holding out his hand for the cup knew the details to be different, as he ran his mind over Maunders' dossier. Maunders, in fact, had been born in 1951, not in Stepney, but in the small market town of Uralsk, on the River Ural in what was then the Union Republic of Kazakh. Born the second son of a granary worker, he had been registered on the town poll as Grigorov Ivan Mahrshazlinsky. Selected at an early age for special schooling, he had been taken from his parents and family and put to training that would some day benefit his glorious Motherland. At the age of twelve, he was already speaking rudimentary English and learning the idiomatic oddities of his new native country. In '70 he graduated from the renowned Marx/Engels Academy in Gorky on the Volga, as a fully fledged 'Londoner', with an accent thick in the vernacular that was his native birthright. He was planted in the new English soil in '71 and later manoeuvred into the present sleeper position.

Maunders looked up. 'Sugar?'

'No.' The man thought for a moment and looked at Maunders. 'You've worked for us three times already, haven't you?'

'Yes, that's right. Seventy nine, eighty one and ninety six.'

'You did, in fact, turn down an assignment. *Yes?*' The man was putting aside his quiet politeness and coming on more hard now.

'Despatching someone with a mustard pellet from the tip of an innocuous umbrella --- at a bus stop crowded with people, of all places --- was not exactly within my field of expertise. My training didn't include that category of work.' Maunders paused to lift out the Tetley tea bag. 'I *was* given the choice of accepting or declining the assignment.' Maunders glanced at the man to see how his statement was being taken.

'This was the *only* reason? There was no *other?*'

'I wasn't aware that another reason was needed.' Another pause. 'So what is it this time? A message or a 'package'?'

'A 'package'.'

'Who is it, then?'

'You know very well I can't tell you that yet. He's an important scientist. We need to pass him on to your cell so that he can't be traced. That's all you need to know for now.'

'I see. Will tonight be soon enough? I've got a few clients to see here today.'

'*Now.* I want it done now, before their intelligence network gets on to us. And they will

eventually. It's inevitably the nature of our work.'

'I see.' Maunders took out the other tea bag and handed the man his cup. 'Cheers,' he said and sat himself down.

While they both sipped their tea, the man looked around the room, openly inspecting the rumble-tumble paraphernalia that made up this man Maunders' carefree existence. 'You pretty well lead your own life here, don't you?' he said at last to Maunders.

'Yes, more or less. I suppose life's like a blank canvass, really. You have to dab on your own colours to make anything of it at all.'

'Hmmm,' sounded the other, not happy with those words. He'd read various reports on the dangers that always had to be born in mind with sleepers. How they could be tempted and become so integrated in a ordinary habitat; so adapted to the softness of the mainly passive lifestyle that they led, as to be firmly rooted there. A waste of the money and effort put into their training, in fact. He looked at the mail basket and picked up a shoddily printed pamphlet bursting with evangelical bleatings from a local mission hall. 'You're not getting interested in this, are you?' The man's suspicions creased themselves into a frown over the bridge of his nose.

'They try to give a truthful picture of what they believe is the Ultimate Philosophy. Or at least, so I'm told.'

'Meaning that others don't? Is that what you're saying?'

'Now that you mention it that way, it does sound a bit like that, doesn't it? Fancy that.'

Maunders' eyes sparkled with harmless fun as he teased the stiffness in the other man.

'You know, you want to be careful what you say. Words like that can be dangerous outside these walls. I'll pretend I didn't hear you say them. In fact, I'd strongly recommend that you forget any ideas you have of attending this Redemptionist Meeting at the local mission hall.'

Maunders laughed. 'I didn't say the words and I'm not going to any mission hall. I'm only repeating what my assistant says when she goes to the hall.'

'You have an assistant? I wasn't told that you have an assistant.' The man was suddenly alert and looking around. He felt that he had been let down by those who compiled the dossier on the sleepers' field section.

'Relax; she's not here this morning. I let her do her shopping this morning, so she won't be in until after lunch.'

'I think it's time we got on with the work,' said the man brusquely and clinked down the cup, with its tea unfinished.

'If you want to. Have you a car outside?'

'No, I left it a few streets away. It's less conspicuous that way.'

'Of course; we must think of everything, mustn't we?' teased Maunders. 'It's just as well, anyway. The place is quite far from here and we can take the dog for a walk.'

'Must we?' said the other, slightly disdained.

Maunders suddenly rounded on him, an unexpectedly seriousness on his face. 'Yes, we must! The dog helps to give everything that ordinary image that we need for cover in our work. Right?' But Maunders was no longer listening for an answer, scrimmaging as he was after the dog, to fasten the leash to its collar. They went out and down the street, two completely opposite types for the same cause. One erect and serious and suspicious of everything that moved. The other stooping and cheerful and cavorting with the dog as it wound the leash round his legs. Both of them part of the plan to hide the who had given the country a deadly ultimatum over life and death.

'He's called Mr Bumble,' said Maunders, referring to the spaniel.

'That's a very strange name for a dog, if ever I heard one,' said the man gruffly. 'Purely fantasy as well. From Dickens, I believe.'

'I suppose you'd rather that I called him Alexander Nevsky, after our own folk hero?'

Maunders abruptly stopped walking. 'Hold on a second.' He felt his side to see if it was there, in his inside pocket. It was. 'It's okay.' They walked on again. He had thought he'd forgotten to put it in his pocket. The small .22 calibre pistol.

Just as they went round the corner, the Vauxhall Corsa came into the street from the other end and pulled into the kerb to settle with a scranching pull on the handbrake. From there, the occupants could view the whole street, including those who entered and left the antique shop. The pretty girl in the passenger seat opened the bag in her lap and set about making her face up. When she had finished, she left the bag open and let her scarf spill out of the untidy interior. That allowed her to get at the 200mm zoom lens Nikon camera that was concealed within the scarf. She had been called out by Broaley, along with the man beside her, who busied himself innocently with a tourist's guide book and street map. But they had just missed the 'site' they had come to see and were bound to waste some considerable time there in fruitless surveillance.

While Maunders and his colleague moved further and further from the area, Sherman and Broaley moved away in a totally different direction, continually relaying their movements back to the departments via Signals. Sir Richard took the news with the cold philosophy that bad timing could play a large part in the dragnet operation and in all else that was to come. As he issued new orders throughout the department, he dismally reflected how Tolstoy had shown that the generals' strategies were not strategies at all, but mere playthings in the hands of chance, so that both sides ran around in futile effort, missing their objectives completely.

8

12.23hrs, 24th June, Buckinghamshire. The giant Nimrod Mr.1 reconnaissance and submarine-hunter plane came in from the sky, screeching its fury to announce its arrival from Oslo. Its enormous wings bounced the roar back down, drowning the striped commotion of military policemen and barrier rails at the camp entrance. The RAF jeep halted before the three policemen, striped in their blancoed webbing and regulation side arms, while the monster Nimrod whistled and whined its way past. For a moment all eyes watched the great fiery bowls receding down the runway, then turned back to more important matters of security. The white stripes and the red and white notices on wire mesh fencing stood out in the sunlight to stop all unwarranted entries: **WARNING: OFFICIAL PASSES MUST BE SHOWN: UNAUTHORISED ENTRY BEYOND THIS POINT IS AT OWN PERSONAL RISK: GUARD DOGS ON PATROL**: Ministry of Defence Notice.

The corporal reached forward for the civilian's credentials. His mate inspected the airman's pass. Sherman eyed the pistol butts with their lanyard rings poking from the two holsters' corners as he sat there waiting. Blancoed anklets bounced brilliantly in the sunlight as the two guards stepped back smartly and saluted. The jeep rolled forward, under the rising barriers, while the man in the glass box spoke into the phone, watching them as they passed. A patrolman watched from the background, holding his fierce Alsatian by his side.

The jeep veered left, and sped out across the open tarmac, where maintenance crews and vehicles criss-crossed hurriedly like ants under a hypnotic spell of urgency. A sausage-link train of bomb trolleys somehow managed to weave and wind its way through the bustle, without actually colliding and exploding. Over in the grass, three missile crews, topped in their white protection hoods, practised with the Tiger-Cat ground-to-air missile launcher. This was the mobile land equivalent of the Royal Navy's Sea-Cat and had three nuclear primed rockets to a battery. At the runway's end, the Nimrod turned with the surprising lightness of a ballet dancer and taxied back up. It moved over into the service bay that was dominated by a large hanger and a hunch-backed goblin gathering of Nissen huts. The hangar's gaunt mouth widened and a long beetle with lots of wheels sped out towards the great silver bird, towing a flight of steps behind it.

Stepping out of the jeep, Sherman crossed over to the plane and stood just inside the shadow of its massive 115ft wingspan. The huge Rolls Royce Spey turbofans whined down like demented banshees as he waited there in quiet awe. At last the Nimrod's side began to bleed out blue uniforms and Sherman walked forward to meet his brother-in-law. Squadron Leader Travis, small and squat, paused a second to pull on his gloves and a sociable face. Slightly more beefy and greyer than before, the man seemed to bear nothing of a likeness to his sister, Maureen, Sherman's 'ex'. But whatever it was that had broken the marriage, Travis had always assumed it to be none of his business. Love was like a dove. Not only did it sound and feel like a dove, but it also flew away frightened, if you spoke too loud in a quarrel. The man had never got on with his sister and rarely spoke to her. He had never hidden his strong dislike for Sherman personally, or more so as his sister's choice of a husband. But he still spoke to Sherman where duty called. The two men, at this level in Her Majesty's Service, could not allow petty family squabbles to come between them in their work, especially in a crisis such as this one.

Sherman smiled and nodded to Travis. He also noted that the man behind Travis was Miller, or was it Mailer, from the same department? That was, in fact, the Directorate of Operational Analysis (RAF), which worked in close conjunction with the Department of the Chief Scientist (RAF). These bodies worked under the MoD's Operational Analysis Organisation, on research tasks impinging on conflict situations such as the nuclear and radiation fields effecting the welfare of the country. That was why they had broken off from the NATO Tactics Review Conference in Oslo, to fly back here.

'Hullo, John,' said Travis. 'Sorry we couldn't come sooner, but we couldn't let it look too obvious without raising eyebrows. You know how it is. By the way, this is Group Captain Morris, if you haven't met before.'

'Yes, we have met before. Hullo' said Sherman, omitting his mistake in names. All three turned and made off for the buildings where the nuclear stockpile was normally kept and where at that moment a cook was wrestling with nothing more ominous than a sack of carrots.

'But tell me, said Travis, 'is the situation really as bad as I've been told? I mean, even in code, the words were hair-raising.'

'I'm afraid so,' said Sherman. 'But you can judge that for yourself, better than me, by having a look at this one we have right here, in our lap.'

'So let's have a dekko at this ruddy great beast of yours, then.' said Travis, smacking a shiny gloved fist into a shiny gloved palm. The Group Captain turned round and dismissed the jeep which had been crawling along discreetly behind them all this time.

'How's Maureen, by the way?' said Travis, straight out of the blue.

'Oh, she's fine; just fine.' Sherman could have said that she'd lost weight, and that she was near to needing medical aid, counselling at least, for her alternating dives of depression and leaps of hysteria. But he didn't. There was no mistaking his awkward feeling over the subject in front of his brother-in-law. So why the hell ask the question in the first place, as if that wasn't obvious. Go on, turn the old thumbscrew a little tighter.

'And the *boy*?'

'Fine; he's coming along just fine. Seems to be taking after his uncle, with his latest craze for model planes. Bought him a radio controlled one.' Sherman managed a smile through his worried expression as he thought for a moment. 'As far as I know, his granny's now compelled to buy him a horse. One of those great hairy Shetland things.'

Travis gave a tut-tut and shook his head. 'That's what I call squandering money, for a boy that age, stuck in the city.'

'We'll see; we'll see.' The way Sherman was seeing things, neither he nor anybody else would be spending much if this terrorist threat amounted to its worst. He also considered it funny, weird even, how such petty talk could occur in the midst of this mad set-up of nuclear destruction, called *defence*, especially with a possible countdown thwarting them. Yet this out of place small talk was what millions were doing right now. Millions who had no idea that they were considered as second only in importance of what was going on. Sherman dismissed the mixed argument as emotional stress points, as the department shrink was apt to say, and concentrated once again on his work.

When they first saw it, it reminded Sherman of a giant sow suckling its litter of piglets. Five of the 'piglets', in white overalls, were kneeling by the bomb's side, while two more stood at the front, where part of the nose cone had been removed. One of the men turned and rose when he saw them. He adjusted his spectacles as he waited.

'Well, Mr Blenning,' said Sherman, 'I hope you've got something good to tell us, for a change.'

'I'm afraid not. But we're working on it. At least the situation hasn't deteriorated, if that's saying anything.'

'It has to be something better than that. Perhaps you could put Squadron Leader Travis and Group Captain Morris, from Operational Analysis, in the picture. I'm not one for bothering with proverbs, but if two more heads can help, we've only fifty nine and a half hours to prove it.'

Blenning led them up to the bomb, where parts of its inner anatomy glistened with omnipotent foreboding. Not at all because it was dark and sweaty, like some mythical devil beast, but all the more so from its gleaming stainless steel assuredness to deliver colossal holocaust. The mythical beast was always unfailingly brought down by the white knight's swipe of the righteous blade; but to destroy the likes of this, you needed -----what? Sherman pulled his mind away from his growing anxiety, or was it despair? What the hell did it matter when it was the same brick wall you banged your head on? He turned his mind back to the others talking beside him.

'I don't understand,' Travis was saying, 'I thought we didn't know where the bombs were? If we have this one, where's the other one?'

'No, no, this isn't one of those two we desperately need to get our hands on, alas. No, this is one which we think Dr Linsdale appears to have been experimenting with --- *practising* with, if you like, before throwing down the gauntlet, so to speak. He seems to have been trying to programme it to explode by radio signals. See here and here.' Blenning slapped the bomb twice and Sherman felt wonder for the man each time. Or perhaps the man was agnostic and didn't visualise God coming so soon in a big flash. Blenning continued. 'And apart from these signals, the bomb had been booby-trapped against any interference by us. We're not sure yet if the booby-trap was going to be radio linked, with feed back to outside transmitters, or was purely internal. But we're working on it.' He gestured in reference to the men kneeling in seeming adoration of the great gleaming godling.

'Couldn't we just dump the bloody things when we get our hands on them?' said the Group Captain.

Blenning closed his eyes for a moment and pushed his spectacles further up his nose. 'No, that's simply out of the question. However obvious a plan it may have seemed to begin with, we're all agreed at this stage that the risk is too great. From the evidence we have here, it's likely that coded signals could be made to come in from more than one transmitter, at irregular intervals, to keep a check, so to speak. Not only that, but if they were being sent out to reach the bombs in their specific locations, movement to a new location for the purpose of, as you say, "dumping", is again out of the question.' He saw the frozen frowns, mistaking dismay for confusion. 'Perhaps I haven't been clear enough. Would you like me to go over any particular point for you? *Any of you?*'

Sherman broke the spell. 'No, I don't think that'll be necessary, Mr Blenning, thank you. I think I speak for all of us when I say we've heard and understood enough to have our darkest nightmares working on overtime with daytime footage.' He didn't bother looking round at the other two for their agreement when the air was heavy with it.

'Halleluiah,' said Travis softly, staring steely-eyed at the great demon adversary.

'We can't simulate the signals ourselves, I suppose, and 'incubate' the things?' said Morris, losing heart before he had finished.

'No,' said Blenning. 'That was also suggested before, but it's quite impossible. The signals kept changing their code as well as their output interval. We can't simulate what we can't predict.'

Morris was persistent. 'How about lead shields to insulate the bombs from the signals?'

'No. As I said, the bombs would be receiving signals to keep them in check. If these signals ceased to come in, there's no knowing the consequences.'

'And don't tell me,' said Morris in bitter humour, 'the transmitters will be mobile, in disguised dustcarts or something, so that they can't be tracked down?'

Blenning laughed and leaned against the bomb. 'No, there's no saying that they'd be mobile. Personally, I don't see them being so. But what of it? Once we find the transmitters -- assuming that we *do* find them, that is --- *then* what? I hardly think that the terrorists would devise such a fool-proof plan so far, without conceiving the possibility of our tackling the problem from that end.'

Sherman couldn't help feeling his irritation rise at the scientist's open satisfaction in succinctly summing up the situation, leaving no loose ends --- all to their disadvantage. Had the bastard forgotten whose side he was on? No, that was unfair; the man was just doing his job, putting them in the picture. Better to get that right, than to make a mistake over it later. He looked round at the other two to see how they were taking it all in. He wasn't alone in his unease, wanting to strike out at something, if facial expressions were anything to go by. He took a deep breath to ease his pent up agitation.

'You think the transmitters will be booby-trapped also, then?' said Travis.

'I would say it's most likely. I'd say they'd probably be automatic too, operating themselves under instructions from their own internal programme.'

'Hell, isn't there *anything* we can do?' said Sherman, clearly perplexed.

'Oh yes, there's lots of things we can do,' replied Blenning with his usual rapid readiness, 'and as the number increases, so does the number of risks of something going wrong, also increase in proportion.'

Damn the man and his ruddy proportions! 'So what *do* you recommend?' asked Sherman, now at a loss.

Blenning folded one arm and kneaded his jaw with his free fist. 'Quite honestly, I don't know yet. It's too early to say, at the moment, but we're working on it.' He swung round suddenly to look at his colleagues as they systematically poked and prodded the ominous bulk with what, to the non scientific minds, didn't look like too much caution. 'Yes, there's an idea we're following, that might just work,' mumbled Blenning, more to himself than anyone else.

Sherman found too much of a hesitant, wandering, tone in Blenning's words, to be convinced that the man really believed them himself. 'Another few hours and it'll be too damn late.' Sherman paused for a second. 'All right, thanks for explaining everything, Mr Blenning. We'll let you get on with your work. I'll see you before I go.' He looked at his watch. 'Probably in thirty minutes or so. In the meantime, we're going upstairs.'

As they stood in the Operations Room, looking at the strategic map of the area, Travis turned to Sherman. 'So what do you think of it?'

'It's going to be a big bang.'

'And?'

'*And?* Well, let's say that if you're an astronaut on the moon, you won't need a telescope to see where the toast has been burned in England.' No-one found Sherman's remark to be very funny. Not even Sherman.

With the technical talk at an end, Sherman and Travis once more became uneasy in each other's presence. Small talk was stilted and unreal. Travis, with his round waxy face and pencil moustache, would have made a fair stand-in as a latter day Rudolf Valentino, but that was where the semblance ended. Whereas that particular Hollywood screen lover would have totally enraptured his women with endearing words, Travis could only capture the cold-blooded fish that abounded in the river of his wife's family's rich Somerset estate. She, too, was a bit of cold fish, so Maureen had said.

Sherman searched his mind for easy, neutral words. 'Look, I've got an important call to put through; got to check in and see how things are. Hold on and I'll be back in a minute.'

'Sure. Go right ahead, John.'

Sherman winced inwardly at Travis using his first name as if they were great friends. He went off to find the radio room. He showed his pass to the operator and gave him the coded message for Broaley that he'd written out. Safer this way than by his mobile.

'Who?' said the operator, pulling his headset back.

'Major Broaley. Have Communications send this message to Major Broaley, and have them demand an immediate reply. Top Priority. Is that all clear?'

'Yes, sir.' The airman couldn't remember the name he'd almost seen flashed before his eyes on the plastic MoD pass a few seconds ago, so he looked up at Sherman. 'Are you Mr Sherman?'

'I've just shown you so. Why?'

'This is for you, sir. It just came through for you a few minutes ago.'

Sherman took the paper message and read it. It was from Monks. It seemed that his CIA colleagues had located the present whereabouts of Linsdale. It was in Bayswater. But that could be ancient news by the very seconds that he'd taken to hold the paper in his hand. He couldn't remember if it was one of the addresses Broaley's people had on their lists, but he wasn't taking any chances. 'Hold on,' he said to the operator, who was preparing to transmit. 'There's something else I want you to put into that message.' Sherman scribbled down the coded message, instructing Broaley to go to the new location. 'Here, get this through, and for God's sake, don't make a mistake.'

But Bayswater was history by the time the message got through, as Sherman had rightly predicted. Linsdale was being moved along from one safe house to another. The manhunt was on, in a joint operation across the country, involving all the intelligence branches as well as Special Branch and CID. Suspension of normal surveillance duties to pull in the personnel needed for the operation was not without protest from the departments. With information and briefings reduced to a minimum, complaints were not dying down too soon. Reports coming in from Langley, in the US, were scant in CIA's usual manner of laying only half their cards on the table. Blenning's estimate of there being less damage to the nuclear defence programme over there had been accurate enough. With the US Forces running a more active schedule, access to their national armoury for subversive purposes had been more limited. CIA was currently on the tail of the suspect. Broaley's hunch had also been on target on that point. They had reason to believe that there was a connection between this suspect and the British saboteur, Linsdale. As usual, CIA would let out no more than this until things improved on their side of the water. Sherman had no regrets about appointing Broaley to run field operations. The Major had that special edge the job required. On a protocol basis, with the task of cementing relations between rival departments, he would have been a disaster. But he was the right man for whipping up teamwork from a bickering lot with his hard line manner. He was never the man to concede to having bitten off of more than he could chew. Sherman knew the Major's philosophy from person experience. You chewed up everything on the plate, provided it didn't move. If it moved, then you beat it senseless, then you chewed it up. That was Broaley's basic never-fail method.

9

14.57hrs, 24th June, Camberwell, S.E. The District Council Lights &
Public Maintenance Dept van turned into the quiet street. It stopped behind
a larger District Council truck of the same department, and Sherman got out.
Dressed in overalls, regulation yellow plastic jacket and white hard-hat, he
looked the part. He climbed into the back of the larger truck. Major Broaley
looked round and then at his watch. 'So you managed to get here? I thought
with your power, you'd have managed to fly over the traffic.'

Sherman ignored the remark and went over to the spy hole in the truck's
side. 'Where are they, then?' he said, looking through the small hole.

'Across the street, nine doors up. The one after the blue door. Third floor
window. The flat above is occupied; so are the two below, so we couldn't get
near them that way, to tap their conversation.'

'And the flat directly across from them, this side of the street? Same, I
suppose?'

'Same. Otherwise we could have used the normal sonic bowl to listen in
on them. It could have looked too suspicious if we'd rigged up something on
the truck roof and parked right across from them. We're better off parked
down here, at an angle.'

'Right, I get the picture; so let's get on with it.' Sherman looked around for
something, saw the rifle and reached out for it. Broaley stepped in to pick it
up before him. 'I'll do it,' said Broaley, adjusting the telescopic sight.

'Sure?' teased Sherman.

Broaley looked Sherman in the eye. 'Just tell him to switch on, and I'll take care of this end.'

Sherman slid the hatch open and told the man in the cabin to go out and switch on the mobile generator that was standing further up the street. The man started the generator up and then played his part by fiddling about with the cables leading from the machine into the open manhole in the road. Broaley took careful aim and fired. The tiny dart from the high-powered air-gun thudded into the upper corner of the wooden frame of the window nine houses up the street. The noise of the dart striking the frame was covered by the din from the generator. A listening bug inside the dart was now relaying all sounds from inside the room back to the monitoring equipment in the truck.

Sherman signalled the man to turn off the generator. Broaley switched on the receiver. The volume and clarity of the Arabic babble coming through was astonishing. Almost as if they were listening from outside the window itself. You almost expected the curtain to be suddenly pulled aside, as the room's occupants looked out at their eavesdroppers. But there was little likelihood of that, the curtain actually concealing the dart from those inside.

'Sounds like two in the room with somebody in the background; probably the next room. Or is that a radio they've got playing? said Broaley.

'Sounds like prayers, with that extended chanting tone,' said Sherman, looking round for confirmation, at the small figure in the far corner of the truck. The woman, their translator, looked back at him, but said nothing, concentrating on the Islamic chanting. 'Prayers are not much good. How long do we have to wait before they tell us anything useful about their plan of operation?'

'If we rush them, they could kill themselves,' said Broaley. 'If we capture them alive, they could still hold back from us in interrogation over the limited deadline time we have left. We have to catch them in their unguarded conversation.' Broaley sat down in a canvas chair. 'We sit and wait.'

'No, you sit and wait,' said Sherman, moving towards the door. 'I'm going for a piss and a bite of something.' He held up his mobile for Broaley to see. 'Let me know if I have to make it a quick splash.'

15.21hrs. 'Sounds as if they've fallen asleep,' said Broaley to Sherman, as they continued to listen in on the terrorist nest.

'Or gone into quiet meditation,' said the translator woman from her corner.

'Two, maybe; but not our third friend,' said Sherman. 'He sure seems happy enough the way he's rattling on. If he were Irish, I'd say he was seeing the day through with a bottle of the old blarney, and not Allah.'

'Sounds as if he's drank half of it already,' said Broaley. 'He's certainly excited about something,'

'They do take their prayers with serious dedication,' said the translator with another of her gems of ethnic information that were beginning to annoy the other two.

As they listened on, two of the three voices had moved into a permanent background position, suggesting that they had, indeed, gone to rest in a backroom. With the background voices gradually stopping, to be replaced only by the occasional cough, it was now an fair assumption that the two in the backroom were asleep, or trying to sleep. The muttering and humming in the foreground, accompanied by the occasional clink of crockery and the rustling of paper, suggested that the third member of the terrorist team was staying awake on guard duty.

From amidst the rabble of fanatical talk that Sherman and Broaley had listened to, only the general outline of an operation --- "the Mother of all Retributions, Allah be praised" -- could be picked up. Nothing more specific could be gleaned beyond that. There was little chance of learning more now.

Broaley stood up. 'It's time we moved. We won't learn any more now; and we won't get them in a better position than this. Time for soldier boys to take over. Time for some *real* action; *right*, Sherman?' You always know when Broaley is digging you, as sure as when the mother-in-law *accidentally* reverses her cute shopping buggy of a Smart car over your new golf clubs.

Leaving Sherman in the truck, Broaley walked down the street to meet the black van that was coming along at his calling. He climbed inside. The four SAS men wore one-piece tunics with body armour designed to withstand armour-piercing bullets. Checking their 9 mm Browning automatics and putting them in their holsters, they attached extra magazines and stun grenades to their belts. Rather than explode into fragments, these grenades were designed to go off with blinding flashes and ear-splitting bangs that would confuse the enemy. They picked up the holdalls containing, along with other gear, their

9 mm Heckler & Koch submachine guns that had a firepower of 10 rounds a second. Finally, they put on the bright yellow municipal works jackets for temporary cover in crossing the street. Checking that all was clear, Broaley led the way, stepping out into the street.

'From what you've been saying, Major' said the SAS commander, as they crossed the street, 'if we go in by their street door, by the time we reach the second floor they'll be on their toes like ballet dancers, waiting for us. So we'll do it our way. Where is it, again?'

'Over there; number eighteen. The first floor flat is empty. If you force the street door, go up the first floor, break into the empty flat, you can jump down from the back window into the back garden. From there you can make your way along to their house, to mount your assault. Would've been better in darkness, but time is not on our side. We can't wait. All right?

'All right, Major. Thanks for the layout. I don't think you'll be needing that.' He was referring to the Major's checking his pistol inside his jacket. 'We'll handle it from here.' He looked round at his three colleagues. 'Ready? Okay, let's go.'

Following Broaley's instructions, the SAS team was in the back garden in minutes. Here they removed their council worker jackets and took their submachine guns out of their bags, slinging them under arm, their loop straps over the head, so as not to fall off. They then donned their heavy rubber gas masks, and fastened onto their belts radio units that were tuned into the receiver in the truck, attaching the head pieces to one ear. This way they could keep a 'picture' of the inside of the flat.

Ascending to the roof of the four storey building, they made their way along the roof until they were directly over the target house. Anchoring the grapnel hooks to the roof's apex point, they moved down their ropes, to hang out in space at the eaves point, their bodies propped out by feet against the gutter pipe. Two would go down the front, and two would go down the back.

Checking in his ear piece that positions had not changed in the flat, the commander tensed himself, gave a sharp whistle signal, and all four abseiled down, pushing themselves out like hopping kangaroos down the wall faces. Passing the top windows, each gave himself an extra hard push out abreast of the third floor target window, swinging out and across, so as to go crashing in feet first through the windows, back and front. The terrorists never knew what hit them, and it was over in seconds and two short bursts of automatic fire dropping the man in his fatal attempt to snatch up his weapon.

The door was opened to let Broaley and Sherman into the flat. Sherman exploded in coughs as the cordite fumes attacked his nostrils and made his eyes smart. Broaley's grin widened at Sherman waving the acrid fumes away. The SAS team wasted no time. Their task completed, they left as promptly as they had come. With curious neighbours' curtains shifting in their windows all around, the four black figures kept their masks on as they sprinted down the street to their van. The dead man was taken away in a body bag by Special Branch officers. The argument over who should take 'possession' of the two remaining Jihadi zealots was settled when it was agreed, at Sherman's suggestion that MI5 should have them for interrogation, so long as a Special Branch officer accompanied them to keep a watchful eye on things. Broaley was clearly not happy with what he saw as Sherman's purely weak-kneed surrendering to Special Branch's bullying, but he said nothing. He didn't reckon that their two prisoners were going to be telling them any more than they had already learned. And that hadn't been much. He saw them as members of a cell that knew no more than MI5 did about where the next cell in the line for this mission was, who was in it and what its specific plans were.

Satisfied that the prisoners were securely seated between MI5 officers in the MoD vehicle, Major Broaley walked back to his own Jaguar. As he stopped to open the door, a car, totally unnoticed in the street's commotion of security people, came cruising along slowly. As it drew near to the Jaguar, a dark youth looked out through the open front passenger seat window. He pointed his Beretta machine pistol at the Major's unsuspecting back. Before he could fire, the bearded mullah leaned forward from the back seat to push the gun arm down. '*Later*, my son; *later*. There will come a better time later. The *proper* time, as Allah so sees it, and so decrees. The one thing we must not do is let our anger overrun our wisdom. Wisdom is a divine gift from Allah; wisdom belongs to Allah, just as anger belongs to Allah. Anger shall be used by us, but must be used *wisely*, in accordance with the Will of Allah. It is so written. Allah be praised.'

'Allah be praised.' The youth's response was a weak copy that lacked the hard conviction of his mentor's words. A young mind's faltering uncertainty, confusion, caught between respect of the mentor's holiness of restraint and primitive animal instinct for violence -- *holy* violence. Holy killing, in the name of Allah, was justifiable. This was what the mullahs were pumping into his mind, and other young minds, in the mosque. To the young mind, not yet moulded into maturity, this mode of violently asserting a creed was most agreeable with his inner urge for releasing pent-up emotions in equally explosive form. He felt his hand tighten on the gun again. But not with enough conviction in him to raise it and fire. That would have offended his holy tutor. But his mind was still muddled.

Young Rasheed Bahsoud had just escaped from his teens by a whole month. But although now a man, he was skinny enough to still be wearing the school jumper he had first donned on entering junior secondary school. His mum had liked the idea of him going on to secondary education. To become something --- something professional. Like her cousin, Atif, who had got his osteopath's diploma and gone back to practice in Lahore. But patriarchal rule had won the day. His father, Hafur Bahsoud, couldn't see why his youngest son, Rasheed, should be spared his duty of supporting the family by working in the family's Catford cash 'n 'carry business. The elder sons had done their duty without complaint. They had gone into their father's business when they were mere boys. Now they were men, still in the family business, with good families of their own to be proud of. All in accordance with tradition. Rasheed had never relished the idea of pre-arranged marriages. 'Matches' that weren't matches at all. His attendances at afternoon and evening classes at the mosque, to make a serious study of the Koran, had only been a ploy to escape the ugly Sateefi sisters. It wasn't their fault that they had great ugly noses to 'match' that of the desert camel. But he had to admit that he liked Hali for her cynical humour. She made fun of both the eastern and western cultures. He knew she secretly adored the western style of clothes. And she adored George Clooney. Said he could pass for Asian with his dark eyebrows and hair. And so Rasheed's mind had meandered between the two cultures for a while. Until these new zealots from the East had come into the area, to the mosque. Their fiery rhetoric had taken hold of his mind and shown him the light --- shown him where his destiny lay --- with the Jihad.

'So why can't we take action now? It would be righteous surely, seeing as they've arrested our fellow Jihad brothers?' His voice, thin with angry excitement, climbed in pitch. 'They've killed one of them.' A trembling finger pointed up the street. ' They put the body in the back of that black Shogun.'

A heavy hand from behind gripped Rasheed's bony shoulder. 'My young son, do you doubt the Will of Allah? Do you dare defy His holy decree, His omnipotent power?' Old fingers dug hard, like steel, into young flesh and bone. 'I know, I know, my son; I know. Their time has passed, and one of them is no longer of this world. But he is already in heaven, receiving his eternal reward. They had a mission to carry out, and now it is over, however incomplete it may seem to our wretchedly mortal eyes. It is their holy destiny. That is how we must see it. They were the fingers, we are the hand. Better the fingers we lose on the hand that we keep, than to keep the fingers on the hand that we lose. Do not worry, and so lose your way with impatience, my young son. Your time will come, most surely as Allah sees it. Allah akbar.'

'Allah akbar.' (God is great)

With no more sage words to offer, the mullah settled back on the head-rest to meditate, as the car moved on.

18.21hrs, Basra, Iraq. The whirlwind of red desert dust died down with the planes's four propellers coming to a halt. The massive Hercules served not just as a transporter, but also as an airborne strategic intelligence relay centre, with its sophisticated satellite and high frequency units sending encrypted information on ground troop developments back to UK command centres from whatever corner of the globe it was in. It was defended by missile-approach warning aids, and anti-aircraft missile jamming devices that released flares and clouds of minute metal particles that 'blinded' enemy radar.

The tail-end door came down, revealing the gaping great mouth of the cargo hold. The Wessex Baker strike vehicle, with its Browning 0.5in heavy machine gun mounted on top, rolled down the ramp first. Next came two 110 Land Rovers, loaded high with everything but the proud regimental silver from the officers' mess, followed by six men and two women in camouflage combat fatigues. Nothing more followed for several seconds, and then a solitary figure came out of the black void. Strictly civilian. Too smooth to be a soldier. The pale safari denims had that refined cut that never came ready-to-wear off the peg --- just like the suede shoes --- strictly Jermyn Street. Telescopic camera lenses and recording equipment deliberately left poking out of the holdall made the statement of 'journalist', as did the ID tag. But the nearest Peter Haldane ever came to journalism was the tall stories he wrote to cover his over the top business lunch expenses claims. The 'newspaper' he worked for sat on the waterfront at Vauxhall Bridge --- MI6.

Stepping out of the cool shelter of the hold into the blazing sunlight, Haldane felt the heat hit him like a broadside blast from an open furnace. It didn't matter how often you came, and Haldane had been here many times, you never could get so used to it as to not feel the first few choking seconds effect of the scorching air on your throat and lungs. He put his hand over his mouth and nostrils and breathed slowly for a few seconds to adjust.

The soldiers from the plane, standing several yards away, looking towards the civilian, were sharing a joke over his apparent discomfort. One of them detached himself from the group to approach the civilian. He had better see if the poor bugger needed any help. 'Not quite the soft balmy breeze of the Hampton embankment on a Sunday afternoon, is it,' the soldier said to the civilian. Haldane saw the freshness of being straight from training camp written all over the young lieutenant's face and in his body language. Along with the nervousness that was carefully hidden behind an over casual manner that didn't quite escape the tell-tale briskness of unsure moments. The lieutenant looked all around, searching vaguely. 'I've a lot to see to, but one of my official instructions is to see that you are provided with transport of sorts.' Not realising that he was biting his lip, the lieutenant once more scanned his surroundings aimlessly. 'A jeep, I suppose, would jolly well do the trick, but just where the hell there's a spare one to ---'

'It's all right,' Haldane cut in, 'I know the way. Give you room to look after your own lot.' As Haldane walked off, he half turned and stopped to call out to the lieutenant. 'By the way, Lieutenant, the engineering guys are over that way.' He pointed for the sake of the other to see.

'*Engineering?* I don't quite follow -----? The voice trailed off, clearly not following Haldane's line of thought.

Haldane pointed in a new direction. This time at a soldier hammering away angrily at the mounting structure of a Milan anti-tank missile launcher in the back of one of the Land Rovers. 'Your man seems to be having some trouble.' He turned and walked off again.

18.30 hrs. Throwing his bag onto the passenger seat, Haldane climbed into the car he had found for himself off the base. A battered, sun-bleached Volkswagen, it would suit his purpose better, drawing less attention, less hostility, than an Army jeep. He looked at his watch. It would still only be about half three-ish in London. It didn't matter that the nuclear countdown crisis was back in England; a massive dragnet operation was underway with all the security services, with everyone, save those who couldn't get at least one foot out of the wheelchair, pitching in their effort. Desperately trawling for vital information -- *any* information -- from *anyone -- anywhere*. With today's traders in terrorist intelligence being one big happy international family, nowhere was too far out to seek information if it helped save the day. An ear to the ground on the remotest outback on the globe was game if it picked up good vibrations.

Turning the engine on, Haldane leaned forward to peer up into the sky. That was another thing you had to get used to here, when just arriving. All the roaring activity of military aircraft overhead replacing that of the squawking seagulls hovering over the Thames. As for the Yanks having 'officially left the country', it was funny how those Apache helicopters, with their Hellfire missiles and rocket pods, still seemed to be around. Just like that one up there. Oh well, let the senators on Capitol Hill argue that one out in front of an irate heckling press audience .He let in the clutch and drove off.

He tried to drive without incident along roads that were primed with an explosive potential for 'incident'. Anything could happen any time. Violence simmered below the surface all around, a bubbling cauldron of dangerous instability. He tensed for a second inside, when he saw the roadblock in the distance, with its crowd of angry gesticulating militiamen. His tension dropped as he drew nearer. It was a market dispute over fruit fallen from a broken down lorry that looked to be in a worse state than the rotten fruit. Slowing down in approach to the crowd, and carefully negotiating his way through a sea of melons, his attention was caught by the boy at the side of the road. A youth of at least twelve, or thirteen, he was having difficulty handling what looked like a .303 Lee Enfield bolt action rifle. A somewhat outmoded piece of equipment that. But that wasn't what prolonged Haldane's stare. It was the fact that the youth was barely half the size of the rifle. But then he had no legs, and half an arm was missing.

Worrying for long enough if the engine would fall out before he got there, the car won the bet, and he arrived. After a third pull at the bell rope and a long wait, the dirty wooden gates on the dirty stone wall finally shifted with a heavy scranching of the lock. The sight greeting the eyes as the gates fell back slowly would have astonished many. In stark contrast with the dry dust-choked desolation outside the walls, that within the walls was a brilliant visual explosion of lush green life. The trees and plants, fed on water pumped from God knows where, filled the courtyard up to the peripheral cloister that was pillared by slender Moorish columns of marble mosaic in gold and blue. Perhaps this colour was meant to match the blue peacock, too proud in its strutting to acknowledge his presence. Only the white parakeet in the tree greeted him with its soft muffled prattle. A small oasis paradise set in a barren wilderness.

But Haldane had seen this place before. Several times. He was reminded how that *first* garden, Eden, in spite of its beauty, had also contained its evil Serpent. Well, this paradise garden also had its wicked snake. A warlord, terrorist, wheeler-dealer in drugs, death, and many other things, call it what you like. And Haldane was here to trade for information. With with what in exchange, though, he wasn't sure. He wasn't sure at all. But he had to try. Even when information was not readily surrendered, an unnoticed slip of the tongue could be revealing. Absolute refusal could also prove to be useful with a little bit of lateral thinking. If you know the shape of the jigsaw piece that's *not* in the picture, then you can work out the shapes of the immediately surrounding pieces that *are* in the picture. A snippet here, a snippet there, anything to build up that complete picture.

The gates were locked behind him by a mute servant whom Haldane knew had no tongue. The master had removed it, for want of a person to blame for his black mood. Bowing down, the mute beckoned Haldane to follow him into the house. The man by the door didn't show any such deference to the guest. He stood stock still, holding his Kalashnikov by its sling over his shoulder. His only movement was in his eyes, watching Haldane pass by him into the dark entrance.

15.33hrs, Lewisham, S.E. The hand poked its way slowly through the booth's canvas flap just as the intelligence man was climbing up out of the manhole. He stiffened when he saw it and tightened his grip on the last rung. Slowly, very slowly, he eased himself out and onto the hole's rim. In a flash of sunlight, the flap suddenly opened before him and the figure stood there. A traffic warden, all nineteen stone of him. Releasing a quiet sigh of relief, the MI5 man got up and squeezed past the uniformed bulk, out of the red and white striped street works canvas booth. 'Just like the Punch and Judy show, you've come to arrest me,' said the MI5 man, playing his innocent cover and putting his thumbs in his dungarees pockets. 'Well, sorry to disappoint you, but maybe next time, eh?'

But the warden didn't think this was funny and fidgeted with his hand meter as he looked around. The MI5 man hid his impatience while the other continued his search for a fault to pounce on. 'It's all right,' he said to the warden, 'we've got permission to park here to do this urgent cable repair job down below. You can check with Head Office, if you want. See for yourself; here's the work schedule sheets.' He held out the papers the Documents Department had fixed up for him.

But the man was being a bastard of a nuisance, ignoring the papers and wandering instead over to the Telecom Engineering van, to inspect its wheels. He leaned down to prod at the tyres. 'These tread depths look critically shallow; they'll need to be replaced,' he said over his shoulder, without getting up.

'Nonsense; they're fine. MOT'd only last month.'

'They need to be replaced.' The warden got to his feet and began fingering through his rule book for a pertinent penalty clause.

Feeling his patience rapidly slipping away, the MI5 man stepped right up to the warden, almost ready to shove his meter down his throat. 'Look, we've a very important job to do down below. It's a major landline junction. If we delay this job, to bother about new tyres, which I still say we don't ruddy well need, half the ruddy well phones in London will go dead. Maybe your own boss's phone. You wouldn't want that on your books, would you?' Not a moment too soon, the warden lumbered off.

The MI5 man moved the red and white wooden trestle over in front of the booth's entrance, to stop any similar interference, and then went over to the Telecom van. He got inside and closed the doors firmly behind him. The tape cassette from his pocket clicked into the machine and wound back with the squealing mirth of a magnetic leprechaun. He then played the tape at high speed so that minutes of speech came out in seconds. The tape recorder was linked to the field transmitter which relayed the message direct to Intelligence HQ. At that end, the message was played at its correct speed and the words put through a decoding computer. Any messages contained in otherwise innocent conversations would be uncovered. In all, the whole process saved many minutes of vital time by dispensing with written reports and slow verbal reports.

Every time a conversation was newly recorded by his mate down in the manhole, the man in the van would take it and send its message through to HQ, while another tape took its place for further recording. This way, HQ was informed as soon as possible and they were also ready to record any further incoming messages.

The telephone being tapped was in number 23, just above the electrical repairs shop, across the street. The man took the tape out again and peered through the window panel at number 23. This was only one of many places being watched and tapped to root out the cell that was hiding rogue scientist, Dr Linsdale. Extra surveillance personnel had been brought in, from other jobs, by Major Broaley, and this was the three quarters of the truth story which he had briefed them with. The man got out and closed the van's doors, so that he was once more a telephone engineer doing an ordinary job on an ordinary day. The van was purely a cover on loan from the Telecom company, but everything that went on inside it was strictly MoD work.

Everything round about in the sunny afternoon was functioning normally. Idyllic daffodils trumpeted out in a profusion of gold along the grass verge. A black mongrel nosed one of the daffodils and the flower jerked its slender neck, to shower an insect with a deluge of tears from its big golden eye. Across the verge, rival 'daffodils' of brilliant brass trumpeted out the glory of *Jerusalem*, from their cyclopean eyes, to the beat of the Salvation Army conductor's baton. The 'telephone' man smiled as he watched the people quickening their paces and casting their eyes down as they passed the SA man, who rattled his collection box like an ancient seer's box of bones. That was good, since it kept the public on the move and discouraged loitering snoopers. He nipped smartly into the booth when the collection man turned and rattled the box in his direction.

Down in the tube, the mate, the listener in the team, sat silent beneath his headphones, reading the week's edition of *Autocar*. He looked up at his returning mate, the team's runner, and shook his head. 'Nothing doing,' he said.

'Hell,' groaned Runner, and sat down on the folding camp-stool. He picked up the started bag of cheese and onion crisps and held it out to his mate.

'Ta,' said Listener. 'How would you get Linsdale out, if you were running the show?'

'Don't know. I suppose the best bet would be to skip the country from a remote part of the coastline. At night, of course. Have a sub or boat standing by. Still, I wouldn't be surprised if they flew out right under our noses, from Stanstead. You know, big handle-bar moustache and wig. Like this. Dah-dah-dah-dah.'

'Yeah, like Groucho Marx, or Broaley.'

'Yeah, Broaley.' They rocked about on their seats, laughing at the mimicry of their boss, Major Broaley.

'Still, it's just as well,' said Listener, 'that that bloody idiot Linsdale hasn't stolen a bomb, to send us all up.'

'Maybe it would be just a bit more exciting than sitting here all day doing nothing.'

'You don't seem very fussed at the idea of being welded to your bedsprings by a nuclear explosion.'

'Listen mate, with my wife lying beside me with her gorgeous twin delights, and the mother-in-law being roasted just across the town, what a way to go!' Great guffaws erupted once more and Runner burst the bag with a violent pop.

'Shhh!' said Listener suddenly, shaking his arm and switching on the tape recorder with the other hand. 'We're on again.' They waited. 'It's that bloke, with another racing tip. Same odds as before. Green Badger at Newbury; four-fifteen. That's all.'

Runner checked the *Express* racing section and found it. 'It's here, right enough. Green Badger. Won its last two. Must be genuine.'

Listener handed him the tape. 'Better check with HQ just the same.'

Runner went through the same process of putting the recorded message through to HQ and when he'd finished, came out once again and locked the door van doors securely. He bent down to pat the young brown and white springer spaniel sniffing at the van's wheel.

'He likes rubber and things like that,' said the man holding the leash. 'He's got to be different, the young scamp.'

'How old is he?'

'Eighteen months. His name's Mr Bumble.'

Runner had no idea that the pleasant gentleman holding the leash was George Maunders, one of the people helping to spirit Dr Linsdale away. He and his colleague had been briefed for surveillance of number 23 only, and he had no idea what the members of other cells looked like. Maunders, in turn, had no idea how close he was to being caught by talking to the 'telephone' man. Just a few minutes ago Maunders had passed his message personally to the 'bookie' down the street, who was his own contact with the next cell unit. The 'bookie' had passed the message by phone to those in number 23. That recorded message had now just been sent via the Telecom van, under George Maunders nose, to Intelligence Headquarters. Maunders said cheerio and walked off down the street, tugging the dog gently.

15.46hrs, Whitehall. Sherman had just managed to get back his office, settling into his swivel chair to punch a number into the intercom, when Pamela walked in. He noted her haste. 'This just came in,' she said. He took the paper from her. His anxious eyes scanned the paper to pick out the words:

CODE: GREEN BADGER // 4.15 // NEWBURY // TRANSLATE:
LINSDALE //
16.15 // FLIGHT HELSINKI // HEATHROW

'Christ!' cried Sherman. He lurched forward to grab the phone.

'We've already put the message out. We got on to Major Broaley as soon as it came in -- just like you told us.' There was her playful smugness in the voice.

'You did? Good.' He sat back in his chair, stretching out his legs full length and tapping the edge of the desk with his pencil. 'Well thank God for that.' His obvious relief dimmed for a second. 'Let's hope there's no slip-ups this time.' The earlier tip-off from Monks about the Bayswater location had been a burst balloon of an operation. They'd already had that on their lists, and a secure check, without arousing the attention of the suspects, had shown that Linsdale wasn't there. 'We've got to get that mad bastard before he gets us, God help us.'

She stood silently, watching his anxiety and relief switching on and off like a flickering light bulb on its way out. He had asked for God's help, but she wanted to give him *her* help. 'The news is supposed to cheer you up, not fret your nerves away.' She continued to study him, worried about his health. 'You didn't come back last night.'

The change of tone in her voice didn't escape him. Here she goes; she was beginning to sound more and more like Maureen every time. When it came to clucking, compared to Pamela, battery hens didn't have a look-in. He leaned forward on his desk to bury himself in his work, not wanting to get involved in another row. 'Yes, I know. I kipped up on the camp bed in the next room,' he said, with his eyes down on his schedule sheets. 'Or don't you believe me? Maybe we should call in the Forensic people to find some of my hairs on the bed to convince you?'

His cold remark, uncontrolled in its hardness, hurt her and she pressed her fingers together tightly, almost breaking one of her brightly manicured nails. 'Oh, I believe you. I can't help but believe you, with that face of yours.' She looked at the fatigue on his face, setting in heavily under his eyes.

'Hell, does it show that much?' He reckoned it did. He could feel the strain of his being knocked about the country, to and fro on helicopters and planes, like a ping-pong ball.

'Yes, it does, she said soothingly, sitting on the desk corner. She ran her hands through his hair, caressing his tired head. Jumping up, she went over to the old kettle plugged in over the filing cabinet, beside the stainless steel corner sink. 'What you need right now is a cup of tea. Haven't you had this ancient wreck replaced yet? I positively swear somebody's going to be electrocuted by it, one of these days. It's time it was thrown out and they gave you a new one.'

'Yes, well maybe you can put in a word to Finance for me. I don't seem to be able to get through to them on that issue.' He threw the pencil down and looked over at her, especially at her lovely bum. 'What are you doing up here, anyway? Shouldn't you be downstairs, hard at work, like a good Section 2 Radio Officer should be?'

'It's my tea-break and Jim Niven's standing in for me with Norma.' She came over and sank her soft bottom onto the sharp edge of the desk, folding her arms. Her voice became quieter and more pleading. 'Do you think you'll manage to get back tonight?'

'I'll make a special effort to get back as soon as I'm free.'

How many times had she despaired in hearing that fruitless promise? But she didn't let him see her disappointment, sighing only to herself inside. 'With the state you're in, I'm not sure if you'll manage to get out of your chair.'

'Yes, well in that case, you can come up to get me and carry me back to the flat on your back. How about that?'

She plumped herself down in his lap with a giggle and they both hugged each other, laughing and shaking. She could feel the nervous release of his tension in his laughter, as he shook against her. He pushed her away, slapping her bottom. 'All right, Radio Officer, Second Class, get back to that kettle, before this place goes up in flames.'

She gave a smart Brownie's salute and turned about. With her back to him, her face was serious again, as she worried about him over-working himself to exhaustion. His face resumed its furrowed look as he worried about *other* things.

10

15.52hrs, 24th June, Middlesex. Major Broaley consulted his watch and shot his eyes skywards in frustration. Twenty three minutes to go and they hadn't reached the airport yet. He turned to the driver. 'For God's sake, don't save it up, man. We want to stop them flying out, not wave them cheerio from the roof.' Thrashing cylinders thrashed faster and the white Jaguar with the maniac driver surged forward, weaving like a ferret through the traffic. Frightened drivers blared their horns in protest, but it was gone, away ahead in oblivion.

Broaley was already in this area, by chance, when HQ had relayed the message through to him. A message sent in by Surveillance, at 15.48hrs, for routine decoding. The computer had taken in the simple betting tip and spat it out again, so that Green Badger was Dr Linsdale, and Newbury at 4.15 was the 16.15 flight for Helsinki, at Heathrow. The fact that Green Badger was, indeed, racing at Newbury was not coincidental. The code's kernel was the time unit and everything else was a shell round about it. This way, the identity and location changed names daily, making things less conspicuous.

Broaley tapped his knee impatiently, hoping to high heaven that this wasn't another wild goose chase, like that earlier, to Bayswater. If it hadn't been for the deadly countdown they were facing, the fact that they hadn't caught the bird on that earlier run wouldn't have niggled him. In the broad experience of the job, he accepted that they had to pass a lot of dirt through the sieve before catching any bright stones. He opened his cigarette case and then stopped, to look round at the driver. Shaking his head in silent exasperation, he snapped the case shut and returned it to his inside pocket, beside the holstered Colt automatic.

They bowled into the airport and jolted to a halt in the official parking space at two minutes past. Broaley went straight to the Special Branch office. The Anti-Terrorist Squad Commander was waiting for him. 'Don't worry, Major, everything's under control. We've had men standing by at all the key-points from the word go. If there's anybody to catch, we'll catch him.'

'You'd better be right, Commander.'

'Of course I am. What's it all about, anyway?'

'I wouldn't want to retire you prematurely with ulcers. Let's just say it's a latter-day defector. A term we haven't been using a lot since the Cold War days; but with what's going on now, let's just say temperatures are falling. Will that keep you happy?'

The Commander was too long in the job to be knocked by being kept in the dark. 'It may keep *me* happy, Major, but I can't speak for others, seeing as your driver nearly ran down two porters when you drove in. All that haste, for nothing more than swapping flags?'

But the Major wasn't in the mood for wheedling. He could have knocked the man aside with a toothpick, but he let it go. 'Let's go and have a look at things,' he said, and led the way out of the room.

Like the Commander had said, the men were everywhere that was important, trying to look normal and blend in with the rest of the people. Whether it was the Departure Gate or the Passengers' Lounge, nobody felt the professionally trained eyes sift through the passports and faces as if they were plain glass. They did their job thoroughly without harassing anyone. Up on the roof, in the visitors' gallery, a young man looked at the planes through a pair of powerful binoculars, while his 'fiancee' clung to his arm. There was nothing about their appearance to say that they were Special Branch officers, except that it was perhaps irregular that she had a large two-way radio in her handbag. Down below, it was like a giant aviary of steel, shining With multi-coloured plumage of international repute or dispute, according to how one's politics leaned. The great birds shifted and circled each other, their tails raised like contending cocks before a fight. Others simply took off.

Broaley and the Special Branch force waited for theirs until it was ready to take off, twenty minutes behind schedule. 'Well, Major,' said the Commander at last, with his hand hovering over the phone, 'do we let it go, or do we stop it?'

Broaley frowned at the podgy hand over the phone and made his decision. 'No, let it go. We'll wait for the next one.'

'Very well, Major, it's your decision.'

Broaley caught the iron tone in the remark. He wasn't sure if it was a compliment or a shirking of blame for a botched job, but he left it at that. He had other battles to fight. They waited for the next flight; and the next one and the next one and many more. Nobody they wanted appeared. Nobody was arrested. At the worst, a schoolboy hugging a radio tuned to air-flight control frequency was escorted from the roof gallery for being a nuisance. But that was all. Nobody had bothered with the gentleman and his springer spaniel, who stood by the incoming-luggage conveyor line, greeting his friend who had just 'flown in'. The luggage they waited on was fake, of course, and had been flown, under redirection, into the country to provide a cover for those waiting for it. Since the airport's security had its eyes on those going out, only scant attention was paid to those 'coming in'. Another friend had come up to them, embracing the new 'arrival', and informing them that security was onto them about their departure plan, so that it had to be aborted. The two policemen patrolling the concourse, walking slowly with their submachine guns cradled in their arms, stopped to let the three men pass by in front of them, on their way out of the airport. They looked round after them. But this was only to admire the sharply-eyed cuteness of the little spaniel trailing behind on a lead.

19.21hrs. Broaley pushed another empty teacup aside and got up to go. 'It's time I went. It seems there was nothing to catch, after all. Sorry to keep your men on the hook. I think we can step down now; but keep somebody on the lookout and let me know if anything interesting develops.'

The Commander plainly didn't like being told like this by 'Five' what he could or couldn't do with his people. Like a schoolboy, not even having been fully informed on the situation. He made sure the Major saw this in his angry response. 'Of course, Major. Perhaps next time you'll even let us know what it is we're trying to catch.'

'Of course, Commander. In the meantime, I'm sorry everything was a waste of time, yours and *mine*.'

'I think God must have said something like that, Major, when He'd finished shovelling the garden for Adam and Eve.'

Broaley found his temper coming to a boil with the Commander's cutting remark, and so he left the room quickly to avoid a scene.

20.41hrs, Whitehall. Sherman was standing there thoughtful over the map, holding a pair of callipers to his teeth, while Meeson beat the hell out of the map for not lying flat on the desk. Broaley walked in. 'Come in, Major and grab yourself a chair or something,' said Sherman, without looking up. 'Be with you in a second. I ordered coffee when I heard you were on your way up. I thought you would fancy a drink after your little escapade at Heathrow. I'm sure you've got lots to tell us.'

'Thanks, said Broaley and sat down. After that endless relay of tea at the airport, he didn't fancy another drink, well, not coffee or tea, anyway. Perhaps something stronger, but he keptthat to himself. He lit a cigarette and blew out. One of his little ways of annoying his 'boss', by smoking in his office. But Sherman burst the balloon on that one, ignoring the smoke and letting him smoke on. You coped with Broaley's iron personality by simply offering no ball for him to bat when you saw he was ready to swing. Broaley studied Sherman's haggard features through the curling grey haze. The tired face nearly matched the pale smoke, and Broaley reckoned he must have been pushing in his fair penny's worth to play that tired tune. In fact, he surprised himself by feeling sympathy for Sherman for pulling his weight on the job, rather than notch up a point against the man. He let out a soft chuckle of surprised praise.

That *did* get a split second reaction from Sherman, when his head half turned in a moment's reflex to see what new mischief the Major was hatching. He bent down close to the map to see what Meeson was marking on it. 'So what happened, Major?'

'Absolutely nothing. No-one turned up, so we nabbed nobody.'

'So like I was saying, Major, tell us about it.' They both straightened up from the map, dropping their preoccupation with Russian bombers once again advancing over the North Sea, to hear what Broaley had to say. Sherman looked at the muscular figure poised on the edge of the straight-backed chair and somehow out of place with all the paperwork that lay all around. For all the dashing about he knew Broaley had been doing, the man looked no more put out than if he'd used an extra hard blow to break his boiled egg. They waited while the cigarette end glowed brightly once more and Broaley blew out again before saying his piece.

'So what's to be said, except that we didn't pull it off? It's the same old inherent factor that goes with chasing a cell. With one individual, there's only one pair of eyes to watch our movements. But with a cell, there's more than one pair and obviously one of those pairs saw us and gave the alarm. So it ends up they clear out, taking Linsdale and all.'

Meeson, who wasn't normally connected with this side of Intelligence's field work, now began to grasp what they were talking about. 'I heard how you nearly grabbed the bugger and then fudged it up at the last minute. A right cock-up. It would have solved a lot if we'd managed to get our hands on the ruddy bugger.' Meeson's words were not intended to be the least critical, but Broaley didn't take it that way. His chest heaved up and the old chair creaked in its tired joints as he leaned forward, short of bounding up at Meeson.

'Now look here, it wasn't our fault! We didn't send them a damned social card saying we were coming. The entire operation was run in accordance with standard procedure.'

'All right, all right, all right,' cried Sherman, stepping between them and shutting his eyes for a second, to stop himself flying off the handle. 'Calm down, Major, calm down,' he said, using the words to quell his own ediginess. With it coming to that, he felt that he really must be needing the sleep that he'd lost over the last two nights. 'Nobody's blaming you. If wewanted to throw the book at you, we could say that it was your operation and let the buck stop there. But we're not looking for someone to pin the blame on. God knows, if all we were looking for was a head to chop off, we wouldn't be playing around with these maps, trying to figure out how to divide the country up into neat slices of radioactive omelette.' He sat on the desk's corner and folded his arms. 'No, gentlemen, our problems are much bigger than that.'

'It's as bad as that, is it?' said Broaley, coming over to the desk to peer down, trying to make something of the mess of papers and maps.

'With just under fifty-two hours to go, wouldn't you say so, Major? But then it's coffee time.' Sherman's interruptive remark had the other two looking round to follow his gaze towards the door. Sure enough, the girl walked in and they all stopped to watch her, grateful for the warm summer air that made her wear a short white cotton frock. She wasn't anything more than simply pretty, but with the full thighs and arms and neck pressing out all around where the dress tightened as she bent over the side table, they had her stripped and pinioned like a butterfly, in their minds, in seconds.

'Thanks,' said Sherman to the girl. The girl smiled back and left the room. Broaley noticedthat there were only two cups on the tray. Sherman was already picking one up. Meeson wasn't. Broaley looked at Meeson.

'It's all right, Major,' said Meeson. 'I'm not having any. You can have mine. I've got to go. Never say stop in this business. ' He turned to Sherman while he zipped up the chrome drawing instruments in their leather case. 'Look, I'll take a run over there now and see what they make of it. See what I can make of it, myself, for that matter. I'll probably be back about ten-ish. So I'll see you then. Okay?'

'Okay.'

'Major.' Meeson nodded to Broaley and was gone out the door.

'Won't we cope, then?' said Broaley as they sat down to drink their coffee.

Sherman rolled his head back, looking across the ceiling and then out the window into the infinite beyond the sky. 'Let's say there will be a big change. The Human Race has come this far only after many changes in the evolution game. In those days our ancestors weren't too fussy about what physical form they took up after mutation. Today, however, I think Mr Man is too fond of his fine physique to want to grow another bunch of fingers, or an extra cluster of ears, after intense radiation dosage.'

'Do you think it will do that?'

'Who knows what it will do, Major.'

'Sounds nasty, all the same.'

'I think the Gurus have the right idea for it, when they see themselves as purely extensions of the cosmic media, manifesting themselves principally as energy forms common to all entities, so that the physical form means nothing.'

Broaley smiled at Sherman's long-winded philosophy. He was good at that sort of thing, with his words like trains in a railway marshalling yard, coming out all organised along the right lines. 'And that will help us, will it? All that thinking, I mean?'

'Probably not, but it's food for thought. And talking of food, ------'

Sherman got up to put on his jacket: '--- is making me feel hungry. All that can be done here has been done --for the moment, anyway. Time for a break, if only for the nerves. Come on, Major, and I'll buy you a last meal before the execution.'

'You give in too easily, Sherman, do you know that? Better let the meal be on me --- at *my* club. That way there's no chance of food poisoning from that Japanese seafood cuisine you're so fond of.'

'Right. And it's *Javanese*, by the way.'

'*Javanese --- Japanese* --- what's the diffe----'

'I bloody well said all right, didn't I! Do you want it in writing?' Sherman's voice was icily sharp.

Anger flared up for a second in Broaley's face, to be instantly replaced by a recovering smile and his steely laugh. The hostility backing down within the sound was barely detectable if you didn't know the man. 'Hey, your nerves *really are* feeling the raw edge tonight, aren't they, Sherman? I suggest we get going --- *if that's all right with you?*"

Broaley's club was an ancient establishment that had the oddity, among establishments of its kind, of favouring the military tie above the school tie. You were unlikely to encounter any females there, not on account of any sexist ruling, but because they were distanced by the austerity of the dark wooden-panelled chambers, where only an old warhorse was as much at home as his charger. Polished steel flashed not only at the dining tables, but also on the walls, where swords, bayonets, halberds and armour guarded smoke-blackened portraits of grim-faced generals. Only the blood from repeatedly retold past battles flowed as freely asthe wine and liquor. When your drink happened to run out, you were never sure if it would be a Cavalier or a Roundhead who would come hurrying in with fresh pitchers of wine and ale to replenish your glass or tankard. And domestic battles were thus averted for a few hours. Not exactly the sort of place Pamela liked being taken out to for dinner. Maybe the Major had a point there.

'Have we had anything else come in from Six?' said Broaley as they went out the door.

'Only from Haldane, so far. Nothing we didn't already know. We know a lot of things, but they're all turning out to be applicable at the wrong place, at the wrong time.' Sherman passed a hand over his tired face in weary acceptance of the cold fact he'd just stated. It didn't help any, reflecting back on the last two frantic chases to Bayswater and Heathrow, both ending with nothing in the bag. 'They're certainly 'passing the parcel' effectively. Is there no way we can intercept the motion, Major?'

'It has to be just before they make the transfer. There's no knowing how many units are in a cell. Only one member of a cell knows of the link member to the next cell. That way, the units are isolated beyond detection by others. When a transfer has to be made, this is done by the one who knows the next cell's link member. That way, the members left behind don't know where he's gone.'

'Sounds pretty watertight.'

'We can cause leaks.'

'How?'

'We keep three eyes open and create pressure at the pipe-line's weak spots.'

Sherman looked at the Major, trying to see the vicious side that lurked beneath the surface, kept in check by his soldierly aplomb that was forged from his bloodline's centuries of grand soldiers. It had to be there, to make his job function. 'I won't ask you how you do that, Major.' He checked to see that his mobile and pager were switched on. 'I think we'd better make that a quick meal.'

Had either Sherman or Broaley looked out of any of the MoD building's windows facing onto Whitehall, they would have seen nothing more conspicuous than a red corporation bus passing by. A very ordinary bus but for the fact that sitting on the upper deck was the man the country's security forces were desperately trying to pin down. Beside him sat George Maunders with his dog in his lap. This was Maunders' method of adopting a low profile by simply being ordinary. Nobody would look for them on a bus. Yet deep down, Maunders didn't feel ordinary. Not with his assignment, as duty demanded. Not any more. Rather, he felt alienated from his work more than he had on his last jobs. But it was over twelve years since that last job. So it wasn't his loyalty that was waning, as he feared. It was simply that he was growing more akin to his cover role of the affable shop owner; with a growing dread of shedding that comfortable role for the more sinister one demanded by his FSB masters.(Federal Security Service; formerly the KGB). The Old Firm under 'new management', with a new name. It was they who had recently come onto the scene to instruct him to act as link man between the cells. As a deeply planted sleeper, he had always worked alone. But this was the FSB's ploy to get under the country's security radar by bringing him in as someone hitherto unknown to the cells to act as the transfer link. He wondered how his new masters would react if they as much as suspected how he was feeling now.

'How you can possibly tolerate all that horrible hair totally escapes me,' came the nervous remark beside Maunders, cutting into his own secret questioning thoughts. The voice carried more than distaste. It carried the psychoneurotic fear of dogs.

Maunders looked round at the scientist and gave his usual disarming warm smile.

'You get used to it. But you have to like it as well; makes it all the easier.' He thought it weird how his words were echoing in on what had been troubling his conscience a few moments before. But he kept his pleasant manner. 'Go on, give it a pat. He won't bite you.' But the invitation only succeeded in making Dr Linsdale shift further away.

11

01.49hrs, 25th June, Kensington, SW7. There was no doubt that some sort of party was in full swing, as Broaley edged his way casually into the room. The stroboscope flashed its light violently, transfixing the the dancing figures in an unreal slow motion of bouncing bums and boobs. In the corner, an oil-film projector gave off its slow turning kaleidoscope of coloured patches onto the ceiling and walls, under the stern scrutiny of Lord Kitchener pointing from the poster. Below the poster, a voiceless discussion group got in the way, so that the coloured patches moved over their bodies and faces like a creeping leprosy. How one could speak and hear in this din was a mystery to Broaley, but it was also a cover. Under the ear-shattering noise, nobody was bothering much with anyone that was too many inches away to speak to. Broaley took advantage of this and moved further into the room, along the edge of the dancing turmoil.

Only one person was moving solitarily like he was, across the room, and she seemed to be the hostess. She looked Latin and slightly overweight. But only a Latin could use that extra fat the way she did. He wasn't looking for her, but he couldn't be a man and not stare for a few seconds. Her flashing white teeth stood out from her dark skin, just like the bra showing seductively through the pale blue chiffon blouse and cutting into her soft sides. Two large water melon breasts bounced as she moved, plunging down in full view with a silken glisten at the blouse's cutaway front. A small man undoing her bra from the front would have been killed in the avalanche. If the body didn't respond to that, one was either gay, or in need of a hydraulics engineer for repairs. Or maybe some Viagra.

A gin-happy face wavered near to Broaley's face and oozed out its words like a punctured sausage. 'Sheesh big, ishn't sheee.'

'She is that,' answered Broaley, not taking his eyes off her. The drunk saw the chance to leech himself onto a new listener, and wobbled round to the front, splashing his drink about like holy water. Broaley jumped back from the drunk's 'blessing' and moved off. He had no more time to waste on distractions. Someone's hand offered some 'pot', but Broaley knocked the cigarette aside and made for the room across the landing.

His way was suddenly blocked by a tall thin figure in a grey moleskin suit. The slender frame, the anaemic complexion and the close-cropped hair reminded one of a stalk of celery. 'Hi, Broaley,' said the American, waving his great flipper of a hand. 'So you finally got here; I thought you were never going to turn up. I've been wanting to talk to you.'

'So I'm here now, Monks; so let's get on with it. Make it brief; some of us just haven't got the time to spare partying around.'

'Hey, don't be like that, Major. We're supposed to be buddies, aren't we? Our guys all working alongside your MI5 boys. Right?'

Broaley's eyes jumped up at the American's loud-mouthed broadcast and he looked around, half expecting the party to come to an abrupt halt. Monks laughed. 'Say, don't let these cute cookies worry you. They can't hear us and we certainly can't be bugged with this racket going on. Most of them are on a trip, anyway. Yeah, I could have done with a bit more fun myself.' He leaned back and looked with feigned disappointment at the long cigarette which could well have conducted the London Symphony Orchestra at the Albert Hall. Broaley just had to smile, even if impatiently, at the American's cheery panache. He knew that Sherman had only told Monks about the country's defence being set back 'temporarily', and that the American and his CIA bosses didn't know about the countdown deadline the country was facing. Or *did* they? There again, Monks' attitude would hardly be so casual if they did know. Or did they know, and were not letting on, just as he wasn't letting on with Monks? Some buddies, for sure. It was the swing-around multi-faced game they all played. When he was with Sherman, Monks used the caustic tongue approach, when he was with Broaley, it was cool clowning.

'Say, something tickling you, huh?' said Monks.

'Sure, but the label's come off.'

'The label, huh? Well let me show you a label, wise guy.' Monks grabbed Broaley by the sleeve, to steer him over to the wall table, where bottles stood or lay among the bowls in an abandoned skittles skirmish. Portions of asparagus, jellied eels, prawns, cold slaw, olives, cheeses and other delicacies that originally had been in separate bowls were now slopped about in all the bowls. Monks swooped down like a hungry gannet and seized up some asparagus, then tilted his head back to drop the asparagus ceremoniously into his gaping mouth. His jaws twisted with scrumptious delight and the sparkling eyes beamed out the satisfaction. 'Good stuff, huh?' he said. Finishing his little private feast, he leaned over to the back of the table and took out his own bottle that had been hidden behind an empty crisps box. It was only cheap plonk, but it was fuller than most of the other bottles. Monks grappled with his knuckles for the stems of two glasses, and started pouring out the red wine. 'Here, get this in your mouth and tickle your taste buds, Major. Back in old Illinois a party hasn't begun until you can tinkle out a tune on your tonsils with your toenails.'

'Thanks.'

'That's right. Finish that one and have another and I'll introduce you to some interesting fun kids. *Real interestin'* people.'

But the Major didn't catch Monks' special tone of voice, behind all his larking around. He'd had his fill of it now. 'I haven't the time. Can we get on with it. Have you got something for me, or not? Your people must be burning a great hole in Uncle Sam's pocket if this is what they're paying you for --- wasting time.'

Monks was unruffled. '*Time*? So what the hell's time, huh?'

'Time is a rock on a secluded lake-shore, sheltering your bottle of delicate bouquet wine from the sun,' said a third voice, which surprised them both. Their faces became slightly serious and they turned round. It was a silver haired Chinese, decked in gold specs, rings and bracelets, who was either a brilliant consultant cardio-thoracic surgeon or an even more brilliant door-to-door tie salesman. He tried to squeeze in and it was obvious that he was only after the booze.

Monks recovered his flamboyant cheer, and his face lit up again. 'Hi, there,' he said, thumping the Chinese on the shoulder. 'Grab yourself some juice. Here, we'll get out of your way and let you have the pick of the table. Mind you, buddy, there's not much to pick from now, huh?' He chortled aloud and ambled lazily over to the banister and sat on the storage heater, crossing his legs. He poured out some more wine and raised his glass in salute. 'Goose feet and pumpkin pickles -- or should it be *pickled pumpkins?*'

'I'm going.'

'Hold on, hold on.' Monks smacked his lips and went on. 'Like I was saying, I'll introduce you to some interesting folks. Like Wally, there. I'm sure you'd like a quiet session with Wally. Plenty to touch there.'

'I never figured you to be gay, Monks.'

Monks rocked back, choking and spluttering on his wine at the joke of the other getting it wrong. He stopped coughing and pointed to the delectable hostess, who was trailing a man by the wrist, into a bed-room. '*That's* Wally,' he said. Wally's short for Waleena. Like I said, there's plenty of room for manoeuvres, huh?'

'So it would seem. But like I said, I haven't the time. Let's leave it there, right?'

Monks looked down into his glass, all serious for a moment. 'It's no use waiting around foryour egg-head Doc guy. He's gone. Vamoosed.'

Broaley's anger shot up. 'You *knew* this? You damn well *knew* this and you couldn't have damn well told me; instead of all this damn well stalling. You bloody ---' Broaley broke off, shaking his head, his fury just held back.

'Jeeze! Quit your hee-hawin', Major. Do you think it's just you guys that are in one right old heck of a hog-tail rumpus over this? We got the spike up our asses, as well, you know, thanks to your Doc.'

'Only after *your* man had poisoned Linsdale's mind. God knows how the bastard did that, but he did.'

'*Our* man! What do you mea ----' Monks trailed off, slapping his forehead in amazement at the dawning realisation. 'Hey, you really don't know, do you? You really don't *know*. Right under your noses, and you don't know. Jeeze, you guys *are slow*.'

'So fill me in. No big words, speak slowly, and I'll try to keep up with you.'

'Okay. You do know your Doc spent time with our guy at MIT and on vacation after they graduated? Great surfboard buddies, smoking 'joints' and roasting chestnuts over the same campfire --- all that stuff, yeah?' Broaley nodded. 'Well, our guy, Ambrose Gerard Bonar-DeWoolfe ---*the Third*, no less, was a bright kid. Ivy-League golden boy. Never short of a dollar. Millionaire parents both from aristocratic New England stock --- as far as American aristocracy goes, you understand. He had everything going for him, career and moneywise. No need for him to do anything out of hand. I guess he felt he had to make his own mark somehow, seeing as his family had already done everything there was to be done --- achieved every honour there was to be achieved. Our shrinks would say that's how the seed was planted in B-D's mind to make a better world. A so-called 'world of peace'. That's all he and your guy were planning to do, and *did* do, in the early stages. Nothing more militant, underhand, than pamphlets, street marches, placards for Unilateral Disarmament; all crazy soft politics.'

'Until *our* man turned the screw on him, coercing him into sabotaging the West's nuclear defence system, no less. Or so *you* say. Why would he want to do that?'

Monks swayed back, slapping his knee and shaking his head. 'Hell, Major, you still don't get it. The man's a goddamned Commie! Never mind the Wall being down --- Commie, Red, it doesn't matter what you call them now, their prayer chants still go East. Poor old God is sure losing out on homage there.' Monks raised his glass to the ceiling. 'Hallelujah!'

Broaley was not feeling too happy, with this revelation hitting him like an arctic blast. And from a damn Yank. 'And this is established as absolute certainty, is it?'

Monks nearly choked from his drink with another laugh. He threw up an arm, letting it flop down at his side. ' "Is it absolute certainty?" he says. Jeeze, Major, he was virtually holding his sacred Party card before he'd dragged his second leg out through the college gates! *We* didn't even know that then. We should have, what with your Cambridge being a right hornet's nest for breeding Reds. Maybe Philby's ghost spooked him one dark night in the cloisters, when his fag ditched him.' Monks paused to gulp down the last of the wine. 'But we did get to learn of this later.'

Broaley had to get something in, to balance up the vacuum feeling he had. 'And you never thought of keeping us informed?'

Monks held his hand to his heart in mock gesture. 'We're both in the same game, Major. Maybe if we didn't have to crane our necks looking up at our flags on their long poles, we'd be able to see each other standing beside each other. Otherwise?'

Broaley nodded in silent understanding. 'And your Bonar-DeWoolfe? Have you got any further developments on him?'

'Tried to hightail it to the Rockies. He thought he could lose himself in the wilds and then through to Canada. The Mounties thought that it was *their* sole effort that nabbed him, but we sure as hell already had him tracked like a cockroach on the cookhouse wall.' Monks raised his eyes to the ceiling to indicate that beyond. 'Eye in the sky satellite.' He looked into his empty glass, possibly wondering why it hadn't filled up again by itself. 'The kid wanted to make his mark on the world; well now he can. If he behaves himself, he can make his mark stamping library books in the state penitentiary. Say, wouldn't the Muslims call that Fate, or Destiny, or something?'

That last remark was jarring reminder to Broaley of more urgent things. He knew Monks wasn't as drunk as he was pretending to be. It was the American's ploy to wind him up with loose chatter and so maybe catch something from a careless slip of the tongue when he lost his patience. Broaley looked at his watch and clenched his impatience in his fist. 'You said something about giving me a hand. I don't see that happening. I'm off.'

'Okay, okay.' Monks put the glass down on the storage heater and took out a pen and a piece of paper. He held the paper at different distances and tried focusing his eyes for several seconds, before deciding that he could still write. 'There we are; that's the number. Your tech guys can trace the address from it. Say, I must be only half drunk if I can still write on a piece of paper this small. I guess you'd choke trying to swallow the piece I'd need to write on if I was really plastered, huh?'

Broaley read the number and put it away in his pocket. 'We'll check it out. And if we're too late -----' Broaley let the rest of the message trail out in the icy look he gave Monks as he turned away.

'Say, hold on there, Major. I'll come along and see that you get there. Call it strictly liaison. I Promise not to meddle in anything that's not mine for the meddling. Scouts' honour. 'Monks saluted with crossed fingers and got up to go, stuffing the empty bottle in the pocket of someone's coat lying over the banister. Just as they were about to go down the stairs, Monks put a hand to Broaley's arm to stop him. He pointed to Broaley's pocket, meaning the number he'd just given him. 'Like you said, Major, that place could just be one heck of an empty stable, horses gone, an' all, by the time we get there. So maybe we can get the guy who sent the 'horse' there. We can maybe knock some information out of him if we use him for a punch-bag.'

Broaley saw Monks' sudden change of heart and felt the paper in his pocket lose its value. He waited for Monks to spill out more. Monks swayed and tapped his nose in cunning, knocking on the bedroom door. The door swung open slowly and there stood their hostess with only a long waist slip and taut bra hugging her body. 'Hi, there,' cried Monks. 'Care if we join you? Make it a real hog-time ho-down, huh?' He slapped the woman's generous bottom. She looked round in question at the man in the bed. He looked very jumpy with nerves. Monks stretched out his arm to point at him for Broaley's sake. Broaley made him sit still by holding out the Colt's muzzle at him. It had obviously been Monks' plan to question the man first, before passing him on as second-hand goods. Broaley glanced with anger at Monks and then looked back with fierce malice glinting in his eyes at the man in the bed. 'You! Out!' He jerked the gun to motion the man to get up and out.

Broaley looked at the man and didn't think that he would have recognised the ordinary face without Monks' intervention. The photograph he'd seen in the files must have been taken 'ages ago' since it bore no strong resemblance to the present face, especially in these low, coloured, party lights. And he had only seen the man from the back, before. Like the typical sleeper, he was nothing special to look at or suspect. A chartered accountant by profession. His *second* profession. His first duty was to the FSB. According to Intelligence, the man's cell had been using the house's basement flat hours earlier; now Linsdale had been moved on to a new safe house. They were going to have to knock some straw out of the 'punch bag'. Even then the Major was worried that it would lead nowhere.

Broaley motioned the man into the corner of the room, to put on some clothes, not taking his pistol off him. Keeping his eyes on the man's eyes, Broaley spoke to Monks. 'Thanks for your help. No doubt you just wanted to pluck a few strands of straw for yourself, before you passed the 'bag' on, right?'

'Gee whizz, Major, that's right! That's right!' Monks held out his hands in cheeky innocence, so ridiculing the Major more than he was being ridiculed himself.

Broaley pulled the man over to the door with his free hand, ready to club him with the pistol in his right hand. He looked at Monks. He still had to goad the American, even though he wasn't drunk. 'Monks,' he said, about to leave with the prisoner, 'you're bloody drunk! Too drunk, I reckon, to be of any further use to us tonight.'

A serious shade slipped across Monks' face for a second, and then vanished again behind the broad grin. 'Well, if you say so, Major, if you say so. But you know, they do say that to the fool's eye, there always seems to be more liquor in the bottle than there really is, huh?' Monks looked at the catch the Major was taking from him, and then at her. She held his eyes with hers, proffering her proud chest forward as she felt behind her back for the bra hooks. Monks' mind went all religious, as he thought of Mohammed moving 'mountains'. He started to close the door on the Major and his prisoner. 'Maybe you're right, Major. Maybe it would be better if you followed up your lead by yourself. I think I could be much more useful staying on here to lend a hand or two. Call it a diplomatic exercise to better the relations between the States and Latin America.' Monks vanished behind the closing door. 'Hi, there,' came the cry through the closed door, followed by the plashy sound of broad hand slaps on soft supple flesh. There was no earth tremor as the bra was unhooked; only a female giggle, followed shortly by a soft low moan as Uncle Sam began to exercise his diplomacy on Latin America.

Broaley took a closer look at his prisoner. Even with clothes on, there was no sharpness of image added to suggest that he was a spy. He was simply Mr Next-Door-Neighbour, with the ordinary air that allowed him to never be suspected of his more devious role. He had been unnerved in the bedroom, naked, with two men and a gun threatening him. Now he was a little more recovered, and so hardened up his resistance. He turned to Broaley. 'Hey, see here, mister, I don't know who the hell you think you are, but you can't touch me without a warrant. I know my rights, if you *don't*. Just try and put the finger on me, and I'll have the newspapers spread you across the front pages like meat paste.'

Broaley thrilled to the man's sudden upsurge, and grinned back viciously, as he would have at a hissing snake. He touched the man's cheek lightly with the cold steel of the automatic. 'Look, son, you'll be lucky if you get a mention in the obituary column.' With that, he pushed the man down the last six stairs onto the floor, almost knocking over the drunk Chinese as well.

10.03hrs, 25th June, St John's Wood, N.W. The Audi TT wheels screeched as Sherman braked and spun the steering wheel, in a lightning decision to veer off course from where he was going -- where he *should* have been going, on prime priority -- to go somewhere else. He had just realised, in a moment's escape from his muddled thoughts, that it was just nearby. It wouldn't take him long. Ignoring the blaring fanfare of angry car horns, he made the dangerous U-turn, mounting the pavement and off again, with the oncoming car missing his wing mirror by a hair's-breadth. Cutting over the pavement corner with another hard bump, he was through the red light, round the corner, and down the side road, with another car only just sparing his paintwork. Brakes rammed on everywhere as he sped off, leaving behind him a cacophony of screaming horns that only the Albert Hall could match in a pre-performance warm-up. You don't bother about counting the penalty points on your licence when you're already counting the hours you have left to stay alive.

Pulling up sharply in front of the house, he got out and bounded up the steps. He tried the handle. The door was not locked, so it was not 'breaking and entry'. He stepped slowly into the dark hallway with a quiet caution. The black movement ahead of him in the dim light was a woman coming out of a room. She turned and started, shocked at his unannounced presence. They stared at each other in a tense long silence, their minds suspended in the surprise confrontation. He saw the pistol in her hand. It was a .38 calibre Sig/Sauer semi automatic.

The spell was broken by the little boy's head suddenly appearing at the room doorway, followed by his little arm reaching up to his mum for his toy G-Man gun. The one he had bought for the boy on his last birthday. About to grab the gun and dash forward, the boy was stopped by his mother's hand on his shoulder. She held the gun away from him, her eyes still on Sherman 'Go and put on your shoes and jacket first, Rudi, and then you can go with your dad to the model train exhibition.' It wasn't his imagination, that the word 'dad' scraped off her tongue with a degree of distaste. And that name, 'Rudi'

-- yuk! Totally her choice, after Rudolf you-know-who, during her phase of hysterical adulation for the silent screen idol, when she was pregnant. A fuse to another of their explosive arguments.

As they talked, nervous words fell more and more on half-deaf ears, she waiting for the boy and he waiting to get away to get on with his operation. Only the dark walls managed to take in all the words without showing any embarrassment. Like they always had done during those infernal rows. Maybe that was why they looked so cold and soulless to him now. You know that feeling when you book into the five star honeymoon suite and then go for a casual stroll in the local abattoir cold storage room.

He saw that Maureen had thinned, skin had sallow, and her mouth shrunken with a dryness of lips that had somehow lost their former bounty. Most unfamiliar of all were her cheeks, drawn in with a sullen pale tightness of reserve that he found he didn't like to acknowledge. But those eyes. They still had that drawing power, there, behind the fiery bitterness that they were silently smouldering with now. He pulled his eyes away from hers.

And to think that he once lived here. He looked around himself. At the walls, the pictures, the furniture --- all the things he had helped to choose, if only because they were opposite to his taste, and hence *her* overriding choice. Almost unbelievable now. They all seemed so strange, alien. Yet not so long ago -- it seemed like ages -- he had known funny things and funny times. He leaned forward to peer at the picture; that ludicrous summer snap of his father-in-law in his skipper's cap. He could have reached out to touch things -- almost did -- but there was a forbidding coolness there too, that kept him in check.

Since their separation, conversation had seemed at times to have flowed easier, freed as it was from their former daily domestic battles. But this didn't seem to be one of those times. She fidgeted thoughtfully with the toy gun while they waited. That very pistol had been the subject of one of their heated debates over suitable toys influencing a child's mind. One of the rare times that he had won the battle; correction: one of the times he had been *allowed* to win the battle.

He had to tell her now. Was this how they felt, putting their heads on the chopping block? 'No, no, I'm sorry, you've misunderstood. I haven't come to collect the lad. I know, I know I was supposed to take him to the exhibition. I

---' He held up his hand to stop her, when he saw she was going to interrupt. 'I know -- I promised the boy. I'm not denying it. I didn't forget.' His hand still held high, he paused, his head and eyes lowered in apologetic pose. 'I wish I could, but in spite of all that's been said --okay, *promised* -- I simply can't manage to take him today. I've got other things, important things to see to. God, if you only knew.'

That familiar cold twitch to the mouth again before she spoke her fire. You were never sure if it was inspired by jealousy or anger. ' Knew what? Don't tell me, she wants ---'

'No! Must you always bring her into everything? This has nothing to do with Pamela. It's nothing personal. It's something else, something very important to do with ----' He shook his hand about in exasperation, unable to fill in the words to the right degree that would be their horrifying truth. 'But you've just got to believe me; something really, really has come up.'

' "Something *really has* come up." Oh, does that mean that something really *hadn't* come up all those other times you said it, then?' She held up the boy's gun, pointing it threateningly at him. 'If only this thing was real.' Anger won over jealousy this time.

There was nothing more he could say to convince her, let alone placate her. You know how you sometimes feel just like Old Blue Eyes Sinatra's 'ram' --- when you're just head-butting that 'dam'. Apart from that, he couldn't face the boy with this crushing disappointment. 'Sorry, I've got to go.' Turning around, he walked sharply to the door. The plastic gun bounced off the doorjamb, narrowly missing his head as he went out, slamming the door closed behind him.

10.03hrs (GMT), 25th June, Tel Aviv. The passengers from Flight 758 from London trooped their way across the concrete expanse, leaving the brilliant blue and white EL AL airliner to sizzle in the sun, while they made their way out of the heat, into the shelter of the Ben Gurion Airport terminal buildings. Stepping up to the Passport Control desk, the slim woman handed her passport to the uniformed officer. Patting down her blue suede skirt, searching for creases, she was annoyed that she hadn't been able to change into fresh clothes before flying out on the assignment. It had been a rushed last-minute switch-over, where current Red Alert had everyone going off on missions like a rocket launcher gone berserk. Peter Haldane had originally been assigned to this one, but had been redirected to fly to Beirut. So she was here in his place.

The passport officer looked up. He waxed up another wide smile. His hundred and 'whatever-th' that morning. Damned if he could remember. 'Clara Tomlin?'

'Yes.' She hoped that her new rimless spectacles, with their needle thin gold side supports, made her look more attractive than she had felt in her old plastic frames. The man nodded, looked at the passport again, then down at the small computer screen out of sight below the desk. He then looked up at the plain clothes security officer standing a little to his right, handing him the passport.

The man made an open study of the passport, before snapping it shut, stepping round from the desk, returning her passport and shaking hands with her, all in one casually flowing suave motion. She thought the bullet wound scar on his left cheek made his broad face all the more handsome. Easy to see how they put him up front on public duties. He turned and led the way. With that oh, so adorable, white-toothed-smile, he could lead her anywhere. Following his broad form through a warren of fluorescent-lit passages, she reflexively, without thinking, touch-tided her mousey brown hair, and undid the top button of her blue chiffon blouse. Restraint, agent Tomlin, restraint. Queen and Country first.

Coming out through a back door and round to a quiet parking area, they found three young men waiting for them. Military green may have been the popular choice among the young men and women of the Israeli populace, but these three men wore civvies. Leaning against a large BMW people-carrier, their languid stance could have had them mistaken for layabouts, skivers from military service. But she could see that they were something quite different. Tension in their faces and eyes betrayed a peak alertness. And one of them just happened to be holding a compact black 9 mm Uzi in his hand. The metal shoulder stock was folded forward to allow for swinging the wrist round suddenly and firing. Useful when surprise attack comes from the sides or from behind. Israel's versatile homemade answer to the fly-swat.

Mr Handsome left her with them and went back into the building. They climbed into the vehicle, she in the back seat beside one of them, while the one with the Uzi rode shotgun in the front passenger seat. The engine made most of the noise as they sped along the sun-baked route, with few words exchanged between them. An occasional smile or nod of reassurance passed across from them to her. Otherwise, they kept their attention focussed on the surroundings outside. It took them just under thirty minutes to reach the city centre.

The driver stayed in the vehicle to take it away after the other three had alighted. Once again there was a marked preference for back passages, away from the heavy volume of babbling crowds and roaring engines. Away from prying eyes. And yet not even down these narrow dark alleys, away from the blinding glare of the wider sunlit main thoroughfares, could they be sure that they weren't being unduly watched. As they made their way along the long winding alleys, they passed before lines of market stalls, open street traders and doorways, where bartering was done with the tongues at Gatling-gun speed, while the eyes searched elsewhere to snatch away your secrets as you passed by. With the din of buyers' and sellers' haggling competing with high pitched Hebrew chanting and the odd braying of an ass, Tomlin gave up trying pick out words from around her to test her knowledge of dialects. At least the Department had refunded here expense claims for all those weekend linguistics sessions.

After ducking under clothes-line after clothes-line stretched across the way, there was suddenly no more need for Tomlin to shield her newly permed hair from flapping sheets. The passage had opened out into a tiny cobble-stoned square, with the route continuing at right angles to the left. Two short dumpy palm tress claimed the centre, each enclosed within its own circular knee-high wall. Small metal tables and chairs sat outside the cafes on the right side and far side of the square. A medley of rich food smells drifting out from the two cafes bombarded her nostrils. The only one she thought she could identify was coffee.

A double armful of brass ornaments was virtually shoved under her nose by a young Arab boy in a sequined Elvis jacket who had run out from a tiny bazaar that she hadn't noticed squeezed into the corner. She shook her head. Not giving up, he whipped up a small phial of perfume with what must have been a third arm. For all she could tell from its pungent aroma, it could have been camel piss. She shook her head again. A low-voiced, menacing, 'fuck off' from one of the men had the boy beating a fast retreat. But not as fast as the stream of obscenities he threw back to scorch the air.

The man with the Uzi disappeared through the beaded curtain shrouding the cafe doorway. A precautionary measure for security. They waited outside. She understood, didn't she? She nodded. Yes, she understood. Did they think she was pea-brained just because she was wearing a skirt instead of trousers? The beads shifted and he was back again brandishing, in addition to his sub-machine gun, a small expresso sized cup of black coffee. Very, very black, like tar. The waiter came out behind him to put down two more cupfuls on the table beside the door. He told them to sit down. Tomlin sat down. But her tall companion picked up his cup and went to join his mate who had gone to sit at a table across the square. It was so she could talk privately with her contact with them out of earshot but still protecting her.

She saw her Mossad contact approaching from the same direction they had come. He was nothing particularly special to look at. But Zaf Ezaika carried that heavily burdened look that characterised his race, with his very own half acre share of deep lines etched into his forehead and cheeks. The man sat down slowly, his eyes on her, studying her all through the long few seconds it took for him settle down in his seat. In contrast to his quiet appearance, the fingers were a give away; soldier's hands, the large hard fingers splayed out in campaign battalions on the table. 'Shalom,' he said, with the same lightness and ease that he would have used sending out his agents to assassinate an anti-Jewish terrorist. Tomlin recognised the irony of this in his words and eyes. They were both in the game that pushed sentiment to the side. She returned the peaceful salutation: 'Shalom.'

The waiter was back, hovering over them while slapping the table top with his cloth. Ezaika shoo-ed him away, then changing his mind, called him back to order a small glass of lemon water and a small plate of olives and dry figs. That wouldn't be too great a torture on his ulcers. His GP, Dr Shorpal, had put him on a diet that would have barely satisfied a hungry flea. But he had to be truly grateful for the old goat delivering his two beautiful grandchildren. The boy would be having his bar mitzvah next week.

They got into their conversation with the usual slow circuitous build-up that went with these sort of meetings. As they did, she could sense that his mind was only half there, only half listening, his deeper thoughts elsewhere.

Not that she doubted his willingness to cooperate in spiking the gun of a Muslim terrorist mission. Israel could hardly have less fervour in staving off Muslim assault than any other country that was experiencing the Jihad tongue of fire. With these thoughts passing through her mind, Tomlin's attention was suddenly caught by an outbreak of dull thuds. Somewhere to her right, uneven in their timing and in the far distance. Of course; rockets. Rockets being fired into Israel from the Gaza Strip. With Israel's blockade on the Strip closing checkpoints, so cutting off food supplies, and cutting off electricity, anger in the narrow coastal settlement was blowing its pressure valves sky high. With the Hamas militants stirring up hatred, homemade rockets were being fired, albeit none too accurately, into Israel.

Ezaika saw the direction of her distraction and smiled, nodding in justification. Another kind of sound filtered through from the distant soft thuds to reach her ear. Harder, sharper, tearing the air with menace, nearer-- nearER -- neARER -- NEARER. The two F-4 Phantom II jet fighters bearing the proud Star of David on their fuselages thundered past low overhead. A second later, two more roared past. She swung her head round to follow their path. All on their way to the Strip to deliver their fury. He watched her face, with its split-second tension, surmising her train of thought. He nodded slowly in heavy thought, biting into the olive flesh to separate the stone and remove it from his mouth before speaking. His heavy-timbred voice carried his words with the same solid conviction as those thundering engines. 'You think, you *say*, we are wreaking *revenge* on the enemy. We do not deliver revenge. We deliver *pain*.' A pause, to chew on another olive and remove its stone. 'You will perhaps agree that pain is, after all, the universal guardian of health, yes? It because of pain that we know something is wrong, that we are ill, that we have sustained injury. And so we halt the action that we now realise will produce further injury.' He looked over at the two bodyguards. 'Take one of those men, for instance. Imagine how hard he would ram his fist into an attacker's face. But would he drive his fist with the same hard force into a concrete wall? The result of *that* action would be immediate pain. I stress the point -- *immediate* pain; the *direct* result of the man's own action. He, in fact, causes his own pain.' He took up a fig this time. 'We send in our planes to attack *them*, as soon as they attack *us*. In that way we can cause them to feel, in reflex, that the bombs that we drop on them are caused by their very own initial rocket attacks on us.'

She didn't argue the point, but simply nodded. It occurred to her that Mossad assassins often cut down their targets well after the 'event' -- months, years, even. Just as the CIA, and 'others' did. But she didn't mention this. The last thing she wanted was to ruffle his feathers. They were on the same side, after all, fighting a common enemy. With all the olives reduced to stones, and only two figs left, she manoeuvred the conversation so that what she was seeking began to come her way. If she got what she was after, her MI6 bosses could pull strings, so that government bosses could set off a domino action all the way across the Atlantic to an effect from which Israel would benefit. Ezaika knew this only too well. No coincidence, therefore, that his information on Maneesh Hassani, the Iraqi nuclear bomb technician, trained by Russian instruction, came out of him with no difficulty -- at long last. Name, details of training, how competent he was expected to be in fulfilling his role as a Jihad modern-day angel of cataclysmic deliverance; even infra-red night photographs of him coming ashore from the dinghy, that had come from the Russian submarine, Yalta. Mossad had long known this, holding it back as a trading card to play at the opportune moment. Now was that moment, and Ezaika was passing it across the table. Now he could tell his government bosses to expect the Whitehouse to convey an appropriate political and military concession on Israel.

They both had what they had come for. Everyone got up. Ezaika went back the way he had come, his own guards waiting for him, just out of sight. Her escorts came across, to take her back to the airport.

12

23.44hrs, 24th June, Clerkenwell EC1. The car seat creaked as its shadowy occupant shifted to look in the rear mirror, carefully watching the figure that had emerged from the lane. Scrutiny held for a few seconds and then the eyes relaxed, as the figure came nearer into the light. The brain registered friend, not foe. Leaning across the seat, the man opened the passenger door and his colleague got in with his paper-wrapped package.

'What kept you?' said the first man, more interested in the package than the answer. 'It's nearly gone midnight.'

'It's not that already, surely, Sergeant?' said the colleague over his shoulder, as he tried to close the door. He turned round and started to open the package. 'I couldn't jump the queue, you know. Besides, I stopped off to have a piss in the scrap yard back there. That one's yours. Fifty five pence.'

Not bothering with words or money, The Sergeant gingerly rescued his pie from its tinfoil tray and sank his teeth into it savagely. It was drier than he preferred and the pastry flaked about in abundance like chronic dandruff. 'Is this the best you could do?'

'That's what you asked for, isn't it? A steak and kidney pie? So what's wrong with it, then?'

'What's wrong with it? Well, I think I've seen more meat on a fat fly. They must have sent this one's kidneys to St. Bart's for a transplant or something.'

'Eat up, Sergeant, that was the last they had. And you still owe me fifty five pence.' He paused to swallow a large mouthful of onion pie. 'Anything been happening?' he said, tapping the 15lb Nocta infra-red camera that was perched on the aluminium support rod bracketed to the dashboard. Not wasting any words, the Sergeant shook his head and gorged on into his pie. His mate leaned forward and looked into the view-finder, switching on the battery power unit for the searchlight. The Nocta had a 35mm single reflex lens and a 300mm long focus lens, giving it a range of one hundred yards. Coupled on either side, like proud ram horns, were the searchlight and flashgun, both with special filters allowing only the infra-red rays to pass through. This made all the difference between night and day with the naked eye and the camera eye. Outside, the night was still dark and shapeless, but the man looking through the view-finder had a brilliant daylight picture of the house they were watching sixty yards down the street, and could count the cracks in the brickwork.

'Anything?' said the Sergeant.

'No.' He swivelled the camera a couple of degrees and then gave up, sitting back in his seat again.

The Sergeant snapped on the radio. 'Hullo, Rufus. Ferret Two, here.'

'Hullo, Ferret Two. Have you anything to report?'

'No, but it's nearly midnight and our relief is long overdue. I take it we're going to be relieved, or has something gone wrong?'

'No, nothing's gone wrong. Don't worry, we'll send your relief round as soon as possible. Just wait a bit longer. There's nothing else, is there?'

'No, there's nothing else, Rufus. We'll wait. That's it. Out.'

As they waited, a cat stalked along the wall and stopped to look at them. The Sergeant's mate shot it between the eyes with his forefinger and a gentle 'Sploof!' Not impressed, the cat twitched its ears and swung its tail back and forth, before moving on.

'Hullo, who's this, then?' said the Sergeant's mate, looking in the rear mirror.

'Where?' said the Sergeant, seeing nobody in front of them.

'Behind us, Sergeant.'

Sure enough, the silver Audi rolled up out of the darkness and parked in at their bumper. Sherman got out and came up to the Sergeant's window. The Sergeant looked at the MoD pass and gave it back smartly. 'Is something on, then, sir?'

'Yes,' said Sherman. 'We're going to raid them. Back-up should be here in a few minutes.'

Just then, the radio came alive, and they all leaned in to listen. 'Hullo, Ferret, are you

there?'

'Yes, we're here. What is it?'

'Stay put. We're sending a raiding party round now. New orders have just come through. We're going to raid your place. We should be with you in a few minutes, so stand by. Got that?'

'Got you, Rufus. Standing by. Okay. Out.'

Sherman was about to go back to his car, when the Sergeant's mate caught their attention, pointing in front. 'Oh, no, that's all we need,' he said woefully.

'What's that?' said the Sergeant.

'A couple of our own beat boys, no less.'

'Maybe it'll be all right,' said the Sergeant hopefully.

'Get rid of them, before they blow the whole thing,' Sherman said sharply, and nipped back to the cover of his own car.

There may have been an urgently increasing need for policemen to be seen on foot patrol, in order to halt an escalating crime rate, but on an undercover job like this, the conspicuous attention of their uniforms was the last thing you wanted. The policemen swayed along up the street, rattling a few shop doors on the way. They drew abreast of the cars on the opposite pavement. They stopped and stood there, staring at the cars with open curiosity, apparently trying to decide if they were animal, vegetable or mineral.

' 'Allo, 'allo, 'allo,' mimicked the Sergeant's mate, in his best Dixon of Dock Green manner. The Sergeant cocked his eyebrow with disapproval at the cheek. At last the policemen came across slowly to the front car, with the front man's radio cackling like a mina bird on his lapel.

The policeman knocked on the window and waited for it to open, while his mate stood back looking at the car's licence plates. The window slid down. 'Good evening, sir. Having trouble with the engine, are we?' That was the policeman's polite version of why were they hanging about like monkeys waiting for tea. He took the Sergeant's credentials and flashed his torch over them. 'Special Branch! Oh, I see, sir. Sorry to bother you, but we were just checking. We thought perhaps----'

'That's all right, Constable. You did the right thing. Can't be too careful, can you?'

'Thank you, sir. On a special job, are you? *Him*, as well?' He nodded at Sherman's car.

'Yes, we are.'

'Anything we can do at all, to help, sir?' He looked about eagerly, but every place looked ordinary and there was no neon-sign in the sky pointing to the villains' den.

'No, that's all right, Constable. We're managing as we are, just waiting here and looking ordinary and not creating a fuss or anything; you understand?'

'Why yes, of course, sir. Still, if there's anything we can----'

'There *is* something you can do,' said the Sergeant's mate, leaning across to the open window. 'You can push off!'

'Of course, sir. Good night.' The policeman sensed at last that he was not wanted, and signalled to his mate with a glum jerk of the head and they moved off. A curtain shifted two doors down, but that was all, and the street became its quiet unruffled self again. More lights went out and the street withdrew itself further from the cars isolated in their lonely vigil.

They waited and the minutes seemed like hours. Sherman checked the time on his watch and thrummed the steering wheel restlessly. Then suddenly, they were no longer alone. With ghostly subtlety, car doors and figures were growing out of the brickwork, where only the night had been, a few moments ago. Clandestine shapes came out of the shadows from different directions and flitted down the street with a common motive in their stealth. Converging on the one point, they melted once more into the stonework, to await the zero signal. The Sergeant and his mate, bored from hours of monotonous watch-duty, were once more revitalised, like the mythical Phoenix itself. The raid was on.

A figure came along beside their car and rapped on the window as it passed by. 'Christ! It's the Commander himself, no less,' said the Sergeant's mate. 'It must be something big.'

'Yeah, and he's waiting hand and foot on Mr Big-Wig, by the look of it,' said the Sergeant, as he got out, seeing Commander Rose wait on Sherman getting out of his car. The Sergeant and his mate went to join the main body of Special Branch men, while the Commander stood taking orders from the Intelligence man from the MoD.

Sherman finished briefing and shook his car keys in the direction of the house.

'That about sums it up, Commander. So can we move in now, if you please?' The statement was polite, but with steely command in its tone of authority.

'Right away.' Commander Rose was much older than Sherman and didn't much like the idea of taking orders from the less experienced man. Nor would he have given a brass farthing for the scant information that Sherman had dressed up in his sum-up, like icing to hide the dull cake. But then it was the MoD's cake, so they could damn well choke on it. Normally Sherman would have been concerned with this cold attitude, since it was his job to liaise between departments, but he was too ill at ease with other matters. With time ticking by like a bomb in his mind, he was desperate to catch Linsdale. That they had snatched out and caught nothing so many times today put him all the more on edge with the operation. It only occurred to him then, in his comparative nakedness in the empty street, that this was the first time that he had ever taken part in a live raid. He had certainly put his signature on paper to endorse many such operations in the past. But apart from that, his normal assignments always called him onto the scene after the pot had boiled over, so to speak. Just like that one earlier, when he had followed on after Major Broaley. Even then, it was the SAS lot who had done the actual job. Not quite knowing what came next in the action routine, it was like facing the lion in the circus ring for the first time, holding the whip and chair in your hands. Do you hit old Leo over the head with the chair, or perhaps you get him to sit down in the chair to talk things over sensibly? He suddenly felt himself wishing for Broaley's experience. The thought chilled him for a second with its implications, and he checked himself immediately.

The Commander could see that the MoD man was not much experienced in outside field duties. 'Do you think you could step in here out of the light, sir,' he said quietly, beckoning Sherman to join him in the shadows between the two adjacent buildings.

13

00.09hrs, 25th June, Clerkenwell EC1. 'Everybody here?' whispered the figure in the Gannex raincoat standing beside the wheelie-bin. The Commander looked around him for confirmation. Heads nodded and body shapes shifted in the gloom of the garden, while the Superintendent took the count. He turned to the Commander. 'Yes, sir. All present. Forbes, Morris and Baxter are round the back.'

'Good.'

'All briefed and ready to go in, sir.'

'Right, Superintendent. In that case, I think we can get on with it.'

The figures turned and moved carefully through the rubbish, while not fully escaping the putrid smells of the unkempt garden which rankled their nostrils. Other odd shapes remained moulded in one great obscurity, except at the big incision made by the alley, where some light had sneaked in between the buildings and scraped itself along the wall in a yellow smudge. The Commander stopped short of the door and turned round. 'Some of us have been issued with arms, I take it?'

The figures stepped closer. 'Riley and Foster, sir,' said the Superintendent. The MoD liaison man at the back of the group hadn't said yes or no, so they looked at Sherman, half expecting him to produce nothing less than a sub-machine gun. But Sherman was unarmed, with only his impatient knuckles to bulge in his raglan coat pockets.

'All right, you two, stay close behind me,' said Rose. 'And remember, no showing of arms unless it is really necessary. I think we can safely leave that sort of thing to the film people. All right, let's get on with it.'

Their knocks rang out loudly on the door and they expected the whole of the street's lights to come blazing on. No lights blazed on and nobody answered the door. They knocked again. Still no answer. The Superintendent banged louder and cried out: 'Open up! Police!' Sherman told the Commander to pass the order to force the door, when magically, it opened by itself. A face peered out. It was Baxter, from round the back. 'We're too late, sir. They've skedaddled, it seems.'

They rushed into the house and spread out into all its rooms, like fresh air into starved lungs. Every single bulb lit up, but the only living thing they found was the loaded electricity meter, turning away quietly beneath the stairs. Otherwise, no great revelations came from the small acreage of doors and drawers that were pulled open. The empty rooms became emptier and Sherman felt his despair mount, so that the butterflies in his stomach were now using pneumatic drills. One man put his hands round the brown teapot on the table. 'Teapot's warm.'

'So's the box,' said another man, with his hand on the television set.

Commander Rose was annoyed and had to pick on someone. 'We didn't come here to collect teapots and television sets for the church sale. Keep on looking. If you've looked in a corner, then look again and count the shadows; one of them might not be your own.'

The Superintendent spoke matter-of-factly, ignoring the Commander's barking at his men. 'Smollie's up under the slates now, sir. I don't think we'll miss anything, working our way up from the ground to the roof.'

'Good, Superintendent, because I want this place taken to pieces and every nook and cranny gone over with a toothpick, until we can count the maggots. God knows, the country's going to lose some sleep if we don't come up with something substantial.'

'Is that what he said, sir?' The Superintendent meant Sherman.

'Something like that, more or less, Superintendent.'

'Didn't he give any specific details?'

'To ask for more, Superintendent, is to cry to the heavens for manna.'

'Quite, sir.'

They both fell silent and looked round as Sherman passed in the hallway.

Sherman ignored the sarcasm and any other remarks intended for his ears, staying as he did in the background, to let the others get on with the search. Any books or papers with markings that could feasibly hide codes were put on a central table for Sherman to examine and confiscate for the experts in his Department to go through more thoroughly.

Suddenly there was a cry in the yard, followed by the sound of scuffling. 'What the hell's that?' said the Commander.

'I'll go and see,' said the Superintendent. He came back in, with his jubilant look beating his great tidings by a second. 'Our luck has taken a turn for the better. We've caught one of them. Caught him leapfrogging the garden walls halfway down the back lane.'

'Good work. So where is he, then?' said Rose.

Two men came in the back door, with a third man in between them. 'He says he hasn't done anything,' said the man at the rear, prodding the prisoner forward. 'Says he wants to phone his lawyer.'

'*Does* he now?' said the Superintendent.

'Oh, he'll get a lawyer all right, have no fear,' said Sherman acidly. 'And by the time we're finished with him, by God, he's going to *need* one!'

The Commander didn't quite like the hostile implication of Sherman's words, not knowing how much of it was sheer bluff, but he said nothing. Sherman, content up until now to stay in the background, had pushed his way to the front, to stand face to face with the prisoner. Everyone could sense the anger throbbing on his face as he scrutinised the man from a few inches. Where there had been a degree of measured reserve before, they all could now feel the violence fuming in Sherman, where he could suddenly erupt and beat the man to a pulp. The man sensed this most of all and forgot his claims for legal protection, falling silent and cringing back under the angry eyes of the man from the Ministry. Sherman jerked his head to the escorts, to motion them off. 'Take him away!' There was a savage tone in his voice that didn't belong in the gentlemen's' clubs of St. James's Street or Pall Mall. When Broaley had stopped playing the Eton Wall Game, all those years ago, you could well believe that he'd taken a brick or two from that wall, to carry with him for use later, to loosen stiff tongues when he wanted quick answers.

'All right, get him back to the yard,' said the Commander. He turned to the Superintendent. 'I think we can get back, too. We can let your men get on with it here, Superintendent.' He looked at Sherman. 'Right?' Sherman nodded his consent. 'All right, let's go, then,' said the Commander.

'Right, sir,' said the Superintendent.

Sherman was angry because they had once more just missed landing the big fish, and had got a mere tiddler, instead. He felt that he could smash somebody's face in, anybody's, but ended up shaking his car keys with agitation and slamming the car door extra hard.

The cars couldn't have cleared the area any quicker if a quarantine flag had been hoisted up the mast. Abandoning their low profile, they roared off round the block, cutting the corners sharply and swerving widely round a blind man crossing the road. Two policemen stepped promptly into the road, but the cars were gone, speeding away before their numbers could be taken down, so they turned to the blind man and his companion, instead. The companion held one of the blind man's arms, while the policeman took the other arm, with its white stick, and they helped him across the road, where a taxi cab purred patiently. All three helped him into the back with his leather travelling bag. They closed the door and stood back to let the taxi go. The Cockney driver leaned out. 'Are you sure you don't want a lift, George? I can easily give you one, you know.'

'No, it's all right, Alf,' said the man in a kindly voice. 'Just see that you get him there and that will be fine enough. I want to give the dog a walk, anyway.'

The taxi moved off and George Maunders turned to the policemen. 'Thanks for your help, Constables. Good night.'

'Yes, good night, sir. And mind how you go, sir. This time of night you can't be too careful, not knowing who you can meet, an' all.' The policeman could have given more warning for the old gentleman's safety, but Maunders was paying no heed, walking away, tugging the young Springer spaniel playfully on its lead. 'Seems a decent bloke,' he said to his colleague.

'Yeah, but a bit loco, if you ask me, walking the streets this time of night with his dog.'

'Yeah, crazy, just like his drunk mate.'

'You reckon the blind man was *drunk*, then?'

'Sure. Didn't you see me nearly getting my eye poked out with that stick of his? Thrashing and staggering about like he'd had a few shorts too many, he was. Drunk. No doubt about it.'

'But he's blind, you idiot.'

'No, no. Blind people have a way with themselves. They can go about just as easily as you or me once they get used to it. He was acting as if he'd just put those specs on for the first time. No, he was drunk, without a doubt. Trust me. And quite right, the poor bastard. I don't fancy being in his shoes for anything.'

'Here, you don't think that ----'

'Think what, Jack.'

But Jack's mental inspiration died away as quickly as it had sparked up. The idea that there could possibly be a connection between a blind man acting strangely, and the Special Branch people doing snoop duty a few blocks away, seemed too remote. Things like that were too far-fetched to ever happen on their humdrum beat. He subconsciously fingered the radio on his lapel. He took his hand away. 'Nothing. Forget it.'

They watched the man wait for his dog at the corner lamp-post. They shook their heads. With road hogs, drunk blind men and mad men and their dogs, they didn't know what the country was coming to. They didn't know, either, that the 'drunk blind man' whom they had helped into the taxi was the very man who had set in motion the landslide that had the country sliding closer to the brink.

While the Special Branch team raced across the city in its own private Le Mans bid to beat the traffic lights, other teams moved about the night with more clandestine stealth. Over in Kensington the gates of the Russian Embassy swung to and fro every so often, like bat wings in the night, as 'cultural secretaries' flitted back and forth surreptitiously on discreet missions. With something obviously astir in the city, all intelligence agencies were feeling the vibrations, and were anxious to get an earful of whatever it was.

00.27hrs, Grosvenor Square. Up on the top floor of the American Embassy, the CIA station chief, Bob Melvin, fretted his way through another packet of Camel whilst pondering over the whereabouts of his agent, Monks. Monks hadn't reported in for some time, and his last report lying on his desk, had been brief and scattered like a sped up reel of Tom and Jerry. What was worse, Melvin was being hounded for a report by the Department's diplomatic advisor, who in turn was being pressed for a report in the morning by the Ambassador, himself. The US Secretary for Defense and the National Security Advisor would both be flying in from Washington later today for a tough parley with the Foreign Secretary and the Minister of Defence. With Ambassador Greene as 'mother', passing the cheese and biscuits between them, a bad report would leave that poor man with no more hair on his head to pull out. And that wasn't all. Melvin would be paying for more than champagne and caviar when he hosted today's lunch at the Dorchester with a hawk-eyed *Time* journalist, to sweet-talk him over the Lancer plane crash and its rumoured dummy nuke. The man was only one of the worldwide network of journalists that the CIA had in its pocket, who could be relied upon to give the 'right story' to the media. Provided, of course, they received their generous perks. And these guys sure as hell developed sophisticated and *expensive* palates, when they knew they weren't paying for the cordon bleu monkey balls. Melvin checked the money in his billfold. He opened the safe to take out some more. Safer to use cash. It was more discreet than the old plastic.

Going over to the window, Melvin peered down into the square at a tall man walking into view from behind the Roosevelt Memorial. But the man wasn't tall enough to be Monks. Melvin went back to his desk and slumped down into his chair. Opening another packet of Camel, he lit one, promising himself, yet again, that he'd stop smoking soon. He watched the smoke wafting up to the ceiling while he waited. When the phone rang, he lurched forward frantically for it, stubbing out the cigarette at the same time. 'Monks, you fuckin' ---' he yelled into it, then broke off to listen to the secretary. '*Who*, honey? Oh, Sir Richard. Sure, honey, sure, -- put him on.'

00.30hrs, Catford SE6. The cold night breeze sent the beer can rattling along before it in an unsure meandering path rolling in and out of the gutter. Stopping and starting again, its erratic clinking cut the night's silence to carry Maneesh Hassani's mind back to a happier time of his responsibility as when he minded the family's tinkling goatherd. That was before the British and Americans had dropped their bombs. Only three of the goats had survived the bombings. That was three more than any of his family had survived. Not that he was unhappy now. He was simply devoid of personal feelings. Strict mujahadin discipline decreed that all his mental energy should be channelled into the success of the mission. Emotions had to be restrained in their lateral wanderings, to be directed forward as a sharpened point that would decidedly pierce the enemy's armour. Hassani was on foot not just because the Underground was not open at this late hour and he was unfamiliar with the city's late-night bus service, but simply because he enjoyed walking. He had walked many miles as a boy, simply to fetch the water for his mama to cook the family's meals. But walking also kept his sinewy body fit for action. And taxi drivers had eyes and ears, and infidel minds for recalling their passengers, and their passengers' destinations. In compromise, he had let himself be driven from the last cell's location in Putney, and be dropped off several streets away, and a good ten minutes from where he was heading now. This way, even his driver didn't know the exact address of this cell and so could not reveal anything under interrogation by the security forces.

The night air was cool after the heat of the day, but Hassani could barely suppress a cynical smile at the puniness of what the British called warm, compared to the heat of those deserts, where Allah's chastisement had burned upon his flesh. Turning into the right street at last, he put the map away in his pocket. It was a very long street. Counting down the house numbers, he was worried whenever a door, or several doors in succession, didn't show any. He didn't want to attract attention by knocking on the wrong door, even if only to ask for some directions, at this late hour. At last, the number he was seeking. Allah be praised.

Hassani could barely squeeze past the great bulk of the Mercedes that took up just about every square inch of the small front garden; and this was only because the low brick wall had been knocked down to facilitate a driveway. His knowledge of cars, particularly those used in the West, was scant. But he could tell by its gleaming parts that it was a very expensive item. An unnecessary luxury. It wasn't hard to imagine that he would find other signs of temptation winning over the faith inside the house. He shook his head slowly in sad disdain. With some difficulty, he refrained from swearing under his breath to himself. That these people, jihadi loyalists, who were pledging their support for him, could at the same time taint their souls by hoarding wealth with its Western luxuries, contrary to Islamic doctrine, was a lot to bear. But this was where he was supposed to come. He could not question the will of Allah.

A thin sliver of bright light sliced the darkness as the door opened a few cautious inches. Guarded suspicion looked out between turban and massive black beard. 'Salaam aleikum,' said Hassani.

'Aleikum salaam,' came the solemn reply. Hassani went in, and the door shut out the light, to let the night reclaim its dark shroud of secrecy.

14

01.46hrs, 25th June, Belgravia SW1. The telephone shrieked with piercing urgency, ripping the skin of silence off the hallway, just as Sherman entered the flat. He heard her get out of bed and so called out: 'It's all right, I'll get it. Pamela came out, nevertheless, to lean against the doorjamb. She was naked but for a scarlet triangular affair trying desperately to stop her bottom and thighs from breaking out. It failed and he was glad. He liked her rounded bottom. It balanced her proud breasts. As he put the phone to his ear, he noticed the little white spots on her pantie frills. Or was that her skin showing through little holes? He couldn't be sure if it was either of these, or if it was spots dancing about before his aching eyes. Decisions like that seemed far away to him now, with his tired brain squealing out for a bed, and the energy draining out of him like water from a sponge.

'Hullo? -- Yes, speaking. -- Yes, well, put him on. -- Hullo, Commander; you want to speak to me? --Nothing out of him yet? Not even with the Pentothal? --I see. -- No, don't let up yet. Keep him under pressure. -- Even if he doesn't know himself, anything could come out of him that could help us. --Anything. Some small snippet of recollection; an underground ticket, a phone number, a name, anything. -- Yes, that's right. Make sure and ring me as soon as you get something further out of him. It's imperative that we strike a lead in this matter soon. -- How far do I mean by imperative? Let's just say that if your means of persuasion fails to prise some information out of him, then you'll *really have* scraped the barrel. Do you understand me? -- Good,

I'm sure you do, Commander. -- Yes, I'll be at this number if you need me. --Yes, all night.' Or should that have been morning? The effort to put his mind across the line to another mind sapped him, and he passed a hand over his weary face. 'Yes, that's fine. Good night, Commander.'

The receiver hadn't quite settled in its cradle, when her arms snaked round his neck and she was upon him like a happy Labrador welcoming its returning master. Perhaps chameleon was more fitting, since her mood had changed, he noted, as her tongue licked his lips with the same seductive cunning of the lizard. Her black expression was a reflection of his own, and had come over her face the moment she saw his worried look, as he turned round in her arms to face her. He ran his finger gently up and down her spine, propping himself inside for whatever mood she was in, hoping that he could manage to step into it and leave his work behind him --- for a little while at least. 'I did phone, you know,' he said carefully, 'to say I would be late, but you didn't answer.'

'I must have been running the water in the bath when you did, and didn't hear you.' Her kisses went too lavishly down his neck, so that she was obviously evading the truth. It was more likely that she had been huffy at the time and hadn't wanted to answer his call. 'Yes, probably,' he said. 'Look, Pamela, you know you don't have to wait around for me, hand and foot.

'Is that how you see me, then? As your convenient footsie, running back and forward to your every beck and call?' She made a low sweeping bow, with arms splayed out mockingly. 'Oh, yes, Master -- no, Master -- anything you desire, Great Master.' The bitterness in her words stung him.

He sighed heavily. 'No, that's not how I see you at all. You know that. You must surely know that.' He sighed again, while he organised his muddled mind. 'There's a big city out there full of fun, if ever you get tired of waiting for me. That is what we agreed upon, isn't it? Give what we can and take no more, with neither of us staking claims or holds on the other? Or am I pulling out the wrong memory tabs?' The last thing he wanted was for her to leave him. But he wasn't sure, in his tired mind, if expecting her to live on with him wasn't tantamount to cruelty, in its situation. He couldn't split himself between her and his work at this time of urgent crisis. While the one was demanding more and more of him, the other was getting less and less of him.

She didn't answer, but simply nestled her face on his chest, beneath his chin, and he held her there, silent and secure. They had, in fact, agreed to live together eight months ago, just shortly after he'd come across her working as an analyst in the codes and ciphers room, in a far flung corner of the building. He couldn't remember what door or corridor that was, except that when that door had opened, what he saw had truly dazzled him. Not only were her vital statistics good, but she had a degree in mathematics as well. He'd liked everything about her, if that wasn't enough. In return for her body, he gave her the luxury and affluence of his regency style flat in this elegant square that shared pigeon droppings with Buckingham Palace. In spite of the fact that she was Lord Teviot's daughter and had a grade one security clearance, he'd still had her screened, not once, but twice, in the last eighteen months as a routine precaution. He had no qualms of conscience over this, since that was what the red tape stringency of his job demanded. Nor did he expect any qualms of conscience from her, for any mistrust she might have of him. Those were the terms they had agreed on, where neither partner held a bond over the other. But it hadn't escaped him that she had been a mite eager to swap her former job with the codes people, for work in the radio section. It was because she didn't like the people in the ciphers department, she'd said. And she wanted to be nearer to him. Was that all it was? What the hell, everybody was checked, screened, call it what you want, in this job.

She looked up at him and caressed his grey face. 'you look so tired.'

'Oh, God; so all right, I look bloody tired!' He'd pulled his head back sharply as he snapped at her. His regret for doing that came a second later, remorse scooping his inside like a great garden hoe. It wasn't that he denied that fact that he looked tired. He sure as hell *felt* tired. But the same phrase thrown at him by countless colleagues over the last twenty four hours was beginning to gnaw his brain like a paranoid woodpecker.

He collected himself as best he could and put his forehead down gently against hers. 'I'm sorry, Pam. I really am sorry.' He said this with all the genuine tenderness he could muster from his leadened emotions. It seemed to work. It wiped the hurt feeling from her face like a magic duster. Or was she just better at this game than him? He made a special effort to pull a funny face in the manner of the tomfoolery that they normally played, and lifted two fingers to his forelock: '*Pals?*'

Her face lit up with a huge smile, and crinkling her nose in her bunny rabbit act, she gave the return salute: 'Pals.' She broke free from his arms and stepped back. 'Coffee?'

He raised his upper lip over his teeth to work his face into a bad Bogart impression and said: 'Here's lookin' at you, Coffee Eyes.'

'Oh, I wish you wouldn't do that,' she said, giggling and threw a playful slap at him, almost beating his parrying forearm. He moved in, through her rain of slaps, to tickle her so that she exploded in squeals. He let her scuttle off to the kitchen, watching her buttocks jostling each other like wrestlers in a bag. While they waited for the coffee, he took out the Andrews salts tin. With all the sweat he'd lost during the day, he needed something to quench his thirst and replenish the salts his body had lost. He plunked the spoonful of salts into the water and watched the bubbles fizz up. He thought of fission then of bombs. His happy mood suddenly drained out of him like a fleeing spirit and he walked off, frowning, into the living room. Taking the small plastic container out of his pocket, he tumbled two of the pep pills out into his palm. He took the pills, as the Medical Officer had advised him, and washed them down with the salts.

Standing with his back to the large window, Sherman looked at his two-walled, floor-to-ceiling collection of books winging in round from the window. His small library had been a gift from his parents on his graduating. They'd not exactly been over the moon at his cantering home clutching only a Second Class. No less peeved had they been at him not jumping onto the carousel of the family law practice; instead, deserting them, to settle for Whitehall's darker side, with its lesser known corridors of whispering shadows. Even then they believed he was a sort of exchequer mandarin with his finger on the national revenue pulse, tracking down rogue bankers to their secret Swiss number accounts. What little they knew.

He smiled. Funny how trivial points like that came to mind, in its sore moments of crisis. The artistic leanings on this side of the room were balanced by the scientific side, on the far wall, with its scintillating assembly of brass instruments, mounted in in glass cases. The pride of these was the gleaming Victorian binocular microscope. His uncle, a G.P, had given it to him on his graduation; a farewell gesture to his not having followed him into the profession. It sat on the workbench, along with the racks of chemicals and the shining forest of glass tubes and bulbous vessels that he had dabbled with lightly in his youth. How he had loved the field of bacteriology. His great boyhood hero had always been Pasteur, followed by Koch and Ehrlich. Brilliant research pioneers. How the hell did he ever get into what he was doing now? He now dabbled in nuclear bombs! He looked at the solemn oil painting of himself in his graduation gown. How would the colours mix, he wondered, when the oils ran down, melting from the heat of a nuclear explosion?

The pit-a-pat of her bare feet on the carpet snapped him out of his morose mood and he turned round. She went straight on through, into the bedroom with the two steaming cups and he followed her, switching off the light.

Sitting on his stomach and straddling his waist, she leaned down and caressed his chest, while he lay there watching the moonlight glisten on her sweaty body. He saw the question coming as she pouted her lips with that demure look and tilted her head slightly. 'Will you be coming back tomorrow night?' she said at last.

'Coming back? I suppose so. Why shouldn't I?' Actually, he could think of hundreds of reasons why he possibly wouldn't be back, but he wanted to hear what she had to say.

'You're in that mood again. It's always the same pattern. Every time you go into this pensive mood and get later and later, you always end up by not managing to get back at all. A repetitive spiral. You usually end up by flying off into the night in the lashing rain. Without a word to me.' Her hands rubbed harder, as she subconsciously worked off her spite.

' "The *lassshing* rain"? ' he teased her playfully. The fact that he could tease seemed to act as an outlet valve for his tension.

'Yes, the *lassshing* rain,' she said, smiling once more and leaning close to kiss him with a splash of lips. She straightened up and started drumming his chest with her fists. 'Lots and lots of rain,' she said.

He caught her by the wrists and held them by her hips for a moment to look at her. If he wasn't awed by her simple beauty, he had to be blind. Reaching up with a lazy hand, he tweaked her nose. 'It's all in your imagination, young lady,' he said, master to pupil.

'I'm sure it isn't, as you know too well, good sir.'

'Oh, but I don't, so why don't you show me, then?' Sliding his hands over her soft bottom, he squeezed her tenderly. Pricking his fingers into her panties, he peeled them off round the lovely smooth curve. She kneeled up and unstraddled her legs, slipping the panties down over her generous thighs and off completely. Cupping her face in his hands, he pulled her back down and kissed her. Their faces parted slightly and he swallowed hard at what he saw and felt. Then, letting a smile creep into his face, and rubbing his nose against hers, he said: 'Me Eskimo. You Eskimo. We make igloo, *yes?*' They both burst out laughing and she lay beside him, while he rolled over on top of her. Just before he made love to her, he noted the time on the alarm clock. There was still half an hour to go before Commander Rose called back again, like he'd said he would.

While she snuggled and contorted her vivacious soft body beneath him, he felt that she was just not getting through to him in his preoccupied state of tension; that he was enclosing her warm flesh like a senseless cardboard effigy. His body wanted to turn its passion on, but his mind seemed remote from his body. Like a distant peninsular extension frozen in its own stupor at the fear of things to come. He had at least given her pleasure, and when her fiery rhythmic wriggling finally subsided, he rolled over onto his back, wondering if she'd noticed his lame performance.

As he lay on his back, his mind fleeted back to distant student days when pre-exam nerves had likewise staved off sex like the besieged on their remote citadel ramparts. He thought of many faces, many people across the land. The ceiling seemed to spin, and he saw endless processions of schoolchildren marching like penguins into the golden sunset of a nuclear flash. Of all the people that passed before his mind's eye, he always came back to Maureen, Pamela, the boy, mum, dad. Why did he think of Maureen before Pamela? With all the mass desecration that could possibly occur in terrifying reality in the coming hours, he wondered if he had the right to think of his own people first. In order to stop his head splitting with trying to resolve philosophical grinders, he supposed that as a mere wretched mortal, he had to fall back on the basic instinct of feeling and fearing for his kinsfolk before all else.

Pamela pretended that she was asleep when he crept out of the bed to make the phone call. 'Hullo, Maureen. -- It's me, John. -- Yes, I know it's three o'clock in the morning, but there's something I've got to say -- Shoosh! Would you just listen a second! I've had this mad idea to rent out a villa in Sicily, for you and the boy to have a holiday there, before he goes back to school. I remember how much you said you wanted to go back there; you always enjoyed it there. -- Why? Well, let's say it's a birthday present for the boy -- No, I haven't forgot that his name's Rudi -- Yes, I know his birthday is not until October; so let's say it's to make up for me not taking the boy, *Rudi*, to the exhibition -- Yes, I know it's unlike me, but miracles do happen -- Never mind why I'm so anxious to get you out of the way -- No, I'm not getting you out of the way so as to have a secret wedding with -- There's no need for you to call her that; *her* name is Pamela. Anyway, just think of escaping from all the noise and dust of London and enjoying all that blazing sunshine -- Yes, I know it's a bit short notice to make up your mind just at this moment, but at least give me a ring later this morning --Promise? -- Good -- Don't you worry about the travel arrangements, I'll see to --- Wait a second and hold the line.' Sherman's soft footsteps came up to the bedroom door and his silhouette hovered in the doorway. He looked in at Pamela's 'sleeping' form. 'Get back to sleep,' he said, before closing the door and going back to the phone.

15

09.01hrs, 25th June, Westminster SW1. '-- and police last night raided a house in the East End of London, in the Clerkenwell district, and a man was later charged under Section One of the Official Secrets Act, at Bow Street Magistrates Court. The man was remanded in custody, pending further enquiries into alleged spying and possible terrorist activities. Home Office spokesmen later today confirmed that they were acutely interested in the case. A Taliban suicide bomb has killed at least forty three people in a mosque in Kabul. At least another seventy one people are known to have been injured in the blast, with the number expected to rise, as work continues in clearing the wrecked building. The body of a young boy wrapped in a tarpaulin has been found behind a garage, in Colchester. Two men and a woman are helping police with their enquiries. The Chancellor, in his address to the TUC Delegation in Stockton, last night declared that whilst inflation was ---

-' Sherman switched the car radio off, having heard enough. So far, so good, with the business still lying low in the background. If it was allowed to swell into the limelight, then pandemonium would snap off its restraining shackles. The horrible thought was easy to dismiss, with only the peaceful dusty facade of Victoria Street curving out in front, with its pigeons fluttering about the upper stone ledges.

Sherman flipped the indicator and made ready to turn in to New Scotland Yard in Broadway, just as the armour-plated convoy overtook him. Four 5.7 ton Fox scout cars howled on past, all bristling with broad-snouted mortars and 30mm Rarden cannons, all in a deadly hurry to get somewhere. The Audi gurgled down in low gear and turned into the Yard entrance. That was the second such military show he'd seen since leaving the flat this morning. It seemed more like the hundredth time, where his mind saw a million such manoeuvres taking place all over the country, in the emergency step-up to counter the rising possibility of major terrorist offensives. Now that the country's nuclear defences were experiencing 'teething problems', and two of its 'nuke pies' were liable to blow the oven door off, a hostile power could easily be tempted to walk in the door, uninvited, without knocking. Need one say Russia, with its claws becoming sharper each day, in its refound hard look to the West?

The engine purred as the car paused in the opening, while Sherman watched the long line of schoolchildren babbling and frolicking along the pavement behind their teachers. So long as they could get away from the classroom for the morning, they didn't care where they were going, or what was in store for them.

'Commander Rose? Yes, sir; if you'll just wait a moment. I'll tell him you're here,' said the policewoman politely. Sherman put his MoD pass away and watched her go through the inner door, once more convinced that tight uniforms worked wonders with women's figures, and to hell with sexist accusations. If he could think like that this morning, the pep pills he'd taken must be doing their job. He may not have felt like an Olympic athlete, and he may still have his worries, but at least they no longer grated through a brain that badly needed oiling. So far, anyway.

The policewoman came back and Sherman noted that her cheerful expression had lost a sparkle or two. The sign of things to come. He went into the office. He hardly needed to bat an eyelid before he knew that he was getting the cold shoulder from the Commander. Rose's manner was brusque, as he darted about the office, speaking over his shoulder and tending to filing cabinets, so that Sherman got the message that he was not a welcome visitor in his office. At last the Commander found time to throw a file down with a bang, onto the desk in front of Sherman. 'That's what you've come for, I believe. It's all we could get out of him.' He then pulled on his Gannex raincoat in a great show of displeasure, so that the collar was improperly turned in, and started to button it up fiercely. The man was clearly angry and was going out, before his temper got the better of him. After all, he was only a policeman, and so couldn't speak unduly to a Ministry man.

Sherman picked up the thin file and pretended to read through it, feeling that the sparse contents of three flimsy type-sheets somehow didn't add up to what was bugging Rose. 'It's not much. Is this all we could get from him?' Sherman used the statement to throw in the bait, rather than voice his suspicions, letting the Commander utter them in his own tongue, instead.

'Not much? Haven't you had enough?' Rose turned his head away to laugh with sarcasm. He had found the fault in his collar and was turning it the right way out, while showing conviction and disgust on his face.

'Perhaps I can be allowed to go down to see him again,' said Sherman, keeping to his polite manner to feign the innocence over what he feared was coming.

'Yes, well you won't be needing my authority for that anymore. It's all out of my hands now. If you want to see him, you'll have to go to the Cardiac Unit at St. Mary's. The poor bastard's just nearly died with a stroke.'

'Stroke? So when they were saying on the radio a few minutes ago that --- ' Sherman let it sink in. 'Right.'

'Exactly. You just heard them say that everything was warm and cosy. Like those millions of others who are not going know an inkling of what is happening. And that includes me; not that I want to now -- not if this is an indication. Anyway, it only happened shortly before you arrived. The strain was too much for the bastard. Well, with all the pressure and all that *stuff* your lot pumped into him. He just collapsed, all white, like a sack of flour. It's a wonder the ambulance never knocked some paint off your car, on its way out. Maybe off your damn conscience, as well. Or is that expecting too much?

'It was all necessary, in the interest of national security, Commander.' Sherman recalled how he'd had difficulty persuading the Commander to allow them to question the prisoner their way, using Pentothal injections. The Commander had relented, but only after they had agreed to do it in a separate room with none of the Yard men present, and with Sherman's own medical man applying the drug. Even then, the Commander had only backed down after Sherman had signed a personal statement that had been endorsed by a Defence Ministry Under-Secretary. The Commander didn't know, of course, about the nuclear countdown, and Sherman didn't let on. To give wind to such information would have caused more panic than if the City were sinking under the flag of the Titanic. He didn't know Rose well enough. And he knew that he couldn't communicate with him like he'd done with his predecessor, Michael Farrow, whom he'd worked with on an agreeable basis, until his retirement two months ago.

'I'm sure it was, but I don't want to talk about it. I've also got to go to a meeting, if only to show my face.' Rose reached round for his corduroy angling hat, with its Zulu fly-baits prickling its band, on the hat stand. He pointed at the file. 'I'd rather that you removed that thing from this office and took it to your own place. You can read it in peace with all the time in the world, over your tea and biscuits. Personally, I think I've suddenly gone off food. I don't think I could eat for a week.' He put on his hat. 'Anyway, like I said, I've got a meeting to go to, to answer some questions. Yes, believe it or not, some of us do have to answer for our actions.'

Sherman was tempted to tell Rose that he wouldn't need to eat after a week, if things were to continue the way they were going. 'You saw me sign that statement, Commander. The responsibility in mine. Let me once again reassure you on that point.'

'If you say so, Mr Sherman; if you say so.' The Commander clearly wasn't placing much faith in Sherman's assurance, even though he had seen the very ink on that bloody piece of official paper. The way he saw it, in his simple policeman's mind, was that any heads to roll would most surely come from a lower level than the Ministry. With a scandal imminent in the Ministry's corridors, the paper statement would be no better than if it were shredded and then flushed down the toilet boil. Right now he could see his pension slipping through his fingers like quicksilver. He stood in dire judgement for a moment, with his chin down on his chest and blowing dejectedly down his nostrils. 'Well, I've got to go now, Mr Sherman. You'll see yourself out, won't you? Good morning.' The Commander was off and out through the outer office before Sherman could reply. He had made it quite plain that he was anxious to get away from a bad smell.

09.30hrs. Big Ben was having a quiet nap and didn't bother to hail Sherman as he got out of his car beside the Parliament buildings and walked towards the St. Stephen's entrance. The policeman saluted as Sherman flashed his security pass, and several excited mothers standing outside the railings were certain that he was the MP who had patted their babies' heads at the last by-election.

Sir Richard Hossley was already with the Minister of Defence, when Sherman entered the wooden-panelled antechamber. The Lowry factory landscape on the wall may have mirrored the Minister's politics, but nothing could have been further from his mind at that moment. That tempers had flared was plain enough from their facial expressions. But Sherman could also see that his boss had managed to ward off, if not completely blunt, most of the javelins of fury that the Minister had thrown down from his privileged peak of higher rank. You needed more arms than an octopus to catch Old Hossley out, when throwing things at him. The voice on the tape recorder was that of Major General Sir James Greeley speaking on details of Operation BLOWTORCH at yesterday's meeting. They all looked up from the tape recorder. Sherman nodded to Sir Richard and looked at the Minister. 'Good morning, Minister,' he said.

'Good morning, indeed, Mr Sherman, if only I knew what was good about it.' After a few exchanged glances, all three looked back at the tape recorder. They listened for another few turns before the Minister leaned down and switched it off. He was clearly disturbed. Tapping on the recorder as he thought for a moment, he turned halfway round to speak to Sherman. 'Sir Richard has been telling me his tale, which I can only describe as utterly bizarre, and Sir James, here, makes a very lucid point of assessing the cataclysmic consequences of such a nuclear ---' he struggled to find words to fit the horrific mental picture, '--- *holocaust*. I find it most frightful, to say the least.' He afforded himself a transient smile and folded his arms. 'I suppose historians could only classify that remark as a gross understatement.' He sat up straight and looked at Sherman. 'I only wish that I could hope that you've come to tell me that it's all a mistake, but you haven't, have you?'

'Not in so many words, Minister, but we are endeavouring to make progress in the matter.' Sherman felt that he couldn't have waxed the words more if he'd been a candle maker. 'We were just one step behind them when we almost apprehended Dr Linsdale, early this morning. We got one of the abductors, instead.' Again, hollow words. He handed the Minister the report from Commander Rose that he'd just read in the car outside.

The Minister would have liked to have shouted at them and said it wasn't good enough for them to have *almost* apprehended Linsdale; but the shock news of the situation had drained most of his bark, and what was left of it had been dulled by his earlier angry encounter with Hossley. 'Ah, yes, my secretary mentioned something about this when I came in this morning. I must be the last in line to hear all these intriguing snippets of information. No, please don't apologise, gentlemen. I'm the last person to deny the fact that I'm only a figurehead in all that goes on in these active field issues. Only by popular vote of the people, and by courtesy of the Prime Minister picking his Cabinet members. I fully appreciate the fact that there are professional heads, to whom a more prompt delivery of this information is more important in its implication. That's why I'm putting my full trust in you, to find these maniacs and save the day.' He gleaned through the typed pages, stopping at the nasty parts. 'Can we use this man we've arrested, to trace Linsdale?'

'This is all we're likely to get out of him,' said Sherman, minding that the report made no mention of the man's last-minute removal to the hospital, following a heart attack. 'He's only one unit of the cell involved. Each unit, or member, is known by codename only, and personal details and background are not allowed. This way, detection of a cell is kept to a minimum and even if a member's cover is blown, the overall plan of the cell continues. In other words, when they met last night to change the 'carrier' of the 'parcel', Dr Linsdale, only the new 'carrier' knew where the 'parcel' was going. Even this knowledge is limited, since the exchange goes on and on until the 'parcel' reaches its ultimate destination.'

'I see,' said the Minister, reading on some more. 'At least he's still in the country. Is there no chance that these people may get cold feet and surrender Linsdale at the last moment, for fear of being destroyed themselves, by the bombs? Or are their dedications so fanatical that their lives mean nothing?'

Sherman puckered his lips and shook his head. 'No, I'm afraid that it's unlikely, since it's almost an absolute certainty that these people know nothing of the bombs, in the first place. You'll see there, in the report, that drugs may have been administered to Linsdale to render him partially insensible. This is an old trick in the trade to prevent the defector being awkward in transit and perhaps making an unwanted scene, by a last minute change of mind, as the final moment approaches for leaving the country. It usually works quite well and makes the subject seem drunk, in fact. It makes it all the easier to shift the 'parcel' about from place to place with minimum resistance. Presumably they put him under before he had time, if ever he had intended, to disclose his own dark secret to his handlers.'

The Minister was having difficulty understanding some point, and they stood watching his clean-shaven professionally pomaded politician's face wrestle with it. Sherman felt his indigestion start up again, to throw its angry acid up his throat. 'Why should they want to drug him? said the Minister. 'I thought he had gone voluntarily with these Russian sleeper people? At least, that was what I was given to understand.' He looked at Hossley, who had just given him this information.

Sherman was relieved to explain a mere technicality instead of the larger issues. 'Yes, as far as we know, Minister, he did go with them voluntarily; to begin with, that is. But the point we mustn't forget is that he isn't our usual type of political defector, making his flight for the usual ideological pains. He was originally flying to Finland; probably to lie low in a backwater village or forest cabin until things cool off and then make his way across the border into Russia. Or maybe he just wanted a bit of peace and quiet to do some fishing on the lakes.' No-one laughed at the joke. 'SUPO were informed, of course. The climate may have been the same there, but not quite the same politics as in Russia. Perhaps a good reason why his new found friends may not fully rely on his co-operation, and so resort to using drugs to ensure a smoother passage.'

'All plucked and trussed like a Christmas goose, in other words,' said Sir Richard.

'SUPO?' said the Minister, puzzled.

'Finland's security police,' answered Sir Richard, amused at the Minister's confused reaction to all these underhand disclosures. '

'I'm beginning to find that to be an apt description for myself. Perhaps I should have stayed on at my old post as Education Minister,' said the Minister, glancing coldly at Hossley. He was in fact, plainly feeling the strain of being involved above his own head in unfamiliar waters. It was all so unlike the comparatively docile duty of apportioning the country's three R's, that he had held before the last Cabinet reshuffle. He looked back through the report and stroked his cheek pensively. 'Y-e-s, I see. So what we've narrowed the situation down to is a search for someone masquerading as a drunk, among all the drunks walking the streets. Am I right?'

Sherman didn't take the remark seriously, but before he could make sure, the door began to open. They waited for the woman to lay her sheaf of papers down on the table and leave. But she didn't go out immediately. She stood for a moment to look pointedly at her watch and then at the Minister. He nodded knowingly. He hadn't forgotten his next official appointment. 'Thank you, Mary.' His secretary went out. The papers she had brought him were notes for his meeting later, with the US Defense Secretary and the National Security Advisor, at twelve o'clock. He wasn't looking forward to it. Satisfied that the door was once more firmly closed, they resumed their talk. 'And there's no chance at all,' said the Minister, leading the way into the inner room, 'of making these bombs inactive, is there?'

'Very little, I'm afraid,' said Sir Richard.

'As a matter of fact, there may be a slight ray of hope there,' said Sherman, surprising the other two. 'Where it was originally considered to be out of the question, there is now the slim possibility that the bombs may be moved. The latest report from our technical team says that there is the marginal possibility of devising a means for moving the bombs so that their signal sensors don't detect any shifting.'

'When did this come through?' asked Hossley, his composure pecked with annoyance at being one fact behind in his report to the Minister.

'I only received the message this morning, ' said Sherman. 'Just before nine. As far as I gather, it involves installing fake receivers which would take in the transmitters' signals as if the bombs were in their original positions. It's all pretty much in the development stage, but it's still an avenue for hope.'

'You seem a little doubtful, yourself. So what are the critical factors?' said the Minister.

'Well, I suppose the first factor is the scientific one itself. Can it be done? The second critical factor is how much time do we have to do it? On top of that, we still have to find out where they are.'

'And if we *do* find them, and *do* move them, *where* do we drop them?' said the Minister.

'There's always the sea, but that wouldn't do our fish industry much good, alas.' No-one laughed at that joke either.

The door opened again, and a different secretary poked his head round.

'Number Ten has just been on to us: the Prime Minister wants you to call back as soon as you find time.'

'All right, thank you, David --- no, wait: have the car ready for me in ten minutes.' Checking the time on the ormolu clock, he looked round at the others. 'As you can see, what little time we have must be rationed. Apart from the Prime Minister, I've also got to decide which is my best foot to put forward, when I see our American friends later today. So, if we could just make the remaining reports brief.'

Sir Richard took the briefest means of all and switched the tape recorder on again. They listened to the Committee's chillingly concise statistics on human devastation and the Minister nervously adjusted his tie that didn't need adjusting. He pressed the switch on the intercom. 'Hills -- Cancel my ten o'clock meeting with the Saudi Ministers. No, wait a minute. Don't cancel it altogether, but have it put back to this afternoon; I'll tell you exactly when later, when I know for sure myself. And keep everything else out of my way in the meantime. I'm going to be otherwise engaged. Have I made that clear enough?'

'Perfectly.'

'Good. You can also put a call through to the Air Ministry. I want to speak to Air-Marshal Wainright. I want to speak to him *immediately*.'

09.59hrs. Sir Richard was glad to take leave of the Defence Minister. Not just because he needed the fresh air, but also because he had shortly to meet the CIA station chief, Melvin, in St. James's Park, as arranged the night before. As a meeting place it was a convenient short walk from the office, and it also saved face for the American, who did not like entering the Whitehall establishment on issues not yet committed in policy by his Government. But what that policy was, Melvin wouldn't specify. That was his way. Not specifying policies clearly was his policy.

Melvin waited in the back of his long black Chevrolet limousine parked under the relative cover of the trees lining Bird Cage Walk, beside the park. Going across Parliament Square and walking along Great George Street, Sir Richard turned into Bird Cage Walk, to see the American car sitting there, with the tall man in dark glasses standing beside it. A tap on the rear window from his man outside told Melvin that the Brit had come into sight. Melvin got out and stood there for a moment to light a cigarette and to let Sir Richard see him, before walking slowly into the park. When Sir Richard caught up with Melvin and they both walked along together, the tall man stepped away from the car to walk along slowly behind them at a distance.

What little did pass between Hossley and Melvin, the ducks beat them by a beak. The points of information that they traded initially were obvious old hash and it was plain that they were being used solely for probing. When they did lay their cards on the table, they could well have been from the same bridge club. That the CIA knew most of the story but not all of it, and were ready to help, was satisfactory to Sir Richard, and they left it at that. Both were anxious to get away on other business. Melvin offered a lift, but Sir Richard declined. Again that satisfied both parties. Pigeons fluttered up as the black thing slid away, and Sir Richard hurried back towards the square and his office beyond.

10.29hrs. Sir Richard was expecting to see the Department's military advisor, who was to put him in the picture, the latest picture, before the committee meeting at 10.45. But the man hadn't arrived yet, and instead, Sir Richard had to suffer five minutes of allegations levelled at him by the puny Home Office secretary over rumours of the Department's recent "monstrous misappropriation of Special Branch police powers to an inhumane degree." Sir Richard could well understand Sherman's present symptoms of nervous exhaustion. The military advisor at last made his appearance, with Sir Richard pointedly taking out his golden hunter from his waistcoat pocket to remind the man that he was late. The man dumped his large bulging file on the desk. 'A few small points I'd like to go over,' he said, preparing for a long session.

'Let's just confine ourselves to the *big* ones, shall we?' said Sir Richard in a tired voice that didn't hide his impatience.

10.30hrs, Catford. Prayers were at an end and the men were filing out of the mosque, most of them not hiding their haste to be away and about their earthly business of making money. Prayers and homage to Allah provided food for the soul, but money provided food for the whole family of nagging wife, rebellious children and scrounging in-laws. Rasheed Bahsoud was in a hurry to unload the two boxes from his small grey Mini van and take them to the imam in his quarters at the rear of the building. It was another ten gallons of the hydrogen peroxide that he had been filching carefully, little by little, under his father's very nose, from the cash 'n carry warehouse over the months. Whilst it sold well to the catering trade as a cleaning fluid, it also served the Jihadi cause well in that it could be used to make bombs. Rasheed had first learned this on the Internet website that was sympathetic to the Jihadi cause. Where his own father had never ever seen him as a worthy son, Rasheed had great need of praise from the imam, and so liked to think that he had earned this when he informed the holy man of this chemical's potentially explosive power. Anyone who went as far as to tell Rasheed that hydrogen peroxide was old news, had to suffer the words falling on deaf ears.

Rasheed was a little annoyed that he didn't have the imam's full attention when he spoke to him, presenting his load. The holy man's mind was elsewhere, held by the words of another young man. A stranger that Rasheed had never seen before, in the mosque or around town. Rasheed's pride fell, while his childish anger rose, as he stood watching the intensity of deep conversation between the other two. At last, the imam introduced the two young men to each other. 'Salaam aleikum,' said Rasheed.

'Aleikum salaam,' returned Maneesh Hassani.

The imam told Rasheed to put the boxes over in the corner, telling him that this was not the time for small gestures. He went on to say that Maneesh Hassani had plans for a gesture that would shake this infidel nation to its roots. As two fine young men devoted to the Koran, they would make a fine team working together. Rasheed could see that the imam meant that he would be *assisting* the newcomer, Hassani. And he was very much irritated to have his work with the hydrogen peroxide described as 'small gestures'.

The two young men looked each other over with discerning eyes, both with mixed feelings at what they saw. Rasheed saw the other as a shadow clouding his light of favouritism in the imam's eye. But he felt great envy for Hassani's mature image and the confident way that he carried himself. Not an arrogant stature; just a quietly contained mannerism that said that he was in control of what he intended doing. He didn't have to tell you. You *knew* he was in control. All this in someone not that much older than himself. Hassani appreciated Rasheed's great fervour for the Jihadi campaign. That was good. But he was more than just a little bit concerned at what he saw was fiery zeal without sober restraint. Energy devoid of sensible discipline was liable to overflow out of control. And that could prove to be troublesome, if not plain dangerous. He saw a definite lack of training there. From what the imam had told him, the 'boy' had never been to a Libyan desert camp for proper training as a Jihadi warrior.

Hassani was especially uneasy over the machine-pistol that the 'boy' had removed from beneath his jacket and was now feverishly brandishing in the air. This was going to require careful handling. He couldn't allow his colossus of a mission to be scuppered by the rash impatience of a 'schoolboy' needlessly letting off bullets at the wrong time. Hopefully he would not have to take *personal* measures to ensure that the overall project was not threatened. But *abortive* measures *would* be taken should that critical factor arise to stand in the way of the end result. In the meantime, he needed someone to drive him around; someone who was familiar with the roads, or could ask for directions in English, free of a foreign accent that would attract undue attention. He needed someone who was familiar with these strange people and the strange ways of this alien country. The imam had recommended the 'boy'. So be it, through the will of Allah. He bowed to the imam. 'Allah akbar.'

'Allah akbar,' returned the imam, bowing back.

'Put that thing away, and come with me,' said Hassani quietly over his shoulder as he turned away and made for the door. Rasheed recognised the latent strength of command in the soft voice and followed his 'commander' out the door.

09.10hrs (GMT) Berlin. Dark grey Cold War memories came back into Major Broaley's mind as the taxi went along Friedrichstrasse, towards where the Checkpoint Charlie border control point had stood, between West Germany and East Germany. It had been the first time he had ventured into their territory on a 'job', so he hadn't been quite sure what to expect. Operations had been directed by Dick Hossley. Broaley recalled sitting in the bus, watching one of the two soldiers unslinging his PPSH-41 Russian version of the Tommy gun. But it was only to hand it to his mate, so he could take out two cigarettes. Further along on the same side of the street, there was the bright yellow Haus am Checkpoint Charlie, where fugitives from the East put up their exhibitions of the Wall. This made Broaley smile inside. He had helped some of these people to escape, and now here he was, under their very window, going the opposite way *into* that dreaded territory.

The column crawled very slowly towards the control point, red brake lights glaring on and off as vehicles stopped and started. Broaley looked across into the Checkpoint Charlie Cafe, searching the faces hovering over the steaming cups and bowls, wondering which one of them would put a bullet in him. They were mostly working class family groups enjoying the best of their pence with a bowl of soup, but any one of them could pull a pistol out of his torn jacket, to shoot him down like an escaping rat. Imagination from heightened tension?

Engines started up and the vehicles inched along, each one nervously dreading its search, like the virgin on her first night. There was no trouble at the British, French and American points, but the Deutsche Demokratische Republic had to show its grim iron hand of authority. The truck in front was stopped and armed guards leaped aboard. Another guard came onto Broaley's bus. He looked at Broaley's forged passport and then peered hard at his face. 'Ernest Klaust?' He looked at the name and the British passport. 'You are naturalised British?'

Broaley shook his head and smiled as best he could. 'English. German father.' The guard nodded thoughtfully, tapping the passport in his hand, along with the other three that he had confiscated. 'Ja.' He understood. But he still didn't return the passports. Turning around, he disappeared with them into the guardhouse. Everyone sat in silence in the bus.

Broaley watched the soldiers swarm over the truck in front like parasites on a host, some of them searching the cargo hold, while others pushed mirrors on rods underneath for a belly shot inspection. Above him, on his right, the bright neon letters of the Axel Springer Verlag building sitting on the Wall blazed out, contrasting the East from the West. The light from the right emphasised the darkness of the buildings on the left, pushing the harshness in hard, and showing the old empty buildings with their black vacant-like eyeless skulls. He could imagine a sniper's bullet picking him off from one of those windows. Checking the tightness in his stomach, he looked away. It was a long wait. Nine minutes, in fact. The guard came back with their passports. But they still had to wait another two minutes for the truck in front to move off. As they finally moved from West to East, past a million sniper positions, Broaley's tension prickled, but still nobody put a hole in his head.

They continued along Friedrichstrasse, Broaley half wondering why the execution squad wasn't lined up, rifles drawn, waiting for him. Two 'gauchos', with their green poncho style capes and shoulder slung rifles, gave him a long look, but their attention was soon diverted to the pretty fraulein, in chic French fashion trench coat, coming out of the Altes Cafe. Passing the Hotel Metropole, Broaley couldn't help steal a nervous glance beyond it, at the American Embassy, as it slid further and further away. Surprisingly, no one uttered a squeak on the decadent ways of the West when they passed the Comic Theatre, this being the modern intellectual mouthpiece for attacking the fat capitalist cousins over the Wall for having too much pork and pickled cabbage in their bellies. From the old academic world of Whelne Kulz Strasse they moved on through the modern blocks of Leipziger Strasse, to turn into the main thoroughfare of Unter den Linden, with its black leafless trees and grimy electric trams. More soldiers greeted them in regular lines, but these were Roman soldiers made of stone, standing on top of the buildings, as they had been doing for a long time.

Broaley swore as he was thrown forward, his head almost hitting the seat in front, when the bus suddenly braked. The driver hadn't been fast enough and a youth in shorts went into orbit over the bonnet in a flurry of limp puppet-like limbs. His bicycle went for a crunch under the front wheels. The father, also with a bicycle, threw his machine aside and rushed in horror to see if the lad was dead. The lad was still in one piece, only shocked and bruised. But that didn't stop the fury, the father setting about the driver, who had got out. A small crowd of people gathered around, and incited by the furious father's hostile cries, began to move in on the bus. Angry murmurs arose, and fists began to drum on the windows. The door was wrenched open and the proletarian workers set upon the bureaucratic bourgeoisie, seizing their sleeves and lapels to rough them up. Broaley waited for a knife to pierce him between the ribs. But nothing like that happened.

Suddenly, the bubble of fury burst as fast as it had blown up. The violence halted and the people moved back onto the pavement, to mind their own business. This was no longer their concern as the grey Polizei truck pulled into the kerb a few yards away, and the military booted figures clambered out.

Broaley's pulse quickened, or so it seemed to him. With all the differences settled, the youth hobbled off with a bruised knee, the crowd shifted away, and the bus drove off, under the watchful eyes of the Polizei. Everything was back to normal in the bus -- except that Broaley now had a small piece of notepaper clenched in his fist. It had not been there before the crowd had invaded the bus. Written on the paper were two words:

PERGAMON MUSEUM.

Caution stuck to Broaley like a fly on gummy paper, as he walked along Am Kupfergraben Strasse, towards the Pergamon Museum. The old building stood back, forever aloof, from the street, its old wooden drawbridge spanning the quietly flowing River Spree. Broaley was so keyed up as he crossed the drawbridge, that he half expected a bayonet to come slicing up between the wooden beams to trim a toenail or two. Going up the stairs inside the entrance, he was met head on by a heavy down-flowing river of people, and again he waited for the sharp umbrella spike to come lancing his way, or a silenced bullet to 'sploof' out of a muzzle concealed in any of the leather satchels or handbags. Searching the river of faces, he found none of them familiar, and none of them found him familiar, it seemed.

The man with the shoulder-slung walkie-talkie returned Broaley's stare for a long while, but that was a normal security routine for the museum. A guide with a Greek god's curly beard and a priest-like garb of black beret and black coat with tight collar gave Broaley a funny look. Broaley didn't return it, deciding it had nothing to do with culture or security. Sorry, mister, no 'fairy' stories today, thank you. Moving across a large room, beneath a brilliant criss-cross ceiling of fluorescent lighting, Broaley stood in front of the enormous blue tile structure that was the awesome arch of the ancient Ishtar (Easter) Gate of Babylon. Beauty was instantly magnetic, attracting a large crowd to gaze upon it. As Broaley gazed up at it, the words came to his ear. 'There is a beautiful restaurant I know on Karl Marx Allee.'

The words jarred Broaley's attention sharply. Not only because they were intrusive in that they had nothing to do with the artwork he was gazing at, but because he recognised them as the passwords of the contact he was to meet. He looked round. He forgot the Ishtar Gate, its beauty blotted out, looking at that face. Its Nordic paleness would have been seen as sickly, except that here her skin was enhanced with a honeyed glaze that made it stunningly beautiful. And cupped by a gorgeous pageboy cut of blonde hair, it caused an electric sensation deep in Broaley's chest. She was Lori Brun, surveillance officer of the Stasi, East Gemany's Ministry for State Security. She was also British Intelligence's double agent, working as a mole within the Stasi. Short, not many inches over five feet, she wore a black sealskin coat. Even though the coat hung loosely, without a belt, he could still see that she came out well in the right places. Broaley didn't speak, held by the vision, so she helped him. 'We can go there, *yes*?' And that low, husky, voice, with its rich syrupy flow.

Broaley nodded his silent consent. 'Ja,' he said at last.

She led the way out of the museum. With him walking slightly behind her, he had a better chance of looking her over, especially her movements beneath the smooth leather coat.

Broaley put away these memories of over twenty years ago, to pay the taxi driver, and turning around, walked towards the Pergamon Museum. Inside, he went from room to room searching for her. She wasn't there. He looked in one direction then another, all to no avail. Then there, in the midst of the sea of floating faces, he saw her. They walked towards each other. She smiled. That beautiful smile. 'There is *still* that beautiful restaurant that I know on Karl Marx Allee.' That same rich voice. They embraced briefly, patting backs and laughing, then stepped apart to look each other over. She was now Kommandant Brun of the BDN (Bundesnachrichtendienst) Germany's Federal Intelligence Service. 'You have put on weight, George; more mature,' she said in her playful critical tone.

'And you look,' he hesitated, 'you haven't changed at all.' He'd lied, of course. The hair was paler, where the blonde had blended, still attractively, into the silver. Her face was heavier but with that motherly comeliness that only the fortunately few women managed to carry into their advancing years.

She read through his eyes, into his thoughts. 'That's silly. I'm mother to a grown up son, now. He'll be twenty three next month. His name's George. He doesn't have a moustache, but he looks like you when ---'

'I know,'

She caught the note of resignation in his blunt reply. They stared at each other, the smiles dimmed for a moment. Slapping her handbag, she broke the suspended silence, with its soft memories of another time. 'But then you have come to talk of *serious* things, right, George?'

'That's right; *very* serious things.' He looked around him. 'What's the quickest way out of this place?' He let her loop her arm through his, and waving aside would-be 'guides' and dubious 'souvenir' vendors, they made their way out of the museum.

16

10.30hrs, 25th June, Westminster SW1. Squadron Leader Travis came out of the Air Ministry a little ahead of Sherman and Meeson, who had stalled in the doorway, scribbling in their folders. Worry was written on all three faces, like the official order of the day, after what they had been through upstairs. Travis scanned the clear blue sky, looking every bit like the symbolic little piece of that sky in his flashing bright blue uniform. Two winking specs returned the greeting, as they etched their way across the blue canvass, at the tips of the fluffy vapour condensation trails. To Travis, they were Typhoons all weather fighters, but to everyone else, they were just specs. Sherman and Meeson put away their pens and came out to join Travis in his skywards gaze.

'Typhoons,' said Travis.

'Really?' said Sherman despondently, feeling that he didn't care what the heck the two dots were, at that distance. Like everything else in this wretched mess, they were too distant to reach or to matter. Just like in those maddening dreams, Sherman felt that he was chasing something frantically without moving a bloody inch.

'Yes. They're damn good formidable little numbers to have around when you need them,' said Travis.

'Let's hope our number doesn't come up and that we *won't* need them, or we may well be *damned*.' Sherman didn't mean to be as pessimistic as he sounded, but it annoyed Travis just the same. This pleased Sherman for a second, then darkened his mind, as he realised it was a sign of his frustration needling him. Even with every man out in the field, doing all that could be done, he was nervous at not being there to see for himself, instead of filling in files and useless figures. He pulled himself together.

They left the planes in their silent flight and started out briskly, thinking of more mundane elements that lay ahead of them. 'I've arranged for Maureen and Rudi to go to Sicily for a short break,' said Sherman suddenly. 'It'll get them away from it all.' There was no need to say more.

'Good,' said Travis. 'I'm sure that was the decent thing to do.' No more words were necessary and they walked on, silent in their private thoughts. Sherman pondered over the wisdom of his sending Maureen and the boy away. Would they, in fact, suffer more, having survived while their relatives had perished? Would they rather stay behind and dance the merry maypole dance of death round Nelson's Column tomorrow night?

With just under thirty eight hours before the 'mushrooms', as the Air-Marshal had put it, the countdown was gathering momentum. On top of that, the Blue Steel crisis was still a sore thumb, and it was on that subject that the Air-Marshal had stressed his points. It was exactly where a show of strength was needed, where strength itself was unnecessary. Like a latter day sword of Damocles. Travis had disagreed. Almost by intuition, he spoke on his thoughts. 'I still disagree, of course. Look, I'm not one to be called a warmonger, but what Wainright's suggesting is hardly going to make a bishop blush.'

'Can you be so sure that your plan would be any more sensible?' said Meeson. 'Would you not say that your plan for direct harassment is applicable only when aggression from them is imminent?'

'Imminent aggression?' fumed Travis. 'So how the hell do you think they're going to react when they find out the truth about Blue Steel?' When they discover it's a glove with frozen fingers inside?'

'I think we should know the answer to that pretty soon,' said Sherman, sobering the other two. 'I would say that they should have caught a whiff of the rumour by now. I'll bet on it.'

'Even money,' said Meeson.

Sherman looked at his watch. The next meeting was at eleven thirty, and they still had to go to the Admiralty. Time was pressing. While half listening to the babble of the other two, Sherman scanned the car park for his contact, who should have been there. They walked on through the usual cluster of official cars, to see the great Yankee monster parked on its own. It was the only way it could have parked. With that acreage of tin, you could make a Mini out of one of its wing mirrors. A tall man was leaning against it. He watched them openly as he spoke to the blue smudge of a US airman that was inside. The airman's cap, with its half acre of badge, bobbed out the window as he spoke, but the tall man didn't move at all. He just kept on staring their way and smiling mechanically from behind the twin-mirrored sunspecs as they got nearer.

'You know what that is, don't you?' said Travis. 'With that type of close-cropped hair, they seldom turn out to be anything else but CIA.'

Sherman could have corrected his brother-in-law on that boy scout presumption, but he let it go. He detached himself from the other two, to go up to his contact. 'You two go on ahead. I'll catch up.'

Monks straightened up and sauntered casually up to Sherman. This relaxed manner, was a new thing to Sherman, where he was used bearing the brunt of hard talk from the American. Monks' flipper of a hand didn't flap up, but stayed hooked by its thumb in his pocket, as he came out with a non-committal 'Hi, there.' With that, Monks waited for the other two to pass by, out of earshot, turning his head to watch them like an eyeless cybernaut. Sherman looked up at Monks, watching the two tiny reflections of Meeson and Travis prance across the convex lenses away into the distance.

Monks turned round and they both assessed each other's state of affairs in silence for a few seconds. Monks looked as if he was going to dawdle on some more idle remarks, so Sherman beat him to it and came straight to the point. 'Have you got it?'

'Sure thing, pal. Sure thing.' Monks flapped a 'flipper' against his inside breast pocket and whistled Beethoven's sinister four bars to mark the shady undertones. He opened the car door and looked around before getting in. 'I get shy standing about in these open places. Too many 'tourists' about with their Walkmans not tuned in to The Beatles.'

Sherman got in beside him in the spacious back seat. He could almost have parked his own car in here. He shut the door. Monks peered over the sunglasses to meet the airman's eyes in the rear mirror. The airman obediently switched on the cassette player's deafening loud blast of rock music. That would put the fear of Babel into any bugging device that had the misfortune to listen in. Monks opened up a black leather wallet and peeled off a thin sliver of telex paper and another of film. He handed them to Sherman, along with a small folding lens to examine the film. 'Now feast your eyes on that, pal. Sure as hell, you should have your eyes insured, along with those precious Crown Jewels of yours, seeing as none but a nickel worth of people outside the Pentagon have seen that memorandum.' Sherman was mainly impressed, with only a little doubt nagging at the back of his mind. In this business, a little doubt could go a long way, with massive backlash. Monks went on. 'And that's just the photo-copy. The real thing's back in the Embassy with the Internal Affairs people.'

Sherman was immediately alarmed. 'You mean to say you've told others about this? About what's going on?' The thought of such knowledge spreading out of proportion to the wrong ears and to disaster was scaring.

'Relax, pal,' said Monks, poking Sherman's shoulder. 'You worry too much. Like I said, our Embassy people have the original copy; but that doesn't mean that they know what it *is* that they have. What those dude diplomatic college boys see and what they understand are two different things. When you've got your hands on the hooker's lovely great ass, what is in the right hand and what is in the left hand is only *half* the story. Right? Gee whizz, pal, it only came in a few hours ago. I'm lucky to have this film copy here.' He pointed to the telex paper. 'That O.K. is from our Moscow station. They're getting ready for a fix-up as soon as we can return the okey dokey without making the place look like a buzzing beehive.'

Sherman re-examined the film, trying to convince himself that he had no doubts over the plan working. The film was a copy of the official statement specifying that the blueprints to the American ground-to-air missile, Skyhawk, were to be leaked to the Russians, in exchange for Dr Linsdale. Skyhawk was top priority in the US home missile defence programme, being only second to Cruiser, the number one missile. To surrender these secrets to the Russians was no mean feat. This was what worried Sherman. Would the Americans go through with it, in spite of what was stated and signed here, when it came to the final moment? 'But are your people going to go through with it, when it comes to the crunch?' said Sherman, voicing his fears. 'After all, this is nothing short of colossal. Why would you give up your Skyhawk defence programme in exchange for our man? Tell me that.'

'Hell, like I said, man, you worry too much.' He playfully punched Sherman's shoulder. Just beyond the sunspecs, Sherman could see crow's-feet lines etching the corner of the eye of this great gaffing Yank who never seemed to have problems. Monks prodded the specs up his nose to the bridge, with a forefinger. 'So what if we do want to help our English cousins step out of the hog swill mess they've created with this Doc guy? In any case, nobody knows,' he paused to smile and emphasise the cheeky secret, 'not even *us two* know that Skyhawk is next to obsolete and is due to be taken off the active priority list and replaced by a superior model within two years. So what's with speeding things up a bit, to straighten things out a bit on the UK side of the big pond? So, okay, Skyhawk goes a bit earlier, but you get your loony boffin back, you repair your dud bombs and the imbalance is removed.' He motioned his long hands up and down to signify the see-saw defence situation between NATO and 'contending powers'. 'The truth is, pal, that whereas once upon a time your little island was all yours, it's now our back gate, and we're mighty particular about who we let in our back yard.'

'We'll have to tread warily, that's certain, said Sherman pensively, handing back the film and telex paper to Monks.

'Sure, sure.' But Monks was more concerned at that moment with setting the film and the paper alight with his Manhattan Bendex lighter. They both watched the flames lick up from the gaping dragon's mouth that was the enormous chromium ashtray in front of them.

Sherman was still worried, but now with a new problem. 'We can't make it too obvious that we want Linsdale back. If we proffer the bait too openly, they'll snap their teeth shut on their own fish and keep Linsdale for themselves, to find out what his newly acquired value really is.'

'Yeah, well, we sure as hell won't be handing out secrets like cookies on a silver tray at an inaugural lawn party at the Whitehouse.' He paused to light two cigarettes, giving one to the airman in front. 'But see here; the final okey dokey has got to come from your people, rather than from me, to set the wheels in motion for the exchange. That's official policy, although I'm quoting off the record.'

So that's why this great pole of a Yank was chirping like a budgie, or one of the reasons, anyway. 'That way you get no axle grease on your fingers.'

'That's about it, pal. Jeez, what more do you guys want in your Uncle Sam jamboree burger! At least we caught our man in the wilds of the Rockies; you guys can't even catch your man when he just walks round the duck pond and out of the park.'

'Fair enough. Leave it with me, and I'll let you know. That will give you time to get things to 'just happen' at the right time, in the right places, about the right rumours of a secrets leak.'

Monks turned his rangy figure away from Sherman and fell back on the seat to blow out his smoke with relief. Sherman saw the tightness that had been around Monks' cheekbone relax, and knew that the man had switched off duty and was back to his old playful self. If only he had the American's ability to turn himself on and off, as he pleased, with the stoical confidence that everything was settled and tied up neat in the bag. Sherman turned his attention to the 'ordinary' airman in front, who, in spite of the noise, had surely heard most of what they'd said. The man had sat impassive through their discussion, showing no more signs of life than a tailor's dummy. He wore only a captain's sparkly bits of insignia on his uniform, but there was too much authority about the shoulders, too much skull, too much austerity about the crags and cuttings in the veteran profile, to hold the man down to such a meagre rank. No, the man's uniform, if he wore one at all, would have a canon's weight of 'brass', and his office more grandiose than this Pontiac's great interior. Sherman couldn't bring to mind any particular person on the US Embassy files, or the US Forces European files. So the man must have just flown in, probably from the Pentagon. Sherman wasn't sure if he was pleased or edgy with this idea.

Monks watched Sherman watching the airman and a sly smile cut slowly across his pale face. He rolled his head back and blew the cloud up to the roof, chuckling softly until he choked on the smoke. Sherman cocked an eyebrow at Monks to question the private joke, and then looked down at his watch. 'I've got to go.'

'Sure, pal.' Monks sat up and held up a lazy hand, while Sherman got out and closed the half ton door.

10.45hrs. As Sherman hurried on towards the Admiralty, he noted how strange the people round about seemed in their unawareness, in contrast to his nervous haste. This thought was interrupted by Major Broaley almost colliding with him as he came out of the gate from Horse Guards Parade with one of his men. Sherman caught a glimpse of the man's light tanned shoulder holster in the second that the jacket flapped open in the breeze. Broaley never used a holster, Sherman recalled from his files. The Major preferred flat automatics that could be carried easily in a jacket or coat pocket. The tangy odours of after shave and hair oil were the first to catch Sherman's attention with their combined assault on his nostrils. He then noticed the subtle shift from soldier to gentleman with Broaley's autumn rust herring bone tweed jacket and dawn grey suede waistcoat, topping a coffee brown shirt and dark sienna leather tie. Alas, the man the man couldn't relinquish the military part completely, it seemed, with his still wearing cavalry twill trousers. Sherman couldn't hold back a cheeky smile. 'So how did it go with *Frau Brun*, Major?'

'Report's on your desk. Nothing we didn't already know.'

'*And?* Nothing else?' Sherman was referring to Broaley's catch the night before. He fell into step with Broaley's rapid pace.

'He's still kicking.'

Sherman could well imagine Broaley plucking the wings off his gadfly in an interrogation. In this situation he felt he could lend the Major a hand to do the plucking, and to hell with the Commander's ethics. But Broaley had things on his mind and didn't seem intent on loosening his tongue beyond a scant report. He checked his watch and then slackened his pace abruptly to cross to the kerb edge. 'We're in a hurry,' he said to Sherman, while watching the traffic for a chance to cross. He tapped the thick folder under Sherman's arm. 'Don't look for my face at the meeting.'

Sherman gave a hard smile. 'Believe me, Major, I shan't *want* to see your face if you've nothing worthwhile to report. In fact, I'd strongly recommend that you don't even consider coming back until you have something solid. Do you follow me?'

'If I followed you, Sherman, the job would never get done.' Broaley rebuffed Sherman's words with the same manner that he cast his cigarette into the gutter and dashed across the road to Trafalgar Square. The lions were still there, not having turned tail yet at the whirlpool commotion of birds, beasts and machines. The beasts, of course, were the ones wearing the clothes. Little wonder that Nelson had been driven to refuge at the top of his lonely perch. Broaley was bristling with suspicion of virtually everyone and everything that moved, hardly stopping short of clapping the pigeons in irons, if he'd had reason to. His eyes scanned the crowd while he spoke to his man. 'And the phone message stated specifically that he wanted to see me, and nobody else?'

'That's right, Major. He wouldn't give his name. But he said you would recognise him on sight. That's all.'

'I think I've an idea who it might be.' Broaley flashed an inner eye over his list of devious 'unofficial' contacts, while at the same time eyeing the people mingling around him.

'Can we be sure it's not one of them up to their tricks, Major? An *old* ploy, of the *new* FSB to sound us out?

'Look, son, the sooner you get it into your head that you can't be sure of anything in this business, the sooner you come to having more sense in your head than one of these damn pigeons.' Broaley swiped at a pigeon wanting to land on his shoulder. He turned to head over to the Underground stairs. 'Keep your eyes peeled for stragglers.'

They took themselves two tickets for Piccadilly Circus and walked on into the tiled corridor. A short ride like that was ideal for contacts to quickly exchange confidences and then scatter. The man who had been fumbling for change for the ticket machine, suddenly had the right amount, and taking his ticket, went on after them. His fumbling had simply been a means of stalling while he waited for the Major. Broaley had recognised him as his contact as soon as he'd gone down the stairs.

As the three of them went round the bend in the corridor, a man darted down from the cover of the twisting entrance steps, where his cigarette had taken an unusually long time to light. Like any ordinary tourist, he carried a bright tricolour map of London and had a camera dangling round his neck. Unlike any ordinary tourist, the snaps in his camera were not of London sights, but of the Major and his companion. Beneath his jacket he had an item that was strictly non-tourist. Issued by the FSB Armoury Department. Taking a ticket from the machine, he went casually into the corridor.

10.46hrs (GMT), Milan. Peter Haldane watched the black legs, with their red side stripes, run beside the car as it was drawing to a stop before the entrance to the Posto di Polizia. The brilliant white diagonal shoulder strap and belt flashed in the sunlight as the *carabiniere* bent forward to open the car door. 'Signore, 'Aldane?'

'Si.'

He saluted as Haldane got out, before turning to lead the way into the building. Haldane followed on, under the watchful eyes of the heavily armed anti-Mafia, anti-Terrorist squad of *carabinieri* sitting smoking, on constant standby, in their jeeps. As was common in sunny lands like this, sun was not welcomed into the building. Haldane removed his sunglasses to see better in the dimly lit hallway. He followed the *carabiniere* towards the stairs at the far end. The young officer stopped halfway up the stairs, to point along the balcony that Haldane only now noticed, looked down on the hallway. 'Tre porte di distanza, signore. Capisci?'

'Yes, I understand,' said Haldane. 'Three doors along. Si, capisci. Grazie.' Haldane walked along the balcony and knocked on the door. No-one answered, so he went in. Empty. Large, with everything that went to make a professional working office, there was a stillness about it that said this was not a 'lived-in' room. But he understood. By courtesy of the police station, the room was being lent as a low profile front for him to meet his contact with Italy's SISMI (Military and Intelligence Security Service). He was scanning the tiny faces in a long group photograph of 'hundreds' of *carabinieri*, when he saw the reflection of the door open behind him and Commissario Baressi came in. Medium height, thickset, with a butcher's chopping block for a jaw. They knew each other well, so formalities were brief. Accents excused, Baressi's English was better than Haldane's Italian, so they spoke in English. 'You'll have to forgive my being late, Peter, but the traffic is absolute hell, driving into the city at this hour.'

'If only that was all we had to worry about.'

Baressi registered the woeful note in Haldane's remark and saw a dark cloud coming. A *very* dark cloud if he judged correctly. And he often did. His doctorate in clinical psychology from the University of Bologna served him well in that aspect. They sat down at the desk. As Haldane was about to delve into his situation, Baressi held up a hand, with a very solemn expression on his face, to halt him. 'First of all, Peter, something very important.' From out of nowhere Baressi produced two minuscule liqueur glasses and a long-stemmed bottle of the powerful Strega that Haldane was familiar with in his meetings with the Italian. 'My son, Reno, has just made his First Holy Communion this morning. So we shall drink to him, before we talk serious. Salute!'

'Salute!

Throats burned. Baressi smiled as Haldane coughed to clear his throat. He could see that what was in the Englishman's mind was burning him far more than that in his throat. 'Now, Peter, perhaps you can tell me which of those Apocalyptic Horsemen it is that you have brought galloping my way.'

17

12.58hrs, 25th June, London SW1. The door slid shut and the lift plunged down the steel wall shaft like a pellet down a narrow gullet. Sherman stood like an idolater, watching the light over the door, while listening to the strange background language of whispers and whines, as the shaft slipped past outside. Looped cables and counterweights raced up through the sinister shadows, like serpents and goblins, while mischievous elves and gremlins spirited down after the lift cage, touching it and making it shudder. Still the lift burrowed down through hundreds of feet of clay and chalk strata that was the London basin, to where the war room lay in secret, beneath the city. Down, down, down, it sank, perhaps not so much into the bowels of the earth, but certainly into its hardened skin of pre-stressed concrete and steel beams and reinforcement plates.

The light over the door flickered for a second and the lift suddenly 'wh-e-e-d' to a halt with its peculiar pneumatic whinny. The door slid open and there was the veteran redcap marine, resplendent in his dark uniform, sprinkled with its refulgent array of buttons that did the glory to half a tin of Brasso. No, he wasn't blocking anyone's way; he was just blocking anyone's unauthorised entry. Anyone who was liable to disagree with this quickly noticed the other two younger marines standing behind, holding their short SA-80 rifles.

'Pass, sir?' said two flaps of rhino skin, hardened by Goose Green in the Falklands and Desert Storm in Iraq. The marine took the MoD pass warily and examined it closely, looking up to make a long careful match of Sherman's face with the photograph. O.K. Iron fingers snapped the leather wallet shut and a ramrod straight arm returned the pass to Sherman. Mercy was being granted. 'Sir!'

Sherman put his pass away and walked along the polished stone passage. It was clearly a military passage, with pipes and phones springing out of the wall every few yards, and demon red bulbs flashing along the ceiling corner. Some of the doors he passed had electronic locks and striped horizontal steel bars running across their middles. No fear of Toby the cat getting out and running off, down here. A naval lieutenant put his coded card in one lock and the steel bar slid out of the door's brackets, disappearing into the wall. The door closed behind the officer and the striped guardian slid back out and through the brackets, securing the door once more against unwarranted entry. All this was seen not only by Sherman, but also by the beetle-eye television lenses monitoring his every move, as he advanced along the passage. The quiet background hum changed to a more precise sound of staccato stutters and discordant drones of computers, as Sherman turned the corner. A young Wren stopped her trolley of Fortran tape discs outside an open door. Inside, the large banks of droning computers gobbled up the data from the Olivetti Vector processor, jerking their tapes round and pausing in the interval to work out the differential ratio between life and death of a NATO exercise.

Sherman turned another corner and the operation room lay straight ahead. This was the Naval Strategy Room, or 'Games' Room, where one played 'Monopoly' with oceans and paid the mortgages with coastlines and computerised contingencies of expendable assault troops and landing craft. Sherman stood just inside the swing doors to gaze at the panorama of giant electronic maps. The room's dimmed lighting brought the Marconi screens out more, to sum up the world's naval situation in a blink. Sherman blinked for several seconds without his becoming much the wiser. Little shoals of yellow-green 'minnows' wriggling about in the two main 'fish-tanks' of the northern and southern hemispheres, were supposedly the two great sea-powers, the USA and Russia. Down here, unofficially, the old tag, Red Fleet, still hung around. Smaller screens twinkling with their 'catches' told the same story on a localised regional scale. Whatever it was, Sherman couldn't fathom it and so gave up. He turned to the Admiral.

The man came up smoothly, without taking his hands out of his pockets.

Maybe that was to stop the gold rings falling off the cuffs. 'How does it look, Admiral?' said Sherman, breaking the pause between them.

'Better than what it could be, I suppose. But bear in mind that this is the early stage. Small mercy that the whole bungling episode wasn't our fault to begin with. At least you can trust us not to be so gauche as to go around dropping secrets and things like a nervous horse.'

'Whatever happened, and indeed whatever happens, Admiral, I hardly think that Devine retribution is going to be meted out according to the degree of guilt.'

'That's precisely my point!' He looked away at the screens for a second to dispel his spasm of irritation and then looked back, managing a smile. A very faint one. The anger was still there, not far beneath it. 'You'll have to forgive the schoolboy in me coming out, but it's hard to play the same old game under these new rules. Or perhaps I should say conditions, to be more fair. I don't know if old sea-horses wear nosebags, like ordinary horses, but I certainly get the feeling that I'm being forced into one, with these increasing cuts in our expenditure. Having to enact the duties of a major sea-power with this sort of budget is simply ludicrous, to say the least.'

Sherman had no time to waste over little points like these and could only agree politely to get them out the way. 'Yes, I know how you must feel, Admiral. But never mind; come and show me what's developing so far.' They moved over into the darker perimeter of the room and peered between the heads of the other observers, at the screens. The Admiral leaned forward on the back of one of the seats, to peer closer.

'See, there; that's the Russian fleet coming in there, and there -- and over there, as well.' He pointed along the luminescent panels. 'With two hundred and sixty or so Russian surface vessels afloat on the globe, this amassing here is outside the usual pattern. And remember that that's just the ships. So we're not counting their submarines. With satellite reports coming in regularly, we can obtain by computer, the normal index drift factor. It's not yet obvious to the naked eye, but the drift factor tells us, at the moment of reading, the predominant drift, or movement, of the Russian fleet at that particular time.'

'And what's that, at this moment?' Sherman felt a tingle of apprehension inside at what he feared the Admiral was going to say.

'At this moment, there's definite movement of their northern arm towards the North Sea. There's also a smaller shift of their Baltic and Mediterranean fleets coming in and up, to complete the pincer movement. As I said, this is not so obvious yet by actual visual effect, but the computers tell us otherwise, in reliable figures. See, over here. You'll see what I mean.' The Admiral spun round sharply and strode over to the large Perspex partition standing out from the corner and running from floor to roof. Each corner had its partition, sitting 45 degrees to the walls, with a 'bookie' perched on a ladder marking in the 'odds'. The man at this corner worked diligently from the figures on his clipboard and marked in the arrows to demonstrate the drift. It was significant, even to Sherman, that the arrows were broader over the back of the Norwegian 'dog', than those from the Baltic and Mediterranean regions. To an ordinary eye, it looked like a simple weather chart. But the bad weather this was forecasting was not hail or snow, but nuclear havoc. Sherman noted that the figures were 2:7/2:5; 2:8/2:5; 2:7/2:4; for the northern 'pincer', and 2;4/2:3; 2:4/2:3; 2:3/2:2 for the southern combined Baltic and Mediterranean 'pincer'.

'Two, seven, as to two, five. What's that?' said Sherman. I notice the seven and five are in red.'

'Yes, that's right. The second digits, seven and five in this case, are the figures giving us the increase ratio or so called drift, of the fleet in that direction. The first figure, the two, is the normal possibility coefficient and remains constant. See how the northern movement is more prominent, obviously because of their comparative freedom to move their vessels in that region. What's also very interesting is the sharpness in variation of the time factor. See here, where he's marking in the graph at the bottom. See the seven over the one. That means that the sudden movement of their fleets in these directions started only a few hours ago.'

'I see. And where are we in all this?'

'That's us there,' said the Admiral, pointing to two tiny arrows curving between the 'dog's head' of Norway and the Shetlands. 'The Dover, Warrior and Atlas. One carrier, the Dover, and two cruisers. We should have another one coming into the area round about now.' He looked at his watch and then up at the long row of clocks on the far wall. Sherman didn't bother trying to figure out which one the Admiral was looking at.

It didn't escape Sherman's notice that the British arrows were as thin as hairs, compared to those of the Red fleet. 'And how long before the 'pincers' reach their position, Admiral?'

'From these figures, I would say twenty-four hours or so.'

'And when, and if, they do pinch?'

'I would prefer to let the computers rummage through their brain banks for a little while longer, before making any firm statements on this aspect. For the time being, anyway.'

Sherman wondered if the Admiral just didn't want to frighten him with horrifying details 'It should be quite an outing, that's certain. The Regatta won't get a look-in, if I guess correctly.'

'Oh, I think you've guessed correctly, all right. It should confuse the seagulls, if anything,' said the Admiral, furrowing his brow as he thought beyond the cynical banter they were both hiding their fears behind.

'Still, maybe if we're quiet enough, they won't notice us in their wake as they pass.'

As they walked towards the Admiral's cubicle, one of the men turned round to call, pulling off an earphone: 'Sir.'

'Yes?'

'Cromwell reporting into Area Nine, now, sir.'

'Good. Excellent.' The Admiral turned to the man on the ladder. But the man needed no directions, and was already marking in the figures at the tails of the skinny arrows. The Wren at the table pushed another little grey model ship into the red hatched area. Did you get two hundred pounds when you passed *Go*? The Admiral beamed. It wasn't a great improvement, but it was an improvement, nevertheless. The ploy was not what one had, but how one used it. That meant contriving ingenious strategies that would make the Trojan horse crumble to dust with dry rot in comparison. Sherman thought of Cromwell and then of Charles I and then of cavaliers. From cavaliers his association of ideas went finally to Don Quixote's futility in attacking those vast windmills.

12.59hrs, Whitehall. Sir Richard put the phone down and marked up yet another appointment for the afternoon in his diary. Handing the sheaf of memo notes to his secretary for typing up, he pressed the intercom, to tell the car pool to have his car ready for him in ten minutes. With the world's pulse throbbing on the UK situation, his office was inundated with calls from the Foreign Office. Some observers saw the East's build up as a threatening aggression policy in Russia's new 'imperialist' expansion plan. Others saw it as pure propaganda by Washington warmongers, to widen the gap in East and West trade relations. Publicly speaking, Uncle Sam's political voice was suffering acute laryngitis. *Sotto voce*, however, there was grave concern for the UK allies with their defence 'balls-up'. The Foreign Secretary sought out the military people. They gave their dire opinions and humped the urgency of finding the rogue atom scientist onto the back of Intelligence. The SIS was spotlighted and the finger pointed at Sir Richard. Meanwhile, the Russian Embassy expressed its strong wish for a spokesman from Her Majesty's Foreign Office to attend and explain the present policies of Her Majesty's Government. Why, for instance, in flagrant violation of the peace treaty, had Russian sailors been fired upon by British warplanes? Never mind that the sailors had been purloining from an American aircraft. Besides, they were a 'rogue' crew, Bosnian sympathisers, commandeering a Russian vessel; not at all the responsibility of the Russian government. A complete U-turn, perhaps? The US Embassy made similar appointments for urgent talks with the Russian Embassy and the British Foreign Office. The Foreign Secretary was at present in deep discussion with the American Defense Secretary and National Security Advisor. He had already despatched a summons for the Russian Ambassador to attend for a separate talk later. Bearing in mind that all this political hotchpotch was of those with the big voices, those with the big power. But what of those who had only little voice, who had no power, except that of Allah? Sir Richard hadn't forgotten that the court of enquiry into allegations of brutal treatment of a terrorist by Special Branch officers was convened for tomorrow. As he hurried out the door and down the corridor, he dialled Commander Rose on his mobile.

18

13.31hrs, 25th June, Whitehall SW1. 'As much as that?' said Sir Richard, sucking the match flame into the pipe bowl. Commander Rose looked on, waiting, while Sherman and Meeson busied themselves with their calculations, more Meeson's, than Sherman's. Rose had been brought in to share the confidence of the situation, where pressure was mounting with the time running out. He was still a bit peeved at not having been shown the light until now, but was coming to terms with it and gradually cooling off. The flame fluttered like a struggling butterfly inside the rim, before Sir Richard was satisfied and settled into a regular puffing routine. 'We have done better than expected,' he said. 'It's certainly an improvement on the dismal tune you were lamenting not half an hour ago.' He eyed Sherman with the old dog red eyed look of appeasement. This meant that things had improved slightly. Sherman couldn't remember when it had ever meant anything better, so didn't bring himself to trust the look. Give the gorilla a banana by all means, but make sure it's on the end of a stick, and you're on the other side of the railings.

'Yes well, bear in mind that these figures from Naval Operations were based purely on statistical factors,' said Sherman, playing with his calculator, wondering if he should feel at all pleased with his figures. 'It simply means that a very small movement becomes a very large movement, when it's made in the opposite direction, if measured from the point of view of the deviation factor.' He looked to Meeson for confirmation.

Meeson nodded. 'That's right.'

'You're surely not trying to tell me that they're only just looking towards us, without doing anything about it?' Hossley took out his pipe and held it wide, to gape at them in a mixture of confusion and disbelief.

'No, you misunderstand us,' said Meeson. 'They're certainly moving in on our defences, all right. Rushing, as a matter of fact. But it's because of the sudden switch in their actions, outside their normal manoeuvres, that the movement is given an exaggerated impetus, or punch.'

'But they're still closing in for that *punch*, as you put it, none the less?' Old Hossley could sure take some strange delight at being right, regardless of the implications.

'Oh yes. But in the meantime, we've dug ourselves in, ready for the onslaught,' Meeson replied.

'The Dover and Atlas were the first two on the spot, in the Artic Circle,' said Sherman. 'Since then, we've improved the situation more than a hundred-fold. Leiffersen has put Operation GLACIER into action, and with NATO's contribution, in numbers alone, we outnumber them. On the surface, that is.' Rear-Admiral Leiffersen was the Norwegian Commander-in-Chief of the Scandinavian northern sector of NATO, and second in command, for this operation, only to the American Supreme Commander-in-Chief of the entire Southern European sector of NATO. Under Leiffersen's command, Operation GLACIER would swing round on its northern, Artic, pivot and sweep back any invasion, through the North Atlantic, by the Russian Fleet. This didn't completely patch up the Iceland/Greenland gap, which carried a constant threat of submarine attack, but relied like most strategies on its good points.

The metal filing cabinet poked out a rude tongue as Sherman pulled the drawer out at the NATO/Neth/Nor/ section. His fingers raked through the 'G' folders and he brought out the file on GLACIER. 'I can't say I know much about this operation,' he said, looking over at Meeson, 'but I suppose now is as good a time as any, to have a look at it.'

Meeson went over to join Sherman in examining the folder's contents. Sir Richard leaned his head back to look up at the ceiling and thought deeply. He took out his pipe and looked over at Sherman and Meeson. 'Like you said, we outnumber them on the surface only. If they should decide on an all out submarine attack, the results could be interesting.' Tension transformed itself to fantasy for a second, in Sir Richard's mind, and he thought of sleek, silver scaled, serpents slithering under toothy crested waves in some ancient mural of some Norseman's mythical tale. Tales in which the just were forever heroic victors with their valiant swords of fire. He came back down to earth. 'And on top of that, there's the tremendous possibility that they'll mount a land attack from the East, across the Rhine. Yes, a most deadly thorn in our side.'

'All this is assuming that we last that long to worry about it, bearing in mind our other little problem, said Sherman, closing the file again.

'There's one damning factor which we must see as being horrifically to our disadvantage, 'said Rose, drawing their combined attention. They waited, ready to measure a new opinion in the game. 'Because of the awesome power of these bombs, *which I've only just been made aware of,* they do not have to be placed anywhere near the target. Up until now the normal police procedure for countermanding terrorist attacks, suicide bombers, has been by special surveillance, monitoring suspects; watching out for suspicious characters, vehicles; watching behaviour patterns, unattended objects near people, near public targets, and so on. But with these wretched things, they can be in the middle of the Yorkshire moors and still do colossal damage. In short, *everywhere* and *anywhere* is a potential target.' All were silent for a few moments. Good for you, Rose, old son; that's made everybody feel a lot cheerier.

'Yes, that's true,' said Sir Richard, 'and it's on that point that I categorically say that we keep an iron maiden's tongue. I know some of the other Chiefs-of-Staff disagreed,' he looked significantly at Rose, 'but like Sir James said, and I'm sure you'll *all* agree with me, it's vital that our domestic problems don't leak out. Not even to our NATO allies. It's in *their* interest, as well as our own. We can hardly be their ally and throw such valuable information to the enemy. There would be little hesitation over striking, in the Russian Command, with that kind of guarantee for incentive.'

'Quite,' said Sherman, putting the file back and leaning thoughtfully on the cabinet's top. He made up his mind and started away from the cabinet, reaching for the phone. 'I think I'll see how they're coming along with this new thing they're brewing up for the bombs.' He looked at Meeson. 'You know, that aerial device you told me about, for maintaining the transmitter's angles.' Meeson nodded. Sherman dialled halfway and then stopped, not remembering if the last digits were 741 or 714. The paper on which he'd scribbled the number earlier didn't seem to be at hand, so he spoke into the intercom. 'Get me the Worcester number for the Royal Radar Establishment, will you.' The intercom sat dead. 'Are you there?' He looked up and saw the secretary standing in the doorway joining the offices. 'Could you look up the number for the Royal Radar Establishment in Worcester. I can't remember if it ends with seven four one, or seven one four.'

'Very good, sir.' She remained standing there.

'Yes, what is it?' asked Sherman.

'There's a gentleman from the press, downstairs, wanting to see someone.'

'What does he want?' said Sir Richard.

'Apparently he wants to know if he can confirm the rumour that Dr Lim---' she checked the spelling in her notebook, '--- that Dr Linsdale has, in fact, defected, and is not just missing.'

'Tell him to go to hell, ' said Sherman. I haven't the time for chit-chat with the press. I'm definitely not in. Tell him I'm not here or something. Anything, just keep him off my back.'

'He didn't seem troublesome, sir,' said the woman. 'He said that he only wanted a firm yes or no, and that he wouldn't keep you after that.'

'The hell he wouldn't,' said Sherman, his hackles rising with annoyance. 'That's what they all say to get a foot in the door. After that you're tied down for hours. Tell him I'm off with the old tonsillitis or something. No, that doesn't sound convincing. Just say he's missed me by a few minutes. Put him on to Winters or somebody.'

'It's all right, I'll handle it, ' said Sir Richard, getting up from his chair. 'I've got to go down to see the PM, as it is.' He took the Commander by the elbow. 'Come on, Robert, I'll see you to your car.'

'All right, just tell the gentleman that Sir Richard will be down shortly,' said Sherman to the woman. 'And while you're at it, be snappy about that number, will you. I need it quickly.'

Hossley had just gone out, when the phone rang. He came back into the room and waited as Sherman lifted the receiver. 'Yes?' said Sherman, listening, while Sir Richard fidgeted with the door handle. 'You have? -- Good. -- Where? -- Right.' Sherman put the phone down and scribbled on a piece of paper. 'That was Army Intelligence. They've just located two of the transmitters. They're both in small houses, rented, it seems, by Dr Linsdale. One's in in Cambridge and the other one is in Abingdon. There's a third one in Monmouthshire, somewhere. But they just haven't been able to pinpoint the exact location yet. It shouldn't be too long before we find it, though.'

'And having found them, how do we then proceed?' said Sir Richard, looking a little more like himself with his customary questioning uncertainty. 'We did issue strict instructions that the transmitters were not to be tampered with, except by experts, didn't we?'

'Y-e-s,' said Sherman pensively, pausing in the doorway. 'I can see your fear of being 'switched off' by some impatient fool. And how do you draw the line between expert and inexpert, except when it's too damn late.?' He closed the door behind them. 'Let's get out of here and get some fresh air. A nip out to Worcester should clear the lungs.' He looked round at Meeson. 'You coming?'

'Sure.'

13.45hrs, Cambridge. Major Broaley got out of the car and hurried down the stone path to the house, with a mixture of feelings knocking his chest. This was mostly mounting expectation coupled with a slight disbelief. He found it hard to believe that all their hectic chasing around could lead to this tranquil patch, where supposedly, the only excitement was that of mad professors chasing butterflies across the meadows with their nets. The quiet little mock Tudor cottage with its oriel windows resting on corbels, was in keeping with the docile image of the street. And yet this was it. Or at least, this was one of the three places where the transmitters were installed, according to the reports.

Broaley's contact in the Underground had only been one of a series of cat and mouse check-ups that had finally led him to this piece of information. During that time, he had had to shake off an FSB tail twice, and that was only after he had made sure that the tail could be no use to him. The Russians here, it seemed, were in the dark about what was really happening at this stage, and were anxious to follow on and find out. The agent who had initially set the Linsdale operation in motion must be operating on direct instructions from Moscow. In total secrecy from the FSB stationed here. Quite possibly had gone back east. Easier that wayfor the 'comrades' here, in their ignorance, to fry in the 'mushroom' omelette.

An Army Bomb Disposal man appeared in the doorway. 'Major Broaley?'

'Yes.'

'It's downstairs, in the basement, sir.'

'Lead on, Lieutenant.'

They clambered noisily down the wooden steps that led to the door with its large glass panel. The lieutenant reached out to open it. There was a sudden cry of alarm from beyond it within, and Broaley's reflexes sent his hand to his pocket. Glass fragments stung their faces as the explosion blasted the door outwards, hurling them back against the stairway. For several seconds they lay dazed on their backs, surrounded by glass shards and wooden strips. The light had survived, but swung nervously to and fro. Fingering his forehead, Broaley felt the blood trickle down slowly from a small cut. He rose and made his way through the thick smoke billowing through from the ugly gap.

Inside was an uglier sight. The place was a heap of twisted metal and wooden strips, where a heavy wooden workbench and metal bracket shelves had stood. Little tongues of fire licked up hungrily in corners, where there was a remnant trace of workshop spirits to feed them. Just perceivable through the smoke issuing from the far corner was a pair of legs. A second form stirred in the smoking shambles and crawled over to its mate. Broaley stepped round them to look at the weird dark rectangle of metal that loomed up in the corner. He knew nothing about transmitters, but his knowledge of this one's significance was so holding that it was tightening his stomach into a hard billiard ball of a knot. The explosion, with its frenzied moments, had told his frightened brain that *the* bomb had gone off. But he had recovered his sense to realise that this was nonsense. What did scare him now was the thought that the explosion could have upset the transmitter so as to trigger off its system for detonating the nuclear bombs. God Almighty! But what *was* the explosion?

'What happened?' Broaley spoke to no-one in particular, but to anyone in the place who could hear him, while keeping his attention on the awesome thing in the corner.

'Would you believe it, the bench blew up!' said the man kneeling over his injured mate. 'The ruddy bench blew up!'

'The bench?' Broaley was puzzled. He turned to look at where the bench had stood.

'Yes, it was standing right there, sir. I reckon we were lucky it was so thick. It gave us a shield as it blew out the other way towards the door.'

'What were you doing?'

'We were nowhere near the bench. We had no reason to be. We were over there in the corner, going over the transmitter like we were ordered to ----' The man swallowed his nerves and broke off to reach in his pocket and pull out the paper chit. 'We got orders from HQ to --'

'Never bloody mind that! What the damn hell happened, man?'

'We were examining the transmitter, going over the regular routine, when we came across the booby-trap wires leading to the bench behind us. It had to be the last place we expected to concentrate our attention. When we realised that we'd set the thing off, it was too late. Luckily we had our backs to the bench.' The man looked at his mate lying there. 'He looks quite bad, sir. I think he needs a stretcher.'

Broaley paid no more attention to the man and looked up at the transmitter and back to where the bench had been. So the cunning devil Linsdale had booby-trapped the bench as a warning to them to keep their hands off the transmitter. The thickness of the bench had been a deliberate means to shield the transmitter, *not* the meddlers. But how could they be sure? Broaley felt the dryness in his throat. How could they be sure that the shock waves hadn't upset the transmitter's programme, to set the other bombs - the *real* bombs - off sooner than intended? He paused in the dazed stupor wondering if he could hear any big bangs outside.

A commotion of feet and voices sounded outside on the wooden stairs and someone rushed in with a fire extinguisher to dowse the mischievous flames. Two more shapes rushed in to help the injured soldier. The lieutenant came in, leaning against the door jamb, holding his eye, where blood was trickling down. He followed the Major's stare to the dark apparatus shrouded in the corner's shadows. 'In God's name, sir, what *is* that thing?'

Broaley shook his head. 'I hope we never really find out.'

19

13.46hrs (GMT), 25th June, Norway. The gull screeched out and took off from its rock, frightened by the storm-class gunboat surging round into sight round the headland, from out of the fjord. Leaping and diving over the waves ahead of its foaming wake, the Norwegian naval boat raced along at thirty knots on its routine patrol, threatening all with its 76mm Bofors gun forward and power-operated 40mm gun aft. Spiking up like porcupine quills were also six Penguin surface-to-air missiles. The sun blinked overhead, as the gulls criss-crossed repeatedly before it. Heads turned up at the birds' irate cries, missing their shadows racing over the curly crested waves. But that was all the crew's Viking eyes missed, passing off the area as 'normal' and speeding on up the coastline, letting the birds fall behind in a squalling retreat.

Far out at sea, a less clamorous swarm besieged a lonely trawler, the white flecks hanging around the fishing vessel like a cloud of midges. Their noisy attack was nothing more than an odd plaintive squeal that was carried inland on a cool breeze. The tumult and the fleeing direction of the motionless boat came with a little thought. With its tanned deck covered in a paraphernalia of rope, seines and balls, the small wooden vessel seemed to just manage to float like a spunky cork. Standing in the hatch, a craggy old man in yellow oilskin trousers lifted out a lobster and threw it into a tarpaulin full of water. The hideous creature squirmed feebly and wondered why another form so creased and broken as itself had the privilege of wearing the trousers.

Another man came along from the aft hatchway, cleaning his hands on an oil rag and sat down on the fish boxes beside the hold. 'Hvordan gar det?' ('How's it going?') he said.

'Jeg er torst,' ('I'm thirsty,') said the old man. 'Det er for varmt.'(It's too warm.')

'Ja.' ('Yes.')

The old man straightened up and paused to feel the dryness in his mouth. 'Jeg vil gjerne ha ol.' (I'd like some beer.')

'Ja,' said the young man and laughed, rolling back, sinking his teeth into his bread and cheese. He threw a piece to the gulls and looked around. 'Det er svaert stille,' (It's very calm,), he said.

'Jeg liker det ikke,' ('I don't like it,') said the old man.

'Hvorfor?' ('Why?')

The old man saw the stranger come out of the wheelhouse and turned back to his work, mumbling gruffly. In spite of the modification of the wellington boots and a donkey-jacket over his city clothes, the FSB man definitely didn't look the part as a seaman. Since he had come on aboard at Kristiansund, nobody but the skipper had spoken to him and nobody but the skipper knew what his business was. The man stood a few feet away and everyone was quiet. While the old man worked on and the young man munched away at his bread, gulls swooped around, displaying their skill in aerobatic manoeuvres with their silent sun-catching antics. The FSB man did nothing but scan the waters around him. He checked the time on his watch.

The young man stopped chewing and lifted his head. 'Hor etter,' ('Listen,') he said.

'Hva?' ('What?') said the old man. The FSB man was interested too, not having the young man's keen sense of hearing.

'Se,' ('Look,') said the young man, standing up.

'Hvor?' ('Where?') said the old man and the FSB man together.

'Se. Der borte,' ('Look. Over there,') said the young man, pointing excitedly.

The seagulls had been more perceptive than the humans and were already swirling and squawking round the small island that was coming up out of the sea. Rising out of the water as a sharp pinnacle at first, the 'island' suddenly became very fat and swelled up and out of the sea to form an incredible shining black island 426ft long. The water cascaded off the submarine Yalta's sides and settled beneath it with a roar that met its mighty tonnage, and had the fishermen staring agog. Far away as it was, the vastness of the submarine made it seem frightfully close. The old man crossed himself and swore at the same time, not bothered by religious differences. He was just in time. 1000 tons of inrushing water welled up and rolled on the surface, rocking the boat and almost knocking the FSB man overboard. Submerged, the Yalta displaced 9000 tons of water, and when surfaced, she displaced 8000 tons, so that the difference could be put down as sweat from her omnipotent body.

Small figures were popping up on the conning tower and looking up at the raucous taunts of the gulls, and down at the tiny fishing boat. One was scanning the sky and coastline with binoculars. At the same time, some 'ants' were clambering down the giant whale's side, into a dinghy, to go and collect the FSB man.

The man checked his pocket for the coded message, before stepping into the dinghy. Nobody uttered a sound, looking on at the solemn crossing, moving to the ritual tempo of the waters lapping on the hulls. Even the gulls seemed far away. The skipper switched off the boat's engine as they waited. Turning to his mate, the young man said: 'Det er praktfullt, nei?' ('It's magnificent, no?')

The old man hawked his throat noisily and spat on the deck. 'Det er for stor,' ('It's too big') he said. 'Det er stygt.' ('It's ugly.')

'Det er skremmende,' ('It's terrifying,') said the young man, resolute in his excitement. The old man spat again and turned away to busy himself with the lobster.

The minutes seemed a long time to the onlookers, but in that time, messages were duly exchanged and decoded and new standing instructions made clear. Passing the final message by hand, after receiving a series of radio messages, was the final act in security. London had sent out the signals to Bergen some hours earlier, and the nearest submarine in the area had been radioed and instructed to rendezvous here. The FSB man now coming back across from the submarine was from Bergen's permanent Russian Cultural Council and had the sole responsibility of organising rural 'business excursions' like this, when the need arose. He came back on board and the Yalta prepared to move off down the coast, where it would lie in wait for tomorrow's mission. Then it would steal into the British waters to pick up the atom scientist, Dr Linsdale.

13.51hrs, London. Back here in the city, swaps were taking place in less dramatic entourage, with diplomats calling on each other with the punctilious regularity of duelling seconds. But professional face meant revealing little. If embassies could admit to vermin scratching away behind the boards, then they could admit to the devious presence of their secret service people behind the scenes. The Russian Ambassador was as friendly as he was adamant with the American diplomat, haranguing him with Russia's right to maintain vigil over the West's naval movements, at the same time carrying out its own naval exercises to guard against the invasion of Russian territorial waters. Ambassador Green listened, remembering from wise experience that sore points were often reached, not by mentioning them, but by patient noting of what was *not* said between the lines. Behind their practised waxy smiles, neither of them knew what the hell was really going on, except that their security people were scurrying about like nervous beavers plugging their dam against rising waters that signalled imminent flooding. When Green passed through the ante-room on his way out, he recognised the man speaking to the Russian naval attache as the British SIS guy, Hossley. Outside, a man stepped over from a limousine to ask the Ambassador if he would care to wait for Sir Richard. When Hossley came out, he invited the American into his limousine, and they rode off, tete-a-tete, into the lunchtime traffic.

13.52hrs, Lambeth. Rasheed felt all the eyes staring - *boring* - into him, when he planted the large heavy duty bolt croppers down on the counter in the builders suppliers store. In his self-conscious mind, burning with guilt, the large tool seemed enormous. It was as if he had on a striped jumper, a mask and was holding a bag marked 'swag', like in those comics that he used to read. And still did, sometimes, but he didn't let on to Hali about that. All these men watching his every move; and they were all white. Bastards! They weren't watching him, but that was how his paranoid mind made him feel. He could have shot them all, every single one of them, with his fantastic Beretta. But Hassani had taken the machine pistol from him before he had left the van. This had been careful insight by Hassani, who had foreseen the danger of Rasheed's tendency to overreact to a situation. Rasheed couldn't wait to get out of the store.

The croppers were the last on the list of tools he had been buying, on

Hassani's specific instructions. All bought from different stores, so as not to draw attention to himself. He had also bought, and they were wearing, boiler suits and caps, so as to look less like Muslims, and so blend in with the scenery as workers on a 'job'. Again, on Hassani's instructions. The one commodity that Hassani had bothered to get out of the van to get for himself, was in the back, in two metal cylinders. He'd insisted on going to collect it on his own, disappearing into a deep metal canyon between mountains of dockside cargo containers. The cylinders looked just like ordinary brewery beer kegs. But Rasheed had noticed the small yellow three-bladed propeller symbol for radio activity on the sides of them. He somehow didn't think that the two cylinders contained beer.

As they drove along the road, Rasheed was half expecting a great line of police cars to be racing after them. But there were no blue lights flashing in his rear mirror or side mirror. 'No marzipan cars so far, it seems; how about that,' said Rasheed, with his boyish chirpiness.

Hassani, disturbed from his deep thoughts, looked round, puzzled at Rasheed. 'Marzipan? Sorry?'

'Yeah, you know -- the checkered sides of police cars; like Battenburg marzipan cakes. Marzipan car -- get it?' But Hassani couldn't understand the 'boy' with his strange ways of the West. Rasheed saw Hassani's puzzlement and gurgled with delight at his being one up on his boss. He put his foot down on the accelerator and throttled on faster up the road. Hassani at once put a restraining hand on the 'boy's arm to get him to slow down again. They could not afford to attract the attention of the authorities with minor traffic violations.

The reason for the bolt croppers became apparent to Rasheed when they drew up in front of the lock-up in the arch under the railway bridge. The large heavy duty padlock glinted in the sunlight. Hassani, in his mind, saw a bigger 'flash' coming soon. His FSB source had given him the locations of the two unfinished bombs, along with the detonator mechanism trigger codes, and transmitter signal codes. This, along with the uranium-238 isotope fission material from the rare radioactive actinide series, which the FSB had also provided him with, was all he needed to get the job done. Or almost. Ironically, out of all this specialisation, his FSB masters had not been able to provide him with the simplest of things. A key to open the lock-up's padlock. Dr Linsdale's sudden need to flee was the cause of this oversight.

Rasheed cursed under his breath, at his lack of muscle power, when he failed to cut the padlock the first time. With a concentrated effort on the long-levered handles a second time, the blades finally cut through. Rasheed couldn't understand why they had needed to buy the two replacement locks, one for this place and one for the next place. After all, once they were in, they were in, surely? Couldn't they just set up the bombs and go? Hassani had to explain to the 'boy' that the bombs were to go off later, so that until then, the doors had to be relocked so as not to look suspicious, as they would, lying open with broken locks, and so prevent any snoopers going inside and interfering with their plans. They went inside, Hassani in front, to make sure that the 'boy' didn't touch anything he shouldn't.

Dark as it was inside, they both saw it instantly, standing out from everything rusting and ancient around it, by its glistening newness. A twenty-first century devil-child held in the dark womb of nineteenth-century brickwork around it. Rasheed was about to step forward to touch it, but Hassani stopped him. Having come this far, it would be a shame to be blown up now, on account of the 'boy's carelessness. Hassani walked round it slowly, making a very careful examination. He saw the work that had to done to make it worthy of Allah's glorious design. But he had been briefed well by his Russian instructors and knew his field well. He would be a worthy executive of Allah's omnipotent will.

They brought the material in from the van and Hassani got to work, while Rasheed stood watch inside the partially closed doors, making sure nobody walked in on them unexpectedly. Rasheed was a little disappointed at the need for this precautionary measure on Hassani's orders. Since Hassani had given him his gun back, Rasheed wanted a chance to shoot some white bastard dead.

Tired of his servile role as lookout, especially when there was nothing to 'look at', Rasheed wandered in to bend down and look over Hassani's shoulder to see what he was doing. 'Get back to the door,' Hassani said sharply without taking his eyes off the delicate wiring in his fingers. Just as Rasheed was returning to the door, Hassani cried out again urgently. 'Come over here. *Quickly!*'

'Make up your bloody mind, will you!'

But Hassani had neither a second to spare for arguing, nor a millimetre's space to spare for movement. He was frozen, holding the vital components that could cause nuclear fission if he moved wrongly. 'Shut up and give me a hand! I need you to hold that little connector rod that's slipping out of that tube there. Can you see it?'

'Where?'

'There, beside the wire where the plate has come away. See it?'

'I see it now.' Rasheed reached out.

'No! Wait! You mustn't let it touch the filament that's beside it in the second compartment -- the one on the right side. Move it slowly back into the tube and fasten it carefully with that clip inside the tube. Make sure it's fastened securely with the clip, or it will swing round and touch that filament.'

'And what happens if I don't?'

The thought of them going up in a flash, annihilating millions of infidel Christians, and so satisfying Allah, would have pleased a suicide bomber. But Hassani saw his scientific skill and knowledge as too valuable an asset to the cause, to be used up like that. His expertise would be needed many more times after this until the Jihadi crusade was fulfilled. 'Just do it!' Quickly; we haven't all day!' Hassani watched the 'boy' secure the rod safely. 'Good. Now just pass me those pliers. No, not those ones; the smaller ones --- beside the callipers. Good.' Hassani worked on quietly, while Rasheed looked on, rapt in awe at the other's calm handling of the bomb as if it were nothing more dangerous than a faulty laptop.

The tense silence and delicate fingerwork ceased at last, and Hassani sat back on his haunches to take an overall broad look at his handiwork. Rasheed judged that the job was done now. 'That's it, then, is it?' So where are we taking it, then? Buckingham Palace ? That would be a good target '

'It stays here.'

'You're kidding me! All this bother just to blow up a miserable dump like this? Rasheed looked around at the filthy walls. 'Who's going to give a damn of a shit if a crap dump like this goes up in smoke at the back of nowhere, eh? People won't even know it's gone off.'

'Oh, believe me, as you do in Allah, when this little creation sings, *everyone* will know of it.'

'*That* thing?' Rasheed looked around himself again. 'Do you really think so, with all these walls around us? I mean, those bridge supports are really massive. They'd take a lot of the blast and ----'

'By the power of Allah --- and a little help from Mr Fermi --- it will be done.'

'*Fermi*? Who's *he*?'

'He was the very man who first split the atom and so gave us the atom bomb. And from that subsequently came --- *voila*! -- the nuclear bomb.'

'You mean ---?' Amazement and shock registered on the 'boy's face. This changed into an internal whoopee realisation of glory at the thought of Hali Sateefi seeing him now, with this great beauty of a bomb, compared to his fucking great manly married brothers. Screw them, screw his dad and the business, and screw all the fucking white bastards who bought his shit-arsed stuff. Damn them all. Another realisation struck him and his mind came down to earth. There was a more sober tone to his voice. 'What about *us*? How do *we* escape the blast? Do we ----' Rasheed's unsettling thoughts of being a suicide bomber without first being asked were cut off by the dark place suddenly going darker. Without turning around, they both knew that someone was standing behind them, in the doorway. Rasheed opened his boiler suit to reach inside for his Beretta.

Hassani stopped him. 'Too much noise,' he whispered, standing up as the man came in.

'Hullo,' said the man. 'So you've taken over from the old bloke? Haven't seen him around here for ages. Reckoned he'd probably kicked the bucket. I'm from the lockup next door. Hassani smiled, with nothing he could think of to say at this unexpected interruption. The man walked over to look at the 'thing', outstanding as it was, in the dark space. 'So what's this contraption you're ----' Those were the last words his brain could manage, with the bolt croppers striking deep into it, mashing it with fragments of skull bone. Even though the man didn't move on the ground, Hassani struck him two more times just to make sure he was dead. Satisfied, he threw the heavy tool aside.

After taking a deep breath, Hassani looked around, making sure that all was well with their important work here completed, and set about gathering up their tools. 'Let's get these tools back in the van,' he said. We've another similar crucial assignment to carry out, about two hours drive from here. Come on, hurry up.'

When they had loaded all the equipment back into the van, Rasheed looked down at the corpse. 'What about him? Are you going to leave him lying there uncovered for someone to find?'

Hassani shook his head slowly, sighing with quiet exasperation at the naive stupidity of the 'boy'. 'Most surely it can only have been through the will of Allah that you were chosen to help me. Otherwise, I should haven chosen differently. *Most* differently! Have you not yet grasped the situation?' Hassani paused, to let his words, and their 'situation', sink into the other's dull brain. 'After tomorrow, there will be *no-one left* to find anything, and *nothing left to find.*'

20

13.52hrs, 25th June, Pershore, Worcs. There were two cars, instead of one, waiting for Sherman when his helicopter touched down on the Radar Establishment's airfield. One of them would be their transport, Sherman figured, but the other one looked like trouble. So what the hell was wrong now? The man stepped forward from the 'other' car and showed Sherman his security card. 'Olcroft. I'm in charge of security at the Establishment.'

'Sherman and Meeson,' said Sherman. Their turn to flash cards.

'A message came through for you on the teleprinter only seven minutes ago,' said Olcroft. 'It's in special code, so I guess it must be important. I thought it best to come and give it to you at the soonest moment, rather than wait for you to drive over to Malvern.' He handed the message over to Sherman.

'Thanks,' said Sherman. Opening up the crackling paper, he recognised the codename at the end as Hossley's, along with the coded letter assembly for Cambridge, but that was all. Everything else needed decoding. He looked up at the cars for a place to work and dithered over the choice.

'It's okay, I'll get rid of the other one,' said Olcroft.

Sherman got into the back seat, along with Meeson, and took out his small ciphers book, while the security officer started the car. They set off for the Establishment at nearby Malvern and Sherman set about translating the message and fearing the worst. Fears came nearer when the first words revealed that a man had been injured. When the next five letters showed themselves, Meeson was ahead of Sherman, pointing at them beginning to form: EXPLO -. 'Oh, God,' he said. Sherman's pimples began to prick. Sure enough, there had been an explosion and Sherman's mind raced over the worst vision. His mind slowed down again as the words DOOR, and after that, BLOWN OUT, emerged. So that was it. An Army man had been injured when an explosion had occurred on their 'affecting an entry onto the premises'. He smiled grimly at the careful choice of words, even in code, for 'broken in'. But he frowned at the rest of the message, in all its brevity. The heart of the matter, the transmitter, had not been mentioned, so presumably it had not been damaged in the explosion. Maybe a layman couldn't detect any effect of the explosion on the transmitter? Sherman thought over the dire situation, letting his imagination run riot for a second and then wished that the car could just sprout wings. He handed the paper to Meeson. 'What do you think?' he said. Meeson threw his eyebrows up, and with no more to say, they both turned to look at the man in front.

'Bad, is it?' said Olcroft into the rear mirror.

'We're not quite certain, yet. Let's hope your Senior Scientific Officer can give us some favourable answers.'

'Oh yes, Mr Springs, is it?'

'Yes, I believe so.'

'Hold on; we'll be there in a jiffy. Well, a few minutes, anyway.'

Sherman sat back and thought of their cloak and dagger dash through this quiet district, with its orchards and pastures, which had looked so lovely from the air; where the occasional noise was a bee buzzing between the neat click of the cricket ball on the bat, or the languid wooden handclap of the spectators, for the contortionist antics of the fielder with his 'duck' catch. Sherman hoped the scientists would have a much bigger catch waiting for his grateful applause.

They drew up outside the Radar Establishment. This was the largest centre for electronic research in the country, providing equipment and significant research developments to the armed services, as well as to industry. Olcroft turned round. 'Where is he seeing you? In hisoffice or in the laboratory?'

'I really haven't the faintest idea.' God, you're 'security', and you're asking me! Sherman cast a despairing glance at Meeson.

'We'll try the office first, I think,' said Olcroft.

'If you think it's best.'

The Senior Scientific Officer, E M Springs, according to the six inches of Formica on the door, was in his office, along with three of his Assistant Scientific Officers. That was three too many for Sherman, who wanted to get on with things. While he waited for the men to finish their discussion and be on their way, Sherman browsed over some of the titles on the shelf: Pyro-Electrics; Electro-Luminescence; Photon Correlation Spectroscopy; Micro-Electronics; Microwave Electronic Devices; Aerial and Microwave Circuitry. The last one looked as if it might contain something on the proposed plan that Blenning had mentioned earlier. Sherman reached out for it. His memory grated like a rusty gearbox at the simplest maxims of his early undergraduate lectures, so he shut the book again promptly. He heartened at the sight of the spectrometer on the side table and he went over and switched on its arc-lamp. Looking into the telescope, he swivelled it round until the familiar double yellow lines of the sodium emission spectrum appeared. Just like he remembered. If only everything was as easy as that.

Everything went quiet in the room and the man was standing over him. Sherman stood up straight and switched off the arc-lamp. 'It's a long time since I handled one of these.'

'Oh, so you're a scientist?' said Springs. 'That's good; you'll understand what I'm talking about, then.'

'Not for a long time,' said Sherman. 'But if I get stuck along the way, my colleague here will give me a nudge in the right direction. He's more qualified than I am for that.' He showed his MoD pass to Springs. 'My secretary phoned, to say we were coming.'

'Oh yes, someone mentioned it to me. We're terribly busy here, you'll understand, and any news from outside tends to reach us only as a draught through the keyhole, so to speak,' said Springs, leaning back against the bench, to adjust the pen in his top pocket.

'You do realise why we're here and the gravity of the situation?' said Sherman.

'Why yes, of course. As a matter of fact, we were just discussing, when you came in, the best way of jumping the next hurdle in the second phase of the project.'

Sherman wasn't sure if he liked the sound of that. *Second phase? Project?* He hadn't expected everyone to be sweating like galley slaves, but he had expected developments of a sort to be getting under full steam. 'You did say "*discuss*"? Is that *all* you're doing? Is nothing practical being done about it? You do realise, don't you, that we now have just under thirty-two and a half hours to remedy the situation? After that we'll really have to pick up the pieces to start again. Perhaps you don't realise that an explosion occurred on one of the transmitter locations less than half an hour ago? How does that strike you?'

The man stood up from the bench and put his finger to his lips pensively. 'An explosion? No, I honestly didn't know that. Was the transmitter totally destroyed? Because if it was ---' He trailed off.

'No, it wasn't, as far as we know, but what were you going to say?'

'Simply that it would have opened up the chasm of possibilities, not all of which would have necessarily been bad.'

'Go on, I'm listening.'

'Well, if these transmitters are sensitised to explode the bombs upon the least variation of their output frequency, then we have the worst to fear. On the other hand, if nothing has happened after one of them has exploded, as you say, then we could have overestimated their sensitivity.'

'There's logic there,' said Meeson. 'But we don't know if the transmitter itself was damaged. Only the location, as far as we know. But that's the question we're putting to you. Could the shock waves of an external explosion cause the transmitter to trigger off the bombs?'

Folding his arms and taking his chin in his hand, Springs walked away a few feet and then turned round. He sighed heavily. 'That's anybody's guess, really. There certainly hasn't been any dramatic change in the signals coming in, as far as we know. We're in constant touch with Buckingham and no noted change has been brought to our attention.'

'That's assuming that Buckingham is still there,' said Sherman.

Springs stopped short of insisting on logical grounds that Buckingham was still there when he realised that his leg was being pulled. 'Quite. I take your point. But for that same point, you'll appreciate our need to tread warily. The scientific problem itself is not so difficult, but the price we will have to pay for miscalculation will be tremendous, you will agree?'

'And if we do nothing, we *definitely* will pay a high price. So I say again, what are you doing about it?'

Springs stepped forward and held up his thumb. 'Look, it's like this. Imagine my thumb is the bomb. Now we attach three strings to it and fasten the other ends of the strings to those three walls. Right?'

'Right.'

'All right, so if I know move over to this fourth wall and, in fact, into that corner, then you can see how the strings will change their angles. Our task is to devise a receiver which can allow the bomb, my finger, that is, to be moved over into that corner, so to speak, without changing the angles of the strings, or radio signals, as they would, in fact, be. Do you follow?'

'You mean like a gyroscopic compass?' said Meeson.

'Yes, I suppose that's similar enough; yes, like a gyroscope.'

'And do you think you can manage to rig up these receivers in time for tomorrow?' said Meeson.

'With booby-traps at our finger tips and elbows, the progress is likely to be slow, but I think we can possibly manage. At least we're preparing the system's layout for our top specialist in this field, Tom Miles. He should arrive quite soon, I'm sure.'

'So where is he, then?' Sherman felt the pangs stab his stomach again.

'He's over in Europe at the moment, on ---'

'Europe! God Almighty!' Sherman put a hand to his forehead and spun away for a moment. He turned back again, subduing his anger on top of his fears. 'All this time and he's still in Europe? So why wasn't he brought here at first notice?'

'Yes, well, we're as frustrated as you are, Mr Sherman, but --'

'No-one's as frustrated as me, believe me, Springs! So can you tell me what the hell's going on?'

'As I was about to say, it couldn't have been done any quicker. Mr Miles has been over in Belgium for the last three weeks, inspecting the radar system for the NATO Air Defence Ground Environment, or NADGE. He went off on vacation from there just at the weekend. He went by car into Holland and that's why we couldn't notify him immediately at the onset yesterday. But your Intelligence people have been after him since yesterday and the last word we had is that he has been tracked down and is being flown in from Holland. From the Schiphol Airport in Amsterdam, I think.'

'I hope you're right, Mr Springs. I hope to God, you're right.' Sherman looked at Meeson for a second, then turned to look out the window, up at the sky. 'I suppose we can be thankful that the West is not plagued by locusts. There again, there's always ruddy Dutch storks to clog up the jet engine's air intake.' Sherman's cold joke hadn't just gone sour, but reflected the sickly feeling he now felt churning up his stomach. It was becoming all too familiar now in a recurrent pattern, as things continually went drastically wrong. He knew that he couldn't allow himself to be irrational, but nevertheless, he felt, no, he *knew*, that something was about to go wrong again.

21

13.48hrs (GMT), 25th June, Amsterdam. While Sherman fretted his nerves away, Dr Miles was at that very moment being driven to the city's Schiphol Airport, located at 13ft below sea level, between the city itself and Haarlem-en-Leyden. Amsterdam, with its ninety-six islands linked by three hundred quaint bridges in a glittering lacework of canals and glass boats, was a sparkling diamond, indeed, to the tourist's eye; but for the MI6 agent driving a government scientist to the airport on a deadline mission, the city was a nightmare. No matter where they turned, there was an octopus of a white-helmeted traffic policeman waving them down to let some wretched pedestrians cross in an endless tide while they waited forever. If this wasn't the case, then it was the tourist bus being too long to turn out of the bridge in one go, or it was the students frolicking with their placards, between the vehicles, across the squares. Whatever it was, it made the seconds tick by, as the MI6 woman tapped impatiently on the steering wheel. She had said in her last phone call that she would get Miles to the airport by two o'clock, but that didn't seem remotely possible now. Still, it was something to be grateful for that, with all the agents put into the field within the last twelve hours, they had managed to track down Dr Miles in his obscure holiday country cottage.

Dr Miles looked at the young woman driver beside him. With her fawn gabardine coat and her chocolate brown beret and shoulder bag, she looked more like a schoolteacher doing her 'classics' vacation. Even then, she was much nicer than the teachers he'd ever had at school. But the more Miles thought of it, the less he was able to fathom the reason for all the fuss. Apparently the Dutch police had been conducting a frantic search for him, and when they had finally located him in his backwater cottage, had politely insisted that he remained there until one of his own people came for him. Then he had received a message from the British Consul informing him that he was required back in England, on the gravest national urgency. The exact nature of this had not been clearly stated, since no-one at the Consulate knew what it was either. Miles had nevertheless been implored to not wander off, but to stay put in his cottage until he was collected. After that, the security woman had arrived.

Miles was used to being whipped off, as top electronics expert, to government installations in the UK and NATO countries. So he didn't mind his holiday being interrupted in this hectic manner. His work was a pleasure in itself, inspecting NADGE's new updated FLS-88 3D radar units and the improvised relays of the new Marconi 5277 height-finder radar systems. His satisfaction with the equipment made up for his annoyance in not having time to see it all. NADGE involved NATO's European members in a defensive umbrella stretching from the western shores through Norway, Denmark, Germany, Holland, Belgium, France, Italy and Greece, to the eastern frontier of Turkey, and comprised eighty-four sites, with thirty-four data processing complexes that interfaced with Britain's air defence network. The complexes had been the most important of Miles' work, with their multiple general purpose computers for analysis and distribution of target information from site sensors, and the correlation of data from other stations, received by data links and conventional communication channels. In all, NADGE was designed for air defence against aircraft flying at heights up to 100,000ft by the control of interceptor aircraft and surface-to-air missiles. The system didn't provide for the detection and countering of missiles, or low level sub radar threats. But that had not been Miles' concern.

Now he had this young thing by his side. He glanced at her ashen-blonde curls and her bronzed skin and reckoned that she was about twenty-five. When his wife had been that age, thirty years ago, she hadn't looked half as pretty. She glanced back at him for a second. To cover her own anxiety, she tried to butter him up with reassurance. 'Not to worry, Dr Miles, the plane is chartered, so it can't take off until we get there. Or should I say until *you* get there?'

'Won't you be coming along, then? Or do you just deliver the goods without handling them?' He patted her leg nervously and felt relieved when it didn't flinch away. His spirits soared.

She examined him again. He was really quite handsome for his age. Probably about the same age as her own dad. She felt herself clicking into the harmless flirting game. It was the easier thing to do to divert his mind, and stop him bombarding her with questions. She didn't know herself what this was all about. Only that all her Department's foreign assignments had been temporarily suspended, and that this operation was top priority, under the command of Major Broaley from MI5. She couldn't understand that bit especially -- MI5 telling MI6 what to do. But hers what not to question why, and all that blah blah. 'Oh yes, I'll be coming all the way, until you're delivered to the doorstep. So long as you're on board, the flight is complete. But I'm sure that you're used to all this VIP treatment the government lavishes on you, aren't you?' She glanced askant for his reaction.

His ego swelled him up like a mating spring frog. 'Yes, that's true, I am, but I'm sure you're not exactly without your own experiences. I can't believe that you really mean nobody cares if you come along or not. I wouldn't have it otherwise on a lonely chartered flight in an empty plane to England. And people usually take my judgment as fairly reliable.' With that, he settled back contented into his seat. 'What is it all about, anyway?' he suddenly blurted out. 'Or have they not said; as usual?' She didn't answer, and they left it at that.

As she painfully waited on the policeman trying his best to 'untie' the traffic knots, she became aware of a man coming from behind their car and looking in for a moment, before walking on. He went up to the policeman and spoke for several seconds. The policeman started instructing the cars in front to move up onto the pavements, to make room for them to pass. Her reflexes tensed as the man came back to their car, first knocking on her window, then opening the door. 'Get into the back, please,' the man said, in a quiet controlled voice that wasn't without its trace of authority. She saw the words: **Interpol: Inspecteur G C Facchini.** Her tension dropped. He put his warrant card away. 'We can get to the airport quicker if you let me drive.'

14.14hrs (GMT). They had arrived at the airport; the Interpol man was gone and the plane was ready for take-off. But she had to make a phone call before they went on board. She shut herself in the soft quiet of the glass and steel booth and picked up the phone. Watching the other air travellers ghost silently past, she waited for the operator to get through for her, on the London code and then a special nine digit code. Only a select few in London's official circles and an even smaller minority outside the city, knew the number. She was part of the smallest minority on the continent to know the number. The BT special codes circuits raced the call through miles of wire banks that were shrouded in the shadowed security of concrete government basements of the Overseas Communications and Signals Division. It got through at last, scrambled, to an office in Military Intelligence, Department 6. There was no pipping sound in the receiver. Only a sharp click and a calm female voice saying: 'Code?'

'Long Weekend, Chelsea,' she replied, following the security screening procedure.

'Transfer; one moment, please.' Another click, and another voice, male this time, spoke: '*Yes?*'

'Hullo, *HAROLD?*'

'Yes?'

'This is your cousin from Amsterdam speaking. I'm just calling to say that I'm bringing you that DUTCH LANTERN that you wanted ever so much.'

'Good. When is your flight?'

'I'm flying out now.'

'Very good. Have a safe journey.'

Having delivered the message, she didn't answer, but put the phone down and walked out.

14.19hrs (GMT). They boarded the plane and she searched it. There was no-one else on board but the pilot, co-pilot and steward. Seat belts were fastened.

14.24hrs (GMT). They took off and circled round to head out for England. With their seat belts off, they looked around. When the steward passed down the aisle, he gave her a funny look that unsettled her. But she couldn't think why and so she let it go.

Miles looked at her across the passage, deciding that the gap was too wide to cross with any flirtatious chatter that he could possibly think up. He turned his mind to his own familiar field and fancied a read at the scientific journal in his briefcase. As he reached over for the briefcase, it suddenly lurched off the seat onto the floor, and he was thrown back against his seat as the plane banked over to one side. 'What on earth!'

When the plane levelled out again, they looked out the porthole to see the grey blanket that was England sliding away behind them. They had turned off on a new course. 'Why are we changing course?' said Miles. But she didn't know. Primitive alarm signals started flashing in her brain and she jumped up to go to the flight cabin. Her way was suddenly blocked by the steward. But for the guise of the immaculate white steward's jacket, his aggressive expression should have told her what she should have known all along. But it was the ugly Chinese semi-automatic pistol growing out of his hand that made that clear enough. Her pupils dilated with fear.

'Hijack.' The curt statement wasn't really necessary.

Miles was stupefied and she wavered between fear and indecision. The 'steward' saw her hesitance as unwanted mischief and jerked up the pistol fiercely. She saw the hardened look in his eyes and her own eyes flew to her handbag on the seat. Her revolver was in it. Just as her hand moved out slowly for it, the huge muzzle exploded, renting their eardrums and sending her crashing back. Miles clasped his face where red splinters from the seat-back showered him. Only when his terrified brain noticed that the red upholstery was unscratched, did his eyes fall on the horridly jagged bone structure that she was clutching at her bloody wrist. He realised that the red 'splinters' were bone fragments of her hand. The electric shock surged through his chest and he felt his stomach catapult up violently into his mouth, choking him with vomit, as he gulped back the burning acid.

She stared at her mangled hand, where only the thumb and half a finger were left. She swayed back against the seat, while Miles flopped back in his own seat, under the prod of the hijacker's gun. Her hard grip seemed to do little good, as the blood welled out rapidly and her face drained paler. She sagged down onto the floor with her eyes closed, trying to catch her breath in dire gasps that never seemed enough when they came. He wanted to help her but couldn't, because of the steel clamp pains in his chest. When Miles looked up, he saw the 'steward' speaking to his fellow hijacker, the 'co-pilot', who had come to see what the noise was about. Miles wanted to tell them that the woman was losing blood badly, but the pain in his chest was too much. She tried, hopelessly, to make a tourniquet with her scarf and comb, but her concentration was interrupted by the bated sobs that she came to realise were coming from herself, breaking through her original composure. The 'steward' kicked her bag down the aisle, then knelt down to apply a proper tourniquet with a wine glass cloth from the galley. He tied another over the jagged mess that was her hand.

Settling into the aftermath of delayed shock, Miles felt the nausea rise slowly up his front and the darkness close in around his eyes, so that the last thing he saw before passing out, was the wine cloth round her hand darkening with its own rich 'claret'.

The hijackers were not Muslims, but FSB influence and money was sufficient persuasion for them to mount this operation. Not only did they deliver a plane for the jihadi cause, but they thwarted a major attempt by the British to save their country from nuclear devastation.

22

15.31hrs, 25th June, Whitehall SW1. 'It's landed in Iran,' said Sherman, dropping the phone heavily in its rest, while fighting down the anger burning inside him. He could almost feel the floor opening up beneath him in his dismay, with this latest disaster. It was really hard to understand why the gods were ganging up on them like this and throwing another dirty trick in their faces.

'So at long last, we finally know where the plane is,' said Sir Richard, not turning away from his window view of the military convey hurrying along on its winding way, below. 'And we're supposed to believe it was independent hijackers?'

'So we're being told by the media.' Sherman stared at the telephone, as if it was to blame, shaking his head slowly with lingering disbelief. He was really appalled at the devilish turn of events. To think they had almost had a part solution in the palm of their hands; and now it had been spirited out of their grasp once again. Of all the planes and all the mad zealots operating independently in the sky, the hijackers just had to pick that time and that plane for their damn joyride. Who are you kidding? It was too incredible an astronomical freak of chance to have been ill luck. No, Moscow was behind this. It was their ideal way of pulling strings far from the field, and so avert blame for any disruptions they subsequently caused in the field. Television and newspapers, in their ignorance, would state otherwise; no doubt Osama Bin Laden would also put in his claim for a prize teddy bear for his part in directing this great coup against the imperialist West. But you could stake your money on the sure bet that it was the FSB who had pulled the carpet out from under their feet.

Sir Richard came away from the window. 'So at least our little domestic crisis still remains our very own privileged secret. Needless to say they'll be negotiating for the usual release of sympathetic prisoners. He's all right, isn't he? Dr Miles?'

'Not sure. Details are scant and slow in coming out. A bit shaken up, so I gather, but still in one piece. So is the pilot, as well. But our agent escort was injured. Shot, it seems. We don't know how badly. No-one has said yet how it happened, exactly. No-one has been allowed near the plane, except the medical team, so stories are still thin on the ground. It was a woman, incidentally, that was wounded.'

'Was she new to the job?'

'I don't know. I'm sure someone can tell us,' said Sherman, reaching for the phone.

'No, don't bother,' said Sir Richard, waving his hand. 'There's a lot more than that they're going to have to tell us, but it can wait until later. How, for instance, it could have been allowed to happen in the first place. Didn't the woman have the sense to search the plane? I mean *really* search the plane, and not just a perfunctory glance?'

'What the mind doesn't conceive, the eye doesn't *see*? said Sherman, tapping his pencil on the intercom. 'They must have played the part well. Probably disguised as aircrew. Fool one, fool all.'

'That may well be, for people like us, but it should never apply to a field agent. And all the less so to the commander in charge of operations. Someone's got a lot to answer for. I'll see to that personally. Whatever the explanation, it still remains that Dr Miles is over in there, when he should be here, helping us, and God knows, we need the help.'

Sherman wasn't sure if he like Old Hossley's classification of 'people like us', and the very implication niggled him into considering doing some more leg work. Besides, they would be lucky to feed a budgie with the meagre information they'd collected so far. He remembered his deal with Monks earlier and saw his desk as a big lump, with himself stoppered behind it. 'They did say it wasn't entirely impossible to complete the project without Miles.'

'No, but slower, and that could mean the difference between the Lord's Prayer and the Lord coming to answer it Himself, on Doomsday, Sunday.' With that remark, Sir Richard had mounted the peak of his brief snapping mood and could only simmer down again. He pulled down his waistcoat and began rolling his sleeves down, in automatic reflex, to resume his usual diplomatic self, while contemplating on the diplomatic difficulties confronting the British Embassy in Iran. 'It's going to be difficult, have no doubts on that. With the frequency of these attacks ever increasing, most countries have resorted to resolute policies of refusing to negotiate on any terms with terrorists. Not many will take kindly to our demanding a possible exchange for only two people, both of them Britons, at that. If our ambassador can pull this one off, I'll drive him to the Palace, myself, for his OBE.' Hossley pondered for a moment over one uncertain point, and looked to Sherman for a similar opinion. 'We are agreed, are we, that we can't send in the SAS to get Miles out?'

Sherman shook his head. 'Too much of a risk. It would only take a stray -- or *deliberate* -- bullet and that would be the end of Miles and our possible end.'

'Unless, of course, we can get Lindsdale.'

'Yes, unless we can get Linsdale.' Sherman frowned as his mind bounded down another avenue of possible solution to the problem. 'I wonder if Linsdale is religious?' It was usually the case that extremists of Linsdale's genre had some religious seed at the centre of theirmania. Whatever it was, the psychologists were working on it now, in the Psychological Warfare Department. But to pinch that seed, they first had to get at it. This aspect was a double-headed barb in the flesh. It was imperative that they tracked down not only Linsdale, but also the Jihadi element involved. According to MI6 reports from foreign sources, a Jihadi operation was currently underway in the country. Its objective was to contact Linsdale and take over from him blowing the place to pieces. But which one should they track down, that was the question. If the Muslim zealots were killed in conflict, that still left the bombs 'ticking'. If they were captured alive, they were unlikely to stop the bombs for the sake of their own lives. Rather, they would see it as self glorification by Allah's will to be literally blasted into that next kingdom. Linsdale, on the other hand, would surely want to save his own skin. So he was the one who had to be found. Sherman sat up and looked down at his desk. He just grabbed what was important off the top and dumped it all, none too meticulously, in the safe. After tomorrow, who cared how disorderly they were?

Hossley was standing over the phone, dialling. 'Hullo, I need you to put me through to our Embassy in Iran. -- Sir Richard from Intelligence -- Yes, I appreciate that it is somewhat out of the ordinary, but this is urgent; I haven't the time to follow the standard protocol for foreign communication procedures -- Yes, I'll wait, but do try and hurry it up; it is most urgent.' Sir Richard tapped on the desk while he waited and looked at Sherman. 'I believe you mentioned something about sending your wife and son to Italy, out of the way, did you not?'

'Yes, that's right. They fly out this afternoon.'

'And your father?'

'No, I doubt if he'd go, even if I explained.'

'Quite, quite.' Sir Richard stopped tapping and lifted his hand to signal Sherman that his attention was back on the phone. 'Hullo, Anthony, Dickie Hossley here, -- No, it's nothing to do with that. As a matter of fact, it's to do with a more recent development. I'm sure that it'll have reached you by now, that one of our chartered planes has been hijacked, to land in your patch, with one of our important scientists on board. -- No, not Linsdale. This is a Dr Miles. But since you mentioned Linsdale, I'm sure you'll appreciate the crucial nature of the situation, if I say it's to do with him. Sorry I can't expand on that, even over this 'safe' line. The task can't be an easy one for you, Anthony, I agree, with such delicate grounds to tread on, but if you can impress upon the Minister the urgency of peaceful settlement over this very sensitive issue, Anthony, you may well save your country from a black day.' Sherman listened in on his half of the deepening conversation, the diplomatic daggers sharpening to a greater keenness, then re-sheathed for political correctness. 'You *will*? That's splendid, Anthony. We really do need this man back as soon as possible. -- Splendid. We may yet all sleep sound in our beds tonight. -- No, I don't think I'll be going to the country this weekend. Rather, I think I'll be spending the time at my club. -- *Hiding something?* Whatever makes you say I'm hiding something? As it happens, I'm a bit concerned at this Linsdale fellow playing truant, and that's my reason for staying in town over the weekend. We still have several loose ends to to tie up, but there's no need to bore everyone with those details, Anthony. If you like, you could just say I'm an old miser for the petrol money.' Hossley laughed with his mechanical promptness and an icy smile, while checking the time on his golden hunter. 'Yes, goodbye.'

But Sherman couldn't help questioning the validity of what Hossley was trying to do. After going to all the bother of abducting Miles, would the Iranians release him that easily? Would they release him at *all*? Would Moscow *let* them release him? It was unlikely. But you had to give points to Old Hossley for trying. He waited in the doorway for Sir Richard to put the phone down and come away, so that he could lock the door behind them, and be off somewhere else. 'I've something in the pipeline,' he said noncommittally to Sir Richard's enquiring look. He was referring, of course, to his deal with Monks over the low key exchange of the Skyhawk missile plans for Linsdale.

'Really?' Hossley plainly wanted to be filled in with more details.

'With everything falling down around us, I don't think it's too soon to spy out the enemy camp and see how the spit is turning over their fire. There could be room for bargaining.'

'And do we have something to bargain with?'

'I think *we* have. But it's whether or not *they* have, that worries me.'

23

15.59hrs, 25th June, Highgate N6. Sherman entered the Russian Trade Delegation building with just a little unease in his mind. Although he would be negotiating for an exchange for Dr Linsdale, he hoped to high heaven that it would look as if it was the other way about, with the Russians making the initial plea. Monks had played his part with his own Intelligence network, circulating whispers of a secret leak, so that the FSB had been quick to raise its head and snap at the bait. A meeting had been called for and Sherman had let them suggest that they have it here. There was some wisdom in coming here, instead of going to the Embassy. Of that, he was sure. It wasn't only because his diplomatic prowess was of a lesser eclat than Hossley's, but also because the indirect approach was less cap in hand. This method of begging bred less suspicion on the beggar and brought down the price of the 'goods'. Moreover, if there were any devious deals to be made, they were made more easily outside the solid bastions of respectability that embassies were supposed to be.

What made Sherman bristle with guilt was the critical time factor and Linsdale himself. Linsdale wasn't exactly the usual brand of character they used as 'currency' in these swaps, so that the very idea of negotiating for him could arouse unwanted curiosity. For those not in the know, that is. Sherman tried to convince himself that this was his nervous imagination playing up on him, and hoped that it didn't show on the outside.

The man went on writing in his ledger, without any apparent awareness of Sherman having entered the room. Sherman sat down opposite Daniloff and watched the figures, dark and thick like their writer, being entered across the page. The man's russet hounds-tooth check jacket and summer brown tie were on a softer line than the army uniform they had replaced, but he didn't seem to mind and had adapted well to his desk job, in punitive exile from his native Moscow. Intelligence reports suggested that he was the real Charge d' Affaires behind the Ambassador. But he liked to act otherwise, making a point of not always sculpturing his words precisely to give the eloquent dialectic abstractions that intellectual diplomats all too often loved to bathe themselves in.

'I won't keep you waiting much longer, Mr Sherman. If you'll bear with me just another few moments,' he said, as he wrote on.

'Take your time; I'm in no hurry,' said Sherman, playing the game, for game it was,with both of them weighing the other up for anxiety and urgency.

Between spasms of cursive writing, Daniloff's fingers danced over the adding machine's buttons and the raw answers swiftly transformed to a state fit for the records. Good solid profit. Writing as he did, with his head full of figures, he still found room for a sideline issue to unnerve the Englishman. 'Indigestion problems can certainly be a nuisance. I know; I've had them myself. Usually a sign of stress, from overwork.' That sly remark was supposed to daunt Sherman with the fact that they heard and knew everything.

'Yes, it's always the same in summer, with longer daytime to hand; stretching eating habits round the clock, and grabbing bites at irregular hours,' replied Sherman, playing nonchalant. He paused, then thrust in his own riposte. 'I hope Mrs Daniloff has got over her pains? It was difficult, I hear?'

Touche! 'Yes, Helga's fine now, thank you. We were all a little concerned with the delivery to begin with, but she managed splendidly. Gave us both a fine little son. Nine pounds, eight ounces. Dark and handsome like his father.' He looked up and beamed. 'Nearly there, if you'll hold on just another second. Finished. I'm really sorry to keep you waiting like this. It's an incumbent chore that goes with the desk and chair.'

'Yes, I know the feeling.'

Daniloff laughed and Sherman played along with an empty laugh of his own. Finishing off the last few lines, Daniloff then slammed the book shut and put it away on top of the wooden cupboard. He looked at Sherman and then at his own cold coffee in the demitasse that could have fitted as a thimble on one of his massive fingers. He pointed to the tiny cup but Sherman shook his head. Pulling a drawer open, Daniloff took out an orange and proffered that in turn.

'No, thanks,' said Sherman, eyeing the bright fruit imprisoned behind the stockade of thick fingers, and noting the familiar purple stamp on its skin. 'Jaffa, I notice,' he said with subtle innuendo.

Daniloff laughed at Sherman's neat insinuation of Jewish oppression, and sat back,

expanding into the large man that he was, without being oversize and bullnecked in the cartoonist's traditional caricature of Ivan. It was easy to see how he had been a nuisance in Moscow's hierarchy, with his handsome features making him a rage among the women --especially those who had geriatrics with one foot in the grave for husbands. 'Never let it be said that we're anti-Semitic or anti-anything, for that matter.' Trapping the orange in his palm, he gouged it through the centre with the other thumb, breaking it into two halves without any juice being spilled. 'As a matter of fact, I have an uncle on my father's side, who makes a point of attending the Orthodox mass on regular dates. That's if he's not getting young girls on the farm into trouble.' They both laughed out their bluff once again and the metal bin in the corner joined in the noise with a hollow clang as the orange peel landed in it.

Their initial remarks on the exchange deal were just as hollow and both of them sensed that the other was just circling round what was really wanted. Like bears edging round a pit of pointed stakes, perhaps. Although Daniloff spoke in perfect English, Sherman could still see the tiny wheels in his mind turning round in a foreign tongue. That was where the printing works really differed, not only in their Cyrillic characters, but in complete ideologies. You could knock a 'Wall' or two down, but old ideas in old minds stayed the same on opposite sides of that 'Wall'. At the same time, he could feel Daniloff's eyes trying to read right through him.

Daniloff studied Sherman with weighted speculation, his eyes twinkling like broken glass and with just as much cutting power. Sherman couldn't help feeling that they were scratching the surface off his cover line. Daniloff pushed in another succulent crescent of orange between his lips to add flavour, before speaking. 'Was it Galileo or Aristotle, who said that given a long enough lever, one could lift up the world?'

'If I remember correctly, it was Archimedes.' Sherman pricked his senses in readiness for whatever it was the Russian was hatching. 'But it's not really that name or even that end of the lever we're thinking about, is it?' Whatever was going on in the Russian's mind, Sherman felt that the baited hook that he'd expected to pull in with the secrets leak, just wasn't working. Whatever he said, whatever he played ear to, Sherman could see that Daniloff wasn't baited so easily.

'Precisely. You catch my meaning well.' The Russian smiled and stretched right back, inclining his head to one side, so that he could study Sherman from a new relaxed angle. 'You're right. We're not so concerned with that end of the lever. What we should ascertain is whose back the lever is being put across, and what precious little stone is being prised up by the lever. Do you agree?' He spat out the pips into his hand, waiting. Daniloff wanted to play ball, it seemed, but something was keeping him back. He wanted the secrets sure enough, but he didn't want to come forward and finalise the deal. All this he betrayed in his wavering questions, while continually plucking away at his lower lip for particles of orange that weren't there.

'Yes, that's the general idea,' said Sherman, waiting for Daniloff to come to the climax he had up his sleeve.

But Daniloff simply dallied pensively with the pips in his palm. He looked up from his pips at Sherman. 'Back in my country there is an old folk remedy used by the peasants, for extracting fish bones or other things stuck in the throat. It involves the warming of a candle until the end is soft, and inserting it down the person's throat. When the candle has hardened again, it is withdrawn and the bone, or whatever is lodged in the throat, comes out with it. Interesting, wouldn't you say.?'

'Yes, very interesting. Poignant, I'd say.'

'Yes, but outdated. We're civilised now and shouldn't need to resort to such means for clearing the throat. *Yes?*'

Sherman could feel his own throat drying up and eyed the bottle of wine on the cabinet, relishing a mouthful. As the minutes had gone by, both had haggled with possible exchange names, knocking them back and forth like ping pong balls. 'All right, then; all right,' Sherman said, almost letting his patience slip for a moment, with his mounting anxiety. 'So do we go ahead with the exchange? Your Kharvensky and Anatolov for our Linsdale?'

'Kharvensky and Anatolov? And to balance the scales: Dr Linsdale? The match is a most peculiar one. But interesting, I must admit.' Daniloff now leaned forward, with his elbows on the desk and his chin on his knuckles. His smile hadn't gone, but he was now seriously using his thinking cap. 'But why those three? And why should you release two of ours for only your one Linsdale?'

'Don't you want Kharvensky back, then? He was your whole hue and cry ten months ago.'

'The point is surely that, whereas you wouldn't release him to our hue and cry ten months ago, now you say you *will*. Why? Or perhaps we should ask why you so dearly wish to have Linsdale back? That is our precious little 'stone', is it not? To be prised like the pearl from the oyster?'

Sherman didn't reply, but listened instead, to the telephone screaming out in the next room. Daniloff threw his pips in the bin while he listened. A low voice in the next room spoke: 'Alo? -- Shto piridat? -- Adnu minuta.' (Hullo? - Can I take a message? - Just a minute) There was a click as someone put through the extension, and the phone came alive on Daniloff's desk. He glanced, annoyed, at the sideroom door and picked up the phone. 'Alo? -- Fchyom dyela? --Ya ni znayu -- Shto eta znachit? -- Nyet, nichive.' (Hullo? - What's the problem? - I don't know - What does that mean? - No, nothing.) Daniloff shifted with irritation, turning away slightly, while listening on into the phone. In spite of his hard features, the embarrassment still showed through at his having this very call, with Sherman there in front of him. Sherman sensed that the call was about him or his people. Daniloff sensed that he sensed this, so that the air was as thick as the desk between them. Daniloff kept his eyes on Sherman as he listened, while his eyebrows did the occasional Cossack dance where news reaching him was puzzling. He put the phone down and thought for a moment, before his mind came back into the room and to the British Intelligence officer in front of him. 'Sorry about that,' he said, resuming his easy cheerful smile. 'But alas, no, to be perfectly frank, we cannot negotiate with you at this time for an exchange for Linsdale for the simple reason that we don't know where he is.' Daniloff's voice had a curt edge on it now to end the parley, where his mind had been made up by the phone call. 'Perhaps we should delay the matter for forty-eight hours?'

The question was loaded and Sherman knew it. That deliberate forty-eight hours was to sound him out and see if he could afford to wait that long, or else shed his feathers in a frantic flutter. 'Fair enough, then. Let's leave it at that. Forty-eight hours from now.' Sherman felt no other option but to play along and keep face, not fully sure if Daniloff had been wholly truthful. The situation was crushing in its finality. From here to where, he didn't know, with the bottomless pit opening up beneath him at the moment. First they had lost Miles, and now they couldn't pull off the exchange deal that had nourished a fair degree of hope. The chair clung jealously to Sherman's trouser leg when he got up, releasing its greedy grip on a thread only after making him feel inept, just like the flopped deal had done.

Daniloff took the wine bottle down from the cabinet and clinked out the yellow seed wine into two glasses. 'It is also a custom of our ancient steppe lands that a traveller is not allowed to depart from beneath the roof of his host without taking the sweat of that soil between his lips .' He held up his glass. 'Na zdarovye!'

'Yeah, cheers -- Na zdarovye!' said Sherman mechanically in his dejected spirit, throwing back the wine, hardly savouring a drop.

Daniloff had been truthful and didn't know where the British defector, Linsdale was. But since the British were so anxious to find him, then so were they endeavouring to track him down themselves. The call had been a field report from their agents on the trail of British agents, on the trail pf their sleeper agents who had gone to ground with Linsdale. What was puzzling Daniloff wasn't the negative run down of the report, but the whisper of a rumour of some urgent deadline that the British had for the twenty-sixth. As Sherman went out, Daniloff called out to his secretary in the next room: 'Kakoye sivodnya chislo?'

Sherman appeared back in the doorway. 'Today's the twenty-fifth,' he said, answering Daniloff's question. It also let Daniloff know that he had understood what he was saying on the phone.

16.21hrs, Whitehall. Sir Richard looked at the general pushing the tiny tank across the large table map and reflected that he bore a faint resemblance to his son, Harry, who would have been about the same age now, had he not been killed on active service in Iraq. But that was as ancient as it was morbid, and about as useful as a free duodenal ulcer on the National Health Service. He shook the thought from his mind and made an effort to concentrate on what the general was saying to those round the table. In rooms all over the globe, men were bent intently over their tables, studying their maps, pushing their tiny tanks. While the Kremlin continued to wonder, Whitehall continued to worry and the Pentagon continued to whistle through its teeth. Russian troops were building up towards the Western borders in massive in land manoeuvres, while Chinese troops shuffled slowly towards the Russian border. Bolder air manoeuvres saw the giant Swallow bomber cast aside its top secret cloak to fly out from its Moscow military air base on flights 'straying' further and further into Western air territory. Flying with these, in greater number, were the great Tupolev TU bombers, scraping the sky with their 164ft wings, like clouds of locusts gathering for a final colossal gorge.

24

16.32hrs, 25th June, Embankment Gardens SW3. Charlie Penrose thought it was all a great farce, and bellowed out his Laughing Policeman's eternal tinny mirth from the transistor radio carried along somewhere in the general stream of passers-by. Broaley didn't share his mirth and cursed as he continually dodged around people in his way, while keeping track of his prey. The man was some yards ahead and didn't seem aware, so far, that Broaley was tailing him. Between him and Broaley was a third man, Broaley's decoy. This man followed without caution, taking the whole of the prey's attention and so shielding Broaley. All the while the policeman tenor in the concert stand continued with his splendid operatic rendering from Puccini's Madam Butterfly, which they sadly ignored. The trio filtered through the standing audience, towards the gate leading into Villiers Street. To pass through the crowd like this was a good thing if you were tailing someone, but it was a pest if you weren't sure if you were being tailed yourself.

The prey wanted to check just this, and the billiard ball scattering of people through the crowd made this awkward. He decided to employ the natural tactics of sharp turns that good old-fashioned street corners and gates readily provided. That way, you could tell if two people were going the same way, without being together or without being pals; just like a fly-paper with its dirty flies. Broaley was ready for this trick and 'coughed' into his cupped hand. Some heads turned at this disturbance, while at the same time a woman alighted from a car in Villiers Street, at the Major's radio directions. It was the same car that the Major had left a few streets back and had been moving round to that position under his directions. While they had moved in a certain direction across the Gardens, Broaley had 'coughed' every so often into the radio microphone, ordering the car to curve round to where they seemed to be going.

Broaley watched the man in his T-shirt turn left through the gate, towards Embankment Place. He 'coughed' once more into the microphone: 'T-shirt left; Embankment.'

'Got you,' said the insect voice in his 'hearing aid'.

The woman was taking over behind the decoy and so Broaley relaxed his pace to make an inconspicuous exit through the gate. When he went through, she was just ahead, clipping along in Scholl wooden sandals and carrying a Chelsea Boutique bag. T-shirt and the decoy were further down the street and didn't seem to be connected with them. T-shirt looked into the back surface of his spectacle lenses, beside the oasis of palm trees and springs that was the enlarged reflection of his eyelashes. Sure enough, the decoy's figure bobbed up and down behind him, in the same blue shirt and corduroy trousers, with the same obvious motive of dogging him. They both carried on, unconnected with each other, except by their inner mental threads, until the Charing Cross Underground station swallowed them up, one after the other. T-shirt took his ticket and joined the biggest crowd he could see, milling around like sheep behind the pen gates and poking in their bright yellow tickets, in some government sponsored quarantine. He was surprised to see his tail not waiting for him, but going off to Platform 6, apparently unconcerned.

The tail had gone off at the woman's signal, so that she could take over. If he had stayed on, T-shirt would have simply played the game and led them on a wild goose chase. But now that T-shirt thought that he had shaken off his tail, he could possibly lead them to somewhere worthwhile. T-shirt was relieved all right, but not before shaking off his natural suspicions. He looked back more than once, on his downward winding way to the Northern Line on Platform 1, before being convinced that he was not being followed and that his fears were imaginary.

Even so, imaginary or not, the reflexes were hard to keep down and he made a check of all those drifting onto the platform behind him. Two business men with brief-cases; a mother carrying her child; a woman in Scholl wooden sandals carrying a polythene Boutique bag; and two hairy youths in decadent denims that clung to their bodies like leper skins. They would probably stink like lepers if they came any closer. But nobody came any closer and everybody was minding their own business. The rest of the crowd had already been on the platform before him and so couldn't possibly harbour a tail. His rational mind no sooner said this, than his nervous mind made a sweeping check of everyone standing there. Negative. He was reassured once more and gave up checking those already there or those coming in.

Broaley kept out of sight round the archway leading onto the platform. He was of two minds whether or not to nab the bloke. If they didn't pounce on him now, there was the possibility that they would lose him. On the other hand, if they grabbed him and beat the information out of his skull, it could maybe cost them hours. Better that they followed him, Broaley decided, for what could possibly only be a few minutes more. All stood there silently, like sacrificial mutes on the giant altar stone, their minds reciting the sacred scripts of the torn posters in a subterranean ritual that was peculiar to the Underground traveller.

T-shirt nearly jumped with nerves as someone spoke beside him. 'Got fifty pence?' said the old man in rag-style clothing. A destitute vagrant. T-shirt took a second to absorb the question through his surprise.

'No,' he said, and the old man ambled off along the platform edge, to annoy someone else and to worry some others with his closeness to the edge. The negro with the Goodyear tyre face and immaculate white collar pulled his little boy away gently from a dirty toffee wrapper on the ground. 'Leave it, son,' he said in a low voice. 'It's dirty.' Beside him, a 'civilised' old vagrant swooped down on a rotting half apple and tested it with his lips. He put it away in his pocket, pleased with his cunning. It would be a long time yet, before the black man became refined enough like the 'civilised' white man, to appreciate such delicacies.

Still no train. Some people swayed and twisted as they waited. The business man looked in his briefcase. The mother patted her child's back. The woman with the Boutique bag felt about inside it. There was nothing in the bag but paper stuffing, but only she knew that. It was all part of her camouflage for surveillance duties. She felt T-shirt's suspicious look coming her way so she turned away, to look at the poster featuring the porcelain exhibition at the Victoria and Albert Museum.

People stirred and papers flapped, as the wind blew in from the tunnel and the giant glow-worm moaned and slid out of the big hole, alongside the platform. T-shirt got on and stood in the empty space by the door. Only the mother and child and the woman with the Boutique bag were with him from his lot, he noticed. They didn't appear to notice him. But it was a common characteristic of the Tube, that people became potentially anything, locked away behind the insular privacy of their minds. So it was pick or choose for plumber or policeman. Broaley stepped through the central door of the adjacent carriage and watched T-shirt through the transparent panels of the adjoining doors. He now had T-shirt between him and the woman.

Everyone held on and they moved off. The worm tunnelled through the city, leaving the Strand, Leicester Square and Tottenham Court Road stations behind. T-shirt noted that the two women were still with him. He moved his head to let a man open his newspaper, and his eye caught the name Linsdale near the foot of the page ----QUESTION IS, HAS BOFFIN LINSDALE FLOWN THE NEST TO ---. T-shirt forgot himself and bent closer to read on. The paper suddenly ruffled itself and eyes loomed up over its top. T-shirt straightened up and looked away, feeling guilty at breaking the Englishman's Eleventh Commandment. Never read another person's paper on the public transport. Be it peace or war, the Englishman was never at variance with this indefatigable maxim that was the creed of all cloths. The ravens could well fly from the Tower, and the Thames could dry up, but an Englishman never read another person's paper on the Tube. Their instructors at the Marx/Engels spy school hadn't included that in the rigorous training programme. T-shirt turned towards the glass panel and caught the reflection of the woman with the Boutique bag watching him just before she whipped her eyes away. It could mean nothing, of course, but his hand still went straight to his back pocket, to feel the outline of the flick knife.

Euston. The doors slid open and everyone squeezed out like parasites from the worm's shiny silver side. T-shirt stepped off behind the crowd. The woman with the Boutique bag got off as well. She dithered about and seemed to be looking for her bearings. He turned to jump on again, just as the doors were hissing shut. Broaley had expected the move and had stayed on the train, waiting for T-shirt. Before T-shirt could get between the doors, an arm shot out on the platform and stopped him. 'Hi, there,' said the tall man in the moleskin suit. 'My name's Monks. I'm American. I'm from Illinois. I'm a tourist here.' Broaley fumed with rage at the interfering American, as the train accelerated along the platform, carrying him away, to block off his view of Monks and T-shirt with the blackness of the tunnel.

T-shirt was flummoxed by the noisy onset of the American and his mind could only register annoyance after the initial confusion. Monks made up for T-shirt's ill-mannered silence with another outburst. 'Gee, but isn't this a swell little town you have here. Isn't it just a swell town. I'm absolutely gone overboard with it. Right whackoo, overboard. You know what I mean?' He prodded T-shirt on the shoulder to emphasize his meaning.

T-shirt tried to crack a smile. 'Sure. I hope you have a good time,' he said and stepped round the stupid loud-mouth, anxious to get away.

Monks grabbed him by the arm and held him back. 'Say, don't let me keep you back, pal, but isn't there a plaque, commemorating one of your great writer guys, near here? Dickie or somebody?'

'You mean *Dickens*?'

'Yeah, sure, Dickie; that's the guy.'

'Sorry. I don't know,' said T-shirt, moving away again.

Monks caught him again, and still smiling, playfully pushed him hard against the wall, like the cat with its doomed mouse. 'Say, but isn't that just like you swell Brits, with your modesty. Always pretending you don't know, when you do, huh?' Walking beside T-shirt, Monks then bounced him against the wall like a rubber ball every time he tried to get away, so that the message became plain. Just to reinforce the message, Monks' eyes glinted through the cheery expression for a second. But only for a second. Otherwise, he was absurdly waggish so as to confound the man. When the knife materialised in T-shirt's hand, Monks suddenly wanted a handshake and 'accidentally' wrenched the man's hand round in a joint-cracking twist. The knife clattered clumsily to the ground and Monks 'accidentally' flipped it with a deft toe so that it slid across the platform to disappear over the edge. 'Gee, I'm sorry. I really am sorry. Say, but what was that thing, anyhow? Some sort of winkle-picker, or somethin'?'

The Intelligence woman had been confused at first by the American tourist's comic antics, but now she began to realise what his game was. Monks stopped beside her, still keeping his twisting grip on T-shirt, and looked down at both of them. 'I know a little place up top, not far from the station, where we can all go and have a nice little chat, over some genuine drinks. Yeah even at this early hour. And maybe some real American coffee.' He looked at T-shirt. 'Give some of us a chance to loosen up our tongues, huh? Come on.' The strange trio shuffled off, as much a mixed bag as those at Alice's tea-party, with the tall one broadcasting to the empty platform's walls. 'Say, and you know what? If you ask for it, they serve you some good old asparagus on golden toasted bread. Do you like asparagus? I sure as hell swear by it, yeah.' They joined the human river flowing uphill against gravity on the escalator. If ever there was an American who could have waded unaided across the Delaware, it was Monks, towering high above all the others in the 'river'.

Upstairs, in the station, weekend travellers bustled to and fro, aware only of their own problems and eager to catch their trains to flee the city for a few days. Monks and the MI5 woman, with their catch between them, had their own worries and paid no undue attention to blind man crossing their path. The man moved giddily between the two men guiding him by his elbows towards the Glasgow Inter-City train platform. His white stick slipped from his grasp, falling at Monks' feet, and a young boy dashed forward to pick it up. Both parties paused to let the boy hand it back to the blind man. Neither Monks nor the woman recognised the swollen face behind the dark glasses as that of Dr Linsdale. The deliberate application of youth drugs had puffed up the old features to bloated appearance quite unlike that on either Monks' or the woman's files.

The two groups went on their separate ways and the young boy turned to wave goodbye to his dad, who was standing outside the station's glass wall. But Sherman had lost sight of his son in the general crowd and so after a last look, turned away to hurry back to his urgent task of finding Dr Linsdale.

25

17.02hrs, 25th June, Bloomsbury WC1. Soft green carpeting padded Major Broaley's feet as he walked into the club, accompanied by two of his officers. American inspired, the decor was purely twentieth century, in contrast to the nineteenth century stonework of the building's exterior. Curved pink walls, aided by hidden lights, threw out a romantic pink shade onto the occupants of the lounge. There were only two. Broaley's agent with her Boutique bag and the barman, *soigne* in his blood-red ruffled front shirt and golden armlets. Broaley caught the man's enquiring glance through the mirror behind the bar and held out his CID cover pass, which he had used to gain entrance to the closed premises. Coppers. The barman was quick to duck away to busy himself with the ice-maker machine beside the corner sink. Whatever itwas that brought the Law and these other people into the place at this time, he wanted no part of it.

Broaley looked around for Monks and T-shirt and then looked back at his agent. He noted the unfinished glasses and the carafe half full of wine. She signalled with her eyes at the little stainless steel jumping man on the door of the 'gents'. Broaley looked at his officers and pointed to the door. They moved in quietly to collect their man. The Major sat down beside the woman and she saw that his face had gone a shade darker since she had last seen him, and she knew that anger wasn't very far from his controlled surface. He was plainly sore about T-shirt being snatched away from under his nose, and she didn't fancy getting on the wrong side of him. When he was in that mood, one got swatted like a fly by his glare, alone.

She offered him a More 'chocolate-stick' filter, but he waved it aside and took out one of his own cigarettes instead. After he had carelessly singed its side in delayed chastisement, he looked at her. 'Anything so far?' he asked her curtly, through his hard frowning scrutiny.

She felt the question split her like a butcher's cleaver, so that neither a yes nor a no would allow her to escape fully without blemish. 'We haven't really had time to work on him yet, sir. We're not long in here, ourselves. I got on to HQ to inform you where we were as soon as we got in. They've not long gone in.' She nodded towards the 'gents'. 'But from what I can see of his reactions so far, it looks much in keeping with the pattern we've been getting up until now, with the others.'

'And that's what, exactly?' He was playing the schoolmaster with her, to see if she had been doing her sums.

'Pretty much a skin of hardened passive resistance on the outside, but soft as sticky toffee on the inside when we put the pressure on. Not quite like the usual professional brand of agents we have to deal with.' She tilted her head back slightly, to blow out the smoke with an ease of confidence.

He had to smile at her 'we', considering her age and inexperience. 'But then, they're not the usual brand of professional agents. They're much more dangerous, in this case. A hell of a lot more damn dangerous unless we stop them.' She didn't understand that, and he didn't bother to explain. After that, the only noise was the soft tinkle of electronic music from a tape. The xylophone's soft Sugar Plum Fairy-like bounce helped to calm tempers that simmered beneath the surface.

Stainless steel jumping man blushed a shade darker as the door opened inwards, and they all came out. After a few seconds of haggling, Broaley's men let Monks take the man over to the Major's table, while they themselves perched on the pink stools lining the bar. Monks pushed the man down roughly into a chair and sat down himself. T-shirt dabbed his bruised lip, where, presumably, a toilet bowl had jumped up all on its own to strike his face. 'Hi there, Major,' said Monks. 'Come to join the party? I'm glad you got here at last. I guess it's strictly your party now, seeing as you've brought your 'regiment' along.'

Broaley looked at her as if she'd betrayed her flag, but Monks put him right on this. 'It's okay, Major. She hasn't flapped her tongue or anything to me. I guessed that she would take the opportunity to phone you guys on her hot line, while I was in the 'John' with Mooselips, here. Anyhow, I overstayed my time in there, teaching Mooselips the difference between doors and walls, but he just wouldn't listen. He just kept squealing and running into the walls all the time, instead of leaving by the door. Ain't that so? Ain't that so, huh?' Monks prodded the man's face where the lips had swollen up to the proportion that could indeed have caused some jealousy among the American elk or moose. Taking up a glass for the Major, Monks splashed out a torrent of wine into it until it almost overflowed. 'I reckon this about makes us quits, huh, Major?' He wasn't referring to the wine, but to his snatch from under the Major's nose in return for the Major's snatch the night before.

Broaley ignored this and swirled the wine round in the glass while he fought to keep his patience. 'Since it's my party, as you put it, I think we can do away with this now, don't you?' He looked at the paper bag on the table, where Monks' tight grip had made a rough outline of the Ruger .357 Magnum revolver that was inside it. The American certainly knew how to get his money's-worth with the paper-wrapped gun as a knuckle-duster. It was a wonder how T-shirt's face was still in one piece with only the lips swollen.

Monks took a sip at his Chablis and looked at the bag and then at the prisoner. 'Say, don't let Mooselips, here, fool you. He can run real wild when he gets trapped. Ain't that right, huh?' Another prod.

'I think the three of us should be enough to handle him,' said Broaley sarcastically. The woman almost chipped in with 'four', but decided that the remark would have backlashed against her.

Monks shrugged his shoulders and picked up the bag. 'Sure, okay. But say, what gives with you, anyway? I'm on your side, remember?'

'Now how did I forget that?' Broaley watched the American take the gun out of the bag none too secretly, and put it into his shoulder holster. Since he himself had more than once caused his department embarrassment with his own indiscreet methods, Broaley didn't really care a damn how open the American was. But he didn't like the American stealing his show. 'If you're going to play our game, we'd appreciate it more if you would let us know when and where you're playing, and more so if you would play it our way. We haven't the time for any points grabbers chasing the limelight and fouling up the teamwork.'

Monks drained the Chablis away and looked at the empty glass in his hand. 'And don't ask me what happened to the bourbon. I find it a pain in the ass, when we Americans are always labelled with bourbon. I guess it's like you English with your bowler hats. 'Say, do you ever wear a bowler hat, Major?'

'It has its place.'

'Oh yeah, and where's that, Major?'

'If I'd known that I'd been called here to discuss the Anglo-American customs of dress and drink, I'd have let you take care of it by yourself,' said Broaley pointedly to the woman, which was as good a way of saying that he was throwing his patience to the wind. He got up sharply and pushed the chair in, ready to go.

'Sure, okay, okay, so no more fooling around, huh?' Monks plonked his glass down heavily on the table and took a long draw from his cigarette. 'Anyway, Mooselips, here, for all his squealing, is an empty shell. I don't reckon he'll give any more, for all that I've given him; not without some of the old juice, that is.' He indicated a hypodermic syringe by moving his three fingers. 'But that's your ball game, pal. Personally I don't think it will go much further than I got.'

'And how far is that?' said Broaley, shifting with agitation and checking his watch.

'Simply that the Doc guy is being taken to Scotland for a pick-up. But where and when --?' Monks shrugged his shoulders and splayed his hands, blowing out a long stream of smoke. 'Oh, yeah,' he said, after pausing to flick a fleck of ash off his cuff, 'and one of his cell pals is based somewhere in the Richmond district. But that's all he knows. The rest are just faces who make contact by dead letter boxes.'

'And most of them might as well be dead, for all they're going to tell us.' Broaley looked down at the back of T-shirt's head and then back at Monks. 'Right. So we'll get to work on that. In the meantime, don't let protocol worry you over any other little hunches you may have buzzing in that head of yours. Don't be shy about sharing them with us. Just spit them out so that we can all see them. Right?'

'So who's worried? Not me, Major.' He grinned at her. 'I'm only a tourist, remember? But say, what gives with this Linsdale guy, anyhow? I mean the *real* low-down?'

Broaley looked at her uneasily, then at him. 'You mean you don't know? I thought everyone knew by now. The way the newspapers are going on about it and ---'

'Yeah, yeah, yeah,' said Monks, waving aside the flippant explanation. 'I know all that. But is that all? The real below-the-belly-button story?'

'Isn't that *enough*?' said Broaley.

'Sure, sure,' said Monks, taking another long draw, and certain now that he was hitting a sore thumb.

Broaley looked round at his men and pointed at T-shirt, signalling them to come and take him away. They took him away with a gentle prod of fingers, rather than frogmarch him. But that didn't altogether put the barman at ease. His boss may have been a friend of the Yank and let him and the other devious lot into the club, but that didn't make the air any easier to breathe. Any moment now the chairs were liable to come flying over his bar and smash his mirror, like they did in his old place in Chicago; or else he would be served with extradition papers for his deportation back to the States. He took care to stand out of the way, in the doorway leading to the kitchen. On cue to the change of atmosphere, the soft plonk of the xylophone stopped, and Frank Sinatra came on with an invitation for them all to go and fly away with him. The idea caught on and Monks and the woman rose from the table. 'Say, if you folks will excuse me,' Monks said, 'I've got a telephone call to make to my Uncle Sam.'

Broaley and the woman went up the stairs, and Monks went over to the bar. He threw down a twenty pound note. 'Gimme some coins for a phone call, pal. And give me another glass of that wine. Have one on yourself, as well.'

'Certainly, sir. Thank you very much, sir.'

'Oh, and say, Lou, while you're at it, how about knocking me up another lot of that swell asparagus of yours, huh?'

'Certainly, sir.' The barman was glad to take the order as an excuse to scuttle out of the way, through the swing-door, into the kitchen. Having deliberately got rid of the barman, Monks put his call through to Langley,

Virginia. Better to use a public phone, than risk being traced on his cell phone.

But neither Monks' call, nor Major Broaley's brutal interrogation methods, was going to stop the minor disaster that was rushing up at them, to horrify them and set them back sooner than anticipated, and in a manner totally unforeseen.

26

18.17hrs (GMT) 25th June, Belgium. Sherman checked his identity papers and the chain on his wrist and case, as the building came through the trees at last. Overlord of that feud for centuries, the tall solitary castle stood off on the hill, with its trees lower down forming a natural perimeter to its grounds. Its massive rounded corners had probably warded off many an enemy in the past, and tonight it was helping to do just that again. The limousine pulled into the base of the tubular tower house, beside the other cars that glinted with the sun's golden mail and bore the pennants of five other NATO countries. Sherman checked them: Germany, Holland, Norway, Canada and Belgium. All the chauffeurs wore military uniforms.

As he approached the small entrance at the foot of the right tower, something flashed in an arrow slit on the battlements. Where once that flash would have been caused by an iron siege helmet peering out over a crossbow, this one came from a pair of silvered sunglasses peering out over a high powered rifle. The overhead guard popped back in when the 'groundsman' handed Sherman back his papers and spoke into a small hand radio. A metal flap opened in on the iron-studded door and eyes peered out, before bolts sounded on the inside. Rough cast walls, with dowsed flambeaux set in iron sconces, opened back to reflect the mood of the grey hall. Sherman left the guard fiddling with the bolts and walked on in, before the guard of honour of generals' busts pensioned off quietly on their pedestals. Bronze skulls glistened peacefully through the patina where martial headdresses had been hung up long ago, like the breast plates on the wall. Two fifteenth century howitzers yawned by the next doorway, bored from the day of their demob. In their line of fire was the iron chandelier, suspended by chains from the intrados. Out of place in all this was the modern master-control radio unit, with its glaring red light and bright yellow flex, twisting like an umbilical cord over the back of the eighteenth century chair, to dangle its microphone beside the second security man's head.

A Dutch aide-de-camp came forward and ushered Sherman into the room. 'If you will wait here a moment, sir. The meeting is already in progress.'

'Who's that speaking just now?' asked Sherman, referring to the muffled voice coming from an inner room somewhere.

'That is General Montford of Canada speaking, sir.' The young officer's accent clicked like a mouthful of sticks; but they were suave polished sticks.

'I see.'

With that, the aide went off through the archway, to the armoury on the left that was flanked by two headless soldiers in brilliant tunics. The room itself was a pageant of arms and battles. Encircled by a shining array of weapons, Sherman took his stand by the wide open fireplace. Above it, a large coat of arms had its motto partly obscured by two variegated regimental flags draped cross-wise across its base. Smaller ensigns and gonfanons shifted with the convection currents as they clung to the crossed ribs quartering the domed ceiling. Sherman followed the countless diagonal rows of varying firearms fanning out along the wall from the fireplace. Matchlocks, wheel-locks, flintlocks and snaphaunces; all rallying to the silent skirmishes behind the wigged commanders in the dark oil paintings. He let his mind float up in the aura of the military past. That was then, and this was now. A desperate rallying of flags was needed once again.

He checked to see if it was time for another pill. It was. The plastic bottle was in his right pocket, so he had to change the steel case over to his left hand to get the bottle out with his right hand. With no water to drink, he gathered the saliva on his tongue first and then took the pill. A little thing like that was enough to restore his sapping energy as he worked under stress with little rest. If only his major problem could be so easily solved like that. Sherman swivelled the naval muskatoon's heavy brass barrel aside to look at the dull photographs. Air reconnaissance shots carried the message better than any written report, and the group sets were nostalgic of the camaraderie formed from the action of those days. Only Foch and De Gaulle stood out from the faded smudge of uniforms, along with one of Churchill speaking to a semi-nude 'desert rat' in the shade of a Crusader tank.

The sound of voices in the next room was suddenly much louder and Sherman turned to see the gap widening between the doors. A fleeting vision of the NATO generals seated and plugged into their earphones, was blocked off again by the blue uniform sliding out sideways between the doors. Squadron Leader Travis turned round and leaned back on his hands on the handles for a second, trying to weigh up Sherman's news before he heard it. He came away from the doorway with a measured stealth in his steps, and spoke in a low, almost whispering, voice. 'I heard you just got in.'

'Yes, a quick, quicker than quick flight, courtesy of the RAF.'

'I think you'll soon have more flying hours than me. So how's the storm brewing now?'

'Pretty black, I'm afraid. They want more time to reconsider the terms.'

'Who? The Ministers?'

'No, the hijackers. They were demanding the release of all the Palestinian prisoners being held in Israel, as well as all Muslims imprisoned in European countries. Our lot in Tehran were swayed by it, but the other Western ministers won't have it. Total deadlock.'

'God Almighty! That's all we need.' Travis swung away to finger the broadsword wielded resolutely by the sentry in a hauberk mail tunic. 'For goodness sake, couldn't we impress on them the urgency of the situation?'

'It's difficult to get them to appreciate the urgency, when you're holding back on the *real* urgency. We tried to sway them, but only halfway. They were prepared to go as far as to release half that quota of Palestinian prisoners, then changed their mind. That wasted time. The hijackers wouldn't accept it. Now that we've actually agreed to shift *towards* an offer to consider releasing more prisoners, they've become suspicious and want more time to think the terms over. Obviously Moscow hasn't told the hijackers the real value of the 'goods' they were hijacking. They can't; not without losing their innocence. And they're not going to allow for the release of Miles. On top of that, Iran is demanding action against us, by the United Nations, on allegations of political suffocation.'

'Yes, I heard rumours going around in there,' Travis nodded towards the closed doors of the conference room, 'about something like that, with the United Nations being brought in against us.'

'To hell with the United Nations! We need to get that man out at all costs. After that we can go back to small things like UN detentes. That's why I've flown in here. Maybe we can get through to the ministers with the military issue to persuade them. That's General Montford speaking now, isn't it?'

'Yes, he's nearly finished. So far he's managed to pull in everyone on last December's agreed plan for general mobilisation of the heavy armoured divisions and atomic weapons units in the European sector, in conjunction with our Operation BLOWTORCH manoeuvres, while Canada itself throws a blanket over the Russian entry in the North Atlantic sector. Everyone at the meeting is in agreement with these proposals and all the necessary phases have been put into action. From what you're saying now, I suppose it's up to us to throw some light on this new development in Tehran, and stress how it affects our overall strategy, even if we can't tell them the full reason.'

'There's no suppose about it. It's an absolute must. It's the only card we've got to play until we get a better deal, and with time running out, that may not be too likely.' Sherman thought of his mess of a meeting with Daniloff. 'There was a chance that we could have clinched a deal with the FSB to get Linsdale back, but that's gone. Even they don't know where he is. No, we've got to get Miles, and get him now, before they decide to hack his head off in another of their jihadi political gestures.'

'I see,' said Travis, scratching his chin with what Sherman feared was some new awkward point brewing up. 'They may want to know why we now want Miles so desperately. After all, it's in their files that Linsdale is our atom bomb man, and Miles is in radio electronics. They know that our air defence programme has been neutralised, but not that some nasty bombs are due for hatching. We know why we need a radio man like Miles, but they don't. They're going to ask questions.'

'So let them bloody well ask! By that time we'll have Miles back in England where we need him. Damn it, man, you're the technical genius who talks shop all the time with this NATO lot; don't ask me to cock up a story for you. Tell them our torch bulb has gone, or something; tell them anything, so long as we get Miles back. All right? So can we get on with it now?'

Travis looked at his brother-in-law, surprised at his unusual show of temper, and then at the steel case he clutched, with its steel chain of urgency. 'Come on; I'll take you in. I think he should be nearly finished now.' They walked over to the double door and Travis held Sherman back while he listened with a knowing ear. 'That sounds like it,' he said, turning the handle. 'Right.' They opened the door and went in, just as the voice stopped and coughs and the rustle of papers erupted. Earphones came out and fell around the necks like rosaries, as the spearheads of Europe's armed forces bowed their heads and held quiet confessionals with their aides and officers. Travis crouched down and whispered with General Laurence, who was consulting his notes before speaking for Britain in a few minutes time. Sherman opened his steel case and handed the report, with its impending death knell, to the General. With any luck, those few minutes could help to save Britain and Europe from disaster. A pencil tapped for order and the loose prattle subsided, in readiness for the next speaker. Someone closed the door and once more the knights of old in their chain-mail and armour were shut out in the silent stillness to swing their swords no more.

But theirs was the only stillness, Sherman thought. For elsewhere, from the castle outwards across the broad expanse of the continent, man was drawing forth his sword from his scabbard and flexing his bow in fine fettle for the coming battle. But whilst ancient archers of Agincourt had sported fine woods and twine, these modern archers of NATO had swifter, deadlier arrows powered by rocket fuel and tipped with nuclear warheads. Even now the soils of the land were stirring in a second coming of spring, where the grasses looked on shyly as the new 'plants' came forth out of the ground and pointed their seeds of doom towards the sky, where pollination would be widespread and radio active. Poachers and shepherds who strayed onto forbidden launching sites and saw what they ought not to have seen, would be sore thereafter for not being believed. Already some country drunk somewhere would be babbling to his fellow villagers that the End was nigh, having witnessed the dead rising from the ground; whilst maybe a witches coven would be declaring the massive phallic symbols as signs of tremendous fertility rites and the accession to power by the Prince of Darkness, Himself. Truth, however twisted, would have found its light, for the fury that would be unleashed by these missiles would far surpass that of Sodom and Gomorrah, or that of Moses when he smote the Golden Calf and cast its followers down into eternal damnation.

27

21.37hrs, 25th June, Whitehall SW1. When the red light flashed on the intercom, Sherman just knew that it would be something that he didn't want to hear. He had only just got back from Belgium, and had just put his hand round the warm mug of tea, and now he knew that it was going to get cold. But not in his belly. He sat staring at the blinking tweeting light for several seconds, before pressing the switch. 'Yes, what is it?' Sherman recognised the defensive hollow ring in his own voice while he waited, hugging his tea mug.

'I'm afraid it's rather bad news, sir.'

'Well go on, I think I can take it. I'm hardly likely to get indigestion, since I've had nothing to eat yet.'

'There's been an accident, sir.'

'Accident?'

'Yes, sir. It's your son, sir. He's dead.'

Sherman forgot about his tea. He forgot about everything, nuclear bombs and all, his mind flying off at a tangent into empty space. Numb space. Leaning forward slowly, he tried to find words. 'How did ---?'

'It seems there was a bad landing at Catania's Fontanarossa Airport. Part of the aircraft's undercarriage failed to come down and the plane went off the runway. Several passengers seriously injured and one ---'The woman stopped there, not wanting to repeat that painful piece.

'And the boy's *mother*? Mrs *Sherman*?'

'Details are still to come in, but we gather so far that she's being operated on. She has already had one leg amputated, and as far as we can understand, is due to lose the other one as well.'

Sherman sat back slowly in his chair, looking around the room, his mind elsewhere, as the message sank in. And he hadn't taken the little boy to the train exhibition. The pang in his chest and the moisture welling up in his eyes wasn't due to work stress alone. He sat silently while the intercom spoke on, its words falling on deaf ears. At last he reached forward and pressed the switch to cut off the voice.

21.40hrs, Preston. The blue beacons flashed on the roofs of the white ambulances, trundling in and out of the hospital like a herd of pukka elephants, in a shuttle line between the grounds and the scene of the train crash. Fire crew rescue teams had cut and heaved away at the wreckage for over two hours. Now at last, the railway line had been cleared and the last of the casualties were being brought in. So far the toll was seventeen injured, eight seriously, and four dead. A porter in the hospital was in the process of pushing the corpses away on their trolleys for storage, when the doctor called out. 'Hold on a second. I haven't finished labelling that one yet.' He went over to the fourth trolley and picked up the file and took out his ball point pen. The porter held up the corpse's tag and read out the letters while the doctor wrote them down: 'L-I-N-S-D-A-L-E. That's it. Linsdale. Dr Linsdale. All right, now, Doc?'

'Yes, I've got it down. You can take it away now.'

The porter started pushing his trolley again, then after a short distance, paused for a moment, as the thought struck him. 'Here, Doc, isn't that the name of the bloke they're looking for? You know, that atom scientist bloke. It's in today's papers.'

'Scientist?' The doctor frowned up from his notes, too concerned with his work to be really sure what it was that the porter was going on about. 'I couldn't say. Is it? Linsdale, you say? I can't say the name means anything to me. But I suppose it could be, for all that I've seen of the papers these last two days. Seems like centuries.'

'Do you want me to get on to the police?'

'If we must, we must. It's the proper thing to do, I suppose. Leave it with me. I'll see to it; when and if I can find the time to, that is.'

22.10hrs, Bromley. Sherman gave the shower spray nozzle another tightening twist with the wrench and then stepped down from the stool to turn on the water. With a hissing dribble, then a splutter, the water suddenly arched out and drenched his arm. 'That's better,' he softly muttered to himself, turning off the water. His father appeared in the doorway, carrying a lettuce from the garden. Sherman turned the water on again to let his dad see. 'How's that? That's better, isn't it?' Neither of them cared in their minds if the shower worked or not, except that it was a charade to allay sore hearts over the tragic event.

'Yes, that's certainly much better. Thanks, John. I've been meaning to do something about that for ages, but Lord knows I couldn't get up on the stool with my arthritis in my knees. My injections don't help too much, either.' He held up the lettuce, with its small clod of earth. 'I thought I'd prepare this and make up a salad so that we can finish off the crab in the fridge.' He walked off to the kitchen, content in his shirt sleeves and waistcoat; virtually retired now, with only an odd hour or two in the office, giving 'advice', to compete with his many hours of pottering in the garden. It had been to his bitter disappointment that his only son had had to abandon his work at the University, to subsequently take up his career in the civil service. But otherwise, they still managed to get along together, like mud and boots. Who was which didn't matter.

Sherman folded the step stool and put it away in the garden shed, along with the tools. His aching mind needed convincing that he could spare half an hour of his valuable time to come out here. He may have failed to persuade his dad to leave the city for a long weekend, but at least he'd been able to deliver the news of the accident personally. His dad had taken the news matter-of-factly, like he always did. Sherman wasn't sure if this annoyed him. But he let himself believe that his dad was feeling the sadness deep down. Sherman felt the acid irony burn his inside, at the idea of those two innocents being stricken down, one dead and one maimed for life. This in their very act of escaping. And that had been his idea. To think that they had been privileged to escape and yet they had been the ones to perish. But maybe that was it. A divine intervention whereby he was not allowed to let millions perish and only save his own folk. Fate? Maybe the Muslims were right after all. He didn't know what to think any more. Not at the moment, anyway. But he knew that he felt hungry. He hadn't eaten for hours; since before his flights. Hunger; that was supposed to be the primitive instinct for survival. A half hour stop here, to grab something to eat, wasn't going to change the picture much, so to hell with it all.

As he washed his hands in the kitchen, Sherman looked at the crab in the plate, with its fragmented shell, and felt himself thinking about the American bomber that had crashed two days ago, to start all this. Two days? It seemed much longer than that now.

'Perhaps it would be a good thing if I flew out with her mother tomorrow, John. Did she say what time the flight was?'

'No.' Sherman hadn't spent more than the necessary few brief minutes on the phone with his mother-in-law. They didn't like each other, and the circumstances didn't make it any easier. Especially bearing in mind that Maureen had finally agreed to go on his dogged insistence. Further irony was that whilst he hadn't tried to persuade to go before, now his dad wanted to go on his own volition. He managed a limp response, feeling somehow trapped in his guilt, between a firm yes or no. ' That would be all right, I suppose.'

'I'm sure it's less bother for me than it is for you, John. In any case, I don't see it as a bother to go and see her in her tragic state.' He held up his hand to stop any interruption. 'No, I insist that you let me go in your place. I appreciate the fact that you have a tremendous work load to cope with. Too much, if you ask me, with all that running around you do. Lord knows, you're not getting your proper amount of sleep, John.'

'It shows, does it?'

'Yes, it shows, John.'

'I'm taking pills for it.'

'What are they?'

'I don't know. I can't remember the name. They're yellow things.'

'Pills are only part of it, John. You must have your natural rest.'

'I'll pay my twenty guineas fee at the door, when I leave,' said Sherman, halting the lecture with a reproving smile. They sat down at the table. Sherman turned the bottle round to look at the handwritten name on the label. Elderberry & Gooseberry 2006. 'Now that's what I call rare vintage,' he said, managing to let a smile break out briefly on his dull expression. 'But where on earth did mum hide all these gooseberries and things in the garden? All I could ever see were her flowers.'

'You just didn't know where to look. You never were a gardener, John. Your mother loved the garden.'

'No, I definitely wasn't that, for sure,' said Sherman, letting his dad pour the wine into the two glasses. He lifted his up. 'Anyway, Merry Christmas.'

'At *this* time of the year?' Mr Sherman couldn't help giving a concerned look at his son's affected cheery manner, and wondered what cursed problem was running his health down.

'Let's say it's to make up for last Christmas, when I was away on a job and couldn't fit in time to come and pull the crackers.'

'Lord knows, you won't manage for this Christmas, either.'

Sherman paused, thinking of tomorrow night. 'Probably not. Anyway, cheers.' He drank a little and watched the red admiral fluttering past the open door, to remind him of those in the North Atlantic. They ate in silence through the simple preparation of tender white crab meat and lettuce, and soft cold slabs of cooked potato dressed in oil and green peppers and sliced spring onions.

'By the way, that reminds me, John,' said Mr Sherman suddenly, leaning his chair back to reach out for the sideboard, 'I found this in the shed the other day.' He opened the drawer and took out a dowdy old frame, putting it on the table. 'It's your old badminton racquet frame.'

'My what? My badminton frame!' Sherman's surprise broke into a choked laugh and he shook his head, laughing all the more. He chuckled on, examining the old scarred frame. Not for modern alloy racquet, but for the old wooden framed racquet. Handed on to him by his old grandad. A good GP would have seen Sherman's humour as a release from tension, and that was what it was, with all the recollections of boyhood flooding in at once. But then he'd grown up. His son hadn't. The floodgate of happy memories suddenly closed. He put the frame aside. 'Thanks. That's just what I need to save the day. Thanks.'

They had finished the salad and were putting the plates in the sink, when the phone rang. 'I'll get it,' said Mr Sherman, going into the hall. 'Hullo? -- Yes, he's here. Hold on a moment. 'He reappeared in the doorway. 'John, it's for you.'

Sherman's mobile was in his jacket, which was hanging up out in the hall. It had probably sounded when he had been out in the garden with his dad.

He went to the phone. 'Hullo? --Yes, what is it, Major? -- No! Dead! Hell! -- Right.' Sherman's thoughts scattered like ninepins under the impact of the news, and he put the phone down. He stood there noisily scraping his stubble, while trying to reassess the situation.

Mr Sherman had heard the word 'dead', and the one thought had leapt into his mind. 'That wasn't the hospital, about Maureen, was it?'

Sherman turned to see his dad had turned a shade paler. 'Sorry? Maureen? No, no, that was something else. Look, something's come up and I've got to go.' My God, the number of times he'd fobbed Maureen off with those very words. He rolled his sleeves down and took down his jacket from the stand, to put it on. He came back to the kitchen and they stood silent for a moment. Sherman picked up the racquet frame and held it up. 'Thanks for the frame.' He stood outside the back door. Some silly pumped up farewell words came to mind, but then he decided to leave that sort of thing to those paid to do it better on the stage. 'See you,' he said, and walked off, along the red chips pathway, under the rosebush arch, and out the gate.

10.40hrs, Whitehall SW1. While the news of Linsdale's death soaked in, to numb the heads of many in their operations, some field operations still surged on under their own momentum, like the frantic antics of a chicken with its head chopped off. This suited Broaley, since he had a few things to try out before his own personal energy dried up.

'It's merely a setback, Prime Minister,' said Sir Richard, trying to sound convincing, while playing down his own dismay. The Prime Minister hadn't thrown up at the logic, but he had looked very worried. True, what had been the *other* chance was now the *only* chance. The Foreign Secretary didn't require any emphasis on the fact that they now desperately needed Miles. He would see to it that Washington made generous arms concessions to the Israelis in return for their releasing of Palestinian 'nationals' held in Israel.

28

01.32hrs, 26th June, Belgravia SW1. 'Dr Linsdale is definitely not dead! I repeat: he's most definitely not dead!'

Sherman stared at the telephone as if it were a black voodoo bone cackling out some dark riddles which he couldn't comprehend. For the second time that night, his mind tried to adjust to the situation in a whirlwind reversal of objectives. With only fifteen minutes of sleep behind him, it was hard enough finding the speaking end. 'That's quite a mouthful, even if it is true, Major.'

'It *is* true, I can assure you.'

'So go ahead and assure me.'

'The man we thought was Linsdale was no more than some business man from Bradford, or somewhere.'

'Really? And what's his part in all this?'

'Nothing, as a matter of fact. Linsdale's papers were found on the man's body and the face obliterated, so it was assumed by the hospital people that the man was called Linsdale.'

'But you *don't*, is that it, Major?'

'We've carried out tests on the teeth and fingerprints, and the man is certainly not Linsdale. These papers were planted on the body as a calculated risk to make us think otherwise.'

'You're trying to tell me something, Major?'

'I'm saying, first that the ruse to use the body as a decoy was an on the spot inspiration by Linsdale's lot, since the crash was purely accidental, as far as we know. I'm also saying that the idea was not to broadcast the fact that Linsdale had expired, and hope it ended there, but rather, to delay us with this thought. Knowing we were catching up on them, they preferred to buy time by diverting us with this false catch.'

'And how much time have they bought, Major?'

'They knew we would carry out the tests anyway, so the time was probably enough to get them into Scotland, where they can lie low until it's time to jump the water.'

'And do you think they'll jump the water, Major?'

'Everyone's been alerted and put out in force up there and we're cracking the cell rapidly, as it is. We'll get the rendezvous soon enough.'

'You haven't answered my question, Major.'

But the Major had already hung up. Sherman's hand stalled on the phone in the cradle when the surge came to him and he lifted the phone back up and dialled for a taxi. With the emergency crisis on, there would be nobody around in the Department's motor pool at this time, to drive him. And he was too tired to drive himself.

When Pamela ghosted into the room in her ankle length flannelette nightdress, he had cast his pyjama trousers aside and was pulling a black crew-neck sweater over his light dark cord trousers. She gathered up the trousers from the carpet and watched him fiddle in the obscure corner with what looked like a tobacco pouch, at his waist. 'These things are surely made for the dedicated masochist,' he muttered to himself in mounting irritation. 'How the hell am I supposed to get behind the wheel and drive with this thing gouging its pound of flesh out of my thigh!' After another try, he at last found the best comfortable position to clip the holster to his belt. He wasn't used to this sort of thing, but now was as good a time as any to broaden his experience. Taking out the revolver and swinging out its cylinder, he fed in the bright cartridges from the cardboard box which still had the Armoury's buff requisition counterfoil stapled to it.

'What in God's name have you got there?' Her anxiety was just noticeable as she clenched the pyjama trousers to her chest.

'What does it look like?' He was offering no mood to mince words, snapping the cylinder in and emptying the box's other cartridges into his hand and putting them in his pocket.

'Haven't you done enough for one night? Can't you leave Major Broaley to get on with that sort of thing? That's his line.'

He slid the revolver securely into the holster and reached for the black cardigan. 'I seem to recall a clause on that piece of paper I signed under the Official Secrets Act which stated specifically that I should be prepared to suspend all normal duties in the eventuation of crisis situations warranting a first hand inspection of the areas of crisis, et cetera, et cetera, et cetera.'

'I don't think it specifically states that you're supposed to act silly and get yourself killed.'

'Oh, but it *does*, sweetie; oh, but it *does*.' Perhaps not by any written word, but otherwise, between the lines, he was expected to carry out all sorts of superhuman duties, as far as his elastic band would stretch, for his Queen and Country.

She bit her lip doubtfully and pulled him by the arm towards the bedroom. 'Come back to bed. You've only just got in it.' But he shook her off with a gruff finality, and went over to the wall cupboard for his anorak. 'You'll never make it to the door before your eyes fall shut.' Her voice was hurt, as well as mocking, in her last bid to keep him with her.

'Try me.' He zipped up the dark blue anorak. He relaxed his tone to make up for his sharp words. 'Besides, I'm not driving.'

01.36hrs (GMT), Hardanger Fjord, Norway. Everything in the vacuous expanse stood still. Movement was measured in geological eons that reduced Man to a nonentity. Man did not feature in the titanic combination of time and strength that had brought forth this scene. Nothing short of millions of years of seismal upheaval had been sufficient to contort and weld the strata together with colossal pressure and heat, to form this indelible sculpture. Enormous boulders reposed with a lethargy that was reminiscent of a slothful Mezozoic Period, where brontosauri had probably weltered in the sun on this very shore.

Heeding this very thought, a giant reptile stirred from its slumber in fjord's dark waters, and slipped out with a gentle ripple towards the sea. The submarine *Yalta* was moving out on the next stage of its mission. Nothing else moved, and the moon was afraid and tried to keep out of sight.

From a mountain overlooking the fjord, two 'snowmen' looked on intently, one with powerful infra-red binoculars of the type issued to Her Britannic Majesty's Armed Forces. Clad in white camouflage dress, the soldiers were a natural part of the snow scene, but for the deathly black sub-machine guns draped across their fronts. Their surveillance orders were to watch without interfering and report when it was necessary. The private snapped on a switch and the white radio pack strapped to his back came into life. Pulling up the artic hood, he spoke into the microphone fastened about his head. 'Come in SNOWDRAGON. Come in SNOWDRAGON. ICICLE calling SNOWDRAGON. Do you read me, SNOWDRAGON?'

A pause, and then SNOWDRAGON answered, with a squeak in the earpiece, asking for location coordinates.

ICICLE gave these precisely. 'Area three, nine six, three six. REDSERPENT leaving area now; repeat, REDSERPENT leaving area now.' The soldier knocked back the hood to look up overhead. Between the crackling squeaks from the headpiece, the two ghostly figures waited silently in the shadow of the pines, their eyes fixed skywards. They were the eyes and ears of Army Field Intelligence for this operation, with a stiff training of waiting and flitting about arctic forests with lone wolf stealth and cunning. Neither of them twitched a muscle until the jiggering chop-chop sound of the helicopter reached their ears from above and beyond the trees. The soldier cracked a smile as the earphone squeaked again, just before the Army Lynx helicopter cluttered past overhead, on its twin Rolls-Royce turbines. Like a twinkling three ton tadpole, it waltzed beneath fifty feet of swirling blades and then corrected itself, to swoop round and follow the line of the fjord.

The rubber-masked figure peered momentarily out of the cockpit while smoothly switching on the Hawker Siddeley Type 201 Infra-Red Lines-canner. This took in infra-red radiations from all bodies below, in rapid strips at right angles to its flight path and recorded the built up picture on standard 70mm film. It also absorbed the variations in infra-red radiations from the thermal 'shadows' left behind by objects which had recently been there. Sweeping down in one swift motion, the helicopter was there and gone, taking with it all the fjord's devious happenings within the last twenty-four hours. That included the movements of the submarine *Yalta*.

01.38hrs, Whitehall SW1. Sir Richard and the Defence Minister sipped their lukewarm tea as best they could while resting for five minutes from the commotion in the war room next door. With land and water now bristling with 'primed steel', both sides were now bristling with fear of pressing the wrong buttons, and so pressed their computer buttons to assess and reassess the situation. If they got their sums wrong, they could end up with more scrap metal than the other side. Either way, both sides ended up with a lot of scrap. The military scientists in London argued themselves hoarse with their points, while the Pentagon experts tut-tutted and shook their heads. In between the messages, the cipher clerks shredded up the code paper like a sideline confetti business. But then nobody ever threw confetti at a funeral. Sir Richard pondered over the message that had come in from Sherman, saying that he was accompanying Major Broaley. The thought of Sherman actively joining the chase would normally have made Old Hossley feel his age; instead, he felt their different ages meant nothing, where time was about to burn out in a dazzling frizzle.

29

02.51hrs, 26th June, Renfrewshire. The landing strip lights prickled the cold night air and danced out on the buttons and pips of the Army colonel standing by the car, waiting on the RAF Nimrod. At last the curved flap opened out on the long fuselage and the figures began to climb down. Two of them were not crew, one of them wearing a dark blue anorak and the other one wearing a sheepskin jacket. Sherman stepped down onto the ground and Broaley jumped down after him, beside the pilot. The back door of the Rover opened behind the colonel, and the First Minister for Scotland got out, blowing into his cold hands and shivering in the cold night air. With only one year to go before retirement, he was becoming a little too old for this sort of clandestine caper at this time of night. Pulling the short woollen scarf closer round his neck, he waited for the two London men.

The old man put out his hand. 'Good morning, Mr Sherman. I trust you had a good journey up. It's awful good of you to come all this way to see us.'

'We came because we had to, Mr Russell. Sorry if we've kept you waiting long.'

'Not at all,' lied the old man, always a gentleman of professional manners and saying what sounded polite, rather than what was felt. 'It's not often at my age that I get the chance to breathe in the fresh air at this early hour. It's quite medicinal, in fact. Moreover, the C.O. has been good enough to lay on some tea for us, so I believe. Am I correct, Colonel?'

'Quite correct, sir,' said the colonel, fidgeting with his buttons. Sherman nodded to the colonel at the introductory remark and looked aside to Broaley. 'Major Broaley, here, has come along to give a helping hand.' Heads nodded all round.

'Glad to have you with us, Major,' said the colonel.

'Thank you, sir.'

The colonel wasn't fooled by the Major's polite 'sir' bit. It was automatically understood that they would wield their Whitehall power to their judgment in running operations, in the interest of national security. He could already see in the Major's face, an urge to get the others to put a step on it. Broaley took advantage of their momentary attention to say his piece. Formalities and mouthwash he could leave to Sherman, while he himself got on with things. 'If I could just have a few words with the Colonel?' He made to move aside and the colonel moved after him.

'Sure, Major,' said Sherman, watching Broaley go off with the colonel, asking if the Rover had a two-way radio, so that he could put out urgent operational instructions that couldn't be delayed much longer. With long extended calls, relying on a mobile phone's battery not to run down was too great a risk. Sherman looked at the First Minister and they both turned round, shoulder to shoulder, and walked towards the landing field perimeter, leaning forward over slow, synchronised strides. A grey mood slid over them, pushing civil niceties aside. 'But let's talk of other things, Mr Russell. Quite frankly, I had to come up and see you, and quickly, too. Our Intelligence Department's report sent to you a few hours ago must have come as a bolt from the blue, and couldn't have helped your indigestion any, I'll bet. I'm sorry about that, as much as I know the feeling. But as you've gathered, I've been sent to keep an eye on the operations; for all the good that will do if things get out of hand.'

'I'm hoping that you'll see that they don't, Mr Sherman.'

'I'm rather hoping something like that myself, as a matter of fact, Mr Russell.'

The old man glanced back with a moment's longing at the comparative shelter of the Army Rover. 'But do go on, Mr Sherman. Tell me more.'

They had reached the lamp beside the first concrete hut and so Sherman handed the buff folder over. 'Perhaps you'd like to read through this. It's the latest information we have.' This wasn't true, of course, but it was all he need tell the old man.

The old crinkling eyes scanned the first few aerial photographs and the no more. 'No, no, you'd better keep this, Mr Sherman. I could never hope to understand it, anyway. Just tell me about it in your own words, if you will. In your own way. I'm sure you can make it sound that much more interesting, however ghastly it may be.' They walked on through, between the concrete huts, so that only the wind whipped out snatches of their classified conversation. The patrolmen were too far away for even their Alsatians to hear.

It's the Russian submarine, *Yalta*,' said Sherman, referring to the photographs, 'and it's heading rapidly in this direction. We weren't too sure at first where it would make its mark, but the latest reports leave only the thinnest doubts, now, that it's heading for Scottish waters. It should be off our north eastern coast pretty soon now.'

'Do we know exactly where?'

'No, I'm afraid not. Not yet; but it's unlikely that it will come in far, considering its size, apart from the risk of it being picked up on our coastal patrol radar. Even if we do pick it up on our radar, there's very little we can do if the party has managed to get on board. It's imperative that we apprehend them before they board the submarine, and that could prove to be quite tricky at night, I'm sorry to say.'

'At night? So you think they'll wait until tonight before they make their move?'

'We're almost certain of it, considering the cut down in risks it means for them.'

'But surely we can cope with night-time conditions? We do have the gadgets and things, do we not?'

'Oh yes, some of the best equipment in that field, if I may say so, but it's still a vast amount of sea and coastline to cover, all the same.'

'You don't seem at all too happy about the situation. Don't you think that we could do it, Mr Sherman?'

'If I can speculate briefly, I'd say our chances of snaring the prey stand a higher chance of success if we concentrate on land manoeuvres. More than that, I'd rather not say at the moment.'

'That's really quite a bellyful you've said so far, Mr Sherman. I'm told that you already have the Army out looking for them at this very moment?'

'Yes, Scottish Command has mounted an all out emergency state of alert, and the country is being scoured coast to coast. But with the state of things as they are, we require the full co-operation of all authorities, military and civil. That's what I want to discuss with you. With the civil element involved, the police especially must be brought in to help matters, especially in the upper eastern constabularies. As a matter of fact, I gather from the radio message we received on the way up, that your Chief Constable for the region is waiting to have a few words with us.' Sherman turned to look around. 'Where is he? Over there, in that main building?'

'Yes. I only learned of that myself, when I was being driven out here. But I hope that you haven't been spreading panic to him and his men. That sort of thing let loose on the public seldom does any good, especially when it reaches the wrong ears.'

'Don't worry, Mr Russell, we've taken every precaution in keeping the matter as hush-hush as possible. The police, as far as they are concerned, are to be on the lookout for escapists, one of them a mediocre scientist; and our own field reconnaissance units are blending in with the local scenery, to be as natural as the pine trees themselves.'

'Yes, I think that sounds just about how I'd put it, Mr Sherman. To be honest, I'd sooner leave any releasing of information to the public to the Prime Minister, in his broadcast to the nation, tonight.' The old man paused with apparent misgivings on this thought. ' He is going to go ahead with it and speak tonight, isn't he?'

'That all depends on what kind of report I give to him later today. If it's a favourable report, there will be no broadcast. If it's a bad report, there will be a broadcast, though God knows what words alone will do to save the situation in that circumstance. So you see, Mr Russell, it can only be a good report that I send in. Do you follow me?'

Russell fumbled with a handkerchief, dabbing at a chronically wet nose for a few moments, before he looked up to stare long and hard at Sherman. 'Yes, I think I understand you, Mr Sherman; all too clearly.' Putting the handkerchief away, he turned and walked away. Sherman stepped quickly after him to catch up, and they walked back together, through the huts, towards the centre. As they emerged once more from the huts, out into the service area, the corporal in the Rover saw them and turned the car round in their direction. Chilly pellets came down out if the dark and the old man tugged at his collar, in a futile effort to shelter.

'Rain, sir?' said the colonel, holding his hand out in the darkness.

'So it seems. That's all we need on top of our present troubles.' Scotland's First Minister peered into the car and round about, in search of the Major, half expecting him to embarrass them with a rude piss behind the boot, or something. 'Where's the Major?'

'He's gone off, sir,' answered the colonel. 'Urgent business he said. Apparently it couldn't be delayed. He radioed for transport and it's just come and collected him.'

'I see. Well, I think it's time we had that cup of tea we've been promised, Mr Sherman. Will you be joining us, Colonel?'

'Of course, sir. Thank you very much.' He turned to Sherman as they got into the car. 'And then maybe you can fill me in on what's going on, seeing as the Major told me little more than nothing. Right?'

They drove off towards the dark buildings, with the wind-sock pointing the way, and the beady raindrops copying out the yellow landing lights a hundred-fold on the windscreen. The soft seats and warmth of the car were more relaxing, and when the First Minister took a quick glance askant, he imagined that he caught Sherman having an enormous yawn.

30

03.05hrs, 26th June, Perthshire. What was still only a gossamer drizzle in Renfrewshire, had developed northwards, through Lanarkshire, Stirlingshire and Perthshire, into a mini 'monsoon' downpour. Icy pellets pelted down in a bitter deluge through the car headlights, and the wheels 'splassshed' on in their plashy humdrum monotony over the wet road, as the car swerved on round the wooded bends. The low black body of the Mercedes glittered under the reflection of its own light from the shiny road, while the moonlight cast a ghostly light upon the car, picking out the chromium fittings and raindrops like sparkling jewels. Inside the back window, the ornamental dog wagged its head as they swayed, beside the huddled form of Dr Linsdale, who also wagged his head. But the Doctor was not wagging his head as much as before, as consciousness began to return and the clouded stupor began to lift. The effect of the drug was lessening and the shock of recent events was also playing the mind up.

The car's interior bubbled with a mixture of voices in Linsdale's head, as a hand slapped him lightly to test his senses. A black distorted mass straightened itself out in his blurry vision, to become a bearded face bent down over him. The voices hushed away at his recovery, and the bearded man leaned away to put his hand in his pocket. 'It's about time we gave him another dose to put him under again, he said, pulling out a flat case and opening it to take out the steel syringe.

'No, hold on,' said the man in the front passenger seat. 'Wait until we get there, first. It'll save us carrying him again.'

'Right; good idea.'

Linsdale peered about through his myopic eyes, seeing strange faces and remembering strange things. Events raced through his mind like an over-sped film reel and he heard moans and screams as steel beams buckled and people died. He saw blood pour out and bodies tossed about just like dolls; his toy puppets kicked about by his drunken stepfather; his CND placard pole broken over his head by the policeman's riot shield crashing against him. The time sequence eluded Linsdale as he confused his unhappy childhood with the recent rail crash and other violent episodes. He held his eyes shut tightly, rocking his head slowly from side to side. 'Going to break,' he whispered to himself. ''Going to break; going to break.'

The others stared at Linsdale for a second as he whispered, remembering the nightmare experience, and then looked away, snapping out of their horror.

'Yeah, that was some nasty crash you had, ' said the driver to his two companions.

'Just as well you came out of it with only a couple of scratches and no more.'

'Our scratches?' joked the bearded man. 'I'll bet you've got more scratches to show, where the wild haggis attacks you.'

'Listen mate,' returned the driver, 'it's so cold here in Scotland that the poor beasts stab themselves to death on their frozen hairs.'

All three laughed and that helped to distract Linsdale from his inner morbid memories and clear his mind a little. But in spite of the laughter, he still felt the alien atmosphere. The total one-sidedness of the situation brought the message home; the way he was ignored as they spoke; the way he was referred to in the third person, and glanced at, as if he was a prize strung ham; their side against his. All this wasn't what he had wanted, or even expected, he had been approached by them and offered their help. Their initial help had turned to forceful persuasion and this was how it had turned out. His throbbing arm, where the needle had gone in, and the stuffy cigarette fumes mixing with the smell of wet synthetic leather, didn't help matters much that way, either.

'Nearly there,' said the driver. Cigarettes were stubbed out and they turned into the dark mouth of a driveway. It was a sinister looking house with as much sign of life as the unkempt garden twining over and around them. A window lit up and a silhouette pushed a curtain back. The silhouette disappeared and the light went out again. They got out and approached the building. A door opened before them with a short monotone groan, bidding them welcome to a large black toothless mouth. The bearded man led the way inside and fumbled around for the switch. The light failed to go on and so they stomped heavily across the floor, their echoing steps telling tales of the colossal hallway surrounding them. Dry dust was in the air everywhere and it was obvious that dry rot was pulverising the place in the dark.

As they clambered up the bare wooden staircase, the depth of the absolute darkness had its effect on Linsdale' already unsettled mind. He panicked, and in a mad frenzy, seized the bearded man's jacket and pulled. Both of them toppled over backwards onto the third man and they all tumbled down the stairs in a ball of violence. The scrimmage ceased with someone banging someone else's head on the floor, and someone else knocking something over with a loud crash. An obscure figure rose from the human scree and groped towards the door. Somebody snatched at its legs, but Linsdale was a second quicker, dashing out through the doorway and running off like a frightened chicken, into the undergrowth.

'Damn it, don't let him get away,' cried an angry voice.

03.15hrs. Perthshire. Snapping twigs in the wood froze Broaley in his position. He could tell the sound was coming from far off, but he still took no chances and dived for cover. It could be anything; a poacher, or Linsdale. He wasn't being too fanciful with his odds for Linsdale turning up here for this was one of the many hot surveillance areas of which he was making a lightning tour of inspection. The noise stopped and he had no real idea of the direction it had come from. He could play the fool of a Rob Roy and waste time searching in the wood, or he could continue on, more sensibly, to the Army Reconnaissance lookout point. Thumbing the safety catch back on the pistol in his pocket, he consulted his luminous compass and moved on.

He was too engrossed in his action to notice the two 'trees' that were watching him. The 'trees' wore green and brown camouflage combat dress and one held a long walkie-talkie. The soldier spoke into the radio and the message raced out to a 'fox' hiding out across the wood. This Fox was steel-plated and had a 30mm Rarden cannon for a snout. A beret with the Signal Corps badge bobbed in the armoured car's chest, below the gun. It turned in as the message came through. 'Sir; message from BADGER. Reports somebody in sector Z-Nine now. Coming this way. That's all, sir. Oh yes, and does anyone want a fine rabbit for breakfast?'

The commander, seated on top, with his head above the armour-plated shell, didn't bother to turn away from his toy. He spoke with his face buried in the knobs and pieces of the Mel Infra-Red periscope. 'All right; relay the message to HQ. While you're at it, better tell them we've seen no further signs of activity at HUB since our last report at 02.00 hours. That'll do.'

He busied himself with the rectangular periscope and focused it on HUB. This was a tiny hamlet mounted on the rolling landscape in front of them. It was the wheel hub, or centre point towards which the soldiers and police were hoping to drive any possible prey, in their search of that area. The periscope functioned in total darkness over a range of 1000metres, so he had a good view. He continued to fuss with the instrument's finer points until the new buzz of activity from the radar below attracted his attention.

'Something approaching fast, sir. Too small for a car. Could be a motorcycle. Or a moped.'

'It *is* a moped. I can hear it coming now,' said a second voice from below. 'It'll be that old gamekeeper bloke. He's got a moped. I was right the last time.'

'You should be wearing a deerstalker, Sherlock, not a flippin' beret,' said the first voice.

The commander rotated the turret so that the periscope faced the road leading to the hamlet. 'So let's have a look, then,' he said, adjusting the eyepiece. 'Yes, you're right, it is a moped.' A squat figure in a white helmet whizzed past and receded in the distance, with only a dark line between its legs to support it. Like a wizard on a broomstick. The rider turned off the road, into the homestead beside the hamlet, and the turret turned back to its original position.

Silence was next broken by the sound of someone coming out of the darkness just beside them. Broaley handed his pass to the soldier in the front hatch. 'Major Broaley; Intelligence, 'he said curtly. Normally he would have barked the soldier down for not making a thorough inspection of the pass, but he was in no mood for barrack-room games. There were more important things to be critical about. He put the pass away in his pocket and looked up at the commander. 'Nothing?'

'Nothing so far, sir. Just a few locals. Nothing unusual from outside.' Broaley looked round about at nothing but darkness for a few minutes and then made up his mind to move on to the next observation point. He was about to knock on the steel hull to signal that he was moving on, when the periscope suddenly swivelled round to the side as a new subject came into the field of view. The commander spoke sharply. 'Get on to HQ. Tell them, new subject approaching HUB from sector Z-Nine.' He remembered the Major behind him and moved his face a few inches to the side of the periscope to speak askant: 'Someone moving in towards the hamlet from the wood, sir.'

The hazy figure danced side to side before settling in the centre of the infra-red viewer. It shed its fuzzy skins, as the focus changed, to become a clear figure stumbling through the brushwood. It didn't look like a poacher to the commander. More like a city gent. He gave a sharp command: 'All right; get that camera out; quickly now! About forty-five degrees right.'

Before the words were finished, the infra-red camera was nosing out from the steel hull. It moved right, wavered, then stopped, before proceeding to suck flat copies of its prey in out of the dark. Frozen forever, by the eye of the long snake.

'Could be one of them, sir,' said the commander. 'Certainly doesn't look like a poacher. Seems to be drunk.'

That triggered off Broaley's reflexes. 'Get them to move in a cordon immediately!'

'Right away, sir. I'll get this thing started, while we're at it.' The commander climbed down inside to start the engine, but Broaley called out to stop him.

'Don't! That'll attract too much attention. We don't want to frighten them back into hiding. Give me one of your men to show me the way down.' He looked at the man in the front hatch and tapped his shoulder. 'You'll do. And step on it!'

The soldier clambered out and went off into the black void where the Major had vanished. He caught the air-cutting sound of the steel slide on Broaley's automatic being pulled back to spring a cartridge from the magazine into the chamber, ready for firing.

31

09.03hrs, 26th June, Faslane Naval Base. '--spokesman said the Foreign Office was looking into the allegation, following an incident in which a British chartered plane was hijacked over Holland and a British woman received serious injuries. National Rail is to convene a board of enquiry into the rail crash which occurred outside Preston last night, in which four people died and seventeen were injured. Eight of the injured have been detained in hospital, with what the hospital described as 'critical conditions'. Among the dead was the driver, who was to have made this his last journey before retiring. Also among the dead was the playwright, Charlotte Rollings. Miss Rollings was best known for her controversial sex play, *White Stallions*, in which Royal horses are said to be implicated. Reports coming in say that the accident may have been caused by rails buckling under heat. The Minister of Transport, Mr Goodwin, has promised to set up an independent scientific council which would look into this matter and so make rail travel much safer for the future. Spokesmen for National Rail have not ruled out the possibility of the crash having been caused by terrorists. And now for today's weather. The day will remain sunny, with occasional showers occurring in -------'

Sherman switched off the transistor radio and went on buzzing the Philips battery razor over his stubbled face. The wood and canvas squeaked beneath him, and he stood up from the rickety camp bed, where he had spent the last five hours in solid slumber, like a block of concrete. Pamela had been halfway there about his not being able to keep his eyes open. He had only just managed to stay awake for another hour after landing, before collapsing in a boneless heap of sleep in this office that the Navy had lent him. If one of Linsdale's wretched bombs had gone off at the foot of the bed, he wouldn't have twitched an eyelid, having been so switched off to the world.

Sherman leaned over the desk as he shaved, to look at the day's headlines in the paper he had asked for. The headlines were much the same as those on the radio, with DEATHLINE DISASTER and AMSTERDAM HIJACK vying for first place. Between contending stories was the faded, badly printed picture of the dead playwright. Further down the page was the blonde woman, described as a civil servant injured while returning from vacation in Holland. Linsdalewas nowhere to be seen on the front page, being no longer that important. The best he could merit was a half column on the third page, which wasn't too important at all. God, if only that was so. But it wasn't so, and it wasn't just the feeling Sherman had in his stomach; it was the harrowing night he'd had, thinking and re-thinking things over on the plane, and here, between phone calls, before sleep had finally clutched him to its black abysmal bosom.

The cup of tea that the petty officer placed on Sherman's desk didn't help much. Sherman ignored the tea and picked up the folder with the plain white ribbon label on its front:

FIELD INTELL REP 801139//GLASGOW//JUNE 26//MAJ BROAL//

It had been lying there with the newspaper, waiting for his attention before he had stirred from his sleep. He opened the folder and glanced at the white teleprint report from Broaley, turning as he did, to his tea. Taking a sip, he read over the cup's rim until he began shaking his head. 'Hell, they haven't. They damn well haven't,' he cursed softly to himself.

'Bad is it, sir?' asked the petty officer, not really concerned with the report, but only trying to butter Sherman up with favours. 'Can I get you a roll and egg, sir? Or maybe a hot roll and sausage? The sausage is very good, sir.'

Sherman didn't hear the offer, being miles away. He went on reading the report, cursing to nobody but himself. 'They couldn't just not find the man. They had to find him and then let him slip through their ruddy fingers again!

I don't bloody believe it!' He threw the empty folder into the wire tray and the report sheet after it. But the flimsy paper floated back out, so that it curled up against the teacup. Sherman picked up his cup for another sip, leaving the paper to lament in disgrace by itself. The petty officer went about his business of tidying up the bed. Sherman watched him fold up the bed frame and tidy the woollen blankets with a swift flurry of primness that he had long since left behind with his boy scout days. 'Have there been any more messages for me, from Major Broaley, apart from this?'

'Who, sir?'

'Major Broaley; from Intelligence.'

The petty officer racked his brains for a moment and then remembered. 'That must be him downstairs, sir, having a cup of tea. I gave him a roll and egg.'

Sherman was a bit surprised. He hadn't expected the Major back on his doorstep so soon after he'd been let loose in the field. Like a good whippet, there was no stopping him once the trapdoor had been sprung open. 'Get him to come up and see me right away, will you.' Sherman waved the bed and things aside. 'Never mind that.'

'Aye, aye, sir.'

Sherman couldn't imagine the hard Broaley eating a sedate roll and egg. Nor did the illusion materialise, for when Broaley did come into the office, he was back on his cigarettes. They looked at each other for a few seconds and then Sherman put his open palm under the report sheet and wafted it up into the air. 'So what the hell's this supposed to be, Major?'

Broaley watched the paper float back down with a final spiral flutter while he took another drag on his Dunhill. He leaned back against the steel cabinet and rubbed his hard lined brow with the back of his thumb. 'You could well say that we all but dissected every blade of grass in that area, looking for him. He was just no longer there.'

Sherman ran a hand over his face in anguish. 'What it amounts to is that you let him give you the slip; you let him get clean away! Do correct me if I misheard you, but did you tell me that you let him get clean away, didn't you?'

'We didn't have enough men in the area to mount a proper cordon, right away. Only a limited number of surveillance personnel, that's all. By the time the cordon had moved in, he was gone.' He paused to inhale and blow out the smoke. 'That wooded terrain and darkness doesn't make it ideal conditions for that sort of manoeuvre, either.'

The sarcasm crept out in a smile on Sherman's face. 'Let me remind you, Major, that we haven't got the *choice* of ideal conditions; not in this morning's fiasco, or in anything else since this whole muddle began. What's more, things are going to be even less 'choicey' tonight, if we don't come up with something pretty smart. We are agreed on that, are we?'

Broaley took in the agitated words and connected their acid bite with the little bottle of bright yellow pills standing on the desk with its lid off. He also noted the camp bed propped up on its end in the corner, and the fact that while he himself had been out all night on the job, others had slept. Sherman leaned over the desk thrumming it hard, while he thought hard. 'Are we even sure it *was* Linsdale?'

Broaley shrugged his shoulders. 'It could have been someone else, I suppose. But it seemed a good enough likeness from what the photographs could show us. Considering the effect of drugs altering his appearance, that is.'

'Photographs?' Sherman couldn't remember any mention of photographs in the report and reached down to claw at the report sheet sticking to the linoleum.

'I didn't include it on that report, but we managed to get some infra-red shots of him on film. Or at least what seems to be a fair likeness of him, according to our artist's impression of what he could now look like. I didn't bring them with me. They're being blown up and circulated among our people throughout the country.' Broaley recalled another point. 'We also had an eye witness; a local forestry worker, to confirm that two men, one with a beard, were in that part of the wood at that time.'

Sherman sat down on the corner of the desk. 'Unless my brain fails me, this could make things much more serious than before.' He looked up at Broaley for agreement. But Broaley simply crossed his legs and folded his arms to wait for more. Sherman held out his hand to count off the points on his fingers. 'Well, the fact that he's broken away from his 'friends' suggests, surely, that he's recovering from his drugging and regaining his senses. So he'll surely remember the peril of his own bombs if he can't escape the country, and be inclined to come forward to the authorities, to save his own skin.'

'So?' There was a mocking look on Broaley's face, at Sherman's schoolmaster manner of recapping the facts.

Sherman ignored it and went on. 'So accordingly, the next natural circumstance would have been for him to have been seen and apprehended by our people. But instead, he vanishes. He hasn't been seen since. That suggests that he has, in fact, been recaptured by his so called 'friends'. Not only that, but having lost him for a short time, they're most likely, I would say, to take precautions against any similar occurrences.'

'You mean re-administer drugs to him, with a heavier dosage?'

'Precisely. And just under fifteen hours to go, at that.' Sherman bit his lip to fight off an even more frightening concept. 'But that's not what's worrying me.'

'Go on.' Broaley's amused expression faded as he waited for that between the lines.

'Well, now that they're under pressure from our people chasing them to ground, there's all the more reason to fear that they'll alter their plans and lie low longer than originally intended. There's no need, after all, for them to hurry, since they don't know about Linsdale's devilish devices. So why not wait until tomorrow, or the day after, or well ---?' He looked to Broaley for spirited response. He got it.

After staring back for a second or so, the Major came to life, stepping promptly away from the cabinet. 'I don't know about that,' he said, making for the desk. 'Let me get at that phone. Sherman jumped up and stood away from the desk to let Broaley get on with it. Broaley cradled the receiver between his jaw and shoulder so that he could flit through his notebook. 'Give me a line through to Army Intelligence in Edinburgh and MI5 in Glasgow.' He gave the password from his notebook. While he waited, he looked round at Sherman, to put him in the picture. 'I'm telling them to put the next phase of our operation into action. We know roughly how the cells in Scotland operate, from our surveillance reports; so now we need to make them move the way we want them to. If they're not already hot-footing it north to meet the *Yalta*, then we use the gillie's technique and beat them out of the bracken.' The Major cast his cigarette at the bin across the room and missed. 'Something's got to happen.'

'*Correction*, Major. Something *good* has got to happen.'

32

09.17hrs, 26th June, Faslane Naval Base. 'Christ! Something's happened!' cried the rating leaning over the teleprinter in the corridor, outside the Operational Analysis Room. He gave a whistle of apprehension as the machine burped up more of its ominous sheet. Ripping off the paper, he stood and looked at it. 'God, they've gone and let the fireworks off!'

'What was that?' asked Sherman, coming out of the NATO Liaison Office and feeling the fear of hell kick up inside himself, at the words rampaging through his brain. The statement didn't seem to affect Broaley much as he sidled up casually to see the message, still more concerned with his notebook of contacts than the prospect of nuclear annihilation. Sherman moved in much faster.

'It's the Gulf, sir. They've gone and blown the lid off the can,' said the rating, turning round with the paper.

'Yes, that's what I thought you said,' said Sherman, trying not to let his fears get the better of him and show on the surface. 'Let's see.' He took the teleprint sheet and held it up so he and Broaley could both have a look at it. 'Yes, you're right, there has been some kind of flare up.' Sherman wasn't familiar with the rest of the code and couldn't take any further meaning from the message. 'What else does it say?'

'I don't know, sir,' said the rating. 'That's all I can make of it so far. I can't make out the code here and here. Slatey'll know; he can tell us; it's his job.' He pointed along the line, at the grouped letters that were beyond his memory. 'But as far as I can make out, missiles have been launched.'

'You'd better get this decoded proper.' Sherman handed the paper back to the rating and looked round at Broaley.

'Do you think it's come to the worst?' asked Broaley.

'We'll find out soon enough. Come on, let's get over there and see what's going on.'

09.27hrs. The Operations Room's atmosphere was no more astir with excitement than it was on any ordinary day, with its sedate rows of ratings sitting hunched over their radar consoles like silver-faced gurus. But there were more officers than usual standing round one of the larger screens. There was also a small white light blinking away above the screen, at one flash and bleep a second, Sherman noticed. The lieutenant acknowledged Sherman's presence for even less time than this, with a curt glance, before giving his attention to the screen once more.

'Trouble?' said Sherman from the secluded rear of the group, and feeling that he could have done with some gold braid rings on his sleeves to get him into the viewers club. The lieutenant turned round, only half surrendered to the idea of talking shop to a civilian. His enthusiasm pepped up a little when he saw the credentials Sherman held out.

'It's an Iranian ship; Russian-trained crew; Russian missiles. We've just had a signal come through; seems their ship was trying to bring the curtain down prematurely.'

'So they fired their missiles first,' said Sherman, trying to pin down something solid and specific out of all the abstract phrases that were going around the room, ten to a tongue.

'They launched their missile first, and we counter-fired with one of ours; a double strike dual warhead model, and it seems they fired another one of theirs at that. All over and done with in seconds. Oh, no ships damaged, incidentally, but a heated moment, all the same. Had our minds racing neck and neck with the computers for a sec, I'll tell you.'

'Do we know what caused the flare-up in the first place?' said Sherman.

'No, as a matter of fact, we don't yet. We don't know what class of missiles were fired yet, either. But we'll know in a tic; the computers are working on the signals now. From what I can see of it, though, I'd say it was some trigger-happy or nervous-fingered fool letting off a target drone, or accidentally over-flexing his muscles in a practice drill on a missile deck. Either way it was bloody stupid. The bloody idiot could have had the whole place blown to smithereens for nothing; absolutely nothing. We can do without that type in the Service.'

Sherman wondered to himself if there was any real difference between the whole place being blown to smithereens for 'nothing', and the whole place being blown to smithereens for 'something'. He looked along the line of Marconi computers and radar systems humming over the problem, without the interfering folly of man's batty logic. It was always fascinating how the big 'boxes' worked on unaided, to specify with incredible accuracy, over incidents like these occurring thousands of miles away across the Atlantic. As it was, the combined effort of satellites and high flying reconnaissance aircraft made this possible, beating the miles in their thousands, to bring home the signals for the computers to chew over. This advanced data display equipment served the function of data gathering (detection, tracking, height finding, target identification and target size analysis); and data utilisation (threat analysis, weapon assignment and weapon controls). Once a target was acquired by radar, the information was transmitted by data link to the Command Reporting Centre, where it would first appear on a display console as a conventional target blip. The data was simultaneously transmitted to a video processor which determined whether the blip was a genuine target, enemy jamming, or simply video clutter. The information was next passed to a correlator, or computer memory unit for generating target tracks for genuine radar returns. These would be returned to the original display as synthetic tracks in the form of digitised track symbols. This would be superimposed upon the raw radar, providing the operator with two means of tracking the target. Target identification was then accomplished by sound identification, or by computer comparison of target characteristics. Potential target co-ordinates were transmitted automatically to surface-to-air missile batteries at interceptor airfields, coastal command stations and naval vessels. Sherman reflected that probably at this moment Monk's lot would also be gawking at such signals, be it just a stone's throw across the loch at the Holy Loch submarine base, or further afloat across the waters in their armada of vessels. As would the Russians.

Broaley seemed slightly scornful of all the faith entrusted to the whole caboodle of humming electronic gadgets, considering that he got all his own results by his own leg-work. 'I think it's quite amazing, all the same, how those little spots can represent so much real danger and devastation,' he said, referring through his near hypnotic stare to the blips on the screen.

'Like the skin spots of a plague, I suppose,' said Sherman. 'Quite harmless enough in their appearance on the surface, but in reality, enough to wipe out nations.'

'I wouldn't worry about it too much, gentlemen,' said the lieutenant. 'It's when that orange light goes on, that you start to worry. That's when the big trouble begins, not before.' They all looked at the orange bulb, inert beside the flashing white bulb, half dreading, half expecting it to go into action. It didn't. Two screens away, white segmented letters that looked as if they had been diced up with an onion chopper began to stipple their way across the screen. 'Ah, here we are,' said the lieutenant, without giving as much as a clue to which one of the many screens he was referring to. 'Well, I wasn't spot on, but I was near enough, anyway, in my guess.'

They watched the classification of the Russian/Iranian missiles shift across the screen:

CLASS:-- SAN-4//--TYPE:--RAM-67A//--NATO CODENAME--GUNI//--RANGE:--16.8km//--VELOCITY:--MACH2//--LENGTH:--4.3m//--MOTOR:--DUAL-THRUST SOLID PROPELLANT///--GUIDANCE:--SEMI-HOMING//

The letters repeated themselves for the second Russian/Iranian missile and then vanished magically. The British missile was next: CLASS:--SAN-4//--TYPE:--RIL-63A//--NATO CODENAME:--GRYPHON//--RANGE:--18.7km//--VELOCITY:--MACH2.5//--LENGTH:--4.0m//--MOTOR:--SOLID FUEL BOOSTER AND LIQUID FUEL RAMJET//--GUIDANCE:--INFRA-RED OPTICAL DETECTION TAIL-FIN STABILISER//

'Ah, yes, the GUNI,' said the lieutenant, 'that's comparable to the old discontinued SABRE. Not as good a performance, though. The old SABRE easily managed about, oh, let me see, seventeen and a half kilometres, compared to the GUNI's sixteen point eight kilometres. We also had the edge over them for velocity, if I remember rightly. They should be making the GUNI obsolete by now. Anyway, we put a prediction programme through the computers, on the Atlantic build-up, and came up with a zero point two possibility ratio forecast of this sort of accidental clash occurring.'

'If I remember correctly,' said Sherman, 'our computers also predicted a similar clash on Europe's growing Eastern/Western divisional tension, on a zero point four three ratio. At least I think that was the number quoted.'

'No, it would be zero point *three four*, actually, but it still leaves room for thought, ' said the lieutenant.

'Yes, I agree, it certainly leaves room for thought.' As Sherman spoke, he noticed out of the corner of his eye, the officer behind the glass in the Communications cubicle pointing them out to a white-shirted rating. The rating approached the civilians, not sure which one was which, handing out a note for a Mr Sherman. Sherman took the note. 'It's Sir Richard. The Prime Minister has been on to him and wants our statements before the President consults him.'

'The President?' said Broaley.

'Yes, he's due on the 'hot-line', from Washington, in fifteen minutes time. Perhaps you'd better come along, Lieutenant, and lend us a hand with those fancy computer figures of yours.'

'All right, but first I've got to go and fix this up on the projector, for all the NATO lot coming over to see it.' He held up the film reel can.

Sherman twisted his head to read the codename on the label. '*DOME*?'

'Yes, it's Phase III in survival counter-measures against radio-active fall-out immediately following a nuclear explosion.'

Sherman noted to himself that DOME could also be short for the Old English spelling of Domesday, or Doomsday. He looked at Broaley and saw that he was anxious to get away. 'Can you hang on, Major, until I'm finished with my phone call?'

Broaley didn't want to wait around and looked at his watch to emphasise this. 'Time's running out.'

'Well, if you do go before me, see and leave me word where I can get you. All right?'

Broaley nodded, took out another cigarette, and disappeared through the swing door.

09.41hrs, (GMT) Moscow. To meet world opinion, the Russian news agency, ITAR-Tass, was putting forth a staunch line supporting Russia's 'new' aggressive policy. Russia, it claimed, wanted war no more than anyone else. But it would not back down lest it should convey the false message that it believed its actions to be wrong. The Kremlin was resolutely unanimous in this, with a call for positive assertion in the face of American imperialism that would leave no one in doubt. It would not only ignore the United Nations Security Council in New York, but it would also step up the military programme by building up and sending out more troops and armoured divisions.

09.41hrs, (GMT) Washington. The President was not at all satisfied with the Security Council's somewhat wrangled handling of Russia's menacing stance. He was feeling a mounting uncertainty over his decision to comply with the UK's request for the United States to convey military support for Israel. And as for that trigger-happy hash-up by the British in the Gulf ---. After Granada and Guantanamo Bay, it made a change for the critical finger not to be pointing at US servicemen for tactical blunder, but at the British. It was a wonder that the Oval Room's massive desk wasn't collapsing under the weight damning reports that had come in -- and were still coming in. Surrounded by seeming battalions of generals bellowing out their advice on how to advise the British Prime Minister, he was not looking forward to the call so much as an allied ear to level out troubles with, than as a landmine to avoid.

09.41hrs, London. In Downing Street, the Prime Minister was nervous over his intended report to the US President, especially over the Navy's botched handling of a missile flare-up with Iranian ships in the Gulf. With Iran's and Syria's now open support of the Hamas rocket onslaught of Israel, it was difficult to see on which side of the scale America's judgment would fall, over Britain's cajoling them into granting military aid to Israel. He looked in dismay at the papers on his desk. The report he'd just had from Sir Richard Hossley from the Secret Intelligence Directorate did nothing to put him at ease. He waited, tensed, for the light on the red scrambler phone to flash its signal that the US President's call was on the line. The heavy ticking of the clock in the silent room increased his tension.

33

01.01hrs, 26th June, Thames Embankment. While Presidents and Prime Ministers talked over their 'hot-lines' on the strategic build-up of their mighty warships Atlantic waters, the two FSB men stood outside the Royal Festival Hall, discussing a chink in the Western armour; the submarine *Yalta*. The crowd of youngsters milling around them with their violin cases fitted the scene well. Like Chicago hoodlums protecting their racketeer bosses. But the only racketeers present were Sergei Daniloff and his first FSB officer, second Assistant to the Cultural Secretary at the Embassy, whilst the rest were genuine members of the Russian Youth Orchestra that was touring Britain that week. Daniloff drew his first officer a little more out of earshot of the youngsters before letting him continue the conversation.

'And are we certain that the *Yalta* will be making a rendezvous off the Scottish coast later tonight?'

Daniloff was about to answer but stopped, as a blond boy came forward and asked him to join a small group for a photograph. Daniloff accepted the offer with a genial smile, stepping forward to join the group and let them take the photograph. He returned promptly to his first officer. 'Of that we are most certain, but exactly where and when the *Yalta* will be making its rendezvous, we do not know. As you know yourself, only the last link in the chain line of cells in Scotland holds this information. And from what you tell me, it is now too late to recall the cell members who are transporting Dr Linsdale. Am I correct?'

'That is the trial technique we are now employing, sir. Once a mission of this degree has been in operation for twenty-four hours, the cells involved become self-perpetuating, by cutting off all help and communications from us outside. This way, there can be no chance of them being tricked into a false recall by a fake signal from the security forces searching for them.'

'Quite,' said Daniloff.

A new wave of spirited bright-eyed youth surged forward, and the two men broke off from their devious topic to pump the youngsters' hands up and down in a great show of cultural solidarity. When they were free after a few seconds, the two men turned to each other once again. 'But can we not simply pick up Dr Linsdale for an exchange when he is on board the submarine, sir? Or even when he is taken back to one of our own naval bases?'

Daniloff beamed down at his man like a patient father instructing his son. 'The simplicity of such a plan would be most certain, I grant you, my friend, but the wastage would be equally so, like the vinegar juices in a badly made wine. The British, it seems, are most anxious to procure Dr Linsdale today, the twenty-sixth. So to make an exchange after today would be too late. Why this is, we do not know; but perhaps we shall increase our wisdom as we progress.' Daniloff smiled and bowed his head to the young Ukrainian girl who was a genius on the first violin, with a hundred years virtuosity in her sixteen-year-old fingers. He tapped his chin in thought. 'There is another point worth bearing in mind.'

'And that is?'

'And that is that the British may be fully aware of our submarine and are deliberately allowing it to slip through their coastal network in order to reach its rendezvous. What I believe the British would proverbially term as 'dangling a carrot'.'

'Sir?'

'Simply that it could be a positive ruse to bring our people out into the open with Linsdale, and so be snared.'

'All the more reason then, that we should go ahead and put Maunders into a parallel cell that will converge on the other escape cells and so allow him to meet up with Linsdale on the last route to the *Yalta*. At that stage, we can intercept and take Linsdale ourselves.'

'Precisely, my friend, precisely.' To push the message home to his officer,

Daniloff laid a large patronising hand, like a great bear's paw, on the man's shoulder and squeezed it. He then gave the man a dull brown package full of instructions and, what felt by its weight, a gun. The man, in turn, handed Daniloff some brochures on the coming music festival, to make things look more innocent.

'And this Maunders?' asked Daniloff, while appearing to read through the brochures.

'A reliable enough person, it seems. I spoke to him yesterday. Perhaps a trifle too naive in his bourgeois complicities, with his acquired leanings of Western ---'

Daniloff cut him off to stop an unwanted lecture on politics. 'But can he see the operation through to its completion?'

'On my better judgment, I'm sure he will serve the purpose ideally. His cover is already blown, so we tell him to flee the country, at the same time as putting a tail on him, to trace him to Linsdale.' The man looked round at the Hungerford Bridge, but couldn't make out any of the distant figures distinctly. 'He's out there now, on the bridge, waiting for me to contact him. It's time I went.'

Daniloff looked over at the bridge and didn't like the proximity of such a contact, with the youngsters so close around him. He put the business at an end by snapping out of their secretive talk. 'Very well, then.' He smartened the lapels of his raincoat. 'Report to me as soon as our hawk has caught its sparrow.'

'I'll do that.'

With their real business at an end and nothing more to share that wasn't a cover, like their supposed interest in the music festival, they nodded to each other, estranged once more. Daniloff went and planted himself in the midst of a group photograph, an oak tree among the seedlings, while the other FSB man went off to meet George Maunders out over the river, on the Hungerford Bridge.

The bridge was a good choice of meeting place, since there was no chance for tails to linger around shop windows or sit in cafes or cars. This was apart from the fact that narrow bridges like this always had the effect of swallowing up people so that they were virtually dehumanised into dots for heads and sticks limbs. The spaniel poked its head out through the bars in the bridge's side, for a peep at the tug chugging out from underneath, as Maunders, at the same time, scanned the banks and the two bridge ends for suspicious characters. He checked the time. Spot on, the man from the Embassy came into view at the far end of the bridge, and Maunders gave a final secret wink to the dog before preparing to restrain his humour. He remembered, after all, from the last meeting, that the man was inclined to be a bit on the grumpy side.

The man stopped short at an arm's length distance from Maunders, like a stranger, and pretended to look out from the bridge, as two women passed by with a pram. Maunders didn't believe much in mind reading, but he sensed a mood emanating from the man, so different from the last time, and wondered if he was being over presumptive in thinking he knew what it was. Rather than probe direct, he decided to play out the simple lines. 'So what tricks do I do this time? Who's it to be now?'

The man stared down at the traffic moving along the Victoria Embankment, to measure out his words before answering. 'It has been unanimously decided that your services be strictly terminated. We can no longer use you.'

Maunders had thought as much, but continued to play out his innocent ignorance. 'What's wrong, then? Didn't I satisfy you with my work?'

'On the contrary, you have rendered a most commendable service to your country, for which you will not go unrewarded. Have no fear of that. But your work must stop there. Your cell has been broken, with a most zealous efficiency I must admit, within the last forty-eight hours. It follows that you couldn't carry out any future operation for us without imposing a severe risk on the operation.'

'And you want me to run? They must be really desperate to lay their hands on Linsdale.'

'Yes.'

'Any idea why he's so valuable?' The man didn't answer why, and Maunders reckoned that he would have had an easier time prising a clam open with a toothpick.

'You must sever all links with the Embassy and our people in the City.' He turned round to face Maunders, passing the brown package over, looking at the package, rather than at the recipient. 'Your directions,' he said, eyes still down and dabbing the package with his finger. 'Expenses, details, and *things*, for your exit north and out of the country.'

Maunders felt the weight of the package and knew it was a gun. He just knew the bugger would take it the wrong way if he said that he already had his own pistol. 'Yes, and *things*.' He was touched by a pang of uneasiness he had never experienced before. 'That'll be the North route, I suppose?'

'Yes.'

'I see.' Maunders had always known, from the very beginning of his training, that a day such as this would come. It was something all sleeper agents were told to anticipate in their majority. Only the times for individual withdrawal varied, according to luck's circumstances. But now that the day had come, he felt strange inside. *Sad*, to be honest. For the latter half of his lifetime, he had lived on English soil, and for just less than that had taken on London, not as an alien city as advised, but as his own native city. He had shared its ups and downs in the later post war climb to social prosperity, and had felt its spirit wafting through its streets and mostly through its people. He looked round at the river's banks and its crowded skyline bristling with 'capitalist' bastions.

The man broke into Maunders' thoughts. 'I strongly suggest you make a point of hurrying.'

'In that case, I'd better get back and pack my bags.'

The man's head jerked round sharply. 'No! You will go *now*! Literally *now*! There can be no going back now. Do you think I would have chosen this location for a meeting place if I could have more easily phoned your instructions, or sent them by post? Your shop is clearly being watched day and night. Your telephone line and mail are being monitored. You must make your departure right now.'

Maunders knitted his eyebrows for a second and then looked down smiling, at the dog. He tugged the lead playfully. 'Just as well that I brought you along, eh? I couldn't possibly leave you behind. Isn't that right, eh? Isn't that right?'

The man's patience snapped and he turned right round to face Maunders, the anger now open in his face. 'Get rid of it!' Maunders looked up with surprise and the man went on. 'You will have it destroyed! That is an order!'

'Hey, steady on a minute, you're asking me to ---'

'You will do as you're told, and have it destroyed! We haven't taken this trouble to arrange your escape, only to have the plans jeopardised by some stupid pest of a dog. The people watching for you must surely know you have a dog, if they know your dossier at all. To tag it along with you will only make you all the more conspicuous. It will also be an inevitable point of hindrance. Or do you really want me to go on and quote our country's quarantine laws?'

Maunders attempted no further words, but looked down at the dog, stroking its smooth warm head.

The FSB man saw a festering bubble of trouble that had to be pricked promptly there and now. Looking both ways to see that there was no one else on the bridge, he took the lead from Maunders and in one ruthless gesture of expediency, picked up the dog and threw it over the side of the bridge. He smiled at the dog's pitiful howl, enjoying it more at the sound of the fateful splash down below. He turned to Maunders. 'Move!'

Maunders would have liked to have slain the man there with his bare hands. But he wasn't fool enough to forget that the man was younger and tougher, with professional training to boot. The man, in fact, scared him. Swallowing his fright and fear, Maunders turned and walked off towards the Embankment end. The man watched him for a few seconds, satisfied that he had spurred the old fogy on with enough fear to do the job, and then went off the way he had come.

Maunders' mind was so caught up in the situation, that he didn't at first notice the two men coming along behind him from the South Bank end. He did notice them when he turned to look behind with casual curiosity at the sound of their steps ringing out on the metal walkway. But what alerted his serious attention was the way the man, while listening in to he mobile, suddenly looked up at him, as if through instruction from the phone. Maunders recognised the movements. He quickened his pace. They quickened theirs. There was no doubt about it. He broke into a run and the Special Branch men started to run as well. Nipping smartly down the Embankment Place staircase, Maunders tore through the crowd of people coming up the stairs, and made off round the corner. The Special Branch men weren't so lucky and had to struggle for a moment to get through the crowd. They followed the sound of Maunders' running feet round the corner and under the steel bridge. Maunders was nowhere to be seen. The Special Branch men looked round at the three identical Hackney cabs haring off up Northumberland Avenue. All three looked empty, but Maunders was obviously crouched down low in one of them, getting away pretty fast.

The tall American cheerfully chewing asparagus while admiring the English architecture, now spoke into a microphone through the window of his parked Mustang. Monks got into the car to follow Maunders, but suddenly found the way blocked by a car which had just as suddenly developed 'engine trouble'. The FSB had just secured the safe release of their homing-pigeon that was to lead their hawk to the sparrow.

Further up the street, beyond the noisy hubbub of the traffic jam, with its honking horns, little attention was given to the two hurrying figures in black burkhas. Only the street beggar sitting on the pavement, looking out from the large cardboard box that was his home noticed the oddity of the two figures. He couldn't help thinking that, whilst the body frames were small enough and thin enough to belong to women, the way that they moved was definitely like that of two *men*. He could see that they were up to no good. The streets had their own 'news' system, so that he knew all about darkie terrorists. He'd been in the Army in India during the Gandhi troubles and had seen what the darkies could do with their bloomin' great parang blades. But he wasn't going to shift his arse an inch to get a copper. If he did, someone else could move in and steal his patch here, where he got a decent lot of money dropped in his tin lid. No, what these bloomin' Indians did with their bloomin' knives was somebody else's business, not his. He cast his eyes down, seeing the commando combat boots beneath the flapping black robes, as Hassani and Bahsoud hurried on past him on their deathly mission of mass destruction.

34

12.17hrs, 26th June, West Lothian. The sky was darkening rapidly with thunder clouds when the black Mercedes crossed the Forth Road Bridge and bowled along the A90 heading for the Scottish capital. It was here that the olive green Porsche took up the tail. At first only a small dot, it grew and gained quickly on the Mercedes, without the driver paying it undue attention. As it nosed nearer, the Mercedes driver noticed it and smiled at the thought of what it could be. He patted his pocket, where his Beretta machine pistol was. Bahsoud's gesture didn't escape Hassani's attention.

Sherman looked aside at Broaley, who was driving the Porsche. 'I think he's on to us now, Major.'

Broaley's face twitched a muscle to show that he was listening above his concentration on the car in front. 'Yes, I think so, too. That's a pity. But we can't afford to lag behind too far in a city. That's all right for country roads.'

'Do you think he could be leading us on? I've got a feeling he is.'

'Maybe. The thought has crossed my mind a dozen turns back. But we'll let him play out his lead, to tickle our onions a little longer, to see what he does.' The chase was part of Broaley's cup and ball rattling game, in a clamp down on all the Russian cells in Scotland. Whilst some cell members were seized for interrogation, others were being allowed to run, so that they could be chased to bigger gains. It didn't matter which direction they ran, so long as the information could be grabbed at the end. They had been chasing this Mercedes with its one passenger for some time now. Maybe it *had* been fooling them all that time as a decoy. 'On second thoughts,' muttered Broaley, 'I think we'll call their bluff and pull them in. Are you with me?'

'Don't let me stop you, Major; just do it.'

As the Porsche nosed up to the Mercedes' bumper, the Mercedes moved away; but not enough, and the Porsche gradually gained on it, sliding past slowly. The passenger in the Mercedes had climbed into the back seat, and was now opening the back nearside window.

'Watch out!' said Broaley, his instinct for trouble prickling. Sherman tensed, half expecting the other car to spit out its lead venom to pock their windscreen with spider web bullet holes. That didn't happen. Instead, a gigantic white 'butterfly' flew out of the open window to attack them. The foam from the car fire extinguisher stuck to their windscreen, flattened down by the slipstream, blocking their view. In a fleeting instant before the view was cut off, Sherman thought he saw a familiar dark face. Was it one of those two Muslim terrorists?

'Hell!' yelled Broaley, slamming on the brakes and upsetting the steering. Screaming tyres slid across the wet surface and Broaley fought for control, swinging the car round to a jarring screeching halt on the oncoming traffic lane. Sherman looked out his window and his mind spun like a fruit machine's wheels. Only seconds away, the giant multi-ton tanker thundered on at them, its driver petrified at the imminent doom. With only inches to spare, the tanker swerved past them and slewed out broadside across the highway, demolishing a lamp-post and crushing a parked car. The coupling snapped under the impact and the great steel lizard rolled over and over, smashing another two poles and belching out its corrosive chemical vomit in dying fury. The cabin sat naked and askew in the middle of the highway, while the driver sat trembling with shock. He was sure it hadn't been his fault. The other bloody drunken bastard in the Porsche had been on the wrong side of the road. He was sure of it. He shook a little and then wasn't so sure, looking at the empty lager can lying on the seat next to him.

He turned to see the other car for proof, but it was already moving away in a hurry.

Sherman sat back, wondering if he was the only one who could hear his nerves jangling like a calypso steel band. He glanced at Broaley and caught his eyes laughing at him. Foot hard on the accelerator again, they sped off into

Edinburgh, to take up the cat and mouse game in the stoney mass sprawling out beneath the skyline castle.

13.20hrs, Army Intelligence Divisional HQ. Khaki had been swapped for civvies, but that didn't make the Army men any less active, pounding away on keyboards and barking above each other's noise, into telephones. The sergeant put his phone down and turned the Major. 'The car's been found abandoned round the back of the Royal Infirmary, sir.'

'For all that's worth, I suppose,' said Broaley, pausing as he looked down at his keyboard, then looking up. 'They're probably miles away, for all we know, or there again, they could still be here, under our very noses, in the city. I wouldn't put a penny either way on a bet.' He looked up for an opinion from Sherman, who was on the phone.

Sherman put his hand over the mouthpiece. 'If it *was* those two, Hassani and Bahsoud, they must have penetrated the cell system somehow, to get help. They were operating independently up until now.'

'Maybe they still are, and just wanted to borrow a car,' said Broaley.

'Well, they've lost it now. So what's their next move?' Sherman looked to the sergeant. 'Have they found out anything from the car's registration number?'

'Yes, sir,' said the sergeant. 'The owner's from Perth. Obscure background; not many too many details. But an Identikit picture has been made up from what we could learn from local acquaintances in Perth. Pictures of the two Muslims are being circulated in the area now.'

'Good,' said Broaley. 'In the meantime I want them to go on turning the city upside down to see if we can still nail the miserable wretches. You've made this clear to the police, I take it?'

'Yes, sir. As a matter of fact, the Inspector was quite angry; hopping mad, in fact, when we got on to him, when he learned that we were involved with the same car that was seen at the scene of the crash outside the city.'

'Hopping mad? Well you can tell him from me, Sergeant, that if he's so mad at this Road hog scratching the municipal paint off his lamp-posts, that's all the more reason for giving us his co-operation to catch these lunatics. If he doesn't, he may well have to deal with a greater crowd than usual attending the Tattoo. In a million smithereens at that, blown all the way up from London, no less. And that's no idle proposition, I can tell you, Sergeant.'

'I'll tell him, sir.'

'You do that, Sergeant.' Broaley typed out the final two lines of his joint Operations Report/ Command sheet and pressed the print button for two copies. Putting one copy, along with two other sheets, into a brown envelope and sealing it, he threw it over onto the sergeant's desk. 'Here,' he said, 'get that delivered pronto to Divisional Command. Who's in charge over there?'

'Brigadier Mirrel, sir.'

'Well get it over to the Brigadier immediately. *Immediately*, do you understand? Apart from the report, it's an outline on the scheme I propose to follow next.' With the other three sheets in his pocket, Broaley moved over to the wall map with the sergeant and looked round to see if he had Sherman's attention. Sherman signalled with a nod and watched the map, while he listened at the same time into the phone. 'So far,' continued Broaley, 'we've been hovering around this central region. If Linsdale's lot are here, or anywhere near here, it can only be for a short lingering spell; a stepping stone to the coast. They've got to come out sooner or later, on to the coast. I want Mirrel to put the word through to concentrate troops here and here, and along the coastline here. Northern Division have already combed this area here, and Southern Division have pretty well covered this lower area here, as you know, Sergeant. That leaves us to move out and upwards, splay fashion, through this region towards the coast; Angus, Kincardine, Aberdeen and the likes, in that fashion. Do you get me?'

'Nail on the head, sir.'

'Right; so get on with it.'

'Yes, sir.'

Sherman put the phone down and came over to the map. 'If they don't come to the coast, but try to jump it by helicopter, I suppose we'll have a counter-measure for that lined up, won't we, Major?'

Broaley was becoming tired of these schoolboy questions, with their piquing mistrust. How the hell did they ever let him out of school. 'We may not have got through the Picts' wall the first time, Sherman, but since then we've stopped using bows and arrows. Yes, we *do* have a plan ready for that contingency. In the meantime --- ' He left that to supposition, and picking up his jacket, moved out the door.

'In the meantime, Major, time marches on. I make it ten hours and thirty-five minutes to go.'

'Ten hours and thirty-*three* minutes; you're two minutes slow, Sherman.' Broaley turned to go.

'Where are we off to now?' said Sherman, reaching for his anorak.

'Tell you in a minute. First, I want to *wash my hands*,' said Broaley, walking towards the WC. 'Sergeant, have your man, Lommax, or whatever his name is, standing by to fix me up another fast car route on the map.'

'Right away, sir.'

35

16.12hrs, 26th June, RAF Leuchars, Fife. If Sherman couldn't see Mr Blenning on the other end of the phone, he could certainly imagine the man tinkering with that ruddy great bomb, until he touched the wrong wire, or whatever, and ended it all with a flash and high pitched whine down the line in his ear. Otherwise, there was an atmosphere of latent tension at other end of the line, Sherman thought, as unsure voices asked him to wait and then abruptly cut off, leaving him suspended. If that was pure imagination, it wasn't pure imagination that there was a line of Tornado F3 fighter planes standing along the airfield, ready for action. Looking at the cockpit covers cocked up in the air in open defiance, you could reckon that you were seeing the Battle of Britain the second time around. There was a sudden flash along the line of gleaming bodies, and Sherman looked round, expecting to see the fighters closing their cockpits and moving off down the runway. But planes had not moved. It was a momentary blocking of the sunlight down their line as an RAF Hercules transport plane groaned past overhead.

Sherman listened in again at a clinking sound, and heard someone coming to the phone. Blenning announced himself on the other end, and also seemed to be cursing. 'You sound as if you're having some trouble, Mr Blenning,' said Sherman, almost praying that it wasn't. 'Tell me it isn't serious, for God's sake.'

'Everything is serious from that aspect. But no, we're simply in a spot of bother with some cutting tools. I've blasted well gone and cut my hand as well, as it happens.'

'I hope that's all that happens, and that you're not going to let things get worse. Will we be able to make it in time? It's just under eight hours to go.'

'I'm hoping we can, but it's difficult to say, working under these unprecedented conditions. We'll all find out for certain, one way or the other.'

'I'd rather find out the one way, and *not* the *other*.' Sherman watched the ground crew technician through the glass partition, who was using a magnifying glass to inspect a micro-electronic circuit that resembled a cake of toffee. That brought him on to his next great worry. 'How is Dr Miles coping with it?' By some miracle of smooth-talking, and probably some hard-talking, diplomacy, their lot in Tehran had managed to secure the release of Dr Miles from the claws of the Iranians. What was Moscow up to? Was it so confident with another trick up its sleeve, that it could afford to let their key scientist go? The thought of that possibility had a chilling effect.

'Not as well as we had wanted, I'm afraid, ' said Blenning. 'His performance is just not his best, as we have come to know it. True, the medical office has given him a clean bill, but his somewhat traumatic experience in Holland still seems to have left its mark on him, alas.'

Sherman didn't like the sound of that. 'Are you trying to tell me that he's liable to fade out on us, or burn out his motors and collapse with nervous exhaustion, or something? Are you?'

Blenning paused for an answer to the biting question, and this made Sherman bite his lip, as his growing dread gnawed into his brain. 'We're trying to fend off such a situation to the last possible moment, with the best teamwork we can provide to assist Dr Miles,' Blenning said at last. 'I think you may have misunderstood me. He's not incapable of doing his work; simply slower. There's no real question of him failing to devise a functional principle from the theory. No, if the plan fails in the outcome, it won't fail on principle, but on account of Dr Miles' condition.'

'Bringing us back to square one, as I've been saying; Miles could be our big sore thumb. So now we can all be annihilated fuss-free in our beds, knowing that the plan was a good one, but didn't get off the ground because of Miles' imaginary spiders chasing him round the ruddy bend.' Sherman thought of the nuclear monster, not in Blenning's carefully calibrated scientific terms, but as a white-hot furnace with shrieks leaping higher than flames, to sear the minds when there was no more flesh left to burn. 'Are you positive that no disused mine shaft could withstand the shock of the explosion?'

'We're not positive of anything; that's why we've decided to take minimal risks. We can never be positive in such situations; only observant in our experiments. And this is certainly a strained experiment which, under normal circumstances, would never have been one of my choosing. No, the margin of error is too great to proceed with the mine-shaft proposal. Even assuming that the mine-shaft walls could withstand the force, there is the problem of placing the bombs in the correct position, first of all. This would require laying out a relay system of receiver units in order to pick up the transmitter signals, otherwise the bombs would explode, as you know, even before they went below ground level. Immediately following this, we have the sealing problem.'

'Sealing?'

'Yes. Obviously we wouldn't have the time to seal up the shafts once the bombs were laid, so that the radiation blasts would travel directly to the surface and into the atmosphere. To make matters worse, the shafts would have a streamlining effect to increase the velocity by a tremendous ratio. Just imagine two bullets being fired; one without a barrel and the other one through a long streamlined barrel.'

'I see what you mean.' You could just see baby Blenning curled up in his cot with his milky rusks and mind-wrenching horror stories. Forget the bloody teddy bears. Sherman looked at the receiver in his hand and could almost visualise the radio-active dust spouting out of it now.

'Well. if we apply these two analogies to the two explosions respectively, we see that in the un-streamlined blast, the atmosphere would tend to cushion the impact and so limit dispersal of radio-active material. In the second type of explosion, the streamlined type, the radiation blast with its greater velocity and concentrated pressure area would cut through the atmosphere for a greater distance, achieving a greater height, before being eventually stopped by the air. This whole effect would make it span out from a narrow stream, to a wider upper lying layer, so that resting on the lower layer of air, it has greater dispersal affects.'

'So instead of all that, we go to sea.'

'Precisely. We go to sea. Assuming we have kept within the time limit, the bombs will be taken by plane out to sea and dropped in the Atlantic, where the elastic power of the water will absorb the impact of the explosion.'

'And the fish perish, and we starve to death.'

'Possibly, along with other side effects which I don't care to go into. Like I said, it's not a theatre of my choosing, Mr Sherman, and given that we can surmount this problem, I would prefer to let matters rest on that.'

'That's if we're not killed in the mad rush for the last fish fingers at the supermarket,' said Sherman, being sarcastic to no-one but the situation.

Someone moaned out loud in the background in the phone, and Sherman's fears stepped up their gallop. 'it's no use, it won't fit in that way,' said a background voice near to Blenning, it seemed. 'We'll have to use a shorter filament.'

'Let's have a look,' said Blenning, as a lathe lowered its whining pitch and came to a halt. The voices dropped to a low, muffled, discussion, revealing nothing to Sherman so that his stomach screwed up as he waited. Blenning came back on the line. 'As you can see, there is an abundance of other problems surrounding us; perhaps only minor ones, at that, but time consuming in their collective effect, no less.' Blenning paused to ask someone for a hammer and set about striking something with sharp ringing blows that made Sherman's brain jump between his ears each time. 'I suppose it would be a tremendous bonus for all, if you could solve the problem for us,' said Blenning, amidst the commotion he was causing on the line at his end. 'Get Linsdale, I mean.'

'Yes, I know what you mean, Mr Blenning, believe me I do.'

'Don't hit it so hard,' said a background voice anxiously. 'You'll break the thread on the angle cap. Hell, it's broken. It'll slide dow. Don't let it slide, for God's sake!'

'It's all right; it's all right,' said another voice. 'I've got it. At least I think I've got it. I can feel something with my fingers.'

While Sherman's mind boggled at all he was hearing, Blenning cut in urgently to say that he was too busy to talk any more. Sherman put the receiver down slowly, realising that he had never before looked upon the telephone as being such an instrument of horror. Listening in on that lot, even at that safe distance, hadn't exactly soothed his nerves. It took guts to have listened on to see if the worst happened. He suddenly remembered that Blemming, with all his intrepid talent for mucking about with hydrogen bombs, was also a father of two children. He also remembered that one of them was about the same age as his own dead little boy. Bonus seemed an infinitesimally small word for an end to all this trouble.

16.29hrs, London. Downing Street had calmed to its quietist for the past few hours, with its flood of worried callers to Number Ten ebbing to a trickle. Pressmen had also faded away, tired of waiting for a new Lazarus to come forth at the door with a message from the other side. Likewise, all the CD-plated limousines had apparently suffered a mysterious attack of 'diplomatic distemper', or some similar contagion, that had wiped them off the streets. With all diplomatic messages having been delivered, hatches were battened down in a stalemate calm before the storm. Sir Richard was spared having to dodge the usual packs of 'D-notice' presshounds, and so continued his talk with the Defence Minister as they walked up the street, on their way to the Admiralty. But behind the city's false peace, a steady clatter of teleprinter tongues stuttered out the latest odds in the one big race where everyone had staked a shirt. Monks ripped the paper off the teleprinter and read the CIA field message from Langley. He quickly put the message through to British Intelligence. Sir Richard's pocket pager bleeped.

36

17.28hrs, 26th June, Glasgow. The sun was coming out again as Maunders made his way furtively across the wide expanse of George Square towards Queen Street Station. But that wasn't the only thing that was coming out, he noticed, glancing around at the sunlight flashing off the diced cap-bands of policemen who seemed to be out in force everywhere. A lot of them were armed. And that wasn't his imagination playing him up, either. It made him feel as if he were walking naked through the square, with all eyes trained on his every movement. It didn't help any, that he was now completely cut off on his own, with only a fugitive's nervous mind to follow the last minute instructions that he had been given. But now that he had started, he had to go through with it. He had just missed the five o'clock train for Aberdeen, having arrived thirty-three minutes late in the Central Station. The question was whether he should wait until ten past six for the next train to Aberdeen, or else take the five thirty-five train which only went to Perth. He didn't think it was too wise to linger around in a strange city, where security men were liable to pounce from any corner.

Conjecture turned to scaring fact, when he eyed the two men who were watching him from the station entrance. One of them was an ordinary police, albeit armed, while his companion was obviously plain clothes CID or Special Branch. Goose pimples jumped up on Maunders' neck as the armed policeman suddenly stepped out towards him. His fright dissolved just as suddenly in surprise when the policeman walked right past him to help an old lady pushing an invalid in a wheelchair up onto the pavement. He was so caught up in this and choked with relief that he didn't see the infant's pushchair until he walked into it. He was saved from falling over as he stumbled, by a firm hand gripping his arm. It was the plain clothes policeman. 'Are you all right, sir?' The policeman's eyes searched the silver-haired gentleman's kind face and registered a touch of nerves; probably travel fatigue. By simple routine inspection procedure the man's eyes went on moving down the old gentleman's form and just happened to be resting on the bulging pocket, when Maunders saw this. His intended words fled his frozen brain and his tongue felt like a mouthful of rope. He suddenly realised that he had been holding his gun tightly in his pocket, so that it must have been sticking out like a barge pole.

Nerves. He was not used to that size of gun, much larger than his own neat model, and hadn't felt happy when he'd been given it in his flurry of panic before leaving London. In fact, he almost couldn't yet quite believe that he had it, or that this was happening. It was a whole new side to his job that he had never really anticipated. In all his years - his *life* - as a sleeper, things had always run quietly and smoothly. Until now. A horrifying crazy thought rushed through his brain for a second at the idea of gunning the two them down. He had the element of surprise to his advantage. But he would never get far beyond that; not in a crowded place like this, with all these people about, and security round every corner.

He drew himself up, taking his hand away from his pocket as naturally as possible, his guilty feeling increasing as his friendly smile widened. Nervous confidence plucked his inside like a harp gone berserk as he tried to think of something to say. 'So who's coming to the city, then, Officer? Somebody grand? The Queen? All *this*?' Maunders gestured vaguely around him, pointing at last, to the policeman's sub machine-gun. His strength for keeping up face waned as the policeman continued to stare into him with hard eyes without uttering a sound. As the policeman tried to match up mental images and features with what he had standing in front of him, his attention was drawn to the crackling in his wired ear piece. He turned away, stepping back to listen to the message. Maunders saw the chance to escape and acted upon it. He made off like a frightened cat glad to have been granted a *tenth* life.

Maunders hurried towards the station entrance, imagining the eyes bore into his back. But contrary to his imagination, he heard no great dramatic pounding of boots on the ground in earnest pursuit of him. But his heart pounded in his chest. If this was a bad dream, he could believe it, more than he could believe it was real.

Minutes later, Maunders clutched his ticket, hurrying along the platform beside the fuming north bound diesel. He climbed onto the throbbing coach and made his way along the narrow aisle to an empty corner. The station started to slide past just as he collapsed with a large sigh of relief into the seat. His mind was on the alert for police and security men, so he had not paid any attention to the two railwaymen who, when they got onto the train, had removed their ScotRail caps and mackintoshes and handed them over to the ticket collector.

Maunders folded his arms and closed his eyes to recover himself and settle in for the long journey north. His mind was miles ahead -- and behind. He thought of the business. Of the custom he had taken roughly thirty-four years to build up. He thought of his young pal, Mr Bumble, whom he had so cruelly lost. What had become of him after he had been thrown in the river? What would happen to *himself*, for that matter? And who *was* that, for that matter? George Maunders? Or 'George' Mahrshazlinsky? His mind floated back to what seemed like another life long ago, with its golden leaves of autumn, where he had been cocooned in a brief happiness of boyhood. Before being snatched away from his family. After that he had belonged to no family, nor country, but merely the files on which his number was entered, in the State spy schools. He had never thought of it that way up until now, where life had been pleasant; but now, with fear raking his mind, his senses were attuned for the worst. It also occurred to him that one was supposed to have these nostalgic recollections when things were coming to an end. A change of sound as they went through the tunnel brought his mind back into the coach.

The first thing that he noticed, on opening his eyes, was that almost all of the people had vanished. The last one was being ushered through the far end door, into the next coach, by the ticket collector. Before Maunders could ask what was happening, he saw the dark reflection of a figure looming up in the window beside him, as the man stepped in from the adjacent doorway. Something metallic glinted for a second in the dark reflection's hand. Maunders turned to see that it wasn't a ticket punch that was gleaming in the man's hand. The Smith & Wesson drooped slightly in the man's hand when he saw no sign of Maunders giving any resistance. Maunders tried to smile through his tight face and pointed to the vacant seats. 'Have a seat; they're not taken.' His hollow sarcasm came out in a tremor of nerves, and when he swallowed, it was as if he had sandpaper in his throat.

Not impressed by Maunders' words, the man sat down silently, staring at him.

Maunders teased on, like a lamb to the slaughter hiding behind its feeble bleating. 'Going the same way as me, to Perth, are you?'

Still the man didn't answer. Words weren't necessary. No time was wasted on names or credentials. Each of them knew what the game was and who was now holding the trump card. The man looked Maunders over and made a bee-line for his right pocket. Maunders didn't flinch a muscle, as the blued steel barrel almost gouged his eye out with its closeness, while the man removed the pistol from his pocket. The man was very casual about his work, putting the confiscated weapon in his pocket, with the same innocence of a handkerchief, and sitting back down comfortably in his seat again. For all the care the man showed, Maunders wasn't even there. The man settled back in his corner for a peaceful ride and put a foot up on the seat, the Hush-Puppy sweating its murky raindrops dolefully beside the prisoner. He just knew that Maunders was going to be a good lad and not give him any trouble.

Maunders studied the face. It divulged nothing of the inner contents. It just looked back fixedly out of the opposite corner. Maunders wasn't fooled. The man would be a lot more cunning than the deliberate vacant expression he was showing. He had to be, to be picked for this type of work.

Maunders considered a test while they waited. He unfolded his arms. The gun jerked up reflexively and a row of teeth came out with a menacing politeness. The man knew his job, all right. At the sound of a sharp coin tap on the glass of the far end door, the man's gun slid beneath his jacket and his foot came down off the seat. The door drew back and the second man backed in, to let the ticket collector pass through up the aisle and out through into the next coach. The man at the far end stepped back out, closed the door, and continued his watch. After all, they couldn't upset the public with any unpleasantness that might occur in the coach, could they? That was strict departmental policy.

The train wasn't scheduled to stop between Stirling and Perth, but nevertheless it did stop officially at Dunblane. When it moved off again in exactly twenty-nine seconds, it carried two additional passengers who had no tickets. They had no need to pay, thanks to the special power vested in them by Her Majesty's Government.

A new man, in a sheepskin jacket, stood in the far end doorway to take in the scene for a few seconds. He came up along the passage and sat down in the inside corner, opposite his catch. After a few seconds further scrutiny, he leaned forward to tap Maunders on the knee. 'I'm Major Broaley, in case you're wondering. I suppose we can call you Mr 'Maunders'; for the time being anyway. I hope you appreciate the fact that we tried to delay you as little as possible with that stop back there. Yes, we reckoned that wherever you were going, you'd want to get there in a hurry. Not only that, but we reckoned we'd tag along with you and keep you company. Wasn't that decent of us?' If ever a bear could smile, Broaley was smiling.

'Charming,' said Maunders, returning the sarcasm. With the real professionals confronting him now, he suddenly felt very old. Although acting out his last scene bravely on the outside, he had already retired behind a fallen curtain on the inside.

'Yes, and guess what, Mr 'Maunders'; we want a little favour from you in return.'

'Favour?' Maunders couldn't help feeling that everything the Major said, even in its jocular form, made him feel very uneasy inside.

'Yes, you know; all those little pieces of information you suddenly don't want to keep to yourself, but would rather share with us. No need to hurry. There's plenty of time.' Broaley looked round, suddenly serious, at the MI5 man. 'How long have we got?'

'About half an hour before we arrive.'

'You see, there's plenty of time for you to remember all the things you want to tell us,' continued Broaley. 'No need to worry about things you *can't remember*. If you have any difficulty remembering things, our friend here will help you by tapping out a little tattoo on your teeth with his nice little gun. That's fair now, isn't it?'

'Have I any choice?' Nothing but fear grated out through Maunders' brave performance of a bold front.

Broaley leaned forward in his seat, letting his playful smile drain away, to leave a message of savage frankness in its place. 'No, Mr 'Maunders'. You haven't any bloody damn choice at all,' he said slowly and forcefully. 'So unless you want us to rip your limbs out, one by one, let's bloody, damn well, get on with it.' Broaley's arm shot out, seizing Maunders' collar, to ram his head back and up off the soft headrest, against the hard wood. 'Starting now!'

Releasing his iron grip, and allowing Maunders to breath again, Broaley looked round as the adjacent door slid open. Sherman put his head in. 'He's in the coach behind us,' he said to Broaley. He was referring to the FSB man who had been put on Maunders' tail. Intelligence had been tipped off by Monks' people, and the information quickly relayed to Scotland. 'I've alerted the police. They'll come on at Gleneagles, to collect him.' Sherman beckoned the agent at the far end to come up. 'You'd better come along and help me keep an eye on him until the police arrive.' Sherman paused before closing the door, for a look at the Russian sleeper agent called Maunders. 'Has he said anything yet?' he said to Broaley.

Broaley looked fiercely into Maunders' face, giving him another hard tap on the knee. 'The curtain is about to go up for the grand finale.'

37

21.12hrs, 26th June, Downing Street SW1. 'You say that Strategic Strike Force Command's Blue Steel power has been returned to an eighty-five per cent potential, Sir Richard?'

'Yes, Prime Minister; according to the latest Air Ministry reports. See here; Air Marshal Wainright's personal memorandum.' Hossley pushed the typesheet across, over the sea of papers already flooding the desk.

'Thank you,' said the Prime Minister, through wearied custom, rather than gratitude, floundering as he was, at the problems surrounding him. He took the report and shifted it about instead of reading it, seeing individual solutions not as glimmers of hope, but as mere pauses before the next problem; like the condemned prisoner saw a chink of light when he was transferring from one custodial vehicle to the next. 'And when can we expect to be at a full hundred per cent of our operational potential?'

Hossley thought for a moment, mixing cold estimation with wishful thinking. 'Roughly, I would say anywhere in the fore of the next twelve hours, Prime Minister.' Even at this late stage, Hossley's diplomatic tongue would not permit him to state anything too categorically, lest he were to be proven wrong later.

The Prime Minister sat back to dry his sweaty palms on his handkerchief. 'Twelve hours, indeed. That's always assuming that we can perform the miracle feat of stretching two and three quarter hours into twelve. I *am* right, am I *not*? It *is* only two and three quarter hours before our other crisis comes to a head, isn't it?'

Sir Richard looked at his watch. 'Yes, two hours and forty-seven minutes, I make it. But we are looking into things developing in that area. In the meantime, there's the brighter news of the strong possibility of our being able to move the bombs out to sea in time.' If Sir Richard wasn't hopeful of anything, he at least made others think that he was.

'Ah, yes, out to sea. And all but for to reap up another mammoth problem in food scarcity. While we gnash our teeth on the sea tonight, to frighten the Russian Navy, tomorrow we will gnash our teeth to drown out the warblings of our empty bellies. Am I right?'

'I sincerely hope not, Prime Minister.'

'So do I, Richard, believe me, so do I. And I'll take your advice and postpone my speech until later. But I'll keep it here, just the same.' He put the dreaded speech in the desk drawer, but didn't bother turning the lock. 'It'll give me time to work in some of my own modifications.' A smile tried to force its way out onto the fatigued face. 'What with elections looming up in ten months time.'

'We're trying our best to stop you needing it, at all.'

'Yes, that's right, you said something about looking into things?'

'Yes, we're working all out on the situation, Prime Minister; most desperately.' Sir Richard would have expanded on that statement had he known more, but he didn't. The last thing he had seen on Sherman's desk was a copy of the requisition form receipt for a firearm, sent up from the Armoury Department.

23.08hrs, Aberdeenshire. The bright spot in the distance gradually grew into a headlamp flux of a car speeding along the mountainside road. It banked down and momentarily disappeared as it entered the wood, reappearing as flashes between the trees as it travelled along the winding road. Flashes sharpened every so often into silver rapiers of light thrusting expertly between the slender trunks, and then withdrawing again with equal adroitness. The car swept round into view like a regal chariot attended on both sides by legions of stalwart pines. A torchlight started waving from side to side some fifty yards down the road, and the Porsche slowed down and halted.

Broaley looked out into the glaring torchlight. 'Major Broaley.' The torchlight moved onto the face beside him. 'And Mr Sherman. Is this the place?'

'Yes, Major. Just down there, by the kirk.'

'Have they got him?'

'No, not yet, Major, but it shouldn't be long. Somebody's bringing dogs in, I believe.' The man looked round at the policeman standing behind him. 'Is that right?' The policeman nodded.

'So let's go and get him,' said Broaley, glancing at Sherman before getting up out of the car. 'God knows, we need him. He's the last link between us and Linsdale.'

'Let's hope so, Major, said Sherman. 'We've had so many links up until now, we could start a chain store.' Sherman was right, but Broaley didn't say anything. He wasn't in a particularly joking mood.

They worked their way down the obscure pathway towards the church, while dark figures skulked about to the right and left of them, scouring the area. As the search went on down the hillside around the church, the black mass stood over them, watching. Parked in front of the huge building was a police van, where a well braided officer was standing, speaking into its radio. He turned round as Broaley approached, putting the microphone back inside the van. 'A bit more light is what we need,' he said to Broaley, looking up at the sifting clouds. 'That'll help us catch him.'

'We've got to get this man *before* the daylight comes. If we don't, it'll be the darkest day this side of hell,' said Broaley, glancing up at the church. But the dark prophecy no more did pull the walls asunder than centuries of bitter sectarian strife had done.

'That's correct,' confirmed Sherman, coming out of the shadows, behind the policeman.

'Of course, sir. The van with the dogs will be here any minute now.'

23.13hrs. Soft wind carried the sound clearly to Rasheed Bahsoud's ears. Snapping twigs. It lasted a few seconds and then stopped. They were coming after him through the brush on his left. A babble of voices rushed out to fill the empty air on his right. And they were coming up at a fast pace from the rear with dogs, by the sound of it. Panic flooded his brain. He looked up the slope. He was getting nowhere pretty quickly and they would soon be upon him. Turning round, he could almost see the dark figures rushing out of the night at him. Snapping out of the expectant trance, he looked around for cover. Extra adrenalin surged through his system and he found himself tumbling over a low wall joining two houses. The ground was lower on the other side, with a thick growth of ferns that offered some hope of cover. Hugging the shadows among the flapping fronds, Rasheed silently awaited his stalkers. Pressed up hard against the cold stone, he felt the fear scouring his mind. Everything was so alarmingly different from how he had originally imagined it would be. In a sickening mixture of shame and disappointment, he realised that all the zeal of his earlier bravado had deserted him. It was one thing to shoot down crowds of people who would not shoot back, or to blow yourself and others up in the service of Allah; this was an act of your own volition. But to have your body cut down by the power of others -- that was something entirely different. The police and soldiers out there who were rapidly closing in on him, would be heavily armed and would cut him down like a sewer rat. He shivered at the thought of their bullets tearing into his body and ripping him apart into undignified shreds. Was he having to accept that as the will of Allah? The pain of doubt racked him. He recalled, with icy revulsion, how Hali Sateefi, in her dull moods, would taunt him for being so skinny, and not manly, like his brothers were. What was it the infidel Christians believed their prophet Jesus said of the disciple Peter? That three cocks would chase him and call him a coward, before he cuts off his own ear and then hangs himself? The machine pistol in his hand now felt puny like a toy, against this march of imminent death that was approaching.

As the search party drew nearer, voices and footsteps became more audible and the man pressed in closer to the wall. The footsteps slowed down and then stopped in a quandary. 'I think we should split up into two lots, here,' said a voice.

'We'll take this side and work our way upwards off the path,' said Sherman's voice.

'Right. We'll work from here downwards towards the road,' said Broaley's voice.

'Are we all organised, then? Good; let's get on with it,' said the first voice. 'Who's got the dogs? Somebody go and tell them to hurry up and bring the dogs along this way.'

The footsteps started up once more and then stopped again, as a close search proceeded, bit by bit. Faltering steps scraped out here and there on the stone path, and the metallic click of a pistol cut the night air. Footsteps retreated across the way and stopped. They moved up and down a short distance and then returned to the hidden man's side of the path. Several volts shot up Raheed's spine as a stick rasped along the wall's coarse stone, in a sweeping stroke above his head. A policeman's head protruded warily over the wall to see if he had disturbed anything with his stick. 'What's over there?' said Broaley's voice.

'I can't see right. Nothing, by the look of it,' said the policeman. 'Hold on; I'll have a better look.' The policeman put a leg up on the wall and was about to haul himself up and over, when a door opened somewhere near, to let out the blare of a radio. All attention was held by the new noise until the door closed and the dark reclaimed its privacy. Suspicion was dampened so that the policeman's stick only made a superficial poke and prod in the wrong places, and then was gone back over the wall. The feet turned round in dithering uncertainty, in search of a new direction. 'Nothing,' said the policeman's voice.

'Right. Let's move down this way,' said Broaley's voice.

Rasheed breathed out more freely again as the steps became fainter down the slope. He got up on his knees and looked about. The night retained its secrecy, refusing to uncover its shrouded black shapes. An electric shock stabbed Rasheed's chest when he saw one of the low-lying shapes was moving towards him. Large glowing eyes spread out into two pointed ears and a double row of snarling teeth. Rasheed lifted his gun to shoot, but like a demon hound from hell, the Alsatian leapt up onto him as he tried to get up and knocked him over on his back. A sharp command rang out and the dog, still growling, stepped back obediently. 'Over here,' cried a voice. 'We've got him. Over here.' Suddenly the night was swarming with policemen closing in to form a tight ring. There were also a couple of plain clothes men, one of them putting away his Colt automatic.

'All right, we'll take over from here,' said Broaley, stepping forward to take a fierce hold of what was only a young lad who was shaking like hell and looked as if he had just stopped short of pissing in his trousers. The Police Chief looked uncomfortable at the Major's action and so Broaley spoke again. 'Right, we'll take over from here, for the time being, if you don't mind, Commander.' Broaley's aggressive temper reared up at the sniff of police red tape blocking the end to his important mission. Sherman wasn't sure if the Major would recognise a difference between friend and foe barring his way in the circumstances. In this case, he would damn well help the Major to rip the young lad's limbs out for information. Even in the poor light he could see, with disappointment, that it was one of the two Muslim terrorists, all right, but not the one they would have preferred to have caught. Damn. They would just have to get what they could out of him.

'Better to do as the Major says, Commander,' said Sherman. 'This is a national emergency of prime priority. It'll be better for everyone if you let us take over from here.'

'Very well, sir, if you say so. I'm sure you know what you're doing, even if it's without my approval, and that you have the full authority to do so.'

'That's right, Commander, we *have*,' rasped Broaley.

38

23.16hrs, 26th June, North Sea. The night was almost as black and tangible as pitch, and that suited the submarine Yalta, as it waited off the Scottish coast for the second time in three days. All around, wherever one looked, the darkness was like a thick heavy blanket. Behind this wallowing medium was the menacing rear guard fleet of NATO's Operation GLACIER, with its long range electric eyes plucking the foe from the night, and the short range human eyes wondering how to pluck the foe from the radar screens. Nerves were tense on both sides, where the last heated moments in the Gulf waters had stopped short of catastrophe, with only the taxpayer losing out on his money's worth of three errant missiles. The next mistake would perhaps not be so venial, and would probably carry a heavier 'tax', with no chance of reclaim. So the great phantom flotillas moved on with stealth through the night, all hidden beneath their forests of steel mast antennae, with their hulls moulded in one great obscurity that was broken by the odd pin pricks of light scintillating over the water.

The *Yalta* had miraculously managed to elude the NATO warships and was now waiting to pick up its passengers. It would worry about slipping through the NATO network once more, when the time came to make the return voyage. That would not be long now. In the meantime it was deploying an evasive zig-zag tactic so as to cut the risk of being trapped in the one spot. Captain Yeltsov consulted his watch as he climbed up into the conning tower. 'Yishco rana. Skakoi skorastyu mi yedyem?' (It's early. How fast are we going?)

'Diviti uzlof, Kapitan' ('Nine knots, Captain.') The First Officer held his binoculars to his chest and looked round at the Captain for his instructions.

'Ni nada yekhat tag bistra. U vas mnoga vryemini.' ('Don't go so fast. You have plenty of time.')

'Da, Kapitan.' ('Yes, Captain.')

The Captain leaned on the steel support and looked around for his bearings. 'Vidimast plakhaya.' ('Visibility is poor.')

The First officer pointed to a gap in the drifting mist. 'Sprava vidyen byerik.' ('You can see land on your right.') He looked round at the Captain. 'Mozhna saiti na byerik, Kapitan?' ('Can we go ashore, Captain?')

The Captain respected his First Officer's eagerness to form a land party so soon after the last hasty retreat from the land. But they had lost two men, and that was two men too many. Rather than give a direct answer, the Captain turned away and looked down at the dark water below them. 'Morye burna.' ('The sea is rough.') That was all he needed to say. It expressed his opinion that he didn't consider it wise for them to go ashore. But at the same time, he was not giving a command that they couldn't do so. The First Officer understood that he was being left with the responsibility of making the final decision.

'Da, kanyeshna, Kapitan.' ('Yes, of course, Captain.')

The sea acknowledged the Captain's words and sent up its foaming cry as it lashed the *Yalta's* sides. The brief sound was lost amidst the shrieking of the wind, howling around the conning tower, battering the sailors' faces and tugging at their caps. Captain Yeltsov lifted up his binoculars and trained them on what shore he could see through the floating mist. Moving along in a slow sweeping search, he stopped at the rendezvous point on the Aberdeenshire shoreline.

23.18hrs, Aberdeenshire. Silence reigned over the shore and in the village and in the rough countryside all around. It was suddenly shattered, one mile away at the crossroads clearing, by roaring engines. The sleek Army Ferret scout car raced out of the woods, chased by two trucks, and made a sharp U-turn before they all rammed on their brakes. Heavy truck doors opened and slammed, while the young lieutenant popped up and out silently from the scout car. The NCOs banged the trucks' sides and the men clambered out and off the backs, the tailboards rumbling like a drunk tart's piss in an empty drum. The sergeant was a bit puzzled and walked to the back of his truck to look in. 'What the blinkin' 'ell are you doin', Fletcher?' he bawled.

'It's okay, Sarge,' replied a cheeky voice.

'Don't you blinkin' *okay* me, son. Get the blinkin' 'ell out o' there, for blinkin' God's sake!'

The last two men jumped down grinning, from the back, with crumpled fags in their left hands and their SA-80 assault rifles in their right hands. Swinging his rifle over his shoulder, the sergeant spun round on his heel to face the lieutenant. 'All present and correct, sir.'

'All right, Sergeant, good. Now this is what we do next. Let's see now.' He hesitated, to look around at the woods. 'Right, Sergeant, I want you to get the men down off the road and move them into the wood silently, so that even the dormouse, or whatever it's called, doesn't hear them. You'll then move the men forward into position B wait there. As soon as I give a signal, you'll advance the men slowly, but slowly, mind you, towards position A and wait for further instructions. That'll put us at eight-eighty yards from the spot. Is that understood?'

'Yes, sir.'

'All right, Sergeant, you have exactly two minutes and forty-six seconds to get the men into position B. Any questions?'

'No, sir.'

'Very well then, carry on.'

'Sir!' Staccato commands rang out, followed by staccato boot-crashing that had the men dashing about like well ordered nags. The noise and motion faded into the trees and the lieutenant looked satisfied at last. He climbed up onto the armoured car and spoke down into the hatch. 'All right, Harris, get on to Field Command and tell them we're here. Confirm that Section Six is moving into position B as directed. Zero countdown for position B is now two minutes thirty-one seconds. Got that?'

'Yes, sir.'

'All right then, Corporal, get on with it.'

Three quarters of a mile off, in front of the advancing Section Six, a civilian contingent of the same operation waited silently in the brush. Being civilians, they had no section number, but as such, they were the vanguard of the operation. As such they were also appropriately armed. Six men to each of the two cars, they had two Uzis to each car. The four of these lay nuzzling the mens' laps like happy pets. What weapons the others had were hidden, like their thoughts, as they waited, tensed.

Sherman fingered the malignant growth at his waist, that was his revolver and wondered if he would have to use it. He wondered on if his secretary had put the requisition form receipt away in the new Inter/Office Miscellaneous expenses file that he was starting in the bottom drawer of the cabinet behind the door, like he'd instructed her. More likely the silly girl had left it lying around on his desk or somewhere.

Broaley made the only noise, turning the pages of his code book when he wasn't checking the time on his watch. At last he leaned over and gave the radio officer a coded message to transmit. The answer came back and Broaley set about deciphering it with what seemed an eternal slowness, while everyone got more anxious. Finishing the code, he put the pencil down and looked up. 'That's it. We've intercepted their message to the Yalta. They're ready to go out to their UNCLE's BOAT, now. So we nail them now, as they break from cover and make for the open sea.' Broaley put the pencil and book away and got ready to move. 'The Army's standing by with six field sections, just in case anyone slips past us. They're throwing a cordon round the place at half a mile radius and less, and will move in when we give them the signal.' He looked round at everybody. 'Right. Everybody know what to do?' The heads all nodded. 'Sure?' Broaley's eyes went to Sherman and lingered for a second on the spot where he knew he had his gun.

Sherman tried hard not to feel out of place among the rest, and held the Major's scrutiny in as calm an expression as he could manage. 'We're all waiting for you to lead us on, Major. Don't worry about anyone having to carry me on his back.'

'Don't worry, we won't.' Broaley nodded to the man at the back and the man knocked on the rear window to signal the others in the second car. Broaley tapped the radio officer on the shoulder. 'Wait until we get halfway down that slope and then send out the zero signal. Right, let's go.' Everyone but the radio officer piled out of the cars and started moving down towards the village.

39

23.26hrs, 26th June, Aberdeenshire. Sherman followed the others down the slope to where it made a sharp incision through the sprinkling of houses scattered around what looked like a quay. Bleak walls were grey and bleached to a blankness that told of endless marauding by the North Sea wind. Tonight was no exception, and the cold current blew in, cutting their faces. It also carried the sound of voices in what could have been Gaelic. But nobody had to be an expert linguist to know that it wasn't.

As they closed in on the boathouse, something moved behind its black window and everyone dived for cover, leaving Sherman standing alone, like a traffic policeman at Brands Hatch. Sherman crouched down beside a pile of fish boxes and fumbled for the safety catch on the finger of steel growing out of his hand. He managed to find the catch and push it off. Broaley gave quiet orders and the four men with the Uzis moved off down to the water, to prepare a reception for any Russian sailors who dared step ashore. The others moved in on the boathouse. Broaley raised the latch softly and eased the door open to peer inside. A great gust of wind suddenly rushed past and slammed something violently inside. Sherman jerked from reflex, while Broaley and the others were up and inside like a herd of buffalo. Sherman followed and almost missed his footing on the narrow plank-walk.

The door which had slammed now shuddered open with a groan, to let Broaley and the others out onto the shingle beach. Sherman followed on, and just stopped himself blasting a lobster pot to shreds as it swung to and fro on a creaking rope. When a sudden single gunshot struck the boathouse door, two short automatic bursts responded, sounding like firecrackers to Sherman. 'Over their heads,' shouted Broaley. 'We need him alive.'

Sherman found it difficult to see who was who in the commotion around the small boat, except that some figures were being pulled about and falling into the water more than others. Someone fired a flare into the sky and night turned into day, catching everyone out, including those from the submarine. The Yalta's dinghies bobbed up and down on the waves like the humps of a visiting sea monster. But this monster wasn't welcome, and warning bullets chopped up the water around its 'humps'. The man standing up to his waist in water beside the first dinghy barked out orders, and flames and bullets spat out from around him, sending stones jumping and skimming about along the beach, in a return warning spray. 'Watch out,'said Broaley to Sherman. But Sherman needed no telling, crouching down for cover beside an upturned rowing boat.

That was when Sherman saw the figure skulking among the prop beams beneath the boathouse. It seemed a strange shape, as if it was turning round. It suddenly exploded in a violent orange flash. The bullet ripped past Sherman's ear with a high scream, almost taking the ear with it. Sherman dropped forward onto his knees on the awkward stones and tried to aim his pistol stretched out at arm's length in a double handed grip. He found that he could hardly see his own gun in the dark, making aiming difficult. Things weren't any better with the two orange spots, from the gun lash, dancing in front of his eyes. He couldn't wait for his eyes to clear, but pressed the trigger once, twice, three times, letting loose his fury into the dark. Something fell with a dull thud in the shadows beneath the boathouse. The wind blew the cordite fumes into Sherman's face and he coughed. He got up slowly, his hands shaking and the cordite fumes smarting his eyes and nostrils. 'Are you all right, sir?' asked one of the men, running past Sherman.

'Never mind me; have we got Linsdale?' replied Sherman, poking fingers into the corners of his eyes, to try and rub away the two orange spots that were still dancing around.

But the man ran on, down to the water to join the others there. Sherman went down among them and looked out into the darkness, where others were wading about in the water. The *Yalta* party had retreated back out to sea. The unfortunates left behind would have to fend for themselves. The two prisoners were half dragged, half marched, back out of the water onto the crunching shingle. Somebody held up a torch to their faces and Broaley inspected them. 'That's not him. That's bloody not him, either!' said Broaley angrily. 'So where the hell is he?' Broaley held the man's jaw in a mad vice grip with one hand, while pushing the man's upper teeth back with his gun in the other hand. The man's eyes bulged with fear, but he couldn't speak properly with the grip that Broaley had on his jaw. 'Where, damn you?' Broaley asked again.

'Somewhere back there,' said the other prisoner, pointing vaguely in the direction of the boathouse.

Horror jarred Sherman's brain. He had just shot Linsdale! Most likely killed him! Sherman ran back, stumbling frantically over the stones, while the others chased after him. The man was dead, sure enough. While two of Sherman's random shots had missed, a third fluke of a bullet had gone through the back of the head. He'd caught the fatal bullet when he'd turned to run off. 'What bastard did that?' shouted Broaley. 'I'll crucify him.'

They turned the body over. It wasn't Linsdale. The forehead had been blown away, with the bullet passing through at an angle, but there was enough face to show that it wasn't Linsdale. 'Look for him, for God's sake; he's here, somewhere,' shouted Broaley angrily, and everyone scattered in a mad search. Sherman could feel the minutes running out like sands in a glass.

'There's something over here,' cried a voice. 'Let's have a torch over here, somebody.' Everyone crowded down into the small inlet hollow, where obscure boat shapes lay aground all around. One of the 'boats' was lying face downwards in the tiny streamlet. Linsdale was silently drowning.

'Get him out of there,' cried Broaley, pushing his way to, the front. 'Don't let the sod drown.'

They all looked down at the figure on the ground, hoping grimly that something other than water would come out of its mouth. Linsdale lay inert, the face like stone, while the man worked over him, pumping the water out. Back and forth the man levered, with Linsdale's arms, until his own arms flagged out. Another man knelt down to take over the task. The brief pause permitted a passing of glances. Nobody's expression was bright. Eyes returned to the operation in hand.

'I don't believe it,' cursed Sherman in anguish. 'How the hell did this happen?'

'The poor bastard's been abandoned by everybody. So much for his compatriots,' said Broaley cynically. 'When they saw the game was up, they dumped him and scattered, to save their own skins. That Muslim bastard, Hassani, must have got away with them; climbing on board for his Order of Putin medal, I'll bet. At least he only left *Christians* behind him on the shore to drown.' Broaley looked up into the black sky for their last hope. 'Where's that damn bloody helicopter?'

'Damn, damn, damn,' fretted Sherman. 'He can't die out on us now, just when we had him. Damn.' He looked at the Major, but didn't bother issuing any threats over the precarious state of Linsdale. No use blaming anyone in particular over a botched operation. Everyone would be paying the same price with the threat hanging over their heads if the man slipped out of their reach now.

The arduous pumping went on and another man bent down to examine the seepage of water from the mouth. 'Try the mouth,' he said. The gawking face rolled over and the man applied his lips to Linsdale's. Two respiratory systems were joined together to become one, the warm vitalising air rushing along to fill the other lungs' cold humid chambers. The new exercise gave fresh concern to the onlookers. Each breath was drawn in and blown through in the same rhythm by all, in a mass subconscious attempt to aid recovery. The torpid body lying on the ground was less optimistic. Soaked in water, it lay there like a fish out of water; so close, yet so far away. He was slipping away, and so was the urgent information with him. The nearness of such a loss, defied by a slim thread of hope, was excruciating. Sherman would have admitted that his nonconcern for Linsdale's life, but for the vital information it held, was downright callous, but that was the least of his worries at this crucial moment in time.

At last, like a true angel of mercy, the sea rescue helicopter from the Lossiemouth naval base descended out of the night in a maelstrom of fury. Someone cantered up and plunked down an oxygen cylinder. The rubber mask was clamped over the face and the gas hissed out. Leaning down closer, the naval rescue man took a look at the face hidden beneath the respirator. 'Touch and go, I'd say. It's a pity you couldn't have called a bit sooner. Who is he, anyway?'

Nobody was in any mood to waste time with names or stories. They all bustled to help load Linsdale onto the helicopter. Sherman went on board also, and the rotor blades whirled them up and away in a swift banking swoop towards the naval base along the coast. Broaley looked at his watch. Twenty-three thirty-one hours. Twenty-nine minutes was all they had to revive Linsdale and get his instructions for stopping the bombs exploding through to London. Just twenty-nine minutes to save the country from a colossal nuclear holocaust.

23.40hrs, Hampshire and Berkshire. Two RAF bombers raced out to sea on vital missions to drop their deadly cargoes down into the depth of the Atlantic Ocean.

23.44hrs, Buckinghamshire. RAF bomber number three raced out for the west coast, following technical delay, with bomb number four. George Blenning was still on board, putting finishing touches to the bomb's radio receiver.

23.55hrs, London SW1. The Prime Minister looked around on his desk for a pencil to alter some words in his speech to the Nation over the coming disaster. When he found the pencil, he was troubled by it slipping through his nervous sweating fingers. More to the point, who would be there to listen to his speech after the disaster?

23.59hrs, Whitehall SW1. Sir Richard looked up from his minutes, along with the other members of the Emergency Council, in a nervous check of the time, awaiting Big Ben's opinion.

00.00hrs. Big Ben struck the hour, midnight to most in the nation, and Judgement Day to the few, announcing that all was well. Those who doubted, sat round the Council table, whispering in hushed expectancy, in a scene from the New Testament, with its dreading disciples. Signals coming in from the planes reported no explosions so far. The pencils tapped and papers rustled as the seconds ticked by.

00.01hrs. The door burst open suddenly and Squadron Leader Travis came in followed by Meeson. 'It's okay, everyone,' said Travis. 'The bombs are dead. They finally switched off the transmitters two minutes ago.'

40

11.00hrs, 27th June, London SW1. As far as London was concerned, it was a rotten day, with drab showers spoiling what could have been the final day to a nice sunny weekend. Anyone who might have questioned this would not have been understood, since the dark happenings of the night had lifted like a nasty fog. Folk moved about the new day, attending their churches and visiting their parks, unaware that a bogey had used their 'backyards' over the weekend for its evil perpetrations. But like all nightmares, things cleared away with the morning. The sudden ominous build-up of the Russian Northern Fleet had checked itself and reversed just as suddenly, dissolving its menace like a child's fantasy in a bad dream.

The CIA got the blame, of course. The CIA was always to blame when sudden outbreaks of violence popped up like sunspots, in any far corner of the globe. Whatever the current image of the Agency was, rumours always took the same form at the outcome of these incidents, to pillory its name with a fresh shuffle of new sensational Washington scandals.

'What time did the reports come in?' said Sherman, leaning over the Audi bonnet to clean the windscreen.

'Just after one this morning,' said Sir Richard, pulling up his collar as the sky spat down its Sunday spittle.

The wrath of the gods had gone from Hossley's face and Sherman could almost have invited him to his own christening, had he not known the man better. 'And they definitely confirm the fighting?'

'Yes, as far as we know, there's been an outbreak of fierce clashes along the Russian/Chinese border, with heavy casualties, it seems, on both sides.'

'All beginning with Russian forces opening fire with heavy artillery on the Chinese frontier posts?'

Hossley shrugged his shoulders and tugged his waistcoat down. 'Artillery fire or planted bombs, who knows, at this stage? All we've heard so far, is that some mysterious explosions occurred in the early hours of this morning, and as a result, a massive land mobilisation force has been rushed in to support the Chinese forces already fighting three miles inside the Russian border.'

'Nasty, but timely, all the same,' said Sherman, putting the duster back inside the car. 'Just when we're under pressure from Russia's naval onslaught, China steps in to attack her tail, to initially distract her, and eventually cause her withdrawal. Yes, I think I would call that timely, regardless of what caused it.'

'Or *who*, for that matter.'

Sherman took the implication and tried to read into Sir Richard's eyes. 'Do you think the original idea came out of Langley?' Sherman smiled inwardly at his own answer to that, as he made a mental note of possibly sending a crate load of asparagus to the American Embassy for a tall crazy-talking man called Monks.

Sir Richard scratched his nose and raised his eyebrows. 'It will inevitably mean trouble for us, whoever is to blame, that's for sure. But I think we can let it lie for a few days. And allow them time to fry in their own fat for a bit.' He pulled open the door of his Jensen and got in. He looked out the window at Sherman. 'When is your flight?'

'Nine forty, tonight; the hospital's quite close to the airport, in actual fact.' He wondered for a second why he'd let out that last piece of pointless information, before accepting it purely as nerves. No more little distractions, like total nuclear devastation, to shield his mind from that tragic accident. 'Got to get back to do a bit of packing.' Car keys danced about in their unease in his hand, like the uneasy emotions in his mind. 'I think I'll take the long way round and run these new tyres in, and get some fresh air, as well. I need some.' It was his mind that needed airing, more than his lungs, but he didn't say that. It wasn't necessary. Both of them were feeling very much drained of energy. 'I've left a four-day working guideline for Janet to give to Aulds when he comes in tomorrow. He should be able to get along on that while I'm away.' They nodded to each other and drove off on their separate ways for the weekend.

Trafalgar Square looked as cheerful as ever, with its casual hubbub of Sunday idlers, having been spared a nuclear roasting, and its only 'vultures' perched on tourists' shoulders, pecking at their heritage of golden seeds. There would always be the dissatisfied, of course; like the man already pestering the bobby over the tap water's warm temperature. There was also a complaint on the new-vendor's sheet, from an MP on holiday in the Shetlands. The MP, according to the radio news, had seen a Russian submarine off the Scottish coast three days ago, and so he wanted to raise a storm over the question of its presence there.

Sherman felt that he wanted to get away from it all, and he thought of the open space of Hampstead Heath, where he could lose himself in solitude for a short while. He could already see the kites in his mind. He smiled as his eye caught a little kite in the Square as he waited at the lights. It was trying to climb up. Two minds alike. But the little boy wasn't managing so well and the kite struggled and stalled. Sherman swept the Audi round into Cockspur Street and was gone out of sight, before he could see the little kite falter to take a dive-bomber turn, to crash down into the ground.